COLD FLAT JUNCTION

COLD FLAT JUNCTION

MARTHA GRIMES

viking

VIKING
Published by the Penguin Group
Penguin Putnam Inc., 375 Hudson Street,
New York, New York 10014, U.S.A.
Penguin Books Ltd, 27 Wrights Lane,
London W8 5TZ, England
Penguin Books Australia Ltd, Ringwood,
Victoria, Australia
Penguin Books Canada Ltd, 10 Alcorn Avenue,
Toronto, Ontario, Canada M4V 3B2
Penguin Books (N.Z.) Ltd, 182–190 Wairau Road,
Auckland 10, New Zealand

Penguin Books Ltd, Registered Offices:
Harmondsworth, Middlesex, England

First published in 2001 by Viking Penguin,
a member of Penguin Putnam Inc.

1 3 5 7 9 10 8 6 4 2

Grateful acknowledgment is made for permission to reprint excerpts
from the following copyrighted works:
"Directive" from *The Poetry of Robert Frost,* edited by Edward Connery Lathem.
Copyright 1947, © 1969 by Henry Holt and Co. Copyright © 1975 by Lesley Frost
Ballantine. Reprinted by permission of Henry Holt and Company, LLC.
"Tangerine" by Johnny Mercer and Victor Schertzinger. Copyright © 1942 by Famous
Music Corporation. Copyright renewed 1969 by Famous Music Corporation.
"Tonight You Belong to Me" by Billy Rose and David Lee. © 1926 (renewed) Chappell
& Co. and C & J David Music. All rights reserved. Used by permission of Warner Bros.
Publications U.S. Inc., Miami, Florida.

PUBLISHER'S NOTE
This is a work of fiction. Names, characters, places, and incidents either are the product of
the author's imagination or are used fictitiously, and any resemblance to actual persons,
living or dead, business establishments, events, or locales is entirely coincidental.

Library of Congress Cataloging-in-Publication Data

Grimes, Martha.
Cold flat junction / Martha Grimes.
p. cm.
ISBN 0-670-89491-5
I. Title.

PS3557.R48998 C65 2001
813'.54—dc21   00-043992

This book is printed on acid-free paper. ∞

Printed in the United States of America
Set in Stempel Garamond
Designed by Jaye Zimet

To Van,
who was there

I have kept hidden in the instep arch
Of an old cedar at the waterside
A broken drinking goblet like the Grail
Under a spell so the wrong ones can't find it,
So can't get saved, as Saint Mark says they mustn't
(I stole the goblet from the children's playhouse.)
Here are your waters and your watering place.
Drink and be whole again beyond confusion.

—Robert Frost from "Directive"

COLD FLAT JUNCTION

A dented cup

1

I'm sitting here where you left me hardly more than a week ago. Every day and nearly every night I've been here on the low stone wall by the spring. I sit near the little alcove where spring water runs from a pipe jutting out of the stone. There's a metal cup dented from years of use that sits beneath the pipe and catches the water so that people can drink it. The cup has been around as long as I have. It's as if the alcove were its room, and people can take it out and drink from it and return it. It's amazing that in all of this time, in all of these years, it's never been stolen.

Why would anyone bother stealing a dented tin cup? Because there are some things that go beyond reason—like the Girl, appearing and disappearing; like knowing Ben Queen didn't kill anyone; like Do-X-machines; like vengeance. Probably, you've forgotten most of what

1

happened, but you might remember Fern Queen being shot and killed over by Mirror Pond. That's on White's Bridge Road. You might remember because people think murder is more important than anything (except maybe sex).

I asked my mother, who's lived all of her life at the hotel, about the cup, and she said, "What cup?" So there doesn't seem much point in asking about it. In the alcove where the cup rests, I found the Artist George tube taken from the Mr. Ree game and put here by Persons Unknown (yet I think it must have been the Girl) to communicate something to me, maybe to tell me, *You're on the right track, keep going,* or maybe just to say, *I'm here.*

I imagine it was *I'm here,* for if I were to tell anyone there was such a person and she was here, they'd say the opposite: *No, she isn't.* That's what Ben Queen said about her, but he had a particular reason: he didn't want anybody, especially the police, to know she was around. He was trying to protect her. So he pretended there was no such person, and I pretended I went along with that, and both of us knew we were both pretending. We both knew *we* knew there was such a person.

When there's a great mystery you wish to protect—that is, a mystery you want to keep people from tearing to ribbons—then you've got to keep the wrong people away from it. You go about solving it in a roundabout way. You sometimes ask questions of the wrong people, people who know nothing, for instance, and although you eventually come to an answer, it will take much longer to get to it.

But why is this? Why would I go about trying to solve it in this roundabout way? Maybe the answer wouldn't mean the same thing to me if I didn't ask the questions in my own way, and of the people I ask them of. Or maybe some part of me doesn't want to know the answer. Or maybe both.

It's been forty years since the Tragedy. That's the way people say it, in that awed, excited way you know means they wish it would happen all over again. Most people seem to have forgotten, or perhaps never knew there were two Tragedies, perhaps because one of them happened in Spirit Lake and one in Cold Flat Junction. Now, if you include the murder of Fern Queen, there are three Tragedies.

———

Cold Flat Junction. It's the kind of place you might look out on from a train window and think, *Thank God I don't live there, what a boring town, what an empty place.* It is an empty place, and maybe even a boring one, sometimes; but I think you'd be wrong to pass it by; you should alight from the train and stay awhile, which is what I did.

There's something about the place itself that I feel when I sit on one of the benches on the railroad platform and look off over the empty land to that line of navy blue trees so far away. The land and all of the woebegone town seem stripped of a protective layer that other places have and can hide behind. It's the layer of busy-ness, profit, community pride; bunting on July the fourth; flower baskets hanging from lampposts in the spring, all ballooning up with civic pride. Cold Flat Junction has shed all of this, if it ever had it.

I cannot let go of them, these Tragedies. I can't let go of a thing—a puzzle, a person, a place. Once it gets my attention, I have to keep worrying it until it comes clear. I have to hang on, and it makes life really tiring. I work on these questions down in the Pink Elephant, a small chilly room which was once used for cocktail parties underneath the hotel dining room. The room's cold stone walls are painted pink, and there's a long wooden picnic bench and hurricane lamps. The candles give the room atmosphere. Cobwebs and dust and ghosts help too.

Ghosts do not frighten me (as long as I don't have to see them). Ghosts are said to haunt places where they died, if they died with things on their minds that they have to find answers to. I hope they find their answers. As for me, I see myself wrinkled and twiglike and dying—well, dying, anyway—still with this weary worrying problem on my mind, and then coming back and haunting the Devereau house, wondering about Rose, Mary-Evelyn, Ben Queen, and Fern—to say nothing of the Girl.

But you've probably forgotten all this as you've been going about your own business. Probably, you've forgotten my name, too, which is Emma Graham. I'm twelve years old. And if you think I shouldn't have waited so long to tell you more of this story, just remember:

I haven't been away. You have.

3

Dervish

2

You must remember the Devereau house. You must remember Mary-Evelyn. One early morning her body was found washed up among water lilies on the edge of Spirit Lake. The rowboat she ventured out in was found capsized and floating in the middle of the lake. She was just my age, twelve.

This was the first Tragedy, and I know it was the reason for the others. Her aunts, the three Devereau sisters, could not explain why Mary-Evelyn would be out at night in a boat. They went, they said, in search of her. When they couldn't find her, it was then they called the Sheriff's office. Why (I keep asking) did they wait so long? There are other questions: Why was she out by herself, and in a rowboat? And why was her body so far from the boat? It amazes me that her death was put down to "accident" without a lot of questions being asked.

There was a fourth sister, a half sister, who was younger and really pretty. Her name was Rose, the Rose who ran off with Ben Queen when they were both twenty years old. The Queens are Cold Flat Junction people, which doesn't mean no-account (except to hear my mother tell it), but just that Ben Queen didn't have the "advantages" of someone like Rose; the Devereaus were educated and if not wealthy, at least well-off.

―――――

The Hotel Paradise is the only hotel remaining from the grand days when Spirit Lake was a famous summer resort. It has been in my family for over a century, or, to be more precise, in my great-aunt Aurora Paradise's family, on my father's side, even though he was not a Paradise, but a Graham. It is owned by Aurora Paradise and operated by my mother and her business partner, Lola Davidow. Aurora herself is ninety-one and lives in style up on the fourth floor, out of sight, but not (unfortunately) out of mind. The hotel might be said to be "family-run." My mother is the cook; I'm a waitress; my brother Will works as a bellhop (when he works at all). These last few years haven't provided either much waitressing or much bellhopping.

The front desk is Lola Davidow's job; the cooking is all my mother's. To say that this division of work is not equal is laughable. Front desk work (the way Lola Davidow does it) is mainly overseeing guests when they arrive, and getting ice and setups to them in the cocktail hour, and joining them for drinks. All of this Mrs. Davidow does to perfection, especially when her private liquor supply is running low. Front desk work is also writing checks and going into the big black safe in the back office out of which I occasionally see Lola take a bottle of Southern Comfort. Front desk work is also getting away from the front desk, like going into La Porte to buy groceries and (if Lola's lucky) meeting up with one of her drinking buddies at the Devon Manor.

The Hotel Paradise has seen better days. You can still see those days reflected in the white-painted, green-shuttered Victorian cottages along Spirit Lake's narrow streets. They have wraparound porches and gabled upper floors and are much too spacious to be called "cottages," but that I guess was the popular term: "summer cottage." Spirit Lake with its summer cottages; Spirit Lake with its pure air. Most of the cottages are a little shabby now, and even the air is stingier; to get those

5

diamond-sharp days, that bright air, you have to get up very early when the air is so clean and rare it makes you feel doped. Early rising is not what I'm famous for.

The Paradises have been around for over a hundred years, the Grahams for over fifty, and the Davidows for five. To hear Regina Jane Davidow tell it, they own this place lock, stock, and barrel. She loses no opportunity to tell me that her mother "saved" the hotel by putting her money into it, and if she hadn't, the bank would have foreclosed and we Grahams would have been out on the street.

Your mother hasn't got any business sense at all. Everything was a mess before we came.

No, everything is a mess now, and you're making it.

Ree-Jane wouldn't know "business sense" if she fell over it, especially since it involves math, a subject she can't seem to pass in school. She is four years older than me, two years older than my brother Will. She is not yet seventeen but tells people she's nineteen. She walks her model's walk, toe-before-heel, and smiles her empty, heartless smile, as if the world were a camera just waiting for her to pass its lens. We are always being compared in the matter of our hair, our faces, our posture, our feet. Since I lose the hair, face, and body contest, I think they should let my feet alone.

Ree-Jane never does any work except for sometimes pinch-hitting as a waitress when there's a crowd (which is hardly ever). Even in the dining room she uses the passage between tables as a kind of ramp on which she walks (toe-down-first) and turns and twirls, modeling whatever she's wearing. She's not forced to wear a uniform like the rest of us waitresses (three, including the head waitress, Vera). I have overheard Ree-Jane tell guests, as she fills their ruby goblets with ice water, that she is the dining room hostess. If there was ever a dining room that didn't need a hostess, it's the Hotel Paradise's. This "hostess" talk infuriates Vera, since, if there were hostessing to be done, she'd do it.

Vera wears a black uniform to set her apart from us ordinary waitresses, who wear white or light blue. She is tall, plank thin, and perfectly groomed: every dark hair hammered in place, uniform so starched it marches when she walks. But the way she is pays off in her expert serving, which is kind of amazing. There's never a movement lost, never a tray clumsily held. She can raise one of the big, metal trays, heavy with dinners, up on her five fingers and waltz it into the dining room, then bring it down to the tray server with a quick one-two, fingers-arm movement that makes me think of a cardsharp toppling a deck of cards one-over-the-other down the length of his arm.

Once I saw a short movie at school about the dervishes, who did a dance of unbelievably complex movements, their arms and legs whipping around and slicing air in more perfectly synchronized movements than the Radio City Music Hall Rockettes. Why do people say "like a whirling dervish" to mean out-of-control when it means just the opposite? In the middle of their semicircle sat a man whose body was as uncontrolled as a Raggedy Anne doll. His head flopped, his arms waved in meaningless movement. I got the picture: the nondervish in the middle was living his life out-of-control.

If ever there was a whirling dervish outside of the dervish camp, it's Vera. That's how practiced, precise, and unwasteful all her movements are.

And if ever there was a floppy doll of a person, one who could hardly even get her feet to go right, it's me, Emma Graham, nondervish.

1

Benchsitting

3

Mr. Root, who often occupies the bench outside Britten's Store, knows the Queens, or at least knows Sheba Queen, Ben's sister-in-law. Mr. Root was with me the last time I went to Cold Flat Junction. The Wood boys were along, too. It's been a long time since they were ever boys, for by now they must be fifty or more; still, "boys" is what people call them, if they're lumping them together. Speaking of one or the other, though, it's "Ulub" or "Ubub." These nicknames came about because of the license plates on their rusty pickup trucks: ULB and UBB. So they were rebaptized "Ulub" and "Ubub." Their real names are Alonzo and (I think) Robert.

The four of us have become sort of a team over the last weeks, trying to solve the mystery of Mary-Evelyn Devereau, which has now become the much bigger mystery of Mary-Evelyn and Fern Queen, and seems to be growing even from that to the mystery of several other people. You think you've solved one problem only to find it's dragging a lot of others in its wake.

We are all four of us important to the team. Ulub and Ubub had actually been around back when the Devereau sisters, together with Mary-Evelyn, lived across the lake in the big house, fog-gray or mist-white, take your pick. Fog and mist are appropriate settings for the Devereau house. As a boy, Ulub did yard work for them—raking leaves in the fall, cutting grass in the summer, seeing to what few flower beds they had. Indeed, Ulub had been there raking leaves the evening before the fatal night when Mary-Evelyn had gone off in the rowboat.

Ulub was the only person I had found who could report on that night. But he has a speech problem that makes it nearly impossible to understand him. It's not a stammer; it's more like sounds getting lost in the cavern of his throat or knotted in his tongue. Ubub, a little older and a lot taller, isn't much help because he also has trouble getting words across. He can understand Ulub, after a lifetime of listening, I guess. They don't try to talk much, and who can blame them, what with people poking fun at them or treating them like idiots, which they certainly are not.

The one person we discovered who is for some reason blessed with a word detangler in his head is Mr. Root. He is a retired person (I'm not sure from what, never having been curious enough to ask him) who, as I said, spends part of every day on the bench out in front of Britten's Store. So do the Wood boys. So do I, lately.

The bench is where we all met. I was sitting on it that first time watching passengers get off the Tabernacle bus that runs from Cold Flat Junction once a week to La Porte and Spirit Lake. I was there because I wanted to catch a glimpse of Toya Tidewater, who had a horrible reputation. I was not to go near any of the Tidewaters and especially Toya, my mother said. So the first chance I got, I set out looking for her, and that's what took me to Cold Flat Junction that first time.

I'm necessary to our group because I'm the one who decided we should all go to the Devereau house. The other three look pretty much to me to be the leader. It's the first time anyone ever thought of me that way, so I try and keep my leadership skills sharpened. The reason I told them we should go to the Devereau place was so Ulub might bet-

9

ter remember and could try and act out what he saw. But the other part of it was I wanted to see inside that old house where Mary-Evelyn had lived and I didn't want to go alone.

Britten's Store is a short walk from the hotel and is the only store around. Often I'm sent there (or Walter, our dishwasher, is) to pick up flour or cornstarch or anything my mother runs out of. Britten's is one of those places where people go just to hang out, drinking Cokes, buying cigarettes, spitting tobacco in the dust around the bottom step. Men like to go there and catch up on the gossip they like to say they're not interested in.

It was in Britten's, when I was looking at cans of beans, that a man named Jude Stemple walked in on the group sitting around in front of the butcher counter arguing about who this dead woman was who was found by Mirror Pond, out along White's Bridge Road. Nobody knew, including the Sheriff. Jude Stemple settled it by saying the murdered woman was "Ben Queen's girl."

Fern Queen. At that time I'd never heard of Fern Queen, only of Ben himself, and that information came by way of my great-aunt Aurora, who couldn't be trusted to tell the truth, and whether she did depended on her mood or on how many Cold Comforts she'd drunk. It was she who told me about Rose Devereau and Ben Queen.

Ben Queen just got out of prison where he's been for the last twenty years, convicted of murdering his wife, Rose. And this is where vengeance comes in. It turned out that it was their daughter, Fern Queen, who was shot over three weeks ago. But Ben didn't kill Fern. I know he didn't because I'm pretty sure I know who did.

Every summer, my brother Will and his friend Brownmiller put on a play for the hotel guests (though it's really more for themselves that they do it). A short while ago, my brother told me about what the Greeks called a "Do-X-machine." This happens when things are in such a mess, or the hero is getting in more and more trouble, that God has to step in—that is, come down in a sort of chair from above, which is the "machine" part—and straighten things out. (God does not seem inclined to do this for the Hotel Paradise, I've noticed.)

The Greeks are important to this story. This is because, although they might've wanted God to come in when things got really messy, they did *not* hang around waiting for God to take vengeance. No, they managed it on their own, which was swifter (and better, probably). Whenever the Greeks murdered somebody, somebody else came along later and avenged the death. Then another Greek would come along and avenge the murderer. So that it went on and on, generation after generation, revenge after revenge. It all seemed fated to happen.

And that's what I mean when I say the Queens are beginning to look like people in one of those Greek tragedies: First, there was Mary-Evelyn Devereau; then there was Rose Devereau Queen; then there was Fern Queen. It's my opinion the person who shot Fern had no choice but to seek revenge and that is why Fern Queen died.

I met Ben Queen. I'm the last person I can imagine such a thing happening to. It was in the old Devereau house across Spirit Lake— that is, the lake itself, for which the village is named. It wasn't too surprising after I thought about it that the Devereau house is the first place he'd go after he got out of prison. That's because he was looking for somebody. Not ghosts, not the ghosts of little Mary-Evelyn or his wife Rose. No, as grieved as he still is after twenty years, he is not a man to be pulled back to a house because he's sentimental about it. He was looking for someone alive, and thought that's where she would go. He might even have thought, when he heard me upstairs, that I was her.

That I was her. It makes me feel a little strange to say it. But that's probably what he did think when he walked into the house. After all, no one had lived there for forty years, not since the drowning of Mary-Evelyn Devereau. And it's not just a coincidence I was there, either. I had been going there in the days following that first trip with the Woods and Mr. Root. That first time had given me courage to go back again on my own. I had begun to feel kind of at home there. I would try on Mary-Evelyn's dresses, which were still beautiful and almost new-looking even after forty years. I examined things in her toy chest, like her Mr. Ree game, her dolls, her picture puzzles, and so forth. It got so I stayed for longer and longer periods of time. I'd take food with me, like my mother's coconut cake, and sit out on the narrow balcony of her room and watch the sun streak the lake with the kind of silver decorations my mother uses on wedding cakes.

Ben Queen: here is a man wild in his youth, in jail for twenty years, and right after he gets out, another person in his family is murdered. You can hardly blame the Sheriff for thinking it might be the same man did it.

11

The Sheriff is someone I never could imagine myself going against. But I did. I didn't tell him I'd seen Ben Queen, much less tell him where. And I think that's spoiled something in our relationship, for in the last couple of weeks, we haven't walked around once to check the parking meters.

No, in all my born days, I never thought anything would be more important than our friendship, the Sheriff's and mine.

Orphans-in-a-storm

4

Where I should have gone first was to the Queen house in Cold Flat Junction, where Ben Queen lived most of his life until he married Rose Devereau, until he'd gone to prison for murdering her.

But remember my roundabout ways.

Instead of going to the Queen house, I went to see Mrs. Louderback, who used cards to predict the future. I had seen her once before, and she is a nice, ordinary woman—nothing like the gypsies you sometimes see along the highway—and also honest. It's clear she's honest because you can "contribute" money or not. The suggested contribution is two dollars, which is certainly cheap enough for all she does. As I said, I went to her once and I'm perfectly aware she isn't the sort of "fortune-teller" who predicts future events, like whether your pig or your apple pie will take the blue ribbon at the local fair.

Mrs. Louderback uses tarot cards. It's the first time I ever knew about them, and I found them very strange indeed. What she does is put them down and turn them up and consider. She's more likely to tell you what's going on with you now than what you'll do in the future. That is not very clear, but then Mrs. Louderback tends to be kind of murky herself. Yet a lot of people, mostly women, go to her, and probably because she is so nice and honest. Also, she's the only fortune-teller in town.

The cards she turned up for me that first time were the Hanged Man and the orphans-in-a-storm cards, which seemed about right for me. But she told me these were actually good cards, and said a lot about what kind of person I am. When I looked at the orphans-in-a-storm card I wondered what she saw good about it. It reminded me of the way adults tell you when you're drowning in a ditch that it's much better than the ditch on the other side of the road.

Mrs. Louderback sees her customers in her house for a couple of hours most days of the week. She has all of her housework to do, after all, and can hardly give her whole life over to other people's fortunes. Her house is as neat as a pin and as clean as the last time I'd been there. Another woman, whose name I don't know, opened the door and went before me into the parlor (a "common" word, my mother says, for living room, meaning language has a lot to do with breeding in my mother's book). Here there was a row of chairs, as in a doctor's office. A woman I don't remember ever seeing in Spirit Lake was waiting for her appointment.

The appointments are usually for a half hour, and if this lady was going in to have her fortune told, I knew I would have to wait for a half hour. This didn't really bother me as I had plenty of time between lunch and dinner. Maybe the person in with Mrs. Louderback right now was really in big trouble and took more time.

The woman who had let me in (and who also lived there) nodded silently toward the straight chair next to the customer. The lady now sitting beside me was wearing a hat with berries and gave me one of those smiles reserved for kids, as if it were every grown-up's duty to try and make kids feel they can go on living, at least for now.

She looked down at me with that simper and asked, "Is that your mother in there now? Are you waiting for your mother?"

I suppose it would have upset her whole world to find out a twelve-year-old kid was having the same problems she was, or made her suspicious of Mrs. Louderback for allowing a kid my age even to enter her parlor. I calculated that the woman in the kitchen (which was where Mrs. Louderback did her "readings") would come out and the woman sitting here now would get up and go in, all done in pretty much one fell swoop. I made an *uh-huh* sound that could also be taken as *nu-huh*, and that covered me in case the woman in there now disclaimed me. I accompanied this yes-no answer with a dopey smile and twined a lock of hair around my finger the way Ree-Jane does, usually with her mouth open a little. It makes her look really dumb. But, then, she is.

The door between parlor and kitchen opened, and another unfamiliar lady walked out. (Where did these people come from?) She smiled at the other one self-consciously. The lady beside me then got up to go into the kitchen and I, of course, got up also to greet the woman who'd just come out. "Hi! Did she tell you interesting stuff?"

The lady going in for her appointment said to the one who was now frowning at me, "She's cute."

When the door closed, I re-sat myself as if I hadn't spoken to her, pretending not to notice the woman was giving me the once-over, perhaps trying to place me. She gave me then a disregarding look. There was no longer any pressure on her to be nice in case some god might be tempted to strike her down. She was free of her fortune and of any obligation to strangers.

I was glad when she left so I could relax. Which I did, sloping down in the chair, oozing down like a snake until my shoulders were almost on the seat. I had a half hour to kill, so I did this for a few minutes and then got up and walked around, looking at things.

I turned to look at some bookshelves behind glass doors. I was very surprised to see a row of Nancy Drew books, my favorites. They looked really old, much older than mine, and I wondered if they were Mrs. Louderback's childhood books. I would have to ask her. I really like Mrs. Louderback and am pleased to think we have Nancy Drew in common. I walked around, picking up and inspecting a strange little carving of three monkeys. The thing they were carved from was a dull brownish-red, and wasn't wood or china or anything like that, more like some sort of stone. I didn't care for it. I also looked the grandfather clock over; I liked its soft chime, which came every fifteen minutes.

There was no sign of the woman who had let me in. She was birdlike and bony, her arms like bats' wings, the skin loose and hanging down from bone, as if the flesh had gone. My own arms and elbows are

15

round and smooth, one of my best features. Opening the door for people seemed scary to her, as if strangers made her nervous. Or perhaps she was being sensible; after all, what kind of people would believe what a deck of cards told them? People—she might think—who weren't much in touch with reality.

I was making all these thoughts up while I leaned back against the narrow case of the clock because I was bored. I don't have any patience and get bored easily. At least that's what my mother and Mrs. Davidow are always telling me. *Don't fidget, Emma; stop your fidgeting.* I think it would make a good name for a bird, "fidget."

As the clock chimed *duuum duuum*, the door to the kitchen was opening. I came to crisp attention.

The lady in the berry hat stood in the doorway saying good-bye, good-bye to Mrs. Louderback (sounding pleased with her future, or her present), and turned and looked at me, puzzled I was still hanging around. Momentarily, I had forgotten I was supposed to have left with my "mother." My thoughts raced around like crazy mice trying to come up with something and what they came up with was, "Hi, Mrs. Louderback. My mom forgot something."

I should have realized that now I would have to come up with something *else* to explain my queer behavior to Mrs. Louderback, but at least the lady on her way out looked satisfied that the world wasn't standing on its head. She nodded and left.

Mrs. Louderback smiled at me, but you could see she was wondering. What could my "mom," who was definitely not a Louderback customer and who likely hadn't seen her in months if not years, have forgotten?

As I breezed past her, too tired mentally to come up with a truly convincing answer, I said, "My mother was going to give me one of her Angel Pies to bring along, but then she *forgot.*" The Angel Pies were famous, as were a number of my mother's dishes.

Mrs. Louderback smiled and said that was very nicely intended, knowing how busy Jen Graham was over at the hotel. She said really nice things about my mother, as she got a pitcher of lemonade from the refrigerator. She poured out two glasses and added some not-so-nice things about the Davidows.

"They're not *real* Spirit Lakers—"

(I agreed.)

"And Regina Jane Davidow walks around as if she's queen of something."

"She wants to be a duchess. She wants to be either that or the countess of Kent. Or a model, or a star reporter."

Mrs. Louderback rooted through the box where she kept her tarot cards and also odds and ends of pencil stubs and paper. Then she swept the cards across the table like one of those casino dealers, saying, "Well, she's in for a big shock, then. There are no duchesses in *that* one's future. Far from it—"

She cut this wonderful news short by apologizing for coming close to breaking a professional confidence. But I tried to keep her going about Ree-Jane's noncountess future. "Jane Davidow says if she was a countess, that made her husband an *earl*, not a count. There aren't any counts, she says."

Mrs. Louderback pursed her mouth. "There certainly are. In Russia, for instance. The writer Tolstoy was a count, I'm pretty sure."

I wouldn't know about him, not being up on my Russians.

"I'm sorry," she said, "I got us off the subject—"

Putting down Ree-Jane was never off the subject.

"—and I think we should go back and finish your last visit because—remember?—you had to leave when we were only half finished."

Inwardly, I groaned. That meant the Hanged Man and the orphans.

"Your cards were the Hanged Man, the Queen of Cups, and—" She was searching for it.

"Orphans," I said, in a dead voice.

"Orphans?"

"A boy and girl in a snowstorm. They looked like orphans to me." One of my favorite books was *David Copperfield*.

"Ah. Of course. But they're not 'orphans.'"

You could have fooled me, I thought, propping my chin in my hands. She turned the three cards face up. I was not happy to see their faces again. Then she placed a finger on the Queen of Cups, whom I'd forgotten about.

She said, "There's a woman who's had a hard life."

That could probably be any female in Spirit Lake, except Lola Davidow and Ree-Jane.

"This woman presents a danger to you. Be careful of her." Mrs. Louderback had her eyes closed when she said this. She is not supposed to be one of those mediums, nor is she supposed to "see things." Whatever information she gives a person comes through the cards. But I wondered about this. For she raised her head and opened her eyes and gave me a blank look and then seemed to be looking not at me, but past me. Her expression was strange.

I remembered then that the one other time I had been here, she had been looking past me in this way, looking at something that must have been outside the window. She was facing the kitchen window and I was sitting with my back to it. And now she made that gesture as she had the last time, with her large-palmed hand, a sort of scrubbing motion.

I could only follow her line of vision by turning around, which I did. All I could see through the window was a spindly top of a mountain laurel or rhododendron, which grew all around her house. It was tapping lightly in the wind. There was no sun, only an even gray paste of light, a blank backdrop for the rhododendron bush. Then in the silence that seemed to get thicker and closer, the 3:05 bore down on us, its whistle wailing.

There are times when life just thunders down like that train, or like one of those waves formed by a tropical hurricane that pushes everything before it—palm trees, huts, people—and leaves behind nothing but stumps and sticks. I felt like that now, two sticks where clothes hung, and the wind whistling through.

But her head was down as if she was afraid to look at me, as if her expression might give something away that she didn't want given. "The Queen of Cups," she said again, as if the card had newly sprung from the deck.

It was making me nervous; the whole *visit* was making me nervous.

She laid out a row of cards, stopping to riffle the deck again and again as she studied them. The Hanged Man she had placed below the row.

The cards in her hands made tiny splatters as she ran her thumb back and forth over them. "I guess that's a pretty bad card," I said, pointing to the Hanged Man

She shook her head. "No, it's a good one."

I frowned. He was hanging by his foot upside down from a tree branch. It didn't look too good to me. I determined to find a book about tarot cards in the library. They were queer.

"It means rebirth. Regeneration."

I was still waiting for the "good" part. I doubled my fists and rested my chin on them, waiting.

"In your case, though . . ."

I knew it. I was the exception and the Hanged Man was putting a curse on me.

". . . well, this is all very peculiar. I don't remember coming up with this before. . . ."

It's my opinion that somebody who's supposed to be a specialist should not be telling you about the uncertainties of what they're doing. It would be dumb for my mother, for instance, to say about her Angel Pie, "There I go putting in too much lime juice," or, "Oh dear, I'm baking the meringue crust too long." That's a sure way of not holding onto your reputation. I slid down in my chair so that only my eyes remained above table level. I wondered if they were mocking her. *Emma, sit up, sit up straight, that's why your shoulders are humped,* I heard the voices of Lola Davidow and Ree-Jane. Mrs. Louderback looked across at my eyes and did not say this. I immediately sat up, probably out of gratitude.

Mrs. Louderback said, "The peculiar thing is that some of these people just don't seem real."

Hadn't she ever been to the Hotel Paradise? "Some of what people?"

Her hand flashed out and shoved the cards around as quick as Aurora Paradise cheating at solitaire. Then she stared at them again. "You are going to be with somebody in a difficult situation."

"That's kind of vague." I permitted myself this criticism.

She nodded. "I know. It's because of this *clouded* area. We are all in each other's magnetic field." She swept up the cards again.

At that I sat bolt upright. Was Ree-Jane rubbing off on me like the hotel cat leaving dander around? "What's that mean?"

"It only means we attract and repel without being conscious of it—"

As long as I could repel.

"—for much of our life goes on without us knowing it."

19

I frowned. "Then what good is it?"

Mrs. Louderback smiled. "Well, it affects things we are conscious of."

This was getting too airy, too "clouded" for me. I'm basically practical. "Do I get to ask a different question this time? Or should I stay with the old one?"

Mrs. Louderback pursed her lips again. "That depends, I expect, on whether you think it was answered."

I thought. "In a way it was . . . no. No, it was." My question had been whether I should tell the Sheriff I'd seen Ben Queen. I didn't tell him; that brought down a lot of woe on my head, for I think he felt swindled. Both of them—the Sheriff and Ben Queen—had entered my "magnetic field" or I had theirs, and they were pulling on me. Ben Queen's pull had been the strongest at that point. I suppose he could have gone by now, but I don't think so. I think he might still be at the Devereau place; it might be a good hideout.

"All right, then ask another."

I closed my eyes, thinking hard. Then what I asked in my mind was, Will the Sheriff ever be my friend again? I opened my eyes.

Mrs. Louderback fanned out the cards, looked at them, then at me. "I don't think the question was put right. It looks like there was no reason for it, really. Can you ask it aloud?"

Aloud? I shook my head. "*Nu*-huh."

News

5

I still had almost two hours until it was time to be in the kitchen fixing salads (and that wouldn't take long, as we had only three dinner guests). I decided to walk the two miles from Spirit Lake to La Porte, which was bigger and had more "amenities." I learned this word listening to people complain about the Hotel Paradise's lack of them.

Peering into the future tells on a person's nerves. There was Mrs. Louderback's queer answer to my question about the Sheriff and there was that moment of seeming to see past me and through the kitchen window. This was so strange that it made me think Mrs. Louderback might be a medium, even though she says she's not. For she seemed to leave herself while something else took over. What did she mean saying my question about the Sheriff was put wrong? That the question didn't matter?

What I needed right now was peace and quiet. I chose the Abigail Butte County Library. I always feel comfortable in it, and Miss Babbit, the librarian, never suggests I go to the children's room. She is smart enough to see that if I like the main reading room, that's my business. Probably, she is so glad to see someone my age come in of her own accord that she wants to make sure I keep doing it.

And of course there's the quiet, broken only by the rustles of newspapers and magazines, or the gentle thud of book on book, or the closing of the file drawers, or the muted voices of people up at the checkout desk.

I always begin by burrowing in among the shelves and have nearly memorized the section numbers on the cards at their ends. This time I went to the travel section, looking for some place far from where I was. There was a big book, mainly of photographs, about China and Japan. That was about as far as I could get from Spirit Lake and La Porte, so I hauled it over to one of the readers' tables.

I rested my head against one hand and with the other turned the pages, lazily looking at pictures of Mt. Fuji. In the chapter about Tokyo, I was surprised to see so much tumult in the streets and so much neon. It was all so quick and bright. I'd always pictured Japan (when I thought about it at all, which was almost never) as being slow, with workers standing up to their shinbones in rice paddies, or pulling rickshaws. Or was that China? I flipped to the China section and there I did see some rice paddies, where women were working with their skirts pulled up and knotted and with faces hidden by those immense platelike straw hats.

My eyelids were heavy, threatening to shut on me. I had been known to doze off in this position, jerking awake and finding that my head was still leaning against my hand. I hadn't fallen from the chair; my head hadn't even dropped from my hand to the book. I was intact. That did not make me feel good. It meant my mind wasn't free to take a vacation. My sentries, upon seeing me asleep, hadn't even gone out for coffee and a doughnut. I was always on guard. It was a strain. Maybe I was the same, asleep or awake.

I shook myself a little to get things going again and turned more pages and came to one of a long undulating wall. This was the Great Wall of China, the text said, so incredibly long that it was the only thing on earth that could be seen from outer space. I guess they forgot about Ree-Jane.

When I was tired of looking at the travel book, I got up and went to the newspapers. I liked the library's way of displaying them, each one afixed to a long pole, which was the way they were handled in France and Germany. I'd seen this in books too, pictures of people sitting in the sidewalk cafés of Paris or Berlin, reading papers on poles. It leant the library a pleasant forcignness. You felt you were sitting in one of those Parisian cafés, sitting at a table in the sun, in dark glasses and very rich clothes with maybe a little dog on a leash lying peacefully under the table. The waiters slipped silently about, very efficient in their movements, as Vera is.

The murder near White's Bridge still took up a lot of space on the front page, which wasn't surprising considering how little happens around here. The shooting must have been like the answer to a prayer for Suzie Whitelaw, who was reporting it in the *Conservative;* her slant was tragedy-bent, referring to "the tragic victim." This column was headlined:

MURDER VICTIM IDENTIFIED, FATHER SOUGHT

It went on from there:

> The police have now been able to identify the tragic victim of the shooting occurring two weeks ago near White's Bridge. Fern Queen, 38, resided with Mr. and Mrs. George Queen of Cold Flat Junction, where the victim lived for most of her life. The Queens, Fern's uncle and aunt, are traumatized by the news.
>
> Sheriff Sam DeGheyn has been put in charge of the investigation, Cold Flat Junction not having its own police force. Sheriff DeGheyn has asked for the help of anybody who may have seen the victim's father, Benjamin Queen. Mr. Queen has recently been released from prison where he served twenty years for the murder of his wife, Rose Devereau Queen. Fern was the only child.
>
> "It's like it's happening all over again," said the tearful aunt, Bathsheba Queen.
>
> Deputy Sheriff Donny Mooma has asked anyone who can help the police with their inquiries to please get in touch with the Sheriff's Office.

23

I come under the heading of "anybody who can help," but I haven't helped, not yet. Whether I do or not I guess depends on how much my conscience is going to hurt me. And how is it I wind up knowing more about this whole thing than any other person? More than the relations and the police do?

Bathsheba Queen, referred to as the "tearful aunt" and "traumatized" is Suzie Whitelaw taking her usual liberties. It would take a lot more than Fern being killed to get Sheba Queen traumatized and teary. But when Sheba says it's like it's happening all over again, she doesn't know the half of it.

It is hard being "anybody who can help" and not doing it. The thing is, Ben Queen more or less put his fate in my hands. I will never forget what he said: *If it goes too hard on you, turn me in.*

This amazed me. It is the most astonishing thing anyone has ever said to me. It's the first time anyone has placed my welfare before their own. I would have done just about anything for the Sheriff, but I couldn't tell him that I knew where Ben Queen was, or at least where he was when I'd seen him at the Devereau house. I do not know who Ben Queen came looking for, but who he found was me.

I would have given him a start if he hadn't been a man beyond starts and surprises. He looked like someone who'd had enough to last him all his life long. You might say of a person such as this that life tastes flat on his tongue like stale soda. He certainly wasn't bothered by me being at the Devereau house. Then I thought, Well, why should he be? I'm twelve years old and he was the one with the gun. I don't know who he would have used it on; he didn't need to scare me off as I wasn't about to arrest him and drag him back to prison. But I can certainly understand why the Sheriff wanted to find him, what with Ben Queen only several days out of prison and his daughter getting killed. That must be too big a coincidence for the Sheriff to swallow; it's certainly a horrible enough one.

And Mary-Evelyn Devereau's house is part of it too, the reason why I held my tongue. I do not want police going into it, some thick-booted, clumsy policeman like Donny Mooma clumping around, opening drawers and looking at sheet music and photos, opening closets and going over Mary-Evelyn's dresses and toys. I do not want them dusting for fingerprints and leaving their own.

The Devereau house is my secret, one that I share with Mr. Root and the Wood boys. If it hadn't been for them helping by leading a way through the woods, I might never have gone there, for the woods are very dense and thick, whatever road there must have been long since grown over. The woods turn day almost to night. Even when the sun strikes light on the lake, making its surface gleam like crushed diamonds, in the woods there is only this green, luminous glow, an underwater kind of light, a decoy, cunning and crafty.

Keeping this secret weighs heavily on me; it weighs more on me than Ree-Jane's snipes and Lola's rages; it might even weigh more heavily than the death of my father, but I don't remember how I felt about that, so it too is like a thicket illuminated by a subterranean light.

Cunning, crafty.

Waitressing

6

It was part of my waitressing job to fix the salads every night just before dinner, which usually started at six o'clock. It was a really boring task and I had asked my mother once or twice if somebody else could do it. She pointed out there were only two "somebodies"—Vera and Anna Paugh—and that Vera was needed in the dining room to check the Pyrex coffeemaker and all of the place settings (as if only Vera could tell where the fork and water glass went). Anna Paugh couldn't do the salads because she couldn't get away from her other job before six P.M. (With what the hotel paid her, I wasn't surprised she needed another job.) So which "somebody" did I have in mind? My mother could be sarcastic that way.

She would say all this while breading the chicken pieces, removing the cigarette from her mouth to rest it on the edge of the counter, which was scarred as black as notches on a rifle. Also, I think she talked like this—in her sarcastic mode—to amuse Walter, our dishwasher, who, wiping plates and pots, waited back in the shadows to hear her say things. Walter's laugh was a kind of gasp, a sucking-in of breath as if each one were his last.

I don't really mind her amusing Walter at my expense; I like Walter and think he should be given more attention anyway, although not so much as to make him fall behind and result in me having to dry dishes. Lola Davidow claims Walter is retarded, for he's a grown man who acts like he has hardly a child's comprehension. But of course he isn't, for if that were the case, how could he understand my mother's sarcasm so well? Sometimes not even *I* get it, and I like to think I am no dumbbell.

So I'm stuck with arranging lettuce in bowls and covering it with tomatoes and onion and pepper rings, taking care to position each of these as artistically as I can. (I am not, however, supposed to get too artistic and make chopped egg and olive faces, which I have done, on occasion.)

The salad makings are kept on a big table with a white enameled top in the kitchen's center. The crocks of salad dressings sit here, together with big serving trays. Whenever my mother announces an order is ready, we grab a tray and load it quickly. She insists the food reach the tables still piping hot and it just irritates the life out of her (she's fond of saying) if we let her plates sit for more than five seconds. It's almost as if she can see heat leaving those plates. She can stare at that drumstick, watching it cool and commanding whoever it belongs to to pick it up before she brings the whole plate down on the waitress's head.

Walter (who would be stacking his clean, dry dinner plates on the metal shelf directly over the big black stove) just about convulses with laughter. He really thinks my mother is a card. He calls her "Miss Jen," which is what nearly everyone does, even Ree-Jane. (When I had suggested Ree-Jane as a salad-fixer, my mother merely gave one of her humorless laughs.)

This dinnertime I had only three salads to make for our three full-time guests (or "regulars" as Mrs. Davidow liked to call them), so I had plenty of time to inspect the stove and countertop to see what was for dinner. To do this I can almost follow my nose, which has become so acquainted with my mother's cooking, it can lead me to answers even

27

if I shut my eyes. That would not do justice to the look of her cooking, though, and I keep them open. A cloud of whipped potatoes sat in the top of a double-boiler, steam rising from the bottom, keeping them moist; a long glass dish of French green beans, onion rings, and mushrooms sat on the counter; fried chicken baked in the oven (fried first, then baked). I inspected the pastry table for desserts and was pleased to see one of the brioche cakes, layered with butter cream, caramel cream, and something like vanilla pudding spiked with brandy. Just looking at it made me feel wonderfully fat and drunk. Sitting beside the cake was a sieve of powdered sugar. I did my mother a favor and dusted the top of the cake with it.

Our "paying guests" (as if the other guests were charity cases) are Miss Bertha, Mrs. Fulbright, and the Poor Soul. His name is Mr. Muggs, but Lola Davidow has christened him the Poor Soul and now all of us call him that. He comes for a couple of nights when he has business around here and always requests the same room. How anyone could get attached to a room at the Hotel Paradise is beyond me. But for the Poor Soul I guess coming back to the same room is like coming home. That thought surprised me and was worth writing down in my journal. Several guests ask for rooms in this way—*I want my old room back*—and Mrs. Davidow will save a particular room for a particular person.

So Mr. Muggs always gets number forty-two on the second floor. There is nothing at all special about it, except it's the one nearest the bathroom. Very few of our rooms have private baths, as the hotel was built back in the 1800s, long before anyone had ever heard of motels.

Sometimes we waitresses have to double as chambermaids when our one maid is sick or doesn't show up. It is a thankless job, for there are no tips. Number forty-two looks unoccupied, even when Mr. Muggs is occupying it. It's amazing. Even the towels on the wooden towel rack look unused. I have to look closely to see any wrinkles in them, have to feel them for dampness. You actually have to open the wardrobe—most rooms not having closets—to see if there are any clothes in it. Even the things people usually set on top of the dresser, the Poor Soul puts in the drawers: brushes, aftershave, keys, and coins.

I can hear Ree-Jane's voice again: *You know his trouble, don't you? He's anal.* She said this smirkily, pleased with her greater knowledge, doubly pleased because it had to do with body parts (which I didn't know until I looked it up). "No, he isn't," I answered. "It's you that's anal." When I don't know what Ree-Jane means, I just contradict her. This infuriates her. "You don't even know what it means!" was her weak comeback. I didn't, of course, but I was expert in looking as if I did.

The dictionary definition goes on in a really complicated fashion, talking about "retentive" and "expulsive" and that these character traits have to do with toilet training. I wasn't about to ponder toilet training, neither the Poor Soul's nor my own. "Anal retentive" is how the dictionary puts it. I practiced the phrase until I was comfortable with it.

I waited awhile, giving Ree-Jane time to forget. One Sunday morning after breakfast I walked out onto the porch where she was surrounded with more than one Sunday paper, pages sprawling around over the wicker rockers and the wicker table. I reached for the comics and she yanked them back and told me to get my own paper.

"I knew I shouldn't ask, seeing how anal retentive you are."

Well. Didn't she ever open her mouth to say something cutting? Nothing came out. Then she said, "You are so stupid. Anal isn't about giving somebody newspapers!"

"Did I say it was? Anal retentiveness includes everything." I leaned my head back against the green rocking chair and gently rocked, not looking at her, but humming a ditty Will and Brownmiller had composed.

She huffed off.

Oh, how I wish Ree-Jane were like the Poor Soul. How I wish she'd slip away like a shadow, leaving no footprint, no scent of perfume, no lock of hair.

Poor Soul.

Poor Ree-Jane.

29

———

I recalled this whole incident while I arranged a green-pepper ring on the Poor Soul's salad. Then I moved on to Miss Bertha's and Mrs. Fulbright's. These two old ladies are friends and together come as soon as the hotel opens in the spring and stay until it closes at the end of September. Since they are a source of steady income, we have to be extra nice to them. It's not hard to be nice to Mrs. Fulbright, who is sweet and not at all persnickety. Miss Bertha is otherwise. She bangs her cane on the floor *thump thump thump!* when she wants more hot rolls or water, complaining that I'm not quick enough: *Dish up my dinner, girl! Thump thump!*—as if anyone but my mother ever does the dishing up. Who else can be trusted to dust a smidgen of red pepper over the satiny cheese sauce which lies in a wide band atop the toast points? No one, that's who.

One of Miss Bertha's problems of course is that she doesn't turn on (or up) her hearing aid, a big beige-colored plastic thing that sits in her ear like an extra ear, making it look deformed, which fits in with (or "complements," as they say) her hump. Her head looks like a walnut, with the same creases and crevices in it. I try to feel sorry for Miss Bertha, who I guess isn't making it through life on looks—neither am I, after all—but the second she starts in tossing rolls around or thumping with that cane, I forget my good intentions.

I looked at the salads and thought they needed sprucing up. On a glass plate on the table were a few narrow strips of pimento which I used to adorn two of the salads. Then I went over to the main counter and picked out a hot pepper sliver and decorated the third salad with that. Only I needed to know which was which and with just three regulars, I would be serving tonight by myself. Vera and Anna Paugh did not have to come in. There was no need for them.

When only the regulars eat dinner, my mother doesn't go to the usual trouble of fixing three different entrees. She thinks they can make do with two. One is a dish she cooks from scratch, and the other, something done with leftovers. Tonight, it's fried chicken and meatloaf, although to refer to her meatloaf as "leftovers" is to do it a serious injury, especially with that Spanish sauce she pours over it, tomatoes mashed with sunlight.

Fortunately, the three regulars always come in the minute the dining room opens up, so I don't have to be wasting time I can put to better use in waiting around for them.

"I'll be leaving in the morning," said Mr. Muggs, sad as sad could be, as he said everything.

As I put down his fruit cocktail, I said back (sadly), "That's really too bad. Maybe you'd like two desserts tonight." My mother's cooking was the remedy for every trouble, including bleeding from your aorta (which I had learned about in science class). I added, "Tonight's Angel Pie and Black Forest Cake."

The Poor Soul sighed. "That would be most appreciated. Perhaps half an order of each?"

I blinked. *Half* a piece of Angel Pie? Solomon could have divided that baby easier. But I smiled and said of course.

Tonight, Mrs. Davidow was at one of Helene Baum's cocktail parties in La Porte, which is lovely news, as it allows the whole hotel to breathe a sigh of relief, and more particularly because it allows me to get at Mrs. Davidow's liquor supply, so that I can make Aurora Paradise her favorite drink: a Cold Comfort.

Sorrowful Places

7

Aurora Paradise does not exercise any right of ownership, like hiring or firing or sending Lola Davidow and Ree-Jane packing. This is not because Aurora is humble or generous or indifferent, but because she doesn't want to bother herself to come down from the fourth floor. She sometimes has her food sent up on the dumbwaiter that travels from the back office up to the fourth floor. I don't know why the dumbwaiter was positioned in the back office, but it works fine and rattles the Hotel Paradise fried chicken and braised lamb and Angel pie right up there.

The fourth floor is Aurora's kingdom, or, rather, what she likes to call her "duchy" ever since I told her Ree-Jane intended to marry a duke so that people would have to call her a duchess. That's assuming, of course, that Hollywood or Broadway or a modeling agency doesn't grab her first.

Up here's as close as that blond floozy'll ever get to a duchy. To Aurora, Ree Jane is always a blond floozy. When Ree-Jane was stupid enough to venture up to the fourth floor with Aurora's chicken dinner, she got a chicken wing thrown at her. It hit her head; and I, pressed back into the shadows of the stairwell, was fortunate enough to witness this. Ree-Jane thinks she rules the world. But even she can't pretend to have conquered Aurora Paradise (who she dismisses as a crazy old coot) or me (who she dismisses as a crazy young one).

I am one of the few people allowed on the fourth floor and that's because I've been entertaining Aurora with the White's Bridge murder, or, more specifically, the Mirror Pond murder, and (more important) because I mix drinks for her. Fancy drinks are my recently acquired skill; the best of them is my Cold Comfort. Aurora has her own liquor, but she would sooner use Lola Davidow's. I complained about this. I said if Mrs. Davidow ever catches me at her liquor supply, she'll kill me. "Just be glad you died in a good cause," she says, "for the duchy is piss-poor! The barons ain't paid their rents!"

I didn't bother asking her why barons were renting, for I knew Aurora didn't understand feudalism and peasants any more than I did, and I'd even studied it in school. Aurora knows as much about running a duchy as she does about running a hotel. So I continue endangering life and limb by using Lola Davidow's gin and rum and Southern Comfort to whip up Aurora's Cold Comfort. (I have to make the drinks in the kitchen when no one is around, as the duchy is out of ice, orange slices, and maraschino cherries.) I wish I could make one of Lola Davidow's mint juleps, for I have an idea they would take first prize in any drink contest. I'll say this for Lola, she is first-rate at drink-mixing.

Aurora has been around forever, longer than us Grahams, and she knows, or at least knew, everyone in these parts. She knew the Devereau sisters and is the one who set me on the right track about Rose Souder Devereau running off with Ben Queen over forty years ago, right after Mary-Evelyn drowned. It wasn't purposeful on Aurora's part, as she has no wish to please me or anybody else. But without intending to be, she was and will be—though she doesn't know it yet—a huge help in my investigation of the circumstances surrounding the deaths of Mary-Evelyn Devereau, Rose, and Fern Queen.

33

Her information does not come easy. She blackmails me into being an audience for her "magical tricks," which consist of pick-a-card or find-the-pea, both of them unbelievably dumb and both of which she cheats at, making it impossible for me to win.

Aurora always sits in the same ancient rocking chair, wearing black or dark blue wool or a shiny gray stuff that looks like thin armor when the light hits it at certain angles. Her lace net gloves have the fingers cut back to the knuckle. She needs her fingers free so she can cheat at find-the-pea. She argues that she never cheats, but of course she does. Up here, she is surrounded by her things—a big old steamer trunk full of really beautiful clothes that she never wears, pictures of horses and grazing sheep, a big 1939 calendar hung on a nail. She writes things in the squares in her stingy little hand. I looked back at April once and there was stuff written there about FDR and other people I didn't know. She told me to get away, *get away!* and not to sully her calendar.

"How can I sully it? I'm not even touching it."

"With your eyes." Then she cackled. The cackle is put-on. "I'll have another drink, Miss!"

I took the glass and said, as sarcastically as I could, "Aren't you worried I'll sully the Southern Comfort?" Then I went downstairs, the glass in my hand preventing me from giving in to the temptation to slide down the bannister as I used to do when I was little.

As I said, I can entertain Aurora with what happened over near White's Bridge. I know more details than our weekly newspaper does and even more than the police. That should give me a sense of power, but instead, it makes me uneasy. I've talked to different people, ones that the Sheriff hasn't because he doesn't know there's a connection.

One of these people is Jude Stemple, who claimed the anonymous victim was "Ben Queen's girl" (and he was right). Jude Stemple is from Cold Flat Junction; so was Fern Queen. She was missing for several days but that didn't worry Bathsheba and George, the relatives she lived with, because Fern had always been touched in the head. There was no reason to connect her to a body found miles outside of La Porte. It was Aurora who'd told me about Ben Queen, and it was Jude Stemple who told me about Rose. But what Jude Stemple says is it couldn't possibly have been Ben who killed Rose, for he loved her too much.

So when I met Ben Queen at the Devereau house across the lake and we walked to Crystal Spring, I must admit I agreed with Jude

Stemple. Not that I wasn't scared running into a man just out of prison, in an empty house in deep woods by a forgotten lake. I was plenty scared. But it only lasted until Ben Queen began to talk.

Someone had murdered his daughter Fern, but it wasn't him.

There are some people born to take the blame for others, he said, and he was one of them. Then he looked at me for a while as if to say, *And you're another.*

It was then I began to tell him about the Girl, the one I had seen in Cold Flat Junction and across the lake at the Devereau house. I had seen her four times, I told him.

She looks, I had told him, *like your wife Rose. Like she was, I mean.*

Well, Ben Queen thought about this for a moment, and then said I must be mistaken, for there was no such person. That this Girl must be a figment of my imagination.

But I think he knew.

———

I have made a list of Sorrowful Places, and the little kitchen ranks number ten on the list. This surprises me because I wasn't that aware I had feelings for the little kitchen. Then I remembered that we use it in the winter when we stay at the hotel all year round, which is seldom. So from the little kitchen's windows I see blue mornings and deep snow, rime on the windowsills and, inside, the smell of biscuits baking and buckwheat cakes just beginning to bubble up before they're turned by my mother's magical hand. Now, I've never had occasion to handle a rosary, being non-Catholic, but from what I've seen, you go over and over its little beads, repeating Hail Marys or Mary, Mother of Gods, and thus you get absolution or get cleansed or something along that order. Me, if I want to do my soul a good turn, I just say *buck-wheatcakesbuckwheatcakesbuckwheat* and my soul is immediately comforted and cleansed.

So the little kitchen is number ten on my list of places I would most miss if I were never to see them again. I rank them from one to ten. I only know which goes where by testing: I have to close my eyes and picture the place vanishing and tell myself I'll never see it again. Then something wells up in me and my eyes spring open and I'm too cold or too warm. What wells up in me is fear, and I wonder if losing something is also the fear of losing something.

Sorrowful Places
1. The big kitchen
2. Spirit Lake
3. The Pink Elephant
4. The Rainbow Café
5. The Devereau house
6. The land across the railroad tracks in Cold Flat Junction
7. The bench in front of Britten's store
8. The Windy Run Diner
9. The Abigail Butte County Library
10. The little kitchen

I had to limit myself to ten items, otherwise I could go on nearly forever. To make sure I wasn't looking at every place I knew as a sorrowful place, I had to choose five places that were opposite, places that could disappear in an eyeblink and I'd be glad to see them go:

1. Ree-Jane's room
2. The part of the porch railing where Ree-Jane likes to pose
3. Miss Bertha's half of the dining room table
4. The salad table
5. "Europa," the expensive store where Ree-Jane buys her clothes

I have to review the first list every week to see if anything's changed in the ranking; usually something has.

It sounds like a strange thing to do, ranking places I'd miss. The way I know when I come upon such a place is that I'm gripped by this awful sadness. And it makes me think this sadness is always right there below the surface, and the surface is easily scratched.

I have to do this, but I'm not sure why. I have to do it in the same way of swallows flighting from cold places to warm ones. It's instinct to do this, it's as if there's a rite I have to perform; then if it comes on that one of these places vanishes, like the little kitchen catching fire and burning into black ash, I will not be wholly unprepared.

Pink thinking

8

The Pink Elephant is where I do most of my thinking. It's underneath the dining room and was once used for cocktail parties, mostly for the tennis players who went along with anything that meant more drinking. I've decorated it with candle stubs stuck in wine bottles with melted wax built up around the necks. There are large pictures which I have checked out of the Abigail Butte County Library and which I can return for new ones whenever I'm in my artistic mood.

No one comes here at all unless it's someone looking for me, which is seldom. Mice, cobwebs, darkness, the thick creaking door, the tall grass and weeds beyond it that always feel wet, even in sunshine. It isn't a place most people want to visit. If they can't find me for some reason, they send Walter. Walter gets the jobs nobody else wants. My mother is, of course, too busy to look for me; my brother Will is up in the Big Garage with Mill; Ree-Jane wouldn't be caught dead looking for me unless she knew it would result in something very unpleasant; Vera is too starched and stuck-up to walk down the gravel road and through the wet grass. So this leaves Walter.

Now, they would never in a million years send Walter to the front desk to check in guests. Anyone but Walter, including Vera and Anna Paugh, would be acceptable. But Walter, as always, doesn't mind he's being discriminated against and goes happily about the task of finding things, including me. Walter can find things. He's like one of those divining rods that locates underground springs.

When he comes to the Pink Elephant, I always offer him a Coke and a bench to sit on. He really likes the socializing, though we don't talk much. I find it soothing to talk to someone who's as slow in his speech as Walter. He can say *umm-hum* as if it had fifteen syllables in it. Words seem to stick in his mouth like burrs, and he peels off one and then another until he gets a statement out. But his trouble is nothing compared to the Wood boys'.

The hotel cat does slip in sometimes to see if there are any mice around. I'm not afraid of mice, but I enjoy the cat's company. He curls up under the table by my feet. He does not have a name, and I'm always reminding myself to think one up. It's possible he's happier without one.

I keep my journal here hidden in a crevice in the pink stucco wall behind a tin sign that advertises Mexican beer. It's decorated with a bull and a matador holding out his red cape. Besides the journal I have a Whitman's Sampler box which I like to go through each time I come here, not because I'm afraid someone has taken something, but just because I like to see the things in it. There's the snapshot of the Devereaus beneath the hotel porte cochere, the three sisters, and Mary-Evelyn. She's standing by herself in front. Now, whenever someone takes a picture of, say, Will and me, Will does something like put his two fingers over my head as if I'm a donkey. Or if it's Ree-Jane posing, I do the same thing to her; it's more to take away the curse of being permanently linked with her in a picture than to give her the donkey ears.

In the Devereau snapshot, though, no hand lies on Mary-Evelyn's shoulder; she's more than an arm's length away from them and no one's called her closer.

Other items in the box: two green marbles I found on the boardwalk that goes down to the Spirit Lake post office. It's a pleasant, leafy walk and I love to pick up the mail, to work the combination on the metal box, and to be the first to see what's there. Then there's a gold locket my mother told me I could have, as she doesn't know where she got it or who the man and woman in the picture inside are. (My mother's memory is not that good; maybe because she has her head so crammed full of recipes, there's no room for strangers.) The man and woman look like turn-of-the-century people; he has long sideburns and she has to hold her chin above a stiff column of collar.

Another thing I keep in the box is the red and black neckerchief Ben Queen handed me when I was in a squall of tears over Mary-Evelyn. I unfolded it now and wondered if tears smelled and gave it a whiff, but it just smelled cotton-y, nothing left over from me or Ben Queen. It bothers me that traces of people can so easily fade, that the red neckerchief held no scent of the person who'd worn it against his skin, and that no one who ever happened across my box sometime could look at the items there and unfold this square of cloth and think, *Oh, yes, Ben Queen. It smells just like him, and Emma Graham, see, here is the stain of her tears.*

It occurs to me that that's what police dogs and mediums with their sixth sense do; you give them a bit of material or a glove or a shoe and just by the smell (I think it's the smell) they go off through brush and brambles and eventually lead you to the person.

But I suppose the whole natural world forgets; the tall grass I plow through beyond the door does not hold onto the imprint of my shoe; the water she drowned in and the lily pads that bore her up have lost all trace of Mary-Evelyn Devereau. We don't leave anything of us behind except in others' memories. And if they forget us, we're finally gone at last.

I folded the square carefully and set it on the table beside the marbles.

What worries me, I think, is that Mary-Evelyn will be forgotten once I'm gone. Her hard little life, and then to be forgotten. She might as well have sunk like a stone to the bottom of Spirit Lake for all the remembering of her there was or will be. It's as if she'd been let go, as if the hand that reached to her from the bank had opened and she had sunk.

The worst of it must have been the knowing she'd been let go. As if the hardship of holding on to her wasn't worth the trouble.

In the Whitman's Sampler box is one other thing of importance. It's a piece from Mary-Evelyn's game of "Mr. Ree." It's a hollow tube about as big around as a nickel with a plastic head formed to look like the face in the Artist George playing card. He's one of the characters, along with Miss Scarlet, Colonel Mustard, and Niece Rhoda. There are six altogether.

If a player gets a murder card he can put one of the four tiny weapons inside his tube and later on kill one of the others. It's quite complicated. The detective is Mr. Ree. This is my favorite game. (I told Aurora about it and she said she wanted to play. She made quite a scene—which pleased me—when I told her it takes more than two players, otherwise each of us would know exactly who has the murder card.)

When I found the game of Mr. Ree in Mary-Evelyn's toy chest, Artist George was missing. I didn't think much of that at the time, not until a few days ago, days after Ben Queen had been at Crystal Spring. I found the Artist George playing piece in the little alcove at the spring where the tin cup is kept. George was slightly damp from lying on wet stone. But he had not lain there long, I knew that, for the night the four of us—that's Mr. Root and me and Ulub and Ubub—had gathered at the spring, we'd all drunk from the cup, and there was no playing piece in that stone alcove.

It's possible that Ben Queen put it there, but that's not likely for it was missing before he came to the house that night. Anyway, Ben Queen wouldn't have any reason for doing it.

But this was another roundabout way. What was the reason for doing it?

I pondered this question for some time. Except for me, no one comes to the spring anymore since the path has gotten so overgrown. No one except for the Wood boys and Mr. Root and Ben Queen that one night.

And the Girl. I had seen her twice around here, once on the other side of Spirit Lake, on the Devereau side; once just outside the house when I was inside.

I figure she left it for me to discover, left it as a clue. Or if not a clue, a message.

Why be so roundabout? That day I saw her when I was inside the Devereau house and she was outside, over by the stand of pine trees, why didn't she come up to the door and say: *This is what happened. I killed Fern Queen because . . .*

For it had to be her, didn't it? Ben Queen as much as said he would be taking the blame for that murder. Who else would he take the blame for except someone really important to him, such as his grandaughter? She had to be, for how else could she look so much like Rose? Even though Jude Stemple said Fern Queen never had children, well, he was only guessing. No, Fern must have had a girl, as I can't see any other way to explain it all. That would mean the Girl shot her own mother, which sends chills down my spine.

Unless she is a ghost—a ghost, or a Do-X-machine.

A short history of Do-X-machines

9

A "Do-X-machine," as I told you, is somebody who suddenly appears in the middle of things-going-wrong to bring order, to right wrongs, to save the day. In Greek plays, it's a god; in *The Wizard of Oz*, it's the Good Witch Glinda. And in a play it's an actor playing God who gets lowered to the stage on a chair or swing controlled by ropes and pulleys.

I learned this from my brother Will and his best friend Brownmiller. They're always in the Big Garage, rehearsing one of their "productions," usually musical, as Mill is such a fabulous musician. They did me a favor recently, but in return they said I'd have to play a part in this production. I agreed. Little did I suspect they wanted me to be the Do-X-machine, sitting in a chair lowered from the rafters. I told them they were crazy and I wouldn't play their damned machine, not me.

My brother stared at me for a while as he slowly chewed gum. Will can look straight at a person, his dark eyes like ten-penny nails, but usually he's looking right through you. It's his "thinking" mode.

"You get to wear tulle," he said.

I was a little taken aback. I liked the picture of me in a tulle gown. But where would they ever get one? I said this.

Will and Mill flicked a conspirator's glance at each other; they do this like they're playing tiddledywinks with their eyes. They were artful in communicating this way. You could see they didn't want anyone in on the details of their precious production.

We'd had an argument before about Glinda, when they'd had her coming up through a trapdoor in the stage, instead of down, on pulleys. They had Paul, the dishwasher's boy, tossing a cloud of flour up to make it look like Glinda appeared out of nowhere. But they decided against that way of doing it in their present production because "it didn't look real."

"*Real?*" I said. "Whenever did you two bother with things looking *real*? Did it look real when you made Paul sit way up in that tree"— I pointed (we were in what we call the "cocktail garden" behind the hotel, surrounded by pines) —"eating a banana and trying to sound like a monkey?"

"He sounds like a monkey anyway," said Mill, pushing his glasses back on his thin nose.

I ignored that. "Did it look *real* when you did that Ku Klux Klan play and tied him to a pole with a lot of newspapers and kindling underneath?"

(I should say that there are no colored people in Spirit Lake or La Porte—or for miles and miles around. I think maybe the entire county steered clear of the Civil War.)

"That production," said Will, "was very educational."

"And we never lit the newspapers," added Mill.

I heaved a huge, trying-my-patience sigh. "Look, I refuse to *endanger my life* being lowered from the Big Garage rafters! How do I know you can work this pulley?"

"We're trying it out on Paul first to see," said Will.

Paul was everybody's guinea pig, including my mother's. If there

43

was something in the refrigerator that had possibly been sitting awhile and you couldn't be sure from just sniffing it whether it was okay, she'd call for Paul to taste it. Then if he didn't fall over in a dead heap, she'd use it.

Paul's mother is the second dishwasher. She's tall and bony and bland looking, like vanilla junket. She has a deep voice like a man's but hardly ever says anything except to threaten Paul. So I see why Paul's strange; he gets it from his mother, unless he learned it from Walter. When the three of them are doing dishes, I like to hang around and listen to the talk, what little there is of it.

Poor Paul (not that I really feel sorry for him; I wouldn't have cared if they *had* lit the newspapers) gets into all kind of trouble. He hid under the pastry table once and when my mother walked away from the beautiful wedding cake she was icing, Paul reached up and just grabbed a chunk of cake in his fist. You can imagine. Once, his mother tied him to a chair to keep him out of trouble and he picked the stitching from his brand new shoes until they fell apart. It's not a good idea to leave his hands free, I told her.

You could say that Paul is the very *opposite* of a Do-X-machine. Things could be running smoothly until Paul comes on the scene, and then it all would go straight to hell.

I often come to the "cocktail garden" and swing on the big swing between two huge trees. It used to be exclusive, used only by the "in-crowd," meaning anyone with a bottle of gin. There used to be a white metal table with a big umbrella in the center and some white metal chairs. People also sat on the two green benches. It's really an elegant place to come and have cocktails in, and when the in-crowd came here, they were always dressed to the hilt in high heels or dark blazers. But like a lot of other things, it's no longer used. I don't know why; I think it's sad. Once it was on my list of Sorrowful Places, but something else more sorrowful beat it out. But you can't tell; it might be back on the list sometime.

I only wish it were harder for me to find Sorrowful Places.

Moses in the bullrushes

10

This bothered me a lot, and I thought about it for the two-mile walk into La Porte. I meant to go to the Rainbow Café, but as I was crossing the street near St. Michael's, I decided to go in and sit down.

I'm no church-goer; none of the family is, though my mother and Lola Davidow claim to be Episcopalians. I like St. Michael's because of all of its stained-glass windows and sculptures. Mostly, though, I think I just like to hang around and talk to Father Freeman, who is high up on my list of adults who don't talk down to children. Also, he's good-looking, very dark and elegant, although not as good-looking as the Sheriff.

Of course, Father Freeman wasn't around forty years ago, but I think he would still be interested in what I had to say about Mary-Evelyn. Probably, he'd at least have heard about the Devereaus and the old Devereau place, and certainly he knows about the shooting over at White's Bridge. I wonder with a kind of fearfulness if I'm the only person who thinks all of this is related. Does that make me more responsible for what might happen?

St. Michael's always strikes me as cool and dark and warm and light at the same time. This has to do with its silence and its windows and the way rays of sun weave color across the floor and the pews. I always stay on my feet and walk around and look at the windows. Even if I'm tired I try not to sit in a pew in case someone might think I'm praying.

Just as I knew he would, after ten or fifteen minutes, Father Freeman came out of one of the little doors near the altar, saw me, and smiled. He joined me in looking at one of the windows. We were pretty quiet. He is one of those people who don't have to be always talking and who are comfortable being around in silence.

I asked him if he was familiar with the case of Mary-Evelyn Devereau, and he said yes, a little. I told him all I knew, the details I'd written in my notebook, but not, of course, about Ben Queen. I did consider it for a moment; priests and lawyers cannot tell what you've told them. They are bound not to.

We fell silent again. And then he said, "That's one of the saddest stories I've ever heard." Sadly, he shook his head. "A little girl rowing herself out on a lake and drowning that way. Why do you think she did it?"

"They said it was an accident."

"Yes, but it was no accident, surely, that she was in the boat in the first place."

It was such a relief to have someone take my side in this. "I know. I've been trying to work it out. There are too many questions left unanswered. It doesn't make any sense the way it happened—" I felt myself rushing headlong into speech, the words tripping over one another. I was breathless.

"You've given this a lot of thought."

I nodded but kept looking up at the stained-glass window.

"Moses," he said.

"Huh?"

"The bullrushes," he said. "You know, when he was a baby."

I have hardly any acquaintance with the Bible, but I mumbled, yes, I knew. Which I didn't. All I knew about Moses was the Red Sea.

"To save him, his mother wrapped him in rushes and then put him in a little boat."

Then he fell silent again and seemed to be in a brown study (a phrase I adored, Maud Chadwick having told me what it meant) over Moses. I didn't see really any similarity between Moses and Mary-Evelyn. It sort of irritated me he had to bring Moses into it. I said, "Well, but Moses got over it and came back and parted the Red Sea." I hoped Father Freeman was impressed with my grasp of Moses's life.

He nodded, and said, "I didn't mean they were literally alike."

"I guess *not*." I said with real authority, although I didn't know what he meant.

I determined then to look up the story of Moses, but I didn't have time to go to the library now, and I'd have to allow myself some time after I got back to the hotel to talk to Aurora Paradise before dinner. Also, I wanted to stop at the Rainbow.

––––––

The Rainbow Café is owned by a bossy woman named Shirley. We call her Shirl. Like Lola Davidow, she is always complaining about her customers. Ordinarily, it's the customer who gets to complain about the management (the rude help, the cold room, the mile-long walk to the bathroom); for the Hotel Paradise and the Rainbow Café, it's the other way around. Shirl and Lola complain about the customers, as often as not to their faces. Once people get used to it, they don't pay any attention.

Shirl sits on a high stool behind the cash register, smoking and barking commands and selling her Heavenly Pie, which is an imitation of my mother's Angel Pie, the one with the meringue crust. Angel Pie is one of the hotel specialties—I guess Aurora would say its "signature pie." For Shirl, my mother threw in a couple of her extra ingredients, in this case a quarter teaspoon of cayenne pepper for the meringue crust and a tablespoon of mayonnaise ("Be sure it's Hellmann's") for the lemon chiffon filling. Who would be nitwit enough to believe this? you might ask. But you don't know my mother. She can lock eyes with you as if she's got a pistol at her temple and lie. Then you might say this is not a trait to want to imitate, but, again, you've never seen my mother do it. It's really not so much lying as *acting*. My mother has a great flair for it (and used to do it when she was young and put on amateur theatricals here at the Hotel Paradise), and she can change selves

47

and accents like Lola Davidow can change martinis for mint juleps. I've heard my mother, among a group of guests from the Deep South, slather on the accent of the most solid Georgia peach-picker that ever lived.

This must be where my brother gets it; his dramatic flair, his ability to stare you down and lie—this must come from my mother.

So Shirl sits in the Rainbow smoking and complaining, her elbows on the glass case in which are housed her Heavenly Pies that no one buys twice. Her cakes and doughnuts, though, are quite popular.

One of the waitresses is Charlene, a pasty-faced girl whose big bust greets you before her eyes do and who's always getting pinched on the behind. The other waitress, one of my two all-time favorite people from anywhere, is Maud Chadwick. She's kind of tall and pretty with silky light brown hair and the clearest face I've ever seen. You can read Maud in her face. I don't know how old she is, maybe as old as thirty or thirty-five, I'd guess. But she has a way of sinking into herself and coming up seventeen, as if she's got all of these past selves right inside that she can call up whenever she wants to. Maybe that's why she seems to know how I feel: her twelve-year-old self is right there at her beck and call. It occurs to me that this is a real gift, almost to become the person you're talking to. In a way, it's my mother's ability to come on as a Southerner, except Maud isn't acting; she just *is*.

Shirl has imposed a ton of rules, tacked up on little signs; one of these is stuck up on the high-backed mahogany booths in the rear of the room warning that booths can only be used by two or more people. But Maud always sees to it I get to sit in a booth; she takes a break when I come in and sits there with me, at least until I get what I've ordered. Once "ensconced" (which is how Maud describes it) with my Coke and bowl of chili, she can go back to waiting tables. "Squatter's rights," she calls it.

The thing is that a lot of the time the booths are completely empty, as the people who come to the Rainbow are mostly by themselves and are regulars who sit at the counter—a lot of them on exactly the same stools, same time every weekday. There's Dodge Haines (who owns the Chevy dealership) and there's Mayor Sims. These are the two biggest fanny-pinchers, which I think in the mayor is disgusting; he should be setting a good example. Then there's Ubub and Ulub, the Wood boys, who do not seem to mind being called by the letters on their license plates. But then, the Wood boys have very even temperaments. I guess they'd have to, getting all the fun poked at them that they do, which I think is terrible.

Maud always waits on them because Charlene likes to make them order, just to hear them say things like "oat bee sanguid" for "roast beef sandwich." But Maud tells them the special and all they have to do is nod or shake their heads, and then she tells them something else until they nod, *Yes, I'll have that.*

One person who won't put up with anybody heckling Ulub and Ubub is the La Porte Sheriff. If he hears Dodge Haines or Bud Hemple or one of the others giving the Woods a hard time, he'll likely walk back out and put a ticket on the person's car. He knows everyone's vehicle and it's not hard to find a reason for a ticket, considering most of them (especially the mayor) park without any attention to signs. They know why they're getting a ticket, though, and when the Sheriff walks in, they shut up from teasing Ulub and Ubub and drink their coffee and talk about other things.

The Sheriff and Maud are good friends; you can sense their closeness even though he's always teasing her and she's always bickering with him. But still, you can tell. Maud's divorced, but has a son named Chad who's away at school. The Sheriff is married to a woman named Florence who I hardly ever see. I've heard my mother and Lola talking about her and how she goes with every man she sees. *Poor Sam,* they say and sigh.

If there's one person I can't imagine saying "poor Sam" about, it's the Sheriff. More than that I can't imagine any wife of his going with someone else. He's very handsome and though he might be a shade under six feet, he looks over it. There is a tallness to him that can't be measured in inches, and I don't think it's the holstered gun on his hip.

The Sheriff seems really glad to see me when I turn up, almost as if someone just shoved an unexpected present under his nose. For me, this is really something, as it is not a reaction I get from people most of the time. I have tried hard to live up to his idea of me. That I guess I failed is my biggest problem.

Moses and Aurora

11

Aurora Paradise is the only one I know who has a Bible. But, of course, she wouldn't let me see it until I made her a Cold Comfort. She called it my "signature drink." Not even Lola Davidow could make a Cold Comfort, for it took not only skill, but imagination. Well, imagination, anyway; skill didn't come into it much. As long as I started with Southern Comfort (from the Davidow supply), I could toss in anything else—brandy, Jack Daniel's, rye whiskey, crème de menthe—in addition to fruit juice. I perfected this concoction as I went along, adding an orange slice, a sprig of mint, or a cube of pineapple, and if I wanted her to really remember, to resurrect people and scenes from the past, I made a whole fruit kabob and tossed in more brandy. The Bible would not test my creativity in the drink department, as it made no demands on Aurora's mind. Just to get a look in her Bible, a maraschino cherry on the ice cubes would do.

She sipped her Cold Comfort and smacked her lips and squinched her eyes shut. "Umm-*hmm!*" she said and sipped some more, first making bubbles by blowing in the straw (which is so childish I hardly ever do it anymore).

"My Bible? Now what do you want that for?" She rocked in a satisfied way, her fingers in their dressy little net gloves, plying the soda straw.

"None of—" I was about to say "none of your beeswax" but caught myself. For Aurora might just know the whole story of Moses. I really didn't want to sift through all of those thin, tissue-y pages. Then I reminded myself that if Aurora Paradise didn't lie outright (as she did about the rules of cards and the find-the-pea trick), she liked to slyly insert a piece of *misinformation* in an account, just to trip a person up. So I said, "I just want to read the Moses story."

"*Moses?* You suddenly get religion, girl? You been over there to the camp meeting with the Holy Rollers again?"

I had gone there once with Will and Mill, who only attended to hear songs they could make up new words for. I ignored that question. Then she asked, "Do you even know which part Moses is in? Old Testament or New?"

It was fifty-fifty so I took a chance. "Old Testament." As I've said, I'm on very shaky ground, Bible-wise. But she didn't contradict, so I went on. "I mean, how many chapters into it is Moses when he gets put in the bullrushes?" I certainly did not want to read any more about Moses than I had to.

Aurora blew down her straw again, but there was little liquid left. "Well, you don't have to read it. I can tell you the life of Moses." She said this while cutting me a sly glance.

"No! I want to read it myself."

She shrugged. "Please yourself, only you got to be careful. Some Bibles don't get the story right."

"What are you talking about? Bibles are Bibles, there's neither wrong nor right ones!"

Elaborately, she placed her glass on the little table beside her rocking chair and fiddled with her net gloves. I just knew she was trying to fill me with doubts and put obstacles in my path. And I stood (I was never invited to sit down) wondering what was the difference really between Aurora and someone like Ree-Jane? I answered myself. Easy. Ree-Jane has no imagination.

Aurora Paradise was much more like my mother giving out recipes with one wrong ingredient in them, like adding cold coffee grounds to the Chocolate Feather Cake. I think this is brilliant and very diplomatic. It makes her out to be generous and at the same time she holds onto her trade secrets.

"Yes, there are. Maybe I'd better tell you Moses's story."

"So which story would you tell me? The right or the wrong one?" I asked this in a put-on-sweet voice. When she cackled, I said, "For a woman ninety-one years old, you act really childish."

"Seventy-nine!" she snapped. "Not a day over, Miss!"

"Oh, well, that explains everything." I took the empty glass and left the room in what I thought was a grand fashion.

Falling out with the Sheriff

12

It wasn't until several days after she was shot and killed that the police were able to identify Fern Queen. There was no identification on her, like a driver's license. Finally, when Sheba and George Queen heard the description of the woman found shot over near White's Bridge, they called the police.

Cold Flat Junction doesn't have a police station or any "police presence" (as the Sheriff calls it), so the state troopers notified ours. Usually, the Sheriff is the one who goes when there's trouble in Cold Flat Junction, and this sure looked like trouble.

I could have told the police who the dead woman was, only I didn't. My trouble with the Sheriff started because I didn't tell him. But more important, I didn't tell him about Ben Queen. The police didn't seem to care too much as to *why* he'd shoot his and Rose's daughter. For if it wasn't Ben Queen, who else would have done it? I got the impression they did not linger over this question.

The Sheriff suspected I knew something; no, he *knew* I knew something when he sat down in my booth in the Rainbow and told me he was just back from Cold Flat Junction where he'd talked to Sheba and George Queen. They had told him, in passing, that Jen Graham's girl (that's me) had been to their house with an Elijah Root, who the Sheriff didn't know and wondered how I did: "I mean with Mr. Root being in his sixties, seventies, it was interesting that you'd be traveling around with him." The Sheriff could be sarcastic. As I'd seen the Sheriff every day since Fern Queen got shot, he wondered that I didn't mention this visit of mine to the Queens and also what else my personal (and unauthorized, he said) investigation had turned up.

All I said was "Nothing," which was hardly the gospel truth, seeing that it had turned up Ben Queen.

It was the night before I talked to the Sheriff in the Rainbow that Ben Queen had appeared at the Devereau house and been just as surprised to find me there as I was to find him. Because Rose had lived there, it didn't seem strange to me that he'd turn up there if he were looking for someone. Did he tell me why he was there? Did I ask him? No, because I thought I knew. I knew he was just out of prison. And someone had shot his daughter. But I knew, after we talked, it wasn't him.

We walked from the house to the spring, and that's when we talked about scapegoats. "There's people put on this earth to take the blame for others." Mary-Evelyn was one, he said; she was the scapegoat for the whole family, the person upon whose head was heaped the sins and misfortunes of the others, of all the Devereaus. It was an accident, he said, an awful accident that had happened to that child.

I believed him then about Mary-Evelyn. But after I'd had time to think about it, I changed my mind. In a way, I would rather not think Mary-Evelyn was so miserable she'd take the chance she did. A blind chance. I hate to think her head was so crowded with remembering things the Devereau sisters had done to her and would keep on doing, that she was driven to escape. The idea that someone our age could find life so hard it drove her to go out on that lake in the middle of the night—well, it hardly bears thinking about.

So the Sheriff and I had been sitting in the Rainbow that day after he visited the Queens. He was waiting me out, waiting for me to tell

him what I'd seen and what I'd heard. What I knew. We sat in silence
while his ice cream melted on top of his peach pie. I still remember the
humming silence, as if everything had stopped except for the jukebox
voice of Patsy Cline.

I was grateful for Patsy. I was grateful to hear someone knew how
it felt. Keeping a secret like that from the Sheriff was hard. The reason
I did it is not because Ben Queen told me to keep quiet about seeing
him. No, he said the very opposite; he said: *If it goes too hard on you,
turn me in.*

I couldn't do it; I couldn't turn in someone who put my welfare
ahead of his. I would do it, too, the same thing, if it had been the Sheriff who'd said that to me.

But no one had ever said it to me.

It is not too late, I told myself as I stood in the rotunda of our courthouse, looking at the frosted glass of the door with SHERIFF painted on
it in white block letters. It's one of several doors arranged in a half-
moon arc around the rotunda. The other half is taken up by a wide
marble staircase with columns on either side. It is an elaborate building
for a town the size of La Porte. There are two dozen broad white steps
leading up to its entrance, and stone lions flank its door. It also has a jail
out back, where prisoners stand around with their hands gripping the
bars of the windows, yelling comments whenever girls walk by, which
I think is pretty disgusting and shouldn't be allowed. I asked the Sheriff once why he didn't crack down on the prisoners. I said it isn't very
pleasant having a serial killer whistle and catcall when you passed. He
could be memorizing your face for when he got out.

The Sheriff just shook his head. "I never heard anybody exaggerate the way you do."

Recalling this, I sighed. For that was back in the happy days when
we were friends and walked all over the town, reading meters and giving out tickets.

Today, it was a little after two o'clock on a Saturday and the Orion
was showing a matinee, as it always did on Saturdays and Sundays. It
was in the back of my mind that if things didn't work out at the courthouse, I might just go along to the movies. I'm not sure what I meant
by "work out." Probably, it meant that the Sheriff would ask me to go
along with him on a meter check. But I didn't go into the Sheriff's

office; I stood and watched shadows move back and forth behind the frosted glass. I didn't know whose shadows. The Sheriff might not even be in there.

I was carrying a white bag of Shirl's fresh doughnuts. There were two plain and two sugared and one iced. The Sheriff likes plain doughnuts and Maureen Kneff, the typist, likes sugar. Donny Mooma, the deputy, likes chocolate iced, so I got vanilla, just to let him know I was losing no sleep over his likes and dislikes. I do not like Donny; I can't stand the way he struts around and puts on when the Sheriff isn't there—sitting at the Sheriff's desk, pretending he's in charge of La Porte and everything else for a hundred miles around. I can't think why the Sheriff keeps him on, for Donny is really dumb. He's always tugging his wide black belt up to make sure you take notice he's got a gun in that holster.

I looked in the doughnut bag, then folded it closed twice over and went to the recessed fountain by one of the pillars. I tipped my head to drink, though I didn't like this water. It was nothing like Crystal Spring; it was flinty from all the chemicals they put in it. I wiped my hand across my mouth as I looked at the frosted glass door again. I was thinking up ways to introduce the subject of Ben Queen, like: *I got the biggest surprise when I was at the lake last week* or *Guess who I ran into?* How stupid. There seemed no way to get out from under not telling him before. I stood there for a while longer. Above me, the clock said two-twenty. It was set in the molding just below the dome that seemed to soar off into the slate gray sky.

I felt doomed. I turned and walked down the marble stairs. Outside, at the top of more stairs I opened the bag and took out the white-iced doughnut. They were my favorite.

Uninvited

13

It was not until after my second helping of almost everything at dinner that I heard about the trip. And, of course, it had to be Ree-Jane I heard it from.

I was resting my stuffed self on the porch. Had I honestly needed that second helping of Mile-High Lemon Meringue Pie? It was so beautiful, the stacked clouds of meringue topping the sun-drenched yellow of the filling, that, yes, I had to have a second slice.

The evening light that seeped through the trees and lay across the porch railing was a paler note of the lemon pie, as if Nature, not feeling up to scratch, waited while my mother put the last meringue loop on the surface of her pie so it could settle down and copy the color. Only a person utterly immune to beauty and one with a leather tongue could have resisted another slice of that pie. . . .

And here was one, and here she came.

Groggy as I was with enough food in me to feed Cox's army (an army known only to my mother, who referred to it as a measure of size), I could still tell that Ree-Jane was going to tell me something that I wouldn't like but that she did. I watched her arrange herself on the porch railing in a dress that was noticeably new. I might as well ask.

"Where'd you get that?"

"Heather Gay Struther's, of course. I got this and four others and an evening gown and a swimsuit. Of course, I'll need more, so I'll buy them at the Beach House."

The Beach House was a shop in Hebrides that specialized in swimwear. "No kidding?" *No kidding* was not at all what I felt. What I felt was an urgent need to kill her. I refused to ask her why she was buying all of this.

So she told me. "I need a lot of new clothes for the trip."

She was watching me closely to gauge my curiosity level. I kept my face as expressionless as I could. "What trip?"

"Oh, didn't you *know?* We're going to Florida. To Miami."

I stilled my rocking. "What? When? Who's going?"

She was clearly pleased by my astonishment. "Three days from now. All of us—mother, me, and Miss Jen."

My mother? But my mother never got to go anywhere. She was always stuck with the Hotel Paradise.

"It's too bad you can't go along." The tone indicated she thought it anything but too bad.

So *I* was to get stuck with the Hotel Paradise. And Will and Mill, I supposed.

I said nothing because I was afraid I wouldn't be able to keep the disappointment out of my voice. I rocked back and forth in the green wicker chair.

"We'll be gone over a week. We want to spend four or five days there and it'll take us a couple of days to get there and back. We'll go down the west coast to the Tamiami Trail and cut over to Miami Beach along it."

Tamiami. For a brief moment I shut my eyes and said that word in my mind. *Tamiami. Tamiami Trail.* It was such a beautiful sound I could almost taste it.

". . . and we're staying at the Rony Plaza in Miami Beach."

Rony Plaza. Another one! I dropped my chin in my palm. Was Florida full of beautiful names? I should say that there is something in my nature that makes me adore certain names of things and places, almost as if the names were enough.

"It's quite luxurious," Ree-Jane went on. "It's right on the beach, so every morning I can roll out of bed and down to the ocean. I'll show you the swimsuit later. Perhaps I'll model it."

"Uh-huh."

"We'll go to the Keys, too."

"Like Key Largo? Did you see that? It had Humphrey Bogart in it." How I remembered the storm, the waves lashing the shore, the furious wind blowing the fronds of the palm trees like women's scarves. Howling winds in which I pictured Ree-Jane lifted off the beach in her Heather Gay swimsuit and hurled at the building. Then picked up and hurled back on the beach. This went on.

Ree-Jane gave a labored sigh. "This isn't a *film.*" That's what she called movies, thinking it much more sophisticated. "This is the real thing. Do you think life is like some film?"

"Yes."

"I suppose you would. You've never been anywhere. Too bad. We'll probably go to Key West, since that's the most famous one of the Keys. You can drive all the way down to it. It's the last one, I think. Those sunsets! I can hardly wait to see them, they're so famous! And that water! It's the color of turquoise. What colors! Like a *film!*"

"Told you." I snickered.

So that evening, after dinner was finished and my mother had changed into one of her good cotton dresses, we all sat on the porch around a green table, rocking. My mother had a glass of sherry and Lola had a tumbler of Dewar's Scotch. I was satisfied to listen as they talked about Florida because every once in a while the Tamiami Trail would come up and the Rony Plaza. And there were other names, like Biscayne Boulevard, and bougainvillea. Everything about Florida had this lush quality.

"Jane" (which is what her mother calls her) had left and gone up to her room to try on her new clothes which she said she'd model for us. From her room, which overlooks the porch, we heard strains of music, a little scratchy, coming from her old record player.

Mrs. Davidow, sitting back in one of the green rockers, leaned her

59

arm on the railing, her hand extending over it to tap ash from her cigarette onto the shrubs. The world is her ashtray. But I shouldn't be so
critical because she was in such a good humor. She called up to "Jane"
with a musical request, a song named "Tangerine." This was a favorite
song of hers, for she associated it with "my Florida years." I didn't
know she'd had any Florida years before I'd heard that song, but she
had, for she'd lived in Coral Gables for a while.

Coral Gables. That had a pleasant ring to it, although not as much
as the other names did. It wasn't right up there with Tamiami Trail;
still, it was worth including. Including in what, I wasn't sure. Apparently, she'd thought up this trip in a sentimental wander through memories of her "Florida years."

"Tangerine" sifted down from Ree-Jane's room. I could not make
out the words very well, though I did catch "lips . . . as bright . . . as
flame." The melody was wonderful, something you could really do a
slow dance to. Mrs. Davidow hummed the tune and sang a stray phrase
here and there, such as "every bar . . . across . . . the Argentine." I wasn't
surprised she liked the song.

So my mother (who had spent time there too, I was surprised to
discover) and Mrs. Davidow talked about Florida—Miami Beach,
Coral Gables, Hialeah, the pink flamingos in its center. *Seabiscuit.*
Whirlaway. I was dizzy with names. And dizzier still to find out that
Whirlaway was a *horse,* or used to be. Lola Davidow was regretting his
loss. With a name like that, so did I.

The first night of driving, they could stay in Culpepper, Virginia,
my mother said. With a word like "Culpepper" I knew we were not
yet in Florida territory.

Perhaps recalling that I was alive, Mrs. Davidow said to me, "You
won't mind keeping an eye on things here, will you?"

"Yes," I said.

For some reason they thought this answer was amusing and
laughed.

"You'll be fine. There aren't any reservations for the next two
weeks. There's only Miss Bertha and Serena Fulbright. And the Poor
Soul might be coming back next week, but that's not sure."

Mr. Muggs. The ax murderer. I said this. That was howlingly
funny. Didn't anyone ever worry about me? I rocked and drank my
watery Coke and remembered the Sheriff had been really mad when
they'd left me alone to watch the hotel once. I was thrilled when I

found out he had *told off* Lola Davidow. Her face was beet red and her eyes were bloodshot when she reported this to my mother, as if some fire inside her were burning through to outside.

I shut my mind to this when Mrs. Davidow mentioned a street in Miami Beach lined with poincianas and royal palms. *Poinciana. Royal palm.* I'd heard of "coconut" palms and "date" palms and wondered how many different palm trees there were. "Royal" must be the handsomest of them all. I would have to research this at the Abigail Butte County Library. Mrs. Davidow called up to Ree-Jane to put on "Poinciana," another record. That it was a song was twice as good.

What did people remember of the past? When I was old, what would I remember of tonight? Would I see us sitting here rocking and talking, but with the actual talk itself vague (at best) or forgotten (at worst), or would I remember royal palm and Tamiami Trail? Would I care less that they hadn't taken me than I'd care about having heard these names?

And if the names were all I needed, I wondered what that meant.

Bunny and me

14

There were only two tables to be served breakfast and only Miss Bertha and Mrs. Fulbright for lunch, so my mother agreed, as long as I waited on tables this lunchtime, to let me off serving dinner, as Vera would be there to take care of a small dinner party, and she could easily wait on Miss Bertha too. I don't know about "easily," but that was fine with me. My plan for the day: to get a ride to White's Bridge and inspect the murder scene. I certainly was not going to take a cab and ride with nosey Delbert, and both the Woods' trucks were being repaired, so I thought of Bunny Caruso, who drove her pickup into La Porte most days to shop. I was supposed to stay away from Bunny Caruso, which made her that much more interesting. Like Toya Tidewater and June Sikes.

When I opened the dining room's double door, there was Miss

Bertha in another of the gray dresses that matched her hair and eyes and made her look armored. She also looked as if she'd stepped out of one of those old pictures called "daguerreotypes," that make even little kids appear solemn and rained on. I'd seen several of my mother and her family when she was small: they were stiff and stern and unsmiling, as if in those long-ago days all pleasure and excitement were forbidden.

"Late again!" snapped Miss Bertha, consulting the silver watch she always wore pinned to her chest. I think she kept it running fast just so she could say this.

Mrs. Fulbright told her, no, it was they who were early, but Miss Bertha was already stumping across the dining room, back to their table for two. (I asked once why they couldn't have been put nearer the door, and Vera said they'd been coming for years and that was their table. They'd raise a fuss if they were moved.)

The other guests were a pleasant family of four, easy to serve, since they wanted to be gone to their exciting day just as much as I wanted them to go. Also, they all ordered the same thing: scrambled eggs, bacon, and toast, which had my mother pursing her lips and kissing heaven, for she always said breakfast was the hardest meal of all to prepare because of all the different things and combinations of things that could be ordered.

Miss Bertha would not give me an order until she'd inspected every single item on the menu, even though only one item had changed—corn cakes in place of yesterday's French toast. I stood and stood with my order book ready, wishing she'd sink in a vat of syrup, when she finally snapped out, "My three-minute egg and sausages."

I said, "But you didn't like the ones yesterday."

"I don't *want* the ones yesterday! I want today's."

"Yes, but that's the way my mother, I mean the cook, makes sausage."

"Tell her to make it another way."

Why was I bothering to argue? Probably because I wanted to. "The sausage patties are already *made*; they're already *seasoned*."

"Well, for Lord's sake, girl, she doesn't have to slaughter a hog, does she?" She turned when Mrs. Fulbright put a hand on her arm. "Leave me be, Serena! All I'm doing is making my *point*." She flung off Mrs. Fulbright's gentle hand. Turning back to me, she said, "Just make me a sausage without all that hot spice in it!"

"And what else?"

"What?" She still had some sausage-arguing left in her head and "what else" confused her. "Oh. Didn't I say? Didn't I say my three-minute egg? And see it's fresh!"

In the way of deaf old people, she barked all of this out so she herself could hear it, which meant the family of four heard it, too, and were enjoying it a lot. It was as good as one of Will's shows.

I told my mother all of this. The "slaughtering a hog" part had Walter laughing so hard he could have washed the dishes back there in his tears.

"And she wants her egg fresh so you better lay another one," I added. That broke my mother up and got Walter, hearing my mother laugh, laughing even harder until he was so overcome with it he had to sit on the floor.

I skimmed back into the dining room on the waves and swells of their laughter, my sails flying, and wondered if I was always on stage, too.

––––––––

Bunny Caruso's truck wasn't hard to pick out, it was so banged up and rusted out. It was parked in front of the grassy slope leading up to the courthouse.

The Rainbow Café was directly across from the courthouse. I wondered if Bunny was in there because she told me once that she didn't want to run into men in town she sometimes saw "under previous circumstances." That sounded mysterious enough, but I didn't question it. Mayor Sims and Dodge Haines were regulars in the Rainbow, plus other men from the bank, the jewelry store, and the telephone company. They had lunch in the Rainbow on a regular basis. Ulub and Ubub usually did too, but now both of their trucks were in Abel Slaw's garage in Spirit Lake being fixed, so they were hanging out on the bench in front of Britten's store. They usually did that anyway, only now they did it more.

It was true that it was almost all men in the Rainbow, as if it were some kind of a clubhouse, like the Rotary. The only regular woman customers were Miss Ruth Porte (a descendant of the founders, supposedly) and Miss Isabel Barnett. People said Miss Isabel was filthy rich, but she never acted like it. She was as nice as could be and she was also a kleptomaniac, which made her more interesting than some. Most of what she stole came from the five-and-dime and hardly amounted to anything. Lipsticks, cheap costume jewelry, hair nets, and stuff. Nobody ever said anything to her about this, as there was an arrangement with the Sheriff that after she'd stolen a few things over a period, she'd go to the courthouse and give him the money and he would pay whatever she owed for the stolen items.

Maud loved that. She said that Sam should be in the United Nations, settling squabbles between countries. She was not being sarcastic, either, when she said it. But of course she didn't say it to him, only to me. Maud said Miss Isabel must really want to be punished. I said it didn't sound like punishment to me, just having the Sheriff go and square things with the store owners. Maud said maybe it's having to admit it to the Sheriff.

I thought about that and sympathized with Miss Isabel Barnett, thinking of what *I* didn't want to tell the Sheriff. "If Miss Isabel would just stop being a kleptomaniac, she wouldn't have to tell him."

How true, Maud had said, smiling. How easy.

Maud was there behind the lunch counter working the old milkshake maker, the aluminum container stuttering in her hands. Charlene was hanging her big chest over the counter with her chin on her linked hands trying to be cute. She was an awful flirt.

Maud looked around, saw me, and smiled. Her smile really made you think that of all the people who might have walked through the café's door, you were the one she wanted most to see. It was the most honest smile I think I've ever seen, except, of course, for the Sheriff's.

I didn't know whether I did or didn't want to see the Sheriff. It was hard facing him, knowing I should be telling him about Ben Queen and yet not doing it. And he knew I was holding back. There were a lot of little giveaways like me not meeting his eyes, or not inviting him to have some of my bowl of chili, and being clearly flustered if he and Maud started talking about the murder. I wouldn't pass a lie detector test, that's for sure. Anyway, the Sheriff wasn't in the Rainbow, hadn't been in for a couple of days, Maud had told me. He was being kept busy looking for suspects. That probably meant Ben Queen.

Bunny wasn't in the Rainbow and I wondered if she was the real reason I'd come in or if it was because I hoped the Sheriff would be there, or if I would at least find out from Maud if any "progress" had been made in solving the murder of Fern Queen. They didn't know anything about the Girl, for they didn't even know such a person existed. Ben Queen and I knew, though. There were times I thought I would collapse under this knowledge, as if a house had fallen in. But I have to admit that at the same time, it was exciting. It was exciting to be the one who knew and could look at what was going on and see the folly in it. For they shouldn't have been looking for Ben Queen at all; they should have been looking for Her.

I finally found Bunny in Miller's Market where she does her shopping. I asked her if she'd do me this favor and explained what it was.

"I sure will, hon." She was over by the fruit stand, shaking a cantaloupe and holding it to her ear. "These darn things is hard as bowling balls. Just see." She handed me the cantaloupe, meaning me to shake it, which I did, though I didn't know why. "You'd know what's ripe and what's not, with all your hotel experience."

Whatever gave Bunny that idea, I can't say. But it was nice to be looked on as an authority. I shook it, but had no idea what was supposed to happen unless it was loose seeds sounding. I smelled it too. "It's not ripe *at all*," I said, as if I knew. Disgruntled, I put it back and picked up another. I shook and sniffed this one and handed it to Bunny so she could, too. "This one's okay."

Finally, we were climbing into her truck. I asked her why she'd parked so many blocks away from Miller's, near the courthouse, and she said because she needed to see Sam. "Only he ain't there today." She sounded wistful, and I wondered if every woman in La Porte was in love with the Sheriff except for Maud and me. I told Bunny he was busy with all of this murder business.

"Oh, God, yes," she said. "I clean forgot that."

As we drove out of La Porte I told Bunny about my dinner date at the Silver Pear, a restaurant near White's Bridge Road. It was with my aunt, I said, from Miami, Florida. She was on her way to New York and was stopping to see us. I reported how this aunt had driven the Tamiami Trail and up the west coast of Florida. She lived every winter in the Rony Plaza Hotel. "Which is extremely luxurious," I added. Bunny exclaimed over all of this, about how my aunt must be real adventurous to do all that driving,

"And rich," I put in, to live at the Rony Plaza. "She also spends a lot of time at Hialeah, that racetrack? With all the flamingos in the middle?"

It was nice to be able to talk like this with no fear of any of it getting back to my mother, since my mother never talked to Bunny. My mother considers her not only common, but worse; even worse than Toya Tidewater or even June Sikes (who lives near the hotel and presents, I guess, a greater danger for that reason).

We drove past fields where cows grazed, lifting their square heads to chew in that dumb way of cows that makes you wonder if they know where they are and what they're doing. ("Is this grass? Do I eat it, or what?") We passed the Christmas tree farm that I thought really disillusioning and that I would never let any little kid see. Past the ramshackle trailer park and a rundown little shopping place.

It was comfortable driving along in silence and surprising, too, as I thought Bunny was more the chatterbox type, only she wasn't. When there was talk, I did most of it, tossing in details about my aunt's days in Miami—the beach just beyond the Rony Plaza, and the royal palms and poincianas. And did she ever hear of Whirlaway? Bunny would just shake her head in wonder, or click her tongue, words not sufficing. And of course that only encouraged me to fill in more awesome scenes such as the Key West sunset and how it would throw its pink and lavender lights across the water.

"My goodness, but it sounds like paradise!"

I agreed and wondered if either of us would ever see it.

Last of the Butternuts

15

The Silver Pear is an expensive restaurant on what the Lake Noir people call the Lake Road, but which is actually just an extension of White's Bridge Road. Maud says the Silver Pear's food isn't a patch on the Hotel Paradise's; she says my mother could cook better blindfolded. Still, the restaurant is in a huge and pretty Victorian house with a wide, wraparound porch, where customers can eat in warm weather. It is painted a soft gray-brown, much like the bark of the trees that surround it. It blends into its woodland setting in much the same way as the Devereau house blends with the trees on the other side of Spirit Lake.

Since Bunny's truck still sat in the driveway after I got out, I figured she wanted to see me safely up the stairs. So I climbed them and stopped on the porch to wave. Tables were set up on the porch and a few diners were observing Bunny and her truck, which looked out of place amidst all of the fancy foreign cars in the restaurant's parking area.

But still Bunny didn't leave, so, waving again, I walked through the open doorway. Was Bunny waiting to make sure my aunt was there? I disappeared from her view and stood by one of the side windows and watched her truck rattle down the gravel drive.

"May I help you?"

The voice made me jump. A man stood behind me with menus clutched to his chest. He was wearing a powder blue linen suit, and his hair was cut in a high silvery sort of pompadour.

I told him I was just watching for my aunt who was supposed to pick me up here. I didn't want to say I was to meet her here or he'd go check his list of reservations. I know enough about how a dining room runs to figure that out.

"I just saw someone driving away out there. Could that have been her in that old truck?" His nose twitched like a rabbit's.

"Of course not," I said, making my tone resentful. Would my aunt drive *that?*

"Oh," he said, and simply smiled and stayed.

If he was the headwaiter, why didn't he get back to his customers? You wouldn't catch Vera standing around in the dining room doorway gawking. And now here came another one. He was clutching menus, too, wearing a powder beige suit and his hair, similarly cut, was more ivory than silver. Then I remembered Maud had said their names were Ron and Gaby something. Something German, I seemed to remember. They did not look at all German. They looked more like the butterfly population out back of Dr. McComb's house. They simply looked flyaway, and I wished they would, but they didn't.

Why is it when you're up to no good, the world wants to visit. And how could they be so interested in a twelve-year-old with no money?

The first man explained to the second why I was there. I said I'd wait outside on the porch and thanked them. Did they watch me go as I'd watched Bunny? It was a peculiar feeling, imagining four eyes riveted on my back. But I couldn't hang around so I just walked down the steps and out the gravel drive.

It was barely a quarter of a mile to White's Bridge, which lay farther along the same dirt road, which I supposed to be White's Bridge

Road, although I saw no sign. The walk was truly pleasant, with the smell of pine needles mixing with the fresh breeze off the lake. I couldn't see Lake Noir from here, but knew it was close by. It's the popular, rich people's lake.

Maud Chadwick lives in a small house on the lake, not far from Bunny. Maud's has a long wooden pier out over the lake. I've never been there, but I heard she has a chair and a lamp (with a really long extension cord) on the pier and she likes to sit there reading and drinking cocktails. The Sheriff is always complaining about that extension cord and the lamp being so close to the water, but she pays no attention to him. Or maybe she just likes the idea of the Sheriff worrying about what happens to her. She keeps vodka out on the pier in an ice bucket. Mrs. Davidow described it all to my mother, both of them laughing fit to kill. Yet, it wasn't unkind laughter; it was more appreciative. Anyway, Mrs. Davidow could hardly laugh unkindly at someone who spent her nights drinking martinis.

I thought about Maud as I pulled up a hayseed and chewed on it the way old-timers do. I pictured the lamp and the book and the bottle in the ice bucket, and wished I could go slowly by in a boat, for in my mind's eye it was such a pretty scene: the lamp shining on the pier and spilling over into the black water. But, then, I guess what your mind's eye sees is often better than the thing itself. I've never seen the Rony Plaza, after all. It probably looks nothing like what I imagine, nothing so grand. It may not be set among royal palms and poincianas, but still I see it that way.

I came to White's Bridge, a plank bridge that rumbles whenever a car crosses it. I was still thinking about Maud, the lamp being the only thing lit against the black night and black water, this image soon surrendering to the one of Mary-Evelyn, floating on the surface of Spirit Lake, her white dress lit like a big candle, floating in the darkness of night, woods, and water. What I felt was what I felt about Maud on the end of the pier, though I could never have said why. It made me stop on the other side of the bridge and ponder as I chewed my hayseed.

And then an image of the Girl came to me, how I'd first seen her at the railroad station in Cold Flat Junction in her dress of such a pale blue it seemed faded out to more a memory of blueness; her hair as pale as moonlight, her strange stillness, so that it was almost as if she was disappearing as I watched. Then how I'd seen her when I was trying to catch butterflies around Spirit Lake. I looked across the lake to the

Devereau place and there she'd stood, where nobody should have been because nobody lived there. To me, she was just "the Girl"; she was one more thing I hadn't told the Sheriff about.

Two hours was how long I'd told Bunny I'd probably be (for she said she'd drive me back) and I'd frittered away nearly a half hour of it between the Silver Pear and stopping to think, so I put on a little speed for the last five minutes of my walk to Mirror Pond. It was a walk on soft marshy ground through leaves and branches that must have lain there since the year zero, so undisturbed did they look. But of course that was another illusion, for the area had been trammeled and sifted over by the police, and before that by Fern Queen and her killer two weeks ago.

The yellow tape that warned POLICE CRIME SCENE—DO NOT CROSS had been taken down. This made me feel sad, for it was as if the place was being returned to its long-gone-and-forgotten self, as if nothing had happened here. And I was sorry too because that canary-yellow tape was bright and cheerful, no matter what its message. It leant the place an air of habitation, of people and strolls and picnics.

This was plain silly; people hadn't picnicked here. I was wasting time. Yet, time, here, seemed meant to be wasted if it existed at all. It was the same sense I got about Cold Flat Junction.

Mirror Pond itself was not, as Suzie Whitelaw reported, clear and tranquil. It was overgrown with rush grass and weeds; you could barely see the water. It was the sort of place to sink a body in, though Fern Queen's had simply been lying at its edge.

Now the place looked returned to itself as if a page had fluttered backward in a book to what I'd read once and now read again. The pond was in a clearing, and two dirt roads came together here, though the one that went straight on was little more than a trail. White's Bridge Road, which I'd been walking on, turned to the right in the direction (at least I thought it was) of Spirit Lake. Going halfway round the lake is an old road no one uses anymore which passes the Devereau house and wanders off in this direction. It was this road Ben Queen must have driven his truck down when he went to the Devereau house that night, driving in on the other side of the lake, miles away.

I picked up a small, dry branch and drew lines in a patch of dirt at my feet, just to clarify this road business to myself. Where these two roads intersect, here, there's an ancient filling station with two bubble pumps and a clapboard building where they probably sold oil and soft drinks and things like that. The name of the place on the sign above the door, weathered nearly to invisibility, was FRAZEE. It's mostly faded out and hard to read, but there are a lot of Frazees around, so it's a safe guess. There were signs in the one window that still had glass in it for Clabber Girl Baking Powder and Mail Pouch Tobacco.

I wondered how long it had been since a car had stopped here. And how could there have been enough traffic to keep the filling station going? Sunlight, in a sudden sweep across the clearing, speckled the glass of the one remaining window. Looking at the pumps, I grew more and more heart-heavy. It was just so deserted. I have this feeling for abandoned places: it's as if they're more real than the ones where folks hang out and the ones people flock to. The bench, the building—Frazee's was like the ghost of Britten's Market.

I shook myself, wondering what I meant and knowing I should stop, for I felt the blue devils coming.

"Hey! Girlie!"

I turned so fast I nearly lost my balance. "You shouldn't sneak up behind a person like that!"

The old man—who I remembered from when Will and Mill and I came here—was standing less than ten feet away. He yelled—certainly louder than necessary—"Ain't you the one came with them po-lice couple weeks ago?"

I nodded and walked over to him so that he'd lower his voice. "I was with them, yes."

"How come you're back here, then?"

"You know how police work is. We've got to go over and over an area where there's been a kill—, uh, a homicide."

He spat into a patch of leaves and fern. I guessed he was chewing some of that Mail Pouch Tobacco. As old as he was, he'd know all about the filling station.

As if arguing this point, he said, "Hell, I live right down there—" He shook his black walking stick off in a direction behind them. "I been here for near ninety years. My name's Butternut."

"I remember. There've been Butternuts around here for over a hundred years."

His eyes squeezed. "How'd you know that?"

"You told us."

Mr. Butternut looked up at the blank, cloudless sky. He seemed to be waiting for God to second what I'd said. "More'n a hunnert years, you're right. See down there?" Again, he took up his stick and pointed off down the road. "My house's down there. Lived in it all my life long. So did my daddy before me. My daddy's name was Lionel. Lionel Butternut lived to be a hunnert and one. I'm the last."

Mr. Butternut wasn't much taller than me. Age must've been shrinking him down and maybe instead of dying, he'd just disappear, blow off like puff ball filaments. Then I remembered Mr. Butternut had told Will (who'd said he and Mill were policemen) how he heard a car or a truck up here the night Fern Queen was murdered.

"Where was that truck when you heard it, Mr. Butternut. I mean exactly?"

"Ain't no 'exactly,' I just did. I was asleep and it woke me up." Impatiently, he said, "I done told all that to them lawmen. That there skinny po-liceman thinks he's God. He said I better tell 'em ev'rthing I seen and heard. Well, a 'course I did, why wouldn't I?" He spat another stream of tobacco against a rock. "They was out here and down the road lookin' for tire tracks, they said."

"Was it a car or a truck?"

"Truck. But there was more'n one ve-*hic*-le."

"You said one of them drove by your house."

"It did."

"What about the other one?" I remembered that Axel's taxi had driven Fern Queen here that night.

He was looking down at his feet, scraping mud off his shoe.

"Mr. Butternut?"

"Yeah?" He didn't look up.

"The *car*."

"What car?"

I gritted my teeth. The Sheriff had to go through this all the time with witnesses. How did he stand it? I meant to ask him, whenever we were friends again. I was seized by a sudden and terrible breath of cold as if all around it had turned winter. Would there ever after be a rift, like the water between a drifting boat and the shore? Would there always be a distance in our friendship?

"You said there was another vehicle."

"Well, there was." He made it sound as if I'd been arguing the point.

"Did it go by your house too?"

For a long moment he said nothing, just looked off down the road to his house. Then he pointed that way with his briar stick. "Randalls lived down there further along from me. Bud Randall, he up and died like four, five years ago. Then there were the . . . what the jumpin' Jesus was their name? Lived here a long time."

I wanted to shake him hard. But then I recalled the Sheriff once telling me you should never hurry a witness, unless it meant someone might die because the witness was too slow giving up the information. *Witnesses have to find their own way,* he'd said. That if you try to yank back from the path they want to go on down, they'll forget something important. Happens all the time, the Sheriff had said.

Mr. Butternut wasn't giving two hoots for whatever I thought; he was still on that name he couldn't remember.

"Frazee!" he exclaimed. "That's the next house, about a half mile down there. Frazees owned that fillin' station—" He pointed his stick in that direction now. "—but that was when there was lots of summer folks lived around here." He was lost again in thought. "There's a old summer cottage back in there, back from the road, but there ain't no path to it no more, it's been so long somebody ever lived in it. Calhouns did once. But you ain't goin' back in there, no ma'am."

"Why not?" It was an automatic reaction with me, that if someone said I wasn't to do a thing, I wanted to do it.

"They's things." He was looking off toward those woods. Now he was humming.

"What things?"

He shied me a glance like a flat stone skipped in water. Cunning, that's what it was. Then he said, "I'm makin' cocoa. Want some? Come on."

Whether I did or didn't, he turned and walked back down the road. I looked at my watch. More time gone and I still hadn't found any new information. I supposed he'd already told the Sheriff or Donny about the car and truck. Yet, Mr. Butternut might still be the most likely source of something new coming to light. If I could just remember to let him find his own way to it. Which I doubted.

For all the Butternuts who must have lived in it, his house was small. It was also cold. In the cold fireplace sat an old pot-bellied stove. Mr. Butternut opened the little metal door and looked in. "Thought so. Them coals is nearly ashes. But we'll get 'er goin' in a minute." He shoveled coal from the bucket through the opening and then took the bellows to it with a lot of enthusiasm. He must have been one of those people who get a kick out of fires. "There goes. Room'll heat up in no time." He stood and watched the black stove, looking satisfied. It was surprising how soon the coals started burning. I could see the flames' reflection on his face, turning it several shades of pink. It was almost sinister.

He rubbed his hands with enthusiasm and said, "Now for the Ovaltine."

"Cocoa, you said." He didn't answer. Pretended, probably, that he hadn't heard. I was sitting at a long wooden table that was probably where all the Butternuts had eaten for a hundred years. Mr. Butternut got a fire in the cast iron stove going; it was a coal or wood-burning one, the kind we had in the little kitchen. This was the kitchen we used when we stayed at the hotel in the cold months. I love that stove. You lift the four black tops off with a special handle. Sometimes I cook mushrooms right on the surface without a pan.

Mr. Butternut muttered as he got the Hershey's cocoa tin out of the cupboard and lined up the sugar and pan and other things he'd need. He was talking to himself as if no one were here at all, which I thought pretty much wasted the visitor experience. I doubted he had many of them. But, then, I don't know—maybe if you'd lived nearly all your life alone, just having someone there wandering around might make you less lonely. Talk wasn't even necessary.

I walked around the room that served as dining and living space— the kitchen was off to the right. There were two big easy chairs near the stove, gathered there for warmth and firelight. They were covered in a faded sprig-patterned muslin. The arms wore those separate little sleeves of the same material to keep the upholstery from rubbing too much. I took one off and the material underneath showed its little flower sprigs in blues, pinks and yellows so much brighter you'd think a garden might have bloomed there on the chair arm.

"Don't take nothin' now," said Mr. Butternut loud as a belfry bell and without turning from the milk pan he was watching on the stove.

"Of course, I won't." I got as much indignation into my tone as I could.

"You got to have a warrant to search the prem-ises, if that there's what you're figurin' on doing."

To his back, I said, "I told you I wasn't part of the police. Anyway, I'm not searching, I'm only looking." He said nothing to this, and I

75

would have said he watched too many police shows, but I didn't see a television set anywhere. Around the walls were stacks and stacks of magazines, mostly *Time* and *National Geographic.* Probably he just looked at the pictures, like I did. I didn't see many books, only six or seven in a small green-painted bookcase. This stood at one end of a camp bed against the rear wall. A gooseneck lamp sat on top of the bookcase positioned for reading in bed. There were other rooms I could see through the door of this one; there must have been a bedroom back there, but maybe when it was cold, Mr. Butternut slept out here, to get the benefit of the pot-bellied stove.

The camp bed was covered with a light blue chenille bedspread, the kind that I've always loved. I sat down on it and ran my hand over the little tufts of cotton that crossed one another in a diamond design. I wondered what it would be like to be completely alone, like Mr. Butternut. I tried to picture myself here, lying at night on the bed with the lamp light falling over my shoulder onto the pages of a book. I looked in the bookcase: *Hiawatha* was there and a book called *The Yellow Room* and some mysteries. I imagined myself reading and listening to night sounds—which I had to make up: whippoorwills, maybe; tiny branches scratching and tapping against the curtained window; a bark, a howl. . . . When the howl overtook my imagination, I snapped my eyes open.

"Whatcha doin'?" Mr. Butternut was standing there with the cocoa mugs.

"Nothing. Just thinking." I got up, took my mug, and followed him to the table. "I guess you don't have anything to eat, do you?"

"Crackers, maybe. There's that fancy restaurant you must've passed."

"I know; I was there. But I didn't eat."

He had risen to get a box of saltines, which he put on the table. We sipped in silence for a few moments. It was not unpleasant, but I was disappointed I hadn't found out more than I knew when I came. Except, of course, what cottages sat along this road and back in the woods.

Things. He had said there were "things" down the road. Probably, he was just making it up. I looked at my watch and saw less than an hour before Bunny was to return to the Silver Pear and pick me up. "What did you mean about 'things' happening in that house?" He better not ask "What things" again.

Mr. Butternut pursed his lips. "Brokedown House."

"What?"

"That there cottage. Brokedown House."

I considered the name. *Brokedown House.* It made a soft explosion in my mind, like a silent firework, showering sparks. *Wow.* "What about it?"

He sighed and ate a marshmallow. "Beats me. Except it's gone pretty much to rack and ruin. I seen lights out at the back." He ate his other marshmallow.

"There's nothing so strange about that. Maybe it was a flashlight or a lantern." I was pleased with myself for coming up with this reasonable view of a presence in the woods.

"You're doin' good considerin' you ain't never seen it."

This really irritated me in the way things do if there's truth in them. "It was probably just somebody hunting."

He cracked a smile at me. "Ain't hunting season. Ain't nothin' much to poach till fall, anyways."

"There's squirrel. There's rabbits. Raccoons."

He flapped his hand at me, impatient with my ignorance. "You don't know nothin' about it."

"Well, I'm *only* a schoolgirl." Here was a defense rarely uttered.

He sighed as if he'd had to put up too long with schoolgirls.

But why did I stray from the point just to defend myself? I'd make a terrible policeman. "When did you see it? This light?"

"Last time's couple days ago. Nights, I mean."

"But when did it start? How long ago?"

He pursed his lips as he set down his mug. "Some time ago, but I don't attend much to time. There's things happened yesterday that seems like they did a year ago. And vice-y vers-y." He chuckled.

"Then how about the truck or the cars you said you heard? Maybe you saw the truck go by and maybe you didn't?"

"Oh, I seen it all right. I'm just not exactly sure when. Gettin' old, I guess. But nothin' happens round here gets by me, no, ma'am."

It was then it occurred to me: Mr. Butternut had been in the road when Will and Mill and I came that first time. He'd been there this time, too. So why not nearby the night of the murder? But he'd already told Donny he neither saw nor heard anything suspicious, except for the vehicles. "Are you sure you weren't—?" No. "Do you think maybe something else happened, something you saw or heard and just forgot?"

"Well, now that's kinda dumb. Ain't you asking me do I remember something I forgot?" He dropped the spoon he'd been fooling with back in the mug. "I'm havin' more o' this cocoa. Want some? I've only got but one marshmallow, though."

Generously, I told him to have it, as I knew he would anyway. "What I meant was, maybe you saw something and didn't *know* it was important."

"Same difference. If a 'coon run by me and I didn't know it was important *then,* how would I know it was important *now,* 'less you told me a 'coon shot that woman?" He thought this was really rich and laughed the milk into the pan and the pan onto the stove.

I said, "Let's go over there."

He stopped stirring the milk. "Over where?"

What a pest. "To that house."

"Brokedown House? No indeed, we ain't."

"I will then." No, I wouldn't; you wouldn't catch me going into woods I didn't know. But I got up and pushed my chair back. My re-solve must have been serious, to make me give up a second cup of co-coa. But I wasn't going there alone. "I'll go by myself, then."

"Now, girlie, that ain't smart." He was putting the one marshmal-low into his cup, ready for the cocoa to be poured. "You got a gun?"

"Do I look like I have a gun?" I spread my arms wide.

He made a disagreeable noise in his throat. "Guess not. Well, okay, then." He pushed the pan away from the burner. His briar stick was leaning against the counter, and he took it up. "Guess I'm ready as I'll ever be."

Brokedown House

16

Down the road we walked, carrying flashlights he had supplied, and arguing who would go into the woods first.

We stopped to argue by a bed of dark nasturtiums looking almost black in the shadows cast by a mossy oak, and I wondered who had planted them, for they didn't appear to belong to any house here. Mr. Butternut said I should be the one to go in first, as it was my idea, and also he had a bad leg and needed his stick, which meant he had only one hand free if he had to shove something. I asked, Like what? He said, You never can tell. I said that he was the adult here, that I was just a kid, that he knew the woods and house a lot better, and even if he only had one hand free, still, he was bigger and stronger than I was. I actually didn't think this, as he wasn't much bigger than me, and probably no stronger. He wasn't as limber, that's for sure.

Like most arguments, this one was never settled; we just stopped talking about who'd go first when we got to a place where the end of a driveway headed off to the right. You could just make out the beginning of it because it was so overgrown with saw grass and moss and a wilderness of bushes. Felled limbs lay across its path; dead leaves were ankle thick. It seemed even denser than the woods surrounding the Devereau house, or maybe it was even part of it. I guess curiosity urged me on and I said all right, I'd go first.

"But you're to come directly behind me."

He agreed, but he didn't do it. I picked my way through what seemed like solid walls of bushes. Rhododendron and mountain laurel were heaped so high I couldn't see over the tops. It was as confusing as a maze. I had gone only thirty or forty feet when I looked back. Mr. Butternut was nowhere to be seen. I called several times, "Mr. Butternut! Mr. Butternut!" Finally he answered, but his voice was distant enough that I just knew he hadn't even started in yet.

To get back I had to pick my way through brambles and briars. Then I saw him; he'd taken no more than a half dozen steps inward, probably only because he knew I was coming back. I was ten feet away and really mad. "You're to stay *close*. You've hardly moved an inch. I can't do all the work!" Since whatever "the work" was wasn't clear, and since Mr. Butternut hadn't wanted to do it in the first place, my argument was pretty weak. But he couldn't remember anyway. He shone his flashlight in my face and I squinted and put my hand up to wave it off.

"It's this here ol' knee that's actin' up."

"Come *on*."

He did, but he was grumbling.

It was dusk, but I could scarcely see light above the tangle of branches and the tops of the black pines. I could barely see the sky.

"Mr. Butternut?"

Rustle of bushes, cracking of twigs, what sounded like thrashing about with his stick. "I'm here! Never did see so many vines and stuff . . ."

I had to go back to where he was. I found him, sitting on a log. "What's wrong?"

"Ain't nothin' *wrong*, except we oughtn't t' be here anyways." He was poking the dark with his flashlight again, making me squint.

"I'm going on ahead," I said. " You're the backup, so come on. It's not that far, you said yourself."

He wobbled up. "Said lots o' things I wisht I didn't."

Brokedown House wasn't big, but still it seemed to loom. Whatever was left over from light outside did not penetrate inside. I switched on my flashlight. The place was still furnished with wicker chairs and tables and a love seat. If they hadn't been painted white I don't think I could have made out their shapes. Then I caught my foot on the corner of a heavy footstool and stumbled and dropped the flashlight. I straightened up. I thrust my arms out the way you do when you're going by touch. For a few moments I felt I knew what it was like to be blind. I passed through an archway that might have been to another part of the living room or parlor. I think there were bedroom doors on either side of this part of the house. I groped for my flashlight, although the sound it had made when it fell told me that it had rolled and was out of reach. Because there'd been light a moment ago, the lack of it made the darkness darker. All I wanted to do was leave.

Mr. Butternut must have shuffled in behind me. There was total darkness until he clicked on his flashlight and shined it right at me. "Get that out of my *face!*" But the light remained. I brushed at it as if it too were cobwebs.

"Girlie! Girlie!" His voice came from a distance.

From outside, from somewhere up the path. That moment looking into that white light must have contained every fright I ever felt. It held the nights when I was three or four and knew my bedroom at night was the most dangerous place on earth (I would have to go sit on the floor outside my mother's door); it held the day I got lost in a crowd of people doing their Christmas shopping, walking around me as if I were a rock in the middle of a stream; it contained the time Mrs. Davidow had gotten so furious with me she lay down on the floor and beat her heels; it held the doctors' needles, the dentists' chairs. The fright was all of that, it was acid, it was all of that distilled into that moment when the light was thrown, like liquid, full in my face.

My voice was a dry rasp in my throat. The air was choked with fear. My feet (which felt like they belonged to other legs than mine) were backing up. After that first lightning bolt of fear, I could think only of getting out. I turned and lurched toward the door. Once outside I moved as fast as the undergrowth would let me. I forced myself finally to stop and listen. There was nothing, no rustle of trees, no animal sounds, no sound to show I was being chased. There was no sound at all. How could there be no sound in such a place? A place where wild animals must hunt at night, where owls must roost in tree-tops. If a cone had dropped on velvet needles, if a star had laid a silver track across the sky, if the dead had turned in their graves—I swear I would have heard it, that's how silent it all was.

Breathing hard, I leaned against the thick trunk of an oak tree, wondering where Mr. Butternut's voice had come from. It seemed to me I should have reached him by now, or at least got closer to him. I knew I was closer to the road and I found my voice at last, cupping my hands around my mouth, I yelled: "Mr. Butternut! Mr. Butternut!"

He couldn't be that far away—unless he'd turned tail and gone home. But I didn't think he'd do that. At most, he'd just go back to the end of the driveway and wait for me. And then I heard it:

". . . lie, *Girl*— . . ."

It was a thread of sound. *Girlie, Girlie,* was what he'd been calling. But half of it was lost in the night air. If there'd been anything to stir up the woods at all—a wind, a falling branch—I'd never have heard him at all.

He was too far away.

I finally realized what had happened; I had left by way of a side door, mistaking it, in blind fear, for the front. Instead of running toward the road, I had run away from it. I had gone deeper and deeper into the woods. Which meant I'd have to go back. I wouldn't have to go *in* the house, but I'd have to go back; I'd have to pass by it, and me without a flashlight.

Go back there? No. I kept on going, slowly, deeper into the woods. I was too scared to have held onto any sense of direction. I looked upward to see if there was any break in this huge canopy of leaves and branches; light was gathering in, I was sure, and anyway the branches looked locked together in some kind of death dance. Because I'd lost direction, I wasn't sure I was going in a straight line away from the house; I could have gone off at an angle—several angles, maybe, a zigzag pattern.

Twigs snapped. I jerked around. It was one of those noises you think someone's trying hard not to make. My stomach seized up. I couldn't tell what direction the snapping came from in this dense place, or whether my ears magnified it, which wouldn't be surprising, what with every nerve and muscle, every cell and filament cocked to hear. I stood perfectly still, worrying over how my calling out for Mr. Butternut could have given away my position. How stupid that had been. But then I'd supposed I was safely near the road.

Carefully, I moved to a huge oak whose trunk and lower branches were so gnarled and deformed the tree looked blasted. The way the branches grew, the tree would be easy to climb, at least its lower branches would. I got easily to the second tier of branches, some of which swooped down so far their ends drooped heavily along the ground. I sat with my legs dangling on either side of a big knuckle of wood; it was like sitting in a saddle. Even though I was not all that far off the ground, I could be well hidden by the drapery of leaves I was now looking through. With some care, I could go even farther up the tree, but the branches directly above me reached upward as if they were beseeching heaven.

Here I was in a place as dense and damp as a rain forest, where there might have been bright birds and unfamiliar foreign flowers, but I saw nothing except my white socks sticking out below my jeans. They were as bright as the light had been in my face. I almost got my feet up on the branch and was taking off a shoe when I heard a shuffling nearby. I froze. Rabbit, 'coon, possum—it could have been anything. Fox, mouse. But it wasn't the startled movement of an animal; it was measured, like footsteps coming across the wet, black leaves and undergrowth.

I was so intent, so *listening*, that I knew every sound must have been magnified and distorted. I forced myself to move my hands and part the leaves. There was a flare of light that showed a man's face, or at least the part I could see from my perch in the branches looking down. He had a shotgun, broken, over his arm, and was smoking a cigarette. The light had come from a match.

Like a coal miner, he had a light attached to a cap. I could see this because he switched it on to bend down and look at something; then he straightened up and switched it off. He was wearing a wool jacket. He leaned against the tree and went on smoking. He did *not* have a flashlight, I was sure, as the light strapped around his forehead would serve that purpose and leave him free to handle the gun. This light was yellow and duller than the one that had shown in my face, but could I be sure he was not the person inside the house? Could I be sure of anything?

But why was he hanging about down there? Then I remembered arguing with Mr. Butternut about poachers. He was probably just a poacher! My body went slack with relief and I sighed and let my head fall against the bump of wood.

"Hey!" Suddenly, he'd stepped back and looked up. Then he snapped the shotgun up.

"Don't shoot me! Don't shoot me!" Quickly, I left the branch for another.

"What the *fuck*?"

I was scrambling down as fast as I could.

"Who in *hell*? . . . What're you doing up that tree, for Lord's sakes?"

Once on solid ground and picking scabs of bark from myself, I told him I'd got lost.

He was taller than he'd appeared, looking down on him. He was also strong-looking; even through the jacket I could see a slight bulge of muscle in his upper arm as he broke the shotgun again (which I appreciated) and leaned it against the tree. It wasn't a jacket he wore but a heavy shirt that did service as one. It was red or blue plaid. In the dull yellow light of his lamp, I couldn't tell colors. I couldn't tell the color of his eyes, either, but he had long eyelashes (the kind Ree-Jane claimed she had but didn't); in the downward reflection of the light, the lashes cast a little fretwork of lines under his eyes. The lamp lit the slant of his cheekbones and nose and the tilt of his chin, making dark slopes of the rest of his face. If he was ever in a lineup and I was the witness, he wouldn't stand a chance. Then he moved and the shadows shifted. He had crouched down and had his hand on a dead rabbit.

"What in the *fu*—?"

(I was hoping he'd say it again, but he caught himself.)

"—in the devil you doing out here in this place to *get* lost *in*? Ain't nobody comes out here, or never has been."

"There's you."

He stopped stuffing the rabbit in the sack (which already held others, I was sure) and just looked at me.

"All I was trying to do was to get to that road. Yonder." It was a word I'd always hoped to say. "Yonder somewhere." For it was the location of the road that had been causing me trouble.

He pointed at a slightly different angle, but not off mine by much. "'Yonder' is that way."

"Maybe you could walk me there. I mean if you're through. What're you doing with those rabbits?"

"Never mind. I ain't going that way." He was really grumpy. I guess I'd butted into his poaching.

"But it's so dark. I'm only a kid." It was going against my principles, but I whined.

He just snorted. "Not too much of a one if you came in here in the first place."

I sighed. "How many rabbits you got in that bag, mister?"

He had slung the bag over his shoulder. The question made him a little uncertain. "None of your beeswax."

I couldn't help but smile. We used to say that in second or third grade. I always wondered what it meant, but this was no time to find out.

He must have thought my smiling meant something else. "What do you care about rabbits? I shot a 'coon, too. In case you got any special feelings about 'coons."

"No. But hunting season's not until October. So you're poaching." This brought to mind the perfect circles of gold and white of my mother's poached eggs; I was hungry after being out here so long.

He just stood looking at me, trying to make me add up. "You don't know anything about it."

"Yes, I do. I'm friends with the Sheriff. He's told me about poaching."

"The sheriff."

It came out a statement, rather than a question. Now, he was sizing me up all over again. I smiled. "To get back to the road, I'd have to walk past that house," I pointed in its general direction, "and I'm afraid to."

He followed the line of my arm. "Brokedown House? There's nothing there."

"There is, too. There's *somebody*." As much as I didn't believe in hunting, I offered to carry the sack. "You've got that gun; you wouldn't want to trip."

"I ain't about to." He'd tossed his cigarette on the ground, pulverized it with his heel, and picked up the sack. "Okay, I'll walk you. Just remember: we never had this conversation."

"Right." Blackmail was a heady experience.

We started back in the direction of the house. Wanting him to have both hands free to handle the shotgun (if necessary), I offered again to carry the bag.

He said, "Never did tell me what you're doing here." The sack bounced on his back.

I tried to think, but it was hard, moving through the trees, getting closer to the house. "I lost my flashlight inside. It rolled away." I told him about the light in my face and Mr. Butternut.

He snorted: "That's one of the most damn fool stories I ever heard."

It wasn't, but it would be. "I'll tell you the truth: I've got this crazy old aunt lives out this way," I filled him in.

Shaking his head, he stopped. "I don't think even Billy Faulkner could come up with something like that."

"Who?"

He pulled the paperback book from the bag and held it up. *Light in August* was its title. "Oh, *him*," I said, hoping I sounded well-read. "You mean *William* Faulkner."

"Yeah, well, I read so much of him, I figure we're on a nickname basis."

"*We* aren't. We don't even know each other's names."

He seemed to be thinking this over. Then he said, "'A shape to fill a lack.'"

I screwed up my face. "What do you mean?" For a poacher, he sure had a way of talking.

"That's what Faulkner says about words. Or some words. Like 'love.'"

I squinted up at him. This talk didn't sound like his other talk.

He told me his name was Dwayne and I told him mine was Emma. He said that was a really nice name, but it didn't match up with me. I did not appreciate that, but didn't give him the satisfaction of asking what kind of girl it *would* match up with.

We were on White's Bridge Road now, and Dwayne said his truck was parked up there in the clearing, near the pond. He offered to drop me at the Silver Pear if I wanted. I'd said a friend was to pick me up there. It was by now nearly nine o'clock and Bunny would have come and gone, but that was all right, as I could always call Axel's Taxis. I didn't tell Dwayne it was past the time for my ride, as I didn't want him to feel guilty for leaving me at the Silver Pear, when, with his own vehicle, he could drive me the ten miles into La Porte. I pondered this, then decided it wouldn't be fair to blackmail him again. Besides we were by way of being pals by now. We were on a first name basis.

He wouldn't tell me his last name in case I forgot and "mentioned" it to "somebody." Why would anyone ever ask me? And even if they did, how many Dwaynes that looked like him and drove a truck were there around here? But I didn't say this so as not to insult his "power of deduction." The Sheriff talked about a person's "power of deduction" and that mine was extremely good. I don't want to compliment myself, but I think this is true, for I can almost always figure out who's guilty before the big courtroom scene on *Perry Mason*. So Dwayne's power of deduction was pretty bad if he couldn't see I knew enough on him to turn him in.

If it goes too hard on you, turn me in, came the voice of Ben Queen; it was the last thing he said to me. That got me thinking about Ben Queen's deductions. Because that's what it came down to; Ben Queen didn't *know* Mary-Evelyn Devereau's death was an accident. He was deducing it from what Rose said must've happened. Rose said it was an accident. And then a thought—more a hint than a thought—struck me almost like the white light flashed in my face in Brokedown House. Rose herself could easily be wrong. But you'd think from living in that house, she surely knew how awful the three sisters were to Mary-Evelyn. Unless—unless what? This was something I had to think about very clearly and I would have to wait until I was alone, back in the Pink Elephant, or on my corner of the porch.

Dwayne asked me what the matter was. He said I looked kind of pale. I told him because of a memory I had, and he said I was awful young to have memories that turned me pale. He said it as if he knew all about memories that turn you pale.

We picked up walking again, this time with me carrying the rabbits. I don't know why I insisted. The bag bounced against my back and I could feel their warm bodies. Or probably I was just imagining this, as I felt somehow guilty for their fate. I asked Dwayne if he'd read about the murder of this woman, Fern Queen, out here. Of course he had, he said, hadn't everyone? What about it? he said. You think I took a shotgun to her? he said. Of *course* I didn't think so. Of *course* not. I only wondered if he'd been out poaching that night—I could've put that better—and maybe saw something that he didn't want to tell the police because then they'd ask what took him over to that clearing that night.

To all of this, Dwayne grunted.

I asked him again if he was sure he'd never seen anybody in Brokedown House, or even seen anything at all, or heard anything. He told me no, and how many times did he have to say it? He was kind of crabby.

We were nearing Mr. Butternut's house and the clearing when we saw the cars and the lights, the domed red lights of three police cars. Several policemen were gathered around the cars. I could see one of the cars was La Porte's, the other two were state troopers. They were all angled in right in front of Mr. Butternut's. I was so surprised by this, I dropped the rabbit sack.

Dwayne grabbed it up and pulled me behind a moss-covered tree by a bed of nasturtiums so dark they looked black.

They were about forty or fifty feet ahead and I was trying to see if the Sheriff was there. I saw Donny standing with the troopers, his hand on his holster, as if he was going to draw at any moment and people better watch out.

Then the screen door opened and the policemen gathered on the road looked up at the porch. The Sheriff stood there and Mr. Butternut was holding the door open and they were talking. I couldn't hear anything except "Okay" and "I'll let you know." The Sheriff went down the steps then.

Dwayne whispered, "It's old man Butternut. What the hell's he been up to?"

"Do you know him?" I whispered back.

"Sure. He's lived around here forever."

What Mr. Butternut had been up to was (I was uncomfortably sure) not the point. What *I'd* been up to was.

The cars passed us and we watched them heading down the road we had just come up. We couldn't see them stop, but we heard them, heard car doors slam and voices raised. They were going to search the woods.

I should have told Dwayne we would have to stop by and tell Mr. Butternut I was okay, but it didn't mean as much to me to be nice to Mr. Butternut as it did to not get in bad with the Sheriff more than I already was.

Dwayne and I left our hiding place and walked on a path he knew that paralleled the main road, passed Mr. Butternut's house, and ended up near Mirror Pond where his truck was parked. He seemed to be under the impression the cops had come for him until I asked why the La

Porte police and the state police would get together just to look for poachers? Dwayne allowed as how that made sense. So they were here for some other reason, and maybe I was right; maybe there was somebody back there.

By the time we piled into Dwayne's beat-up truck, I wasn't so concerned any longer about the person in Brokedown House as I was with whether the Sheriff knew I was the one Mr. Butternut had called in about. (I guess I should have been more grateful.) But he didn't know who I was. I'd simply forgotten to introduce myself. All he could do was describe me, but there was nothing about me particularly describable. As the truck bumped over White's Bridge, I looked down at myself as if that might turn up something a person would remember about me and me alone, but I found I was perfectly ordinary. And my face looked like a lot of other faces so no one would recall anything particular. (Now, if it'd been Ree-Jane Mr. Butternut had met up with, I could hear him telling the Sheriff: *Pale blue eyes, look like they never had a thought behind 'em, and a real dumb expression, you know, emptylike, and this blond hair come out of a bottle. Skinny, too.*

We got to the Silver Pear, whose parking lot was crowded, for it was a fashionable hour for the Lake Noir people to eat, I supposed. All I needed to do was hop inside and call up Axel, and tell him to get here quick, since I was needed back at the hotel right away. For if the Sheriff *did* give it some thought, he might wonder what other child would be inspecting a crime scene (his powers of deduction being a lot more advanced than anybody else's). Well, I wanted to be home and in bed in case people came looking.

"Thanks a lot, Dwayne," I said, holding out my hand. "It was really interesting."

He turned in his seat to look at me, and I realized he was very good-looking. It was really my first opportunity to rate his looks. He was dark like Ben Queen, his hair and eyes much darker than the Sheriff's, and on the basis of looks alone, it would be hard to say who was the handsomest. I wondered how I came to be surrounded by handsome men—or was it just that they looked that way up against my plainness?

He said, "You sure do have a peculiar life for only being twelve years old."

"I'm actually nearer thirteen."

"Oh." He nodded. "Oh, well, that explains everything."

The silver-headed owner was very obliging about letting me use the restaurant's telephone, mostly, I figured, so he could listen in. For he was lavishly excited when he saw me, because hardly a half hour ago the sheriff's department had come in and asked if he'd seen a little girl in the vicinity. Well, of course he said yes, and asked what had happened.

"He—the sheriff—said you'd been reported as lost somewhere near here. Lost in the woods, he said."

I stood there frowning, holding my mouth open a little and breathing in an adenoidal way. At least I think I was; I've never been sure what an adenoid is, but I think it affects your breathing and makes you look sort of out of it. I shook my head in a wondering way, as good as asking, Are you stupid, or what?

I said, "Why do you think it was me? Do I look lost?"

He blustered. "No, no, not *now*. You don't look lost *now*."

"Well, I didn't look lost before, did I?" I spread my arms out. "Do I look like I was *recently* lost?"

He sighed heavily and looked about to give up. It's interesting about adults, how little it takes to make them just roll over and refuse to deal with it. Talking to me, I can't say I blame them. "There are other kids around here, aren't there? I mean, I don't even *live* here. So it must be some kid who lives here and just wandered off into the woods."

He pursed his mouth and shoved the telephone toward me. We'd been standing by the wooden column with the little light where he kept the reservation book.

I called Axel's Taxis and was told he'd be at the Silver Pear in a jiffy. I went out onto the porch, where diners sat at tables lit by candles, every once in a while flicking moths away. I rocked and munched a roll I'd taken from one of the breadbaskets lined up on a side table. The roll was cold and hard, a roll that would never have seen the inside of my mother's kitchen.

The cab pulled up in just twenty minutes, Delbert driving. I slammed the door and told him I'd like to get back to the hotel in a hurry. He took another road to Spirit Lake that was quicker than the highway to La Porte. Then I told him to go around by way of Britten's on the road that leads to the rear of the hotel so as not to wake anybody. He thought this was very considerate of me.

If the Sheriff had, for some reason, suspected the "lost girl" was me (and I don't know why he should, as far out of town as White's Bridge is), he apparently hadn't called to ask if I was here, since no one appeared to be up waiting for me. Probably, though, he was still out in the woods there searching; it made me feel guilty.

After I ate a bowl of potato salad in the kitchen (not turning on the lights), I went carefully up to my room. I lay in bed staring up at the ceiling, going over that night's events. So much had happened, these events seemed stretched out over nights and nights, over years of nights. I lay very quietly, my hands folded on top of the turned-down sheet, so as not to jar any part of the night loose into forgetfulness. Even this soon after it all happened, I had forgotten things like the exact color of the Silver Pear owner's hair, or the shadows of the leaves that had quilted Mr. Butternut's old face. And in time I would forget the way the light caught at Dwayne's eyelashes, or the smell of the rabbit bag.

Memory is slippery. I wondered, as I had wondered on the porch amidst all the talk of Florida: would the larger memories net the smaller ones and haul them back? Not just the memory of Mr. Butternut and his briar stick, but also the skin on his cup of cocoa? I read somewhere that we never completely forget a thing, that there are the imprints of everything we've ever seen or done, all of these tiny details at the bottoms of our minds, like pebbles and weeds that never surface from a river bottom.

Lost girl
17

My eyelids flung themselves open like a blind snapping up, afraid I might have forgotten even now what I'd been thinking before I went to sleep. So I checked everything over: Mr. Butternut, Silver Pear, silver hair, Dwayne's shotgun, police, Donny swaggering around—check. Check. Check. Check. Yes, it was all there. (Of course, if there was something I *didn't* remember, how would I know?)

I would go into La Porte as soon as the breakfast chores were done, which would have been a lot sooner had Miss Bertha not sent back her three-minute egg, not once but twice, complaining it was overcooked. My mother was holding a heavy frying pan and hefting it, and I hoped she was going to brain Miss Bertha. But she set it down, removed her apron (which meant she was going into the dining room!), picked a fresh egg out of the bowl, and marched out of the kitchen, me dancing behind her.

She smiled in that dangerous way she has of smiling, greeted Mrs. Fulbright kindly, then said, "Miss Bertha, this should be soft enough for you." Whereupon, she broke the egg onto Miss Bertha's plate, then turned and marched back into the kitchen, me pausing just long enough to catch Miss Bertha's reaction, then again dancing out to hear Walter's braying laughter back there in the shadows.

On that high note, my mother told me not to even bother with the damned old fool any more that morning and I almost sailed right out of the kitchen until I remembered my own breakfast. It was French toast and sausage and I ate it at the table with Walter, who was enjoying Miss Bertha's two rejected three-minute eggs. Walter said, "Tastes twice't as good, being the damned old fool's." Walter loves the way my mother puts things.

Delbert taxied me into La Porte and dropped me at the Rainbow Café. I had to find out about the police visit to Mr. Butternut and the woods. Since I wasn't supposed to have been there, I couldn't ask directly. The Sheriff generally stopped in the Rainbow midmornings to have coffee, so I would find out one way or another.

Maud was just taking her morning coffee break when I walked into the Rainbow and past Shirl, seated as always on her tall stool in front of the cash register. The morning coffee drinkers and early lunchers were there, including Ulub and Ubub (who must have walked to town, for their trucks were still in the garage). They gave me a cheery hello (though it came out "uh-o"). It was going on eleven A.M. Maud was just the person who would know about the White's Bridge incident, knowing the Sheriff as well as she did. Also, she was one of the few people in La Porte who had a lot of sense.

"Want some chili? It's just made."

My French toast breakfast was still crowding my stomach, so I said no thanks. But I needed something to do with myself in case the Sheriff walked in, so I said yes to the offer of a Coke. Maud stubbed out her cigarette and went to get it. It was nice being waited on for a change.

After she'd set the Coke before me, with a straw, she settled back into the booth and said, "There was something going on over near White's Bridge last night. In the woods there."

"Did someone else get murdered?" I asked that to let her know how far from a lost child I was thinking.

"No. Some man out there—named Butterfinger, I think—called up Sam and said this young girl had disappeared. Or got lost, he feared."

"No kidding? How did he know? I mean was she a relation of his or what?"

Maud shrugged. "I don't know. That was all Sam told me."

I wondered what Mr. Butternut had said to the police, whether he had played down his own role in this chapter of my life for fear he would be suspected himself of something awful. "Well, but did they find her?"

Again, Maud shrugged. "I guess we'll have to wait—Good! Here he is now."

She always sounded kind of joyful when the Sheriff appeared, no matter how she talked to him afterward. I kept my eyes down and sipped my Coke. My heart thudded, bumping around in my chest as if it only wanted a way out of its trouble. I still did not look up when I felt him standing by the booth.

"Emma."

He was just saying my name by way of hello. My eyes felt fastened to my glass, as if I couldn't raise them no matter what. I made a "hello" sound. Thank heaven Charlene was coming with his coffee and doughnut so that Maud didn't have to leave the booth. I did look up then to where Charlene simpered and managed to brush her chest against his arm when she set the cup down. He thanked her. She swayed off.

The Sheriff was looking straight across the table at me, smiling, but was the smile exactly what it used to be? I blinked. He raised his coffee cup.

Maud said, "*Well?*" in that tone that suggested he was holding out on her, being deliberately secretive, which he wasn't. She used that tone with the Sheriff a lot, and it was completely opposite of her earlier joy. I wondered a lot about Maud and the Sheriff.

"We didn't find her," he said, munching his doughnut. He liked plain doughnuts, not the iced ones or sugar ones. I didn't much see the point of a plain doughnut.

"What could have happened to her off White's Bridge Road?"

"Don't know." He sighed and took another bite out of his doughnut.

"You don't seem awfully *worried*, Sam!"

"If I worried about everything that came over my desk, I wouldn't have time to go out and search for people."

Maud was offended. "But you're the law!" There was that accusing tone again. You could almost see the words standing with their hands on their hips.

I was even *more* offended. After all, this poor girl could've been me. I almost said so, but thought better of it.

Maud asked, "How old was this girl? Did he say?"

" 'Bout Emma's age. He said around eleven, twelve, at most."

At that, my eyes snapped up from my empty glass. I don't look anywhere *near* eleven. My age has even been mistaken for fourteen by guests in the dining room.

The Sheriff regarded me with a bland expression as he polished off his second plain doughnut and picked up his coffee cup. "He said she could've been ten, even."

Ten! I had to wipe the indignation from my face and replace it with my dumb look, the one I'd copied from Walter: mouth slightly open, eyes partly closed. Walter would stand near the dishwasher shadows like this, thinking (or not thinking, seeing it was Walter).

"But what about the child's folks? Hasn't anyone reported her missing?" Maud asked

The Sheriff shook his head. "Nope, not so far. This Mr. Buttercup who called—"

"Butter*n*—," I nearly corrected him.

He raised his eyebrows. "Yes, Emma?"

"It's just a funny name, that's all."

"Mr. Buttercup said he'd seen her near Mirror Pond, and that he'd talked to her and she wasn't from around where he lived."

"Then what on earth was she *doing* there?"

"I don't know, Maud. He said she seemed interested a lot in the murder of Fern Queen."

"Sam, this sounds *very* strange. It doesn't sound quite right."

"No, but it doesn't sound quite wrong either. Can I bum a cigarette?"

As she slid the pack toward him, I wondered what he meant.

"Are you sure this man's telling the truth?"

"No."

"Then he might have . . . done something to her himself and he's throwing you off the scent this way. I mean by calling the police himself."

"Possibly. But he sounded really worried."

I was glad *somebody* was.

"He seemed to blame himself for allowing her to go into the woods in the first place."

"Well, he damned well should!"

"He said she begged and *begged* just to see this derelict house."

I did *not*!

"But why would she want to see it?"

The Sheriff laughed. "Maud, you keep asking me why. I don't know. To me she sounded like one very curious kid." He pinched the match out he'd used to light his cigarette. "This Buttercup did tell me she said she'd been at the Silver Pear. He said it just didn't occur to him until they got separated in the woods that she must have been there with someone, her family or some adult. Little kids don't ordinarily eat out by themselves in restaurants. Like Emma, here."

"I'm not a little kid, anyway."

The Sheriff smiled. "Did I say you were? When I asked them, Ron and Gaby, they said, yes, a girl had been there but they didn't know her name."

I'd forgotten I'd told Mr. Butternut I'd come from the Silver Pear. It was the truth, too, which was even more annoying. "They should pay more attention to the customers instead of standing around."

"You've been there?" He sounded mildly surprised.

"Me? No." But then I thought, I might slip and say something that would show I'd been there, so I said, "I mean, not in a long time. Once I drove out to Lake Noir with Mrs. Davidow, and on the spur of the moment, she decided she'd like to have lunch there, and so I got to go too. The food is so—" What was Maud's word for it?

"Pretentious," she said.

"Pretentious, yes. Anyway, if this Mr. Butternu . . . Buttercup . . . murdered her and buried her, well, you'd have to get a lot more policeman out there searching than just four. I saw in an English movie where Scotland Yard got a whole long line of policemen—there must have been fifty or even a hundred—going over this field, and they all had to move forward at the same time. You'll have to get the dogs out too. They can sniff out the grave." I rather liked this scene as I was painting it, all of this trouble taken just to look for me.

"My God, Emma! Don't let your imagination run away with you!" said Maud.

"Always has before," said the Sheriff.

I didn't like the way he regarded me over the rim of his coffee cup. Just those blue eyes. And I didn't like some of the things he said; it was as if there was something underneath it, underneath the words he was saying. There was a phrase for this kind of thing, but I couldn't remember what.

"We did find some fresh footprints near that derelict house. There's been poaching going on in those woods."

Dwayne! Would the Sheriff find Dwayne if he really looked into this poaching? I don't think I was worried about Dwayne all that much, just how well he could describe me if the Sheriff talked to him. I must have groaned a little, for Maud asked me if something was wrong. I just shook my head.

"What are you going to do now?" Maud asked.

"There's hardly anything we can do, except maybe Emma's right. We could get up more men—get some from Cloverly if they can spare them. Trouble is, that would be pretty presumptuous when no one's reported a missing girl. I mean no family member. Without any evidence—" The Sheriff shrugged.

I was glad he wasn't going to bring anyone else in. For if he went to even more trouble to find out who the girl was, I hated to think how he'd react if he ever found out it was me and I let the police do all that for nothing.

"Wait," said Maud. "There's the owners of the Silver Pear. They must have described her, too, and at least if their description was like this Buttercup's, that at least would tell you he wasn't making it up."

The Sheriff had a studious look. "The description doesn't amount to much. She could've been a hundred girls. There was nothing to set her apart. Light hair, hazel eyes. But you're right, of course, they described the same person."

I looked down at my straw wrapper, ashamed there was nothing memorable about me. I was really disappointed. My eyes, that I liked to think were green, were only hazel. I rolled up bits of the wrapper and considered spitballs.

The Sheriff continued, "Now, one thing I did think might help is a composite drawing—you know, where the witness describes the subject and the artist draws him or her accordingly. Then show it around."

Well, I couldn't help myself; I looked up wide-eyed. But I quickly dissolved my fearful expression and looked down again.

Maud gave him a little punch on the arm. "That's brilliant. Only, you don't have a police artist, do you?"

"La Porte doesn't, no. But I'm sure I could find one if I want to proceed."

Imagine: my face, or near enough my face, shown all over kingdom come, maybe even pasted up on windows or tacked on poles, maybe in the Cold Flat Junction post office, next to the Drinkwater brothers who're still wanted for armed robbery.

HAVE YOU SEEN THIS PERSON?

Just imagine what Ree-Jane would do with *that!* It was then I remembered Bunny Caruso: why, she didn't even need a picture. She knew who I was and what if she just happened to mention in passing to the Sheriff (who I think she had a crush on) that she'd driven me to the Silver Pear? I kept my head down for I knew I was blushing furiously. I started tearing up the straw, having finished with the wrapper. All I seemed to be doing was getting in deeper and deeper; it was like a snowball rolling downhill that I didn't know how to stop, except by telling the truth, and I didn't want to do that, obviously. I heard the Sheriff say

"... in the *Conservative.*"

That made my eyes snap up. "What?"

Maud said, "Sam says they could run something in the paper about this girl—"

"Wait a minute!" I said, coming to my rescue. "Remember the Girl that I saw in La Porte?"

The Sheriff frowned. He was thoughtful. "I remember something about that but I never saw her."

I hated doing this; I hated "using" the Girl. I'm surprised I even brought her up, for I didn't want to let other people know anything about her. She was very mysterious and I was part of the mystery, I think. Not only that; I'd be endangering her, and Ben Queen too, which was unthinkable. I'd almost even rather tell the truth than that. "No, no. It couldn't be her. She's nearer . . . she's too old. But there's something, *someone* . . ." My hand gripped my forehead; my eyes were closed, and I must have looked like Mrs. Louderback over her tarot cards. "Listen: I remember now. I saw a girl walking the highway to Lake Noir. She was around my—she was eleven or twelve, I think. The only reason I noticed is she was alone. I mean, it's strange to see someone that age alone, isn't it? They're always with a gang of kids or a grown-up, at least. Someone." This made me wonder about myself. How must I appear to people? I saw her in my mind, walking along the highway by herself and she looked not so much lonely as left behind. Unclaimed, like a suitcase left in the Lost and Found. I set to wondering what her family was like. She had a family of sorts, it was just the wrong family. But I came to the conclusion family had little to do with her reason for walking out there by herself. No, it was something else.

I thought again of that day in Cold Flat Junction when I waited for the train back to Spirit Lake. I guess I was waiting for the Girl to turn up again. In that great stillness, I looked out over the flat empty land across the tracks, off to the line of dark trees where the woods began. I had seen this several times since, and it had never lost that look of land far away, unreachable, as far as imagination or the moon.

But all of Cold Flat Junction is like that. I remembered the small girl inside the empty schoolyard that I played Pick Up sticks with who had not said a word the whole time. On another day, there was a boy shooting a basketball by himself, and when he saw me, he stopped. Then there was the woman in black who I later learned must be Louise Landis, standing on the top step outside the rear door of the schoolhouse, shading her eyes with her hand and looking off toward that far horizon that surrounded Cold Flat Junction. What was she looking for? Ben Queen, perhaps. But way out there in the same emptiness I saw from my bench at the station. I had moved from that bench to the one directly across the tracks, for I was going in the opposite direction. Sitting there looking at the bench opposite, seeing myself still sitting there. I had felt either desolate or afraid, or perhaps they were in this case the same thing.

"Emma?"

I started, as if waking, surprised I was in a booth in the Rainbow Café. Both Maud and the Sheriff were looking at me.

"You seemed to be thinking so hard," said Maud.

"I guess I was in a brown study."

She smiled. "Well, I have to get back to the counter."

The Sheriff said to me, "Come on. Let's check the meters."

I was suddenly flooded with happiness. It was what we used to do before the Ben Queen business came up. I had arranged my spitballs on the table and now wiped them into my hand and dumped them on the empty doughnut plate.

But as I followed him to the front of the café I felt a little of this joy slip away. I thought it would never be exactly the same between us, me and the Sheriff, and this wasn't his doing, it was mine. It was the price I had to pay for keeping quiet about Ben Queen, and now maybe even for Dwayne.

I followed the Sheriff through the door, hardly bothering to do more than glance at the pastry display. But my eye did land on a Boston Cream Pie that I might come back for.

We walked down Second Street and had no sooner ticketed Dodge Haines's shiny new truck for parking in the loading zone of Mc-Crory's, than I saw Bunny Caruso coming out of Rudy's clothing store right across the street. She was trying to balance one of the Rudy's bags with a load of dry cleaning from Whitelaw's, trying to hike one up with her knee to get a better grip.

No! I thought. As she was on the other side of Second Street, I might be able to get the Sheriff's attention so he wouldn't see her.

"Looks like Bunny needs some help," he said, making to cross the street when I caught his sleeve.

"Oh, she's a lot stronger than she looks and we've got nearly all the meters to do."

"I'll just give her a hand. You can go on ahead for a minute."

So, of course, I had to follow him to try and stop Bunny from saying anything about giving me a ride. This was all becoming such a load on me, a lot heavier than the cleaning bags. I guess when your conscience bothers you it's like bags filled with bricks.

"Well, hi, Sam! Hello, Emma. I swear, Sheriff Sam DeGheyn, you are the absolute last gentleman left on this planet."

I said, "He sure is. My mother and Mrs. Davidow always say so." Then I launched off on an account of Sam's changing a tire for Lola Davidow. Just taking up talking space. The Sheriff looked at me quizzically, as I was being pretty effusive.

Then, as I feared she would, Bunny smiled at me. "Did you have a nice dinner? I know the Silv—"

I jumped all over "Silver." "Oh, yes. There's nothing like my mother's fried chick—."

Bunny jumped all over "chicken." "No, but I mean with your—aunt? Was it an aunt?"

The Sheriff was holding both the dry cleaning and the Rudy's bag. "You both seem to be talking at cross purposes."

Bunny squinted up at him; so did I. It's one aspect of our nature we have in common, Bunny and me: our squints.

"Maybe if you'd stop interrupting each other—" He smiled.

Bunny laughed, opening the door of her truck. "Oh, it ain't nothin', just small talk."

I agreed eagerly as the Sheriff stowed the bags and shut the door. "I just remembered, Bunny, you live out on Swain's Point. There's a young girl was reported disappeared in the White's Bridge area."

"How *terrible*." It was not empty words of concern; Bunny sounded sincerely troubled. "When did that happen?"

"Last night, sometime around eight, nine o'clock."

"Well, who was she?"

"That's just it. We don't know."

I had stepped back into the shadow cast by Rudy's awning, creating the scene which I feared was coming: Bunny would say, *Why, last night's when I drove you out to the Silver Pear.* They both look at me. I put on my dumb expression; the Sheriff mightily surprised/angry/disappointed. He demands to know: "Why didn't you tell me you were near the scene of the crime?"

None of this happened, except I did put on my dumb expression, which turned to sheer amazement when nothing like this took place.

Then the Sheriff and Bunny said Good-bye, be seein' you, and we went back to walking our beat. My mouth still must have been open, for the Sheriff asked me what was wrong.

"Nothing, nothing," I said. I vowed to go immediately after the meter walk to St. Michael's and kneel down before whatever was there, and tell Father Freeman that now I believed in miracles. He might suggest I join a convent later on, and I'd probably agree, for joining would be many years away and by then he'd have forgotten I agreed. (It would certainly be preferable to making any promises to the camp-meeting Christians, for I'm sure they'd suck you right in and not give you a chance to change your mind.)

I said, "I guess it's going to be nearly impossible to find this girl. I can't imagine nobody missing her." Actually, I could. I could imagine it six ways from Sunday.

The Sheriff nodded thoughtfully. "It's sad, really."

"Why?"

He was slotting change into Miss Isabel Barnett's meter. He never ticketed her because I'm sure he realized how forgetful she was. "To think a girl could go through all of that, and no one ever know about it." Sadly, he shook his head.

It was easy for me to pick up on her trials and tribulations. "And she'd have been scared to death. There's hardly anyone lives out there excepting Mr. Butternut—"

"Buttercup."

"Buttercup. And those woods are really dark, I mean *really* dark. Not just your average night-dark, electric-out-dark, cave-dark, or even blind-dark—"

"You know a lot about the dark."

And suddenly, I remembered that I was *not* supposed to know a lot about the woods. "Will told me. Will and Mill, you know how they like to nose around whenever something happens. They went out to Mirror Pond after the murder."

"They shouldn't be doing things like that. Tell them."

"Uh-huh." That didn't interest me at all. "But getting back to this poor girl, why, a lot of things could have happened. She could have starved or died of exposure."

"Oh, I doubt she's dead. There's more than one way out of the woods. She sounded smart, the way Mr. Buttercup talked about her. He said she was as stubborn as Abel Slaw's mule."

I was *not!* I stopped and put my hands on my hips.

"Something wrong?"

"Well, *no!*" I shrugged and walked on. "But it doesn't make any difference. No family's reported any missing girl."

"Um. There is a good reason why they wouldn't have."

"What?"

"She's not missing anymore."

Once again, I stopped dead. "*Not* missing?"

He nodded. "She might by now be right back where she came from." He'd stopped and was writing out a ticket for Helene Baum's canary-yellow car. Above the law, she thought she was. He ripped it from the book and stuck it on the window, making a little rubbery twang with the windshield wiper.

"But—well, wouldn't you be furious if that's so?"

"No. No harm done." He smiled. "Would it be better if the poor girl was still missing?"

"But all the *trouble* she caused you! Getting the state police out there and having to talk to Mr. Buttern—, Buttercup, who's probably a hundred and talks a blue streak about his family—I mean he *sounds* as if he does." (*That* was close!) "I mean, you would have to be awfully disappointed after all of the trouble you went to."

The Sheriff stopped and adjusted his black glasses and looked skyward. "The only thing that disappoints me is I'll never know her. She sounds like a girl worth knowing." He sighed.

I gaped. I felt like a firecracker sent sparks of its hot self racing through my veins.

Then we walked on, left Second Street for Oak Street, walked and walked in our old friendly way, with me trying to figure out a way to let the Sheriff know the girl was me.

A new decor

18

The Abigail Butte County Library is a building of pale brown brick, and one of my favorite places. Miss Babbit doesn't talk down to kids the way most adults like to do, as if our puny brains could only take in information spoken very slowly and clearly. It's the same way adults talk to old people.

After serving lunch, I had gone down to the Pink Elephant to think about Florida. It was then that I decided to take my painting of flowers and water back to the library to exchange it. I handed over the Manet or Monet—I couldn't keep them straight. I think when they both discovered they were going to be painting pretty much the same things, one of them should have changed his name. But then they might have thought it was fun confusing people, like twins who let you think they're each other.

Miss Babbit asked if I'd enjoyed the painting and I said yes, I was going to look at some others, which I did. But none of them looked like Florida, except possibly one with a palm, some fruit, and two naked women. Miss Babbit came to stand beside me and said that the painting was a Gauguin. I was amazed she seemed not at all embarrassed for us to be staring at the naked women. I asked if it was supposed to be Florida and she said, no, the South Seas. She went on to tell me about Tahiti and Gauguin taking off—quitting his job, leaving his family in Paris to run off to Tahiti. Eyeing the naked women, I thought, no wonder.

Miss Babbit had to leave to take care of Helene Baum and Mabel Staines, who I would be surprised to hear ever read a book.

Under "Travel, U.S." I located two big Florida books, full of photographs, which I dragged over to a table to leaf through. I was searching for palm trees, mainly the royal palm. I wasn't disappointed; stately palm trees lined avenues and beaches, grew in profusion in parks, eclipsed the sun and moon with their black trunks and dark green fronds silhouetted against a sky full of melting crayon colors, so vivid the scene looked artificial, unreal. I found a royal palm in daylight, taking up the whole of one photograph, that was just perfect. I marked the place and looked for the Tamiami Trail. I found sections of it in the next book. Some bits of it were really not that pretty, so I ignored those and marked a picture which was, showing palms unreeling down a highway, into the blue distance.

I was suddenly very tired, as if a load of flour had just been dumped on me. I figured I was thinking about Paul and Do-X-machines again, so I rested my head on my outstretched arm on the table and looked at the pictures sidewise, lazily turning the pages. It was an interesting angle that gave the palm trees the appearance of moving when I slowly turned the page. And then there were pictures of beaches and buildings, and interior shots of rooms. One of a hotel lobby caught my eye. There were white pillars around which sat poincianas with flame-red blooms. They were truly beautiful, especially with the white backdrop of the pillars. This lobby was quite luxurious, with crystal chandeliers and bamboo furniture and a deep-looking dark green carpet. The photograph was not identified, but I decided this had to be the lobby of the Rony Plaza. I continued looking until I found the outside I wanted. This sat directly on the beach, surrounded by royal palms and coconut palms (and probably others I didn't know), a towering pink and white building that reminded me of one of my mother's birthday cakes.

105

I felt my time had been well spent and took both books over to the copy machine. Not only could you copy, but you could enlarge on the machine, which is what I did, first copying one-half of each image and enlarging as much as I could, then doing the other half. I read the message about how it was illegal to copy pages of a book without prior permission, but since I had no idea how to get that, I figured I could take my chances. The halves I could scotch tape together later.

Now all I had to do was buy poster board and crepe paper and take a taxi back to the hotel. I walked to the stationery store (which was really more of a jumble store that sold comic books and regular books besides typing paper, ink, pencils, and pens in addition to stationery) and bought these with tip money that I always had a supply of in spite of Vera's keeping the big tippers for herself.

I almost got weary again thinking of all the things I had to do: I had to wait tables, I had to go to Cold Flat Junction, I had to solve this mystery of Fern Queen and the Girl, I had to find a new decor for the Pink Elephant.

Life certainly wasn't about to leave me alone.

———

Back in the Pink Elephant I settled down to copy the two halves of the royal palm picture. I had green crayons and brown and gray with which I filled in the tree on the poster board. It was hard to draw, since the palm, even enlarged, was still smaller than what I wanted. But I finally got the outline right. I finished coloring the trunk and then cut up the green crepe paper and pasted wide strips to the top of the tree. I also colored and cut out a few coconuts to attach beneath the palm leaves. Finally, I cut around the tree as well as I could, leaving the extra at the bottom, which I then folded back as a support. It worked very well.

I had the missing coconut that my mother had been looking for, one of three brought back from town by Mrs. Davidow, and now took it up to the kitchen, which was empty except for Walter. I got a hammer and a screwdriver from the storeroom and asked Walter if he'd help me open up the coconut, and he was pleased to do it. Soon, he'd got it open and I poured the milk off into a cup. Then we each ate a piece and agreed it was "real good." Walter said come dinnertime, I should take a piece on a platter into "the old fool." Walter laughed his gasping laugh.

It was nice having the kitchen to ourselves with nobody to neb around and ask what we were doing. I sat on the stool my mother kept near the stove, and Walter leaned back against the serving counter. We ate another piece of the coconut. He asked where they came from and I told him coconut palms, as far as I knew.

"They're all along the Tamiami Trail, rows of coconut and royal palms." I didn't know this, of course, but it offered a chance to say "Tamiami."

"Where's that?"

"In Florida." I bit into my piece of coconut. It had the most wonderful cool and unsweet flavor. I could hardly wait to turn it into the drink my mother described. Probably I could do it in a blender.

"That's where Miss Jen and Mrs. Davidow are going." He made it sound like some huge coincidence.

I told him that was right. "Ree-Jane, too."

Walter shook and shook his head. "She's gonna drive that there white car straight to hell."

Knowing Walter, he meant literally.

"Wish't I could go to Florida." He sighed.

"Me, too." To keep him company, I sighed too.

—————

I needed a number of other things, one being a fan and a bucket of sand. I decided to visit the Big Garage, even though Will and Mill didn't welcome visitors. On my way across the backyard, I stopped at the sandbox kept there for the small children of guests. The spade and sand bucket were a weathered blue, and rather small for my purposes, but they'd do. I filled the bucket and set it down on the walk to collect on my way back.

I knew Will and Mill had at least one fan in there, for I had seen them use it. As there was no electrical outlet in the Pink Elephant, I would just drop a long extension cord out of the dining room window above it.

As I walked up to the Big Garage, I took comfort in the knowledge that Will was being left behind, too. Still, I couldn't kid myself into believing they thought of Will and me in the same breath. Will was another thing altogether for most people. He was only there in spurts, when he'd appear to carry someone's bags or bus the dishes. Most of the time, he was either gone (with Mill, over to Greg's for Moon Pies and Orange Crush and to play the pinball machine) or they were both up in the Big Garage. Since Will didn't seem to be around, people had a chance to miss him. He'd come and go in an almost magical way. I'd guess you could say he was the pure performer. He was always on stage.

I heard the piano going, and they were singing some old gospel song, interrupting it now and then with hysterical laughter. When I knocked on the door that seemed bound shut from the ivy growing on it, the laughter stopped suddenly, as if I'd dreamed it. Then there came noises of the sort that went with whisking things out of sight. I knew Will would come to the door and open it only a half inch to keep me from seeing in. It was all so melodramatic.

"What do you want?" he asked through the narrow opening. He spoke to me sometimes as if he couldn't remember who I was, or what I was doing on his planet.

I scratched my elbow. "I just wondered if I could borrow that fan."

"The rotating one?"

I wasn't sure, but I just said yes.

"You'll have to bring it back. We use it for special effects."

"Bring it back when?"

He shrugged. "Whenever. We're not using it right now."

I waited while he went to get the fan. When he returned, I asked him about Florida and how he felt about not being allowed to go.

"I could go."

That stunned me. What did he mean?

The door opened a bit wider as he shoved the fan through, and I could see him shrug. "I just didn't want to go. Why would I want to spend days in a car with Ree-Jane?"

I stood there, staring. When he asked what else, I shook my head. Then he closed the door.

The fan was taller than I was, but it didn't weigh much. Holding it up a little from the gravel road, I walked back around the rear of the kitchen to the Pink Elephant. I felt it was awful of my mother not to tell me that I wasn't going to Florida with them, and that Will had been asked, but said no. I knew my mother could hardly ever bring herself to talk about anything fraught. I felt I was of no account. Then I saw Walter on his way back from the mint field with a bouquet of it in his hand. It was a relief to see here was someone of even less account than I was. When we met up, I asked him to go and get the sand bucket.

Their Florida vacation

19

The next day they left. And what a leave-taking it was; it had started three days before they all piled into Lola's station wagon and actually went. My mother was, of course, too busy doing real chores to participate in the preparation. Ree-Jane modeled her new Heather Gay Struther clothes again, and that took quite a bit of time in itself, as she'd finally bought three dresses, a pale yellow linen suit, an evening gown, and three bathing suits.

Mrs. Davidow's preparations consisted mainly of getting in a new case of Bombay gin and one of Wild Turkey. Over the past three days, she consumed a lot of this as she discussed the route they would take and where they could stay over, while my mother fried chicken or made Angel Pie or slapped Paul away from her coconut cake. She had made the icing for this cake with real coconut, instead of Baker's canned, giving Walter the job of shaving and shredding the two co-conuts that she still had. She had been quite surprised that Lola had found coconuts in La Porte, and so was I. My mother was also sur-prised that the third coconut had disappeared.

Lola Davidow would follow my mother around the kitchen with a martini in one hand and a map in the other, plotting their course through Maryland, Virginia, North Carolina, and South Carolina. She meant to do nearly all the driving, which I was sure the state police would like to hear in Maryland, Virginia, and the Carolinas.

I knew the route as well as they did. On my own map, bought at the stationery store in town, I had marked each place Lola had said they would stop at night, the first town being Culpepper, Virginia. I wanted to feel I had some control over the trip, especially over when they hit the Tamiami Trail. I'd marked it in red.

The day before they left, Ree-Jane had found me in my favorite spot on the porch where she modeled her evening gown. She said, "This is what I'm wearing to dances." She twirled, actually twirled, floating the light blue silk and chiffon in waves around her legs.

"Do they have them in Culpepper?" I refused to look up from my Key West sunset photo.

"Oh, for *God's sake,* no. In Miami *Beach.*"

Then she started doing a dance step and singing, "Palm trees . . . are gently swaying . . . They seem to hear me say-ing . . ." She swayed along, holding out the thin, tissue-y blue of her skirt, going back and forth, back and forth. As she was close to the top step of the porch, I was hoping she'd go over, but she didn't.

Ree-Jane never could carry a tune, but it made me remember her phonograph. "Would it be okay if I listened to your records while you're gone?"

Freed from the thrall of her invisible dancing partner and back on planet earth again, she asked (suspiciously), "Why?"

"Because I like your records. They're nice and old. Old songs are comforting." I don't know where that notion came from. Except maybe it was true. My mother liked to sing "Red Sails in the Sunset" sometimes, and I found that comforting.

She balanced herself and her long full skirt up on the porch railing, thinking it over. Then grudgingly she said, "Well. Seeing you have to stay here, well, I guess so. Only, *don't touch one single thing in my room!*"

"Uh," I grunted, meaning nothing.

"You can sit in my room and listen, but *nothing else.*"

To think I'd pay attention to that warning only showed her ignorance. Anyway, why would I want to mess with her stuff? I'd sooner go through Walter's belongings, which would be more interesting, I'm sure. Anyway, anything Ree-Jane owned that she thought would make me jealous she'd already shown me, so there wouldn't be much point in rummaging through her drawers. I had, of course, no intention of sitting in her room and listening. The phonograph was to go down with me to the Pink Elephant. I needed atmosphere.

While she posed there on the porch rail, I asked, "Are you going to model for Great-aunt Aurora?"

"What? Not after the last time I was up there. That crazy old bitch!"

The "last time," was, of course, the chicken-wing incident. But Ree-Jane clearly had forgotten she'd never admitted what had happened and had, instead, come back to the kitchen and said Aurora had complimented her on her beautiful self.

Then she added, with a slippery smile, "But I guess it figures, since she's a Paradise." Meaning all my back family was crazy.

Innocently, I asked, "Why? What did she do?" Ree-Jane wasn't about to tell me Aurora'd thrown a chicken wing at her and called her a "blond floozy."

"She's just crazy, that's all."

"Oh. Well, that's too bad. I mean she especially wants to see your Florida clothes."

Ree-Jane stopped pleating the chiffon of her skirt. "I don't believe it!"

Neither did I. "She does, though. She likes clothes, if you've noticed. And she's got those two steamer trunks. She still hangs her clothes in them. So she really likes travel, too."

Now, the trouble with vanity is you always want to believe something or someone so much that you'll believe it no matter how much it's against good sense or reason. But at this point, there was nobody left to model for. There were Will and Mill, but even Ree-Jane knew better than to try and get in the Big Garage. That place was like a fort. I was probably the only Zulu who dared even to knock on the door.

"Too bad," I said, sighing (as though I cared), "for she likes Heather Gay Struther's clothes a lot. She'd especially like to see this

111

blue evening gown. Her favorite song is 'Alice Blue Gown.'" That was the only truth I'd told. Of course, Aurora only sings it when she's stinking drunk, but she still is really fond of it. "Listen: I'm taking her up her lunch in a little. Why don't you come with me?"

As I said, only a fool would have believed this, but of course, we're talking about Ree-Jane, who finally said, "Well, all right. When?"

"I'm going right now to get it and I'll bring the tray back through. So you can just wait."

My mother was dishing out creamed chicken over biscuits for two of Anna Paugh's customers and I said I could take up Aurora's lunch. "She wants a stuffed tomato."

My mother frowned so that her forehead took on the look of bean rows ready for planting. She pointed out that Aurora disliked stuffed tomatoes. "They're stuffed with tuna-fish salad, and she hates tuna fish as much as the tomatoes."

I was leaning against the countertop with my shoulders bunched, the heels of my hands pressing down as my feet did a little jig. "She changed her mind."

My mother just looked at me, almost as suspiciously as Ree-Jane had, but when I didn't look away, she set about getting the tomatoes from the ice box and arranging one on a little bed of salad. Then she added hot rolls and a small dish of peas. I transferred this to a tray and hotfooted it back to the front of the hotel, where Ree-Jane was waiting, flicking through one of her fashion magazines. Her blue evening gown was really very pretty. The hem was cut in a kind of zigzag, and fell over a silk underskirt. It was a beautiful shade of blue, a shade I imagined the ocean to look like, sweeping up on the Florida sands.

The last time she'd seen this tomato-stuffed-with-tuna-salad dish, Aurora had poked it around on the plate and said the Hotel Paradise was going to hell in a handbasket, serving these tomatoes. Why, if she, Aurora Paradise, were down there overseeing things, she'd have fried chicken and Angel Pie every night.

Anyway, the nice thing about the stuffed tomato was it fit your hand as good as a tennis ball. So up the stairs we went, Ree-Jane behind me, to the fourth floor.

The minute I walked into her room with the tray (I'd told Ree-Jane to wait outside) Aurora asked, "Where's my Cold Comfort?" She seemed to think I had twenty-four-hour access to the bar in the back office. The fact I'd brought Ree-Jane instead of her cocktail would not sit well at all.

"You hear, Miss? I want my Cold Comfort!"

"I'm sorry. I couldn't find the Southern Comfort."

"Don't be ridiculous. Lola Davidow wears a bottle on a chain around her neck. What's *this?*" She was wearing her gray net gloves, with the fingers cut out, and she poked at the tomato. "That's one of Jen Graham's goddamned stuffed tomatoes!" She waggled a mittened finger at me. "You know I can't stand these. I'm onto you, Missy!"

Aurora was a lot smarter than Ree-Jane (as Ree-Jane was about to see). I kind of fluted, "Somebody's come to *seeee youuu.*" Aurora wanted visitors about as much as Will and Mill did. "Come on in, *Jaaaane.*"

Here came Ree-Jane, waltzing through the door, her blue chiffon skirt held in thumb and finger, spread out like a fan. She hummed and pirouetted all around Aurora's chair—eyes closed, arms waving, as she'd done on the porch. It couldn't have been better (or worse, depending on your point of view).

Aurora followed these movements, gap-mouthed, speechless—but not for long. "You blond-headed *bimbo!*"

Ree-Jane's eyes snapped open and she quickly rose from a Cinderella curtsy she'd made, looking completely white.

"*Floozy!*" Aurora's mittened hand curled around the tomato, lifting it from the plate in that slow-motion way of awful things about to happen.

It was then my heart, which twenty-three hours out of the twenty-four yearned for Ree-Jane's ruination, turned tail on me and fled. Ree-Jane backed away, her hands in her blond hair like the heroine on the cover of a cheap detective novel. I grabbed Aurora's hand just as it was rearing back to let the tomato fly. It dropped from her hand, and the tuna salad plopped onto the tray as she yelled at Ree-Jane to get the hell out.

And I, really disgusted with myself, said something soppy to Ree-Jane, who had, of course, run out of the room, her face such a mottled pink above the sea-blue gown, it could have been the sun going down into the technicolor waters off Key West. Why had I stopped Aurora after all of my plotting and planning? I guess I'd felt sorry for Ree-Jane, or maybe for Ree-Jane's dress. I did not like confusing feelings or

113

going back on myself. It could get to the point where I'd think *She's only a poor old lady* the next time Miss Bertha dumped her basket of rolls on the floor.

To shut up Aurora (who was heaving insults right and left at the Davidows) I told her I'd go down and make her a drink. On the way down the stairs—Ree-Jane had fairly flown down them and slammed the door to her room—I wondered why I felt that little drop of pity for her. I decided it wasn't all that much of a change of heart; I figured if the blue dress had wound up covered in tuna fish, there'd be hell to pay. And I knew who would pay it. My mother was no fool.

So I continued on my way to the kitchen to make the Cold Comfort with a cold conscience.

———

Will and Mill joined Walter and Vera and me to see the three travelers off. Will and Mill carted all of the luggage downstairs and out to the station wagon, but it was obvious none of this registered on them. Their minds were back in the Big Garage no matter where their feet were. This was especially true of Will, who Moses himself would have sworn was up on the mountain with him when Will wasn't even in the same country. I've never known anyone who could look you right in the eye and nod and not be hearing a single word. Mill wasn't much better. His fingers moved up and down his pants leg, so you could tell he was playing the piano in his mind.

114

But they both called good-bye, and have a nice time, as if they meant it, and waved until the car was down at the end of the drive. Then they turned and hotfooted it back to the Big Garage.

Sauerkraut

20

Roast veal and Salisbury steak were the entrees for dinner; before she left I'd heard my mother giving very specific instructions to Mrs. Eikleburger as to how the roast should be cooked. My mother's main fret in life is leaving the cooking to somebody else. I wonder if she isn't like Will—even though she'll be driving the Tamiami Trail, she'll still be back in the kitchen, overseeing the roast.

Miss Bertha knew that my mother was to go to Florida and she hadn't liked hearing that at breakfast, not one bit. The "other two" (meaning, of course, Ree-Jane and her mother) could "drive their car off Table Rock into a flaming pit" as far as she was concerned. This was one of the very few times I found myself in accord with Miss Bertha's feelings. But the absence of "Jen," well, that was a catastrophe. For who was this "Eikleburger" person? Miss Bertha was really hot under the collar and it took

Mrs. Fulbright some convincing to get her to believe that she wouldn't be eating German food for several days. After she'd simmered down, I took the opportunity to un-convince her by saying that it wasn't *only* German cooking Mrs. Eikleburger did, for she sometimes cooked American dishes. But not often. Mrs. Fulbright winced, but still smiled at me.

"I'm of German extraction, myself," said Mrs. Fulbright. Mrs. Fulbright would have turned herself into an Eskimo if it would have helped me, she was that sweet.

So that afternoon when I'd finished putting up my pictures in the Pink Elephant, I got Walter to help me look through the cookbooks up on a shelf above the pastry table. He looked in *Foods of the World* and I looked in *International Cooking*. Walter was slow because he stopped so long to stare at the pictures. He said, "Here it says weiners, but it don't look like them. But it's from Germany, it says."

I looked over his shoulder. It was Wiener schnitzel and it was veal. I congratulated Walter on finding the very thing. We kept going to see if we could find German Salisbury steak, but the closest we could get was sauerbraten, which made my mouth pucker up to read about all the vinegar in the recipe. But sauerbraten was a piece of beef; it didn't look like hamburger. I scratched my elbows and considered this. The beef was covered with a lovely dark gravy, and Walter could probably make that from one of the ready-made packets. I could have, but I had entirely too much to do as it was.

I went to the stove to see what was bubbling away under the top. Sauerkraut! Probably that was to be one of the vegetables, and Mrs. Eikleburger, being, I now supposed, "of German extraction," would be cooking something like that. Now, my mother cooks sauerkraut like nobody else in the world. My mother can make sauerkraut haters (which most of us are) into sauerkraut lovers—nothing less than a cooking miracle, but that's my mother's cooking for you. Many people have tried to get that recipe out of her, but, again, I'm one of the few who know it. What she does is to wash and squeeze out canned sauerkraut, then spreads it on paper towels to absorb the moisture, *then* does the same thing all over, twice. After that she cooks it with white wine, and, I think, juniper berries.

Mrs. Eikleburger's sauerkraut was just cooking in water, the old sauerkraut everyone hates. Good. I went off to type the menus. I wanted to catch the afternoon train to Cold Flat Junction. I wanted to find Louise Landis.

Diner people

21

There are some words that can set up in me a kind of homesickness for a thing other than home. The feeling is such a close kin to fear, it could convince you that fear is what it is. The Florida words seem to have done this and made me homesick for a place I've never been and probably never will be.

I am easily haunted. If any spirit wanted to, it could take me over without any trouble at all, slipping in through the invisible cracks in my skin. We all have cracks but don't know it; we are all pretty windy.

Places, words . . . *A space to fill a lack.*

Cold Flat Junction is like that. It has something to do with the silence and the distances. The distances are all around me—north south east west. Wherever I look is endless; nothing stops my looking. Something should; you'd expect something to stop it, a wall or a mountain, but Cold Flat Junction land just seems to go on forever. There are houses, of course, though even these are kind of spread out. There are a·few businesses, like the Esso station and Rudy's Bar and the Windy Run Diner. There are these, but it's the stretches beyond these that I'm talking about. From the railroad station, I look across the tracks and the land beyond and those dark blue trees that are its horizon and this homesick feeling comes over me.

Cold Flat Junction seldom sees passengers either coming or going. The reason the train makes the stop at all is because of the old railroad station, which I think is called by some "an architectural gem." I guess it is Victorian.

"The Junction," as people who live around here sometimes refer to it, was originally expected to be a bustling, busy place, with the two roads intersecting there—a junction through which much traffic was expected to move, but none ever did. I had been here three times, twice aboard the train, once with Mr. Root and the Woods boys. The train compartment was pleasantly stuffy, with worn, burgundy-colored and once flowered horsehair seats. When the conductor came, I handed him the ticket that I'd bought last time. It had never been collected and I expected him to refuse it, but he didn't.

I was the only person to step down to the Cold Flat Junction plat-form; I stood and looked at the imposing red brick station, which be-longed in a much bigger, more interesting town. As always, it looked closed but wasn't, although the blind was once again pulled down over the ticket window. I waited for the train to pull out, and when it had gone, I looked out again over that cropped, empty land on the other side that stretched away to that far-off line of dark woods. Then I set my feet in the direction of the diner, which stood across from the Esso station and which was the place I always stopped for information, and of course, food.

Its interior was by now familiar to me; I could see it perfectly in my thoughts when I was somewhere else. The counter, where I always sat, was a kind of half-horseshoe design with four seats going around the end curve. There were tables with chrome legs and different-colored Formica tops; a few booths were installed in the corner nearest the door. The booths were dark red Naugahyde, and one torn seat back was bandaged with silver duct tape. It all gave the impression of being furnished with leftovers, not enough of any one thing to fit the place out correctly. Skimpy flowered curtains too short to reach the sill hung at the small windows. I took my usual seat at the curved end of the counter and pulled out a menu. It was the same.

So were the customers. I recognized all of them, including the married couple in a booth. There was Billy, the one who looked like a truck driver but probably wasn't, as he spent so much time in Cold Flat Junction, at least in the diner. Down the counter were the two whiskered men wearing the same blue caps that looked like those old railroad caps you see in pictures. One was named Don Joe; I think the other was named Evren. There was a heavy-set, chain-smoking woman in thick glasses who sat at the counter. And of course, the one waitress, "Louise Snell, Prop." (This was on the badge she wore on her uniform.)

Now, here I came, blowing in like the dry wind that carries grit and sand across the railroad tracks, and no one seemed to think it peculiar that this was the fourth time I'd been here, unaccompanied, as usual, by any adult. The first time, Louise Snell had asked, in a friendly and not nosy way, where I was from, or what I was doing here in her Windy Run Diner. My reason had been that my dad's car had broken down and it was being fixed over at the Esso place. The times I had come before today had been information-gathering events. Once for Toya Tidewater (who I never found) and again for Jude Stemple (who I did).

"That car done been fixed yet?" asked Billy.

This question was not asked in a joking manner, but in a small-talk way. Would that car still be at the Esso station after nearly three weeks? But this didn't faze them one bit. Nothing much did. Things just didn't seem to change here, at least that's my impression. It accounts, I guess, for the mysterious quality of Time, as if Time had been misplaced and we all had to get along as best we could without it. I remembered one of our hotel guests who explored a lot, talking about his travels in Tibet: the farther up he went into the mountains and the villages in them, the more time rolled back until he got to one so far up he felt completely outside of time.

I'd finished looking at the menu, still making up my mind as I waited for Louise Snell to come for my order, and she did.

"What'll it be today, hon?"

Thinking of the ham pinwheels with cheese sauce my mother had left for our lunch, I had to check with my stomach to see how it felt about the hot roast beef sandwich. It told me the roast beef would be too much, and I had better just settle for pie and a Coke. The pies were displayed in a cupboard behind glass. The chocolate cream looked really good so I ordered that.

Instead of starting right off with asking Louise Landis's whereabouts, I decided that mentioning Ben Queen would be the best route to take to her. After all, it'd been all over the papers that police were looking for him "to assist in their inquiries" into the shooting death of Fern. Since Ben Queen came from here, they'd regard the place itself as more or less famous and would be glad to talk about it. I smiled at everybody to get them feeling friendly toward me, but it was a wasted smile, as they were always glad to see a stranger here, even if the stranger was a kid.

I asked, "Doesn't that man police are looking for live in Cold Flat Junction?" I mustered up my dumb look. But as soon as the words were out of my mouth, I knew it really *was* dumb, for the question set off a spate of reactions that would go on and on until doomsday and would never get to Louise Landis.

"Those policemen got it all wrong," said Billy, who, as usual, led off. "Ben Queen never killed nobody, and that's a fact."

The woman in the booth put in, "Ben'd never kill anyone and sure not his own *child.*"

Everyone nodded and muttered words of agreement.

Louise Snell said, "There's just some folks in this life that've got to be scapegoats."

Scapegoats. It's exactly what Ben Queen and I were talking about that night by the spring.

The husband part of the couple in the booth turned around and said, "Well, but Ben *was* kind of wild."

His wife slapped the hand holding his spoon of soup and all the others more or less turned on him. It was not a popular opinion.

"Where you goin' with this, Mervin?" Billy turned on his stool as if meaning to make something of it.

"He ain't going nowhere, Billy." Mervin's wife whispered something to him and gave his hand another crack.

"I was only *sayin'*—"

Billy waved a dismissive hand at the two and turned back to the counter. Just as Louise Snell passed him with my pie, he said, "Don't know his ass from a hole in the ground."

Louise Snell stopped and leveled a look at him as she pointed her head in my direction.

Billy slid a look off me and said, "Oh. Sorry, ma'am."

Ma'am? *Me?* Mervin sticking his nose in had kind of calmed things down, so I stirred them up. "Maybe he's hiding out here somewhere—some*wheres.*" (I thought it would make them take to me more if I adopted a few little habits of speech.)

"Round here? You mean in Cold Flat Junction?" Don Joe's voice slid up on a rising scale of notes, ending in a kind of astonished squeak.

Up and down the counter they regarded one another as if this was crazy but interesting. "I just thought if he came—*come*—from here, well, it'd be where he'd want to hole up." "Hole up" was good, I thought.

Don Joe frowned. "It'd be the first place police'd look."

How naive, I thought.

Don Joe went on: "If I was Ben Queen, I'd've hotfooted it right to the border." He slid one hand off another in imitation of the speed he'd fly off with.

"What border?" asked the woman in the thick glasses.

"Who cares? Alaska. That's where I'd go. Yes, sirree. To get me back to the U.S. of A. they'd have to exterdite me."

Louise Snell was leaning against the pie cupboard. "That's part of the United States, Don Joe."

"Since when, woman?"

"I don't know *when.* It just is. Has been for a long time."

"Twenty-one years," I put in, thinking if I appeared knowledge-able, they'd be more inclined to pay attention. I didn't know how long Alaska had been a state. I'm not even sure I knew it was. I knew there were two states added on to the forty-eight, but they could have been Nova Scotia and the Florida Keys for all I knew. For all any of us knew. They turned to me with something like respect. I looked around at their softly blinking eyes. What they reminded me of was the forest creatures' eyes peeping into the dark where Snow White lay asleep. But I felt more like Cinderella than Snow White, for Cinderella had those evil stepsisters. It would take two to make up one Ree-Jane.

I told myself to stop thinking about fairy tales and get back to the real world and its problems. But then I wondered, looking into the sleepy-seeming ring of eyes: were the seven dwarfs any more of a fairy tale than what we'd got going here in Cold Flat Junction? I shook myself a little, for I felt spellbound, or about to be.

They seemed to be waiting—Billy and Don Joe and the others—

121

for further historical revelations. I remembered Hawaii. "Number fifty's Hawaii. That's been a state for, oh, ten or eleven years, at least." We were way off the subject. I squinted my eyes up and said, "Now, what were we talking about? Oh, this Ben Queen. But if he's from here, he must have . . . kin (a good word) around here."

Evren entered the conversation. "Well, now, I dunno whether he's still got kin or not in the Junction."

How could anyone not know everyone who lived in Cold Flat Junction? Especially the Queens?

"Of course he does, Evren," said Billy. "Queens has lived here long as we have. That big house over on Dubois Road. Ben's brother and sister-in-law, that Sheba, live there. Ben lived there with Rose and Fern when their house was gettin' built."

"Who was Rose?" As if I didn't know.

"Pretty girl from over Spirit Lake way. Yeah, ol' Ben, he really give us a surprise there." Billy was fingering a cigarette from the pack in his shirt pocket.

I was hoping someone would nose in with "What surprise?" but all they did was nod and murmur, so it was left to me. I imagine I knew as much as they did about Rose Devereau Queen.

But my purpose in coming here hadn't yet been served. "I'll bet this Ben Queen's got some kind of good friend here who'd help him out."

They pursed their lips and looked thoughtful. For heaven's sakes, why was it so hard to remember Louise Landis had been Ben's steady girl before Rose?

Louise Snell, who had lit another cigarette, leaned her weight against the glass-enclosed cupboard again and said, "Well, if Ben wanted help, there's always Lou Landis."

At last!

"Yeah, Lou, she was always sweet on him," said Billy.

"Hard to think," said the chain-smoking woman in glasses, "she'd be living all these years in the Junction."

Don Joe leaned so he could look past Billy and down the counter. "Why's that? The Junction ain't a bad place. I growed up right here all my life!" He slapped his small hand on the counter.

She turned to him. "I never said it wasn't a nice place. But Louise Landis, shoot, she's too smart and educated to spend her life here teaching in that little no-account school. She graduated college. *Then* she went to some big university and got herself a—whaddayacallit?—an Advanced Degree."

I could hear the capitals she gave those words and wondered what kind of degree.

The husband in the booth put in his second contribution. "Master of Arts, that's what."

Wow! I thought. What was Louise Landis doing in Cold Flat Junction? "Is Ben Queen? Educated, I mean?" I knew he wasn't, but I wanted to hear more about the two of them.

Billy snorted. "Hell, no—'scuse my French—Ben, he couldn't hardly sit still for stuff like that. He was one wild kid," he added, obviously forgetting he'd laid into the man in the booth for saying just that.

I waited for more on Ben's "wildness," but Billy just clammed up, not giving thought to Ben Queen, but merely to the fact everyone here knew him. I drew little but air and ice through my straw and said, "I hate school." They all smiled and nodded because that was what a kid should do. Hate school. But they didn't say anything more about Louise Landis. "This Miss Landis, she must be a good teacher."

"Absolutely," said Louise Snell. "Of course she's wasted here because she's oversmart, even though she's the principal. And the school only goes up to fifth grade. Then they have to go to Cloverly to the big school."

"Real nice person," said Billy. "Ev'ry year she has a treat for them orphans that live up to that institution outside Cloverly, takes 'em out to lunch and stuff. Real nice woman."

There was I guess you'd say a "respectful silence." Then Don Joe asked Louise Snell, "Does Lou Landis still live over there in the Holler?"

I could have *clapped*. Here's the information I wanted. At the same time, I felt just a trifle irritated because I myself hadn't wormed it out of them.

Louise Snell nodded. "Surely does. Same house her folks lived in all along. They're dead," she said to me, as if it was information I might need. "It's an awful big house just for one person."

"That's over where Jude Stemple lives," said the woman with the thick glasses. "You got to go on a ways from his house."

I stayed looking down the length of my straw and hoped it wouldn't jog their memory that I'd been here not long ago asking about an Abel Stemple. But they didn't remark on that.

"There's some really big houses here," I said. "I guess hers is one of them." But it would be no problem at all to find out which it was, as all I'd have to do is ask Jude Stemple. We were by this time by way of being friends.

"Kind of pretty. Sort of a leaf-green," said Louise Snell as she began to polish glasses with a tea towel.

With a final clatter, I set down my Coke glass. "Well, it's real nice talking to you. I guess I better be on my way." I smiled brightly and slid from the stool, then looked up at the big clock, gasped, "Oh, I'm late," and rushed to the cash register with my check before they could ask where I was off to.

Flyback Hollow

22

I walked along Windy Run, which meant passing Rudy's Bar and Grill on one side and the Esso station on the other, sitting in its own couple of acres of sandy ground. There were no cars in sight being fixed or filled up with gas. A wind tunneled down the road (which is where the road got its name, I guess), and blew a Milky Way wrapper against my foot.

As I looked across at the Esso station and wondered how business was, I asked myself why I hadn't just gone there to find out where Louise Landis lived. Gas station attendants always know everything. Why had I gone to the diner and more or less created a lot of confusion? For I knew they'd all disagree about any topic, including the whereabouts of some villager. I suppose Lola Davidow would put it down to just being "troublesome" (which she'd told me I was on many occasions).

But this was my roundabout way. I think it had to do with what the answer came out of, how it came about. Yet, what difference does it make if the answer comes out of a long, out-of-the-way conversation, or just comes out as a simple answer? I don't know; it just does.

It's said the older you get the more philosophical you become. I'll be thirteen in a couple of months. I have always looked forward to my teens, but now I'm not sure. I really don't want to get more philosophical than I already am.

As I passed Rudy's Bar, I stopped to look in the window. I couldn't see much but my own reflected self right above a blue neon sign that said BEER—EATS. I would have liked to cup my hands around my face and peer through the window—it was really dark in there—and see if anybody was "drunk and disorderly." (I enjoy police terms, when the Sheriff says them: "drunk and disorderly" sounds almost poetic.) But I didn't stare in. I told myself it was because I respected people's privacy, but it was more because I didn't want Rudy coming out and yelling at me to get away from the window. I am not a risk taker.

Walking on, slowly, I kicked up leaves that skittered along the pebbly ground. Why were there dead leaves on the path in this early summer? The land all around looked as if it were between seasons. Or you'd think the place had only a single season that had to make do for all four. I had this sinking feeling as I always did in Cold Flat Junction when I was alone, just looking around. Often, there was no one else around, and when I did see others, they were few and far away. There was something collapsible about all of this, as if it were a plan of a village, a mock village, or a replica, a village cut from cardboard and put up as an experiment in lastingness. And everyone was surprised it had indeed lasted, the way that tall, thin people outlive dumpy, fat ones (or at least that's what Ree-Jane keeps telling me).

I had come to Schoolhouse Road. The school always looked to me more like a church than a school, with its white clapboard and steeple bell. The playground was empty even of the girl I'd played Pick Up sticks with the first time I'd been here. That was scarcely three weeks ago, yet it seemed like months, years even. Time, here, stretched to breaking.

I knew exactly where Flyback Hollow was and where the Queens lived on Dubois Road, and the post office, too—a square, gray, cinderblock building. I went in and found no one about, as there hadn't been before—no one at the window selling stamps or anything. I stopped at the bulletin board where I was glad to see there was no "Wanted" poster for Ben Queen. The Drinkwater brothers were still up there looking mean, and I wondered if the FBI had forgotten about them. I also wondered how effective the FBI was, as the Drinkwaters had been "at large" for nearly a year now. They might be up in Alaska.

"At large." I supposed it meant being all over, being out there in some helter-skelter way, hardly visible, anonymous. I left the post office and walked on, wondering if this was a good description of me.

On Dubois Road, I stopped out in front of the Queen house. I wound my hands round the white and peeling fence pickets, and leaned back and wondered if they were home and could see me. Would they remember me from being here with Mr. Root? Of course they would, for hadn't they told the Sheriff about me? It felt as if months had passed since I'd seen them, and I wondered if Time were like a glass of water or a Cold Comfort: if you poured too much into it, it would spill over onto any available surface. If Time has to contain too much—too many murders or lost people found or chicken wings thrown—does it have to expand to take care of it all?

I walked on, thinking about this, until I got to Flyback Hollow.

If Cold Flat Junction was a place where Time worked in strange ways, Flyback Hollow was its midnight. Dubois Road ended here, where the name "Flyback Hollow" was painted in whitewashed letters on a large rock. Trees and foliage grew around the place where it began. It had got nearly all of the trees in Cold Flat, as if they'd got together as saplings and decided to stick together and Flyback Hollow was where they stuck.

The branches above me lapped across the narrow road and created a tunnel of coolness and partial dark. It was like a little park in here, almost, the road dividing and arcing around a couple of acres where Jude Stemple's house sat. There were other houses, little ones, square and uninteresting and dropped about as if Aurora Paradise had tossed playing cards on the floor, which she sometimes did.

I slowed down and picked a black-eyed Susan, humming and pulling its petals. It was so nice not having to be anywhere, not having anyone to serve at dinner except for Miss Bertha and Mrs. Fulbright. I turned around and around in quick circles like a skater, my arms thrown out and my head back. I did this until I was too dizzy to stand and had to go and lean against an oak. Then I did it again, this time moving the circles forward down the road. I suddenly stopped, won-

127

dering why I was dawdling this way and making myself dizzy when I had important things to do, like talking to Louise Landis. I hadn't even given thought to what I was going to say.

Jude Stemple had been building the wooden fence around his house, sawing wood, when I first came across him. The fence was finished and I opened the gate. I didn't see him outside, or hear any sawing noises coming from the shed behind the house, nor did I hear noises coming from inside, either. His hound dog was lying on the porch as usual. I walked the path up to the porch and the dog beat its tail, though it did not rise. There was a screen door and behind it the front door was open. I knocked on the doorjamb and called out, "Mr. Stemple!" I knew the open door didn't necessarily mean anyone was home; people didn't bother locking their doors around here.

Wearily, I sat myself down on the step beside the dog. He was really old and tired. I scratched his ears, knowing how he felt, though moments ago I'd been dancing crazy circles down the road. Again, I had that strange feeling of Time lying heavy and gathering itself together, as at a formal dance a woman might stop to scoop up the train of her gown. Time wasn't passing, it was bunching. Bunching before me and this old hound.

What I really wanted to do was lie down on the porch and go to sleep, too. I can't recall ever feeling so tired. Maybe once I did before in the Rainbow with the Sheriff sitting across from me, waiting for me to tell him what I knew. I saw again Ben Queen walking away that night from Crystal Spring and heard him say, *If it goes too hard on you, turn me in.* It wasn't dog-tiredness I felt now, it was a tiredness all my own. I leaned over and put my chin on my knees and studied the gray porch step.

"I don't have to do any more. I didn't *have* to do all this," I said to the dog, who beat his tail against the porch. I guess he understood.

I did not understand the reluctance I felt as I left Jude Stemple's place and got farther back into Flyback Hollow. The road had come together again and continued on its way. Masses of trees divided this part of the Hollow from the part I'd just left. I thought of Brokedown House and that white light in my eyes, and I stopped dead amid the unfamiliar, glad it wasn't night. Even so, the trees seemed to have drunk in last night's darkness and were throwing it off in blue shadows along my path.

"*You got to go on a ways,*" the lady in the diner had said, and I wondered just how far. I looked back, anxious that the road might be closing up behind me. It was ridiculous. Still, I surely did wish Dwayne were here, even if it meant I'd have to carry a sack of rabbits.

Then I saw the house, up on the right; it had to be the Landis place, as there was no other, and it did—as they had said—melt in. Its dull olive-green paint and dark green roof separated themselves from their surroundings like the figures finally seen in one of those cloud puzzles. You have to look hard. If I hadn't been looking for it, I would have passed the house right by.

Now there was another road, narrower than the one I was leaving, a driveway, I guessed, for I was sure an educated person like Louise Landis would drive a car. I did not take to this road very quickly. I stopped to pick some more black-eyed Susans and tiger lilies and thought as I did it (though this had not been my clear intention) that Louise Landis might appreciate a bouquet. Then I realized they were her flowers in the first place and dropped them by a tree.

I told myself to stop acting like I was the Gretel part of Hansel and Gretel and that Louise Landis was a perfectly normal person, not someone to stuff little kids in an oven, and that she wouldn't have changed over the years, despite yearning after and maybe even waiting for the man she had always loved (except it hadn't done the Phantom of the Opera any good, all that waiting around). With a firmer step I walked on, recalling I'd seen her three weeks ago, the woman in black who'd stepped out of the school to look off into the dense beige distance of Cold Flat Junction.

But wait: I stopped again, feeling I'd walked miles and the house was receding before me. How did I know that woman was Louise Landis? It could have been just another teacher. But I didn't think so. The woman I saw standing on the top step and shading her eyes against the sun had an air of certainty about her that went along with being a school principal.

I still hadn't decided what to say and thought I'd better hurry up about it. My brain paraded several choices before my eyes: one, I was lost, or two, I used to live here (which she'd know was a lie, since *she'd* lived here all her life). Three, I just moved here and was walking around—only, that would lead to being lost again; four, I was visiting—

The door opened before I'd settled on something and it was the lady in black I'd seen, just as I knew it must be, only now she was wearing blue. Her skin was like mine: no matter what color we put on, it looked good.

Five, I was selling subscriptions; six, I lost not me but my dog . . .

She looked down at me with one of the pleasantest smiles I'd ever seen and said, "Hello." It might even have been her second hello, offered in a warm and friendly tone, but my mind was still busy: *seven, I was collecting for the First Tabernacle Church; eight, I was helping the Humane Society and did she have a pet?* She was a person you just knew you could put your trust in, and so I did: "Hello. Jude Stemple sent me."

"He did? Well, you'd better come in then, and tell me all about it."

My mouth was open to deliver whatever the next part of this lie was, but when she said that, I was completely stumped. I mean that she seemed to be so accepting in advance of the queer people who turned up on her porch. After I entered, she closed the door and I watched her back as she led me from the hallway, scented by furniture polish and roses, into the living room. Her hair was coiled into an elaborate scroll at her neck. It was shiny, pale brown, almost blond, maybe that color called ash-blond. I thought it was very nearly the color of mine, but hers certainly wasn't mouse-brown or dishwater-blond, as Ree-Jay said mine was. Just before I sat down in the armchair she indicated, I pulled a lock of hair around and looked at it out of the corner of my eye and thought, yes, we did have similar hair. Skin and hair, two ways we were alike. I wondered if she ever had a hankering to go to Florida.

We were in her "parlor"—a word I preferred to "living room" but one which my mother thought to be "common." "Parlor" suited this room better, as it was so comfortably old-fashioned, like the hotel music-parlor. (I would have to ask my mother why "music-parlor" was okay.) Hers contained a piano, upright against the far wall, and velvet upholstery on a settee and several side chairs in a red so deeply touched with blue it was almost purple. A fireplace with orange flames that seemed on the verge of going out, licking around and turning to ashes a few blue coals. There were pictures and portraits on one wall, and more books than I'd ever seen outside of a library on the other. They covered an entire wall and looked, as books always do to me, warm and colorful and inviting.

The whole room was that, really. The walls were papered with village scenes—little people walking in little streets past tiny houses on tiny squares. Wide mahogany moldings shone with that same polish that scented the hallway.

We were sitting in armchairs covered with a brown, flowered chintz that didn't match but didn't clash with the velvet and the wallpaper. There was a little ball of yarn between the cushion and the arm of my chair and I pulled it out. Maybe she had a cat. My eyes traveled back to the books. We sat in silence and listened to coals sifting and sputtering; somewhere, a clock chimed, and for once I didn't have to count the chimes.

The silence surprised me. Here was an adult person who just sat, her elbow on the arm of her chair, chin supported by her hand, waiting for . . . well, whatever I had to offer, I guess. All of this, you would think, would edge me closer to telling the truth of why I was here, but, strangely, it didn't. Maybe the room seemed so overwrought with imagination—all of those writers hidden in all of those books, all of those villagers in the wallpaper—that I moved instead toward greater foolhardiness. That was the danger of imagination; you could so easily fall right on your face. But it was like, well, writing a play, the way Will and Mill were always doing. Writing it *and* performing it, so for once I had the lead.

I said, "I've got—kin around here." This was not a good start on why Jude Stemple sent me. I frowned and picked at a loose thread on the chair arm.

Surprisingly, she picked up on this. "Are the Stemples—Jude—relations?"

"The Stemples?" Now I was looking up at the ceiling, thinking that I might not want to be related to Mr. Stemple, as he was definitely what my mother would call "common." I didn't want to be unkind to Mr. Stemple, but I didn't want to be related to him, either. "No, not directly. He's more by way of being a cousin of a cousin." She had not asked me my name or where I'd trucked on in from, or where I went to school, or how old I was.

In her just waiting there, seeming fully prepared to wait if she had to forever, and not making any judgments, I knew who she put me in mind of: Ben Queen.

"My name's Emma," I said, surprised at this little bit of truth escaping me, just as it had with Ben Queen.

Orphans

23

As I looked around, I felt mired in the past, lost in something old I couldn't identify, other than in the photos on the wall, the stiffened collars imprisoning necks, the cameos pinned to shoulders, the hair skinned back. Her question hadn't quite gotten through to me. "Pardon me?"

"Jude Stemple," she said. "He sent you here?"

"Oh, I nearly forgot!" I scratched my head, thinking hard.

But Louise Landis rose and asked me if I'd like tea, that she was going to have a cup. Except Miss Flagler, who has the gift shop, and Mr. Butternut giving me cocoa in their kitchens, no one had ever offered me a cup of tea like that. "Do you want me to help?" I asked, remembering my training.

"No. You just sit there and relax. Or look at the books, if you want. I'll only be ten minutes."

After she left, I sat for a moment, my mind empty. Beside my chair was a knitting bag with some orange yarn lying loosely across it. I picked up a loose piece and wound it around my finger. I should have sat there and worked on my Jude Stemple story, but instead, I looked at the bookshelves. Besides, I had already managed to get inside the house. I was tired of thinking; it seemed to me I had to do so much of it. Not easy thinking, either, like what to have for breakfast—French toast with sifted maple sugar and fresh berry compote or walnut pancakes. (I'd had both that morning, so that wasn't much of a decision.)

What was it about food? I liked it so much, mostly my mother's, of course. But there were also Dr. McComb's brownies, and there was the chili at the Rainbow Café, and the hot roast beef sandwich at the Windy Run Diner. So this liking must be connected to something else, or someone.

I had been standing before the wall of books, reading the spines. I had taken down and returned *Huckleberry Finn* to the shelf, promising Mark Twain that I would read his book one day soon. I bounced on the balls of my feet to get more eye level with the shelf above. My eye fell on the dark spine of a book by Wilkie Collins called *The Woman in White*. I remember trying to read this book when I was a child, but it was too hard for me. I do recall the woman, who appeared suddenly on the road, her face as white as her gown, frightening the hero (and me).

I took the book down and stood looking at the cover, which pictured the woman in white. Suddenly, I drew in breath and thought of the Girl. Her dress was such a pale color that it might as well have been white. I saw her again, standing in the rain at the edge of the woods just beyond the Devereau house. I'd just put a record on the old phonograph of a French song, the singer's voice hollow and reedy, but the words, soft and elegant. The Girl watched the house for a moment. Maybe the music had drawn her; more likely she had wanted to go into the house, but, seeing me, she stopped. She had this *waiting* air about her. Then she'd turned and walked away.

The only person I had ever told about the Girl was Ben Queen. I seemed to be keeping her to myself; I don't know why. Except for that one excited time in La Porte, when I had seen her and followed her and

133

fairly flown into the Sheriff, I had never mentioned her. And even with the Sheriff, I caught myself before I'd really told him much.

I was sure the Devereau family was cursed. If I ever told that to anyone I would be laughed at. I don't care. Rose was murdered; her daughter Fern was murdered. And Rose's little sister, Mary-Evelyn? In my mind's eye I see the three Devereau sisters, moving through the woods by lantern light. The sisters had told the police they were looking for Mary-Evelyn. Were they? Only Ulub had seen this strange procession and he didn't know what it meant. It is too heavy, too weighted, to have been an accident. It is—really—too mysterious.

A tray rattled and I shook myself, drawn back from that scene by the sound of clinking china. Miss Landis was carrying the tea tray in and setting it down on a small table. She said, "I was hungry and thought you might be, too."

"I am, a little." I didn't see how I could possibly eat anything else—not after the walnut pancakes, French toast, ham pinwheels, and chocolate cream pie—but since she'd gone to the trouble, I couldn't refuse. I said yes to both milk and sugar in my tea, since that was what she was taking, and I wanted to be thought accomplished at tea drinking, which I wasn't. I took my cup and picked up a sandwich half. It was chicken, and all white meat. I almost expected Mrs. Davidow to come by and snatch it out of my hand. With my tea and sandwich, I sat down again.

"I like that book," she said, nodding toward the chair where I'd left it. "Have you read it?"

I wanted to say a plain "yes." But I didn't want to be caught out if she asked me something about the ending. "Some of it I have."

"Did you think she was a ghost?"

For one frightening moment, I thought she was talking about the Girl. But then I realized she meant the woman in the book.

"The woman in white," she said, nodding toward the arm of the chair where the book lay.

"Maybe. I don't know."

"I did. That white face." She shook her head, as at something hard to accept.

During the brief silence that followed, I wondered again why she wasn't asking me why I was here. She was certainly polite not to. But after all, it *was* her house. Perhaps, I thought, it was because she'd been a teacher for so many years and had gotten to know the ways of children pretty well and how they didn't like being questioned. Adults did, nearly all the time, because they never seemed to know what else to do.

She sat, looking into the blue firelight, peacefully eating her sandwich. I couldn't get over this October feeling, the fire, the glazed look of the windowpanes. Asking me nothing, she treated my visit as if it was what she'd planned to do for today. I studied her. She had the kind of smooth good face that makes you think either nothing had ever ruffled her or if it had she knew so well what to do that any disturbance left her face untouched. It put me in mind of lake water, the placid center of Spirit Lake.

And to think she must be sixty! I hoped I could be that way when I got older. She had a calming effect, like the Sheriff, like Maud. Even when people like that go against themselves and get angry or fearful, there's still that part of them at their center which remains untouched.

Drowsily I watched the fire and almost forgot the second half of my sandwich, which was not like me at all, especially where the white meat of chicken was concerned. I wound the yarn, trying to make a cat's cradle, and thought about Jude Stemple and came up with, "I didn't mean Mr. Stemple actually sent me here; no, I should have said he gave me directions."

Louise Landis nodded and waited.

"See, it's really—" I stopped to pick up my tea cup and had this choking fit and spilled it. On myself, not on the chair or the rug. I was careful. I finished coughing and said I was really sorry. Miss Landis went to get a kitchen towel.

In her brief absence, I remembered Billy talking about the orphans. I wiped at my shirt and said, "It's really my mother who sent me." Since she was driving through the Carolinas about now, Louise Landis couldn't very well check on what I said. "She wonders if you'd like to have your annual lunch—the one for the orphan children—at Hotel Paradise." Well, it must've seemed to Miss Landis an awfully roundabout way (which, of course, it was) of getting to this lunch business. My mother could easily have phoned her instead of sending me along. "We could even supply entertainment."

She smiled. "What a wonderful suggestion. What kind of entertainment? Like a magic act?"

"More like part of a show that's going to be put on. Or maybe music. Piano playing, maybe."

"That's a fine idea. How much would all of this cost?"

"Oh, don't worry about that." I waved cost away as I finished my sandwich.

"I'm sure they'd love that. They have, well, as you can imagine, not a very happy sort of life."

Wide-eyed, I hoped with concern, I said, "It must be hard for them." I wondered who they were, but that was only my general nebbiness. I was much more concerned about how hard things were for me. I was a little ashamed at this reaction; I felt I should be better able to identify with the less fortunate. My mother was always telling me this when I complained about things like having to eat the dark meat of chicken: "You should remember those less fortunate than you." I pointed out to her that Ree-Jane wasn't one of the "less fortunate," and my mother said, "Oh, really?" I hate it when my mother is quicker than I am.

So whenever I see newspaper pictures of floods or hurricanes wrecking things and killing people, I sometimes bow my head and say a brief prayer, usually for the dog sailing atop some sinking building, moving downstream. I have a particular feeling for animals.

My mind had been so busy with false reasons for coming here that I nearly forgot the true one. Now I was trying to figure out how to work Ben Queen and White's Bridge into the conversation. So I just plunged. "We had a murder not far from La Porte, I guess you know."

"Yes. That must have been an awful shock to you. The woman who was murdered was from here."

"It was really horrible," I said enthusiastically. "Everybody's still talking about it. She was somebody's daughter from here. What was his name? . . ." I pondered.

"Ben Queen." She looked around the room, as if the name might call him up.

It was strange the way she said it, unadorned, you could say, the name without any other words around it explaining. It was as if the name itself had the power to acquit him.

"But she was his daughter. A person wouldn't kill their own *child*, would they?" As the chain-smoking lady in the diner had said.

She hesitated, as if familiar with child killings and not wanting to tell me. "I imagine it's possible, but not for him." She looked at me, abashed. "I shouldn't have brought this up. I'm sorry."

No, no. "Well, but you didn't. *I* did. Anyway, it's all right; it doesn't scare *me.*"

Her smile was quick, gone in an instant, like a bird lighting and flying off. "Oh, I bet it would take quite a bit to scare you."

I took this as a compliment, as they were few and far between for me. "And wasn't he the man that went to prison? For killing his wife?" For someone who didn't even know his name, it struck me I was being pretty quick handing out details about him. I put on my dumb look.

"Yes." She nodded.

"I guess everybody in Cold Flat Junction must know him. I guess you do too?"

"Nearly all my life."

I shook my head in a wondering way. It was sincere wonder, too. To think you could stay friends all these years! I wondered if the Sheriff would still be friends with me when I was sixty, though I didn't see how I'd ever get there. Not to mention how *he* would. He'd be ninety or around there. And what if Ree-Jane was still here? The two of us hanging around like Miss Bertha and Mrs. Fulbright? The few friends I had now, like Hazel Mooma (a distant cousin of Donny and just as swaggering), I couldn't imagine being that old. Especially when Hazel, passing Miss Ruth Porte on the street, said she'd kill herself if she ever got that old. We were all afraid of it, I guess, age and the loss of our looks and charm (what little there was). Hazel would be staggered by Louise Landis, I bet, and refuse to believe she was as old as she was. Hazel would probably say Miss Landis had been turned into a mummy ages ago and all the wrappings had preserved her. Hazel would believe this too, as she could believe anything better than that she was ever wrong, including about mummies.

I cast about for a way to bring up Fern Queen. "Mr. Stemple says Ben Queen's wife was a Devereau from Spirit Lake." I held my hand up toward a shaft of sunlight to see its transparency and the blood in it.

"Rose Devereau was her name. She was a beautiful girl, certainly beautiful by our standards around here, where there isn't much of it."

I watched her look around the room and then out of the window, as if she were trying to find even a trace of that vanished beauty, and had to report back: Gone.

"And Fern was her daughter? Hers and Mr. Queen's?"

"That's right."

Then I came to the part which always made my heart lurch; it was one of those dreadful, full-of-dread things. Anything could bring it back—a black twig snapping, the yowl of a dog. It was the image of Brokedown House and that bright white light. If it wasn't for Dwayne being there and the rabbits, I think I'd have had a harder time believing in it than in mummies. I chewed at the inside of my lip and said, "That was out near White's Bridge where she got murdered."

"That's right."

"There's a family of Butternuts who've lived there for a hundred years, at least that's what Mr. Butternut says." But what could I say or ask to set her feet on that road or in those woods? What really *was* I asking? I had to admit it: I was asking for help. I could feel a welling up of my unhelped and helpless life. It took me by terrible surprise, the threat of tears.

"Are you all right, Emma? You look a little—peaked." She did not wait for a reply, but got up and said, "I'll get you a glass of water."

I took this to be her way of not embarrassing me, in case I wanted to be left alone. Water. What good would that do? For once I could see the advantage of a Cold Comfort or a plain old glass of gin.

Louise Landis was back in a minute, handing me the water. I took a drink and set it on the table and then sort of scooted down in the chair, making a plane of my body. This position looks uncomfortable but isn't; it's mainly an unconcerned position. Anyone sitting this way could hardly be on the verge of tears or haunted by something in her mind. I twined some more yarn around my fingers and listened to Miss Landis carry on with the talk of White's Bridge.

"I've been to Lake Noir a few times, when I went to dinner at a restaurant out there. The Pear Tree?"

"The Silver Pear. I was there too. A man with silvery hair owns it. Well, two men with silvery hair. Do you know somebody that lives out that way? There's this Mr. Butternut, but he's the only one I know." I finished fashioning a cat's cradle. My heart was pounding as if I were coming too close to a thing I didn't want to see.

"No." She shook her head. "One time I did go for a walk along White's Bridge Road. It's quite beautiful. It seems pristine, almost. You know, untouched and uninhabited."

I just looked at her over my fingers. Untouched? She sure didn't know Dwayne. Uninhabited? She *really* didn't know Mr. Butternut.

138

He was inhabiting all over the place. He was born nebby. "How far down that road did you walk?"

"Not far. Why?"

I pulled my fingers apart to tauten the yarn. "Did you see that old, falling-down, worn-out house back in the woods to the right? They call it Brokedown House?"

"No, I didn't," she said, frowning slightly, as if worried she'd missed something important. "Why? What's there?"

"Oh, nothing. I just noticed it, is all. Mr. Butternut and I went there, but he doesn't know who owns it. Nobody lives there; it would make a good haunted house." Again the image of that blinding light rose up before me. The more I thought of it, the more strange and mysterious it became, until I was almost ready to believe the house was a figment of my imagination. But Mr. Butternut and Dwayne, they weren't figments, that's for sure.

She smiled. "You weren't frightened, though."

I wasn't? Tell that to my feet that felt like two cement blocks, as in a dream when you want to run. "Me? Oh, no." I held my hands before me again and pulled at the cat's cradle.

"Whose house it it? Or was it?"

"Mr. Butternut says some people named Calhoun lived there once. But what was Fern Queen doing in that place? That's what the police wonder."

"You seem to wonder, too."

I shrugged, which was kind of hard to do in that position, but I managed. We were silent for a moment. "Did you know Rose Devereau's sisters?"

"I knew of them. I know the little one drowned. That was terrible."

I was glad she brought it up instead of me trying to work my way around to the subject. It was like digging with a shovel; it was hard work. "Mary-Evelyn." And as usual when I spoke it, I felt that weighted sadness. I kept my eyes on the cat's cradle for fear of giving more away than I wanted to.

"I remember, now. She apparently went out in a rowboat and the boat capsized. But it sounds strange, doesn't it? Why was she out at all and dressed the way she was?"

I stared at Louise Landis. Here was another person who had really thought on the matter. "She didn't have any shoes on, either. And the Devereau sisters left it until morning to report it. But Ben Queen—" I stopped.

Now it was her turn to stare at me. "Ben Queen?"

"I . . . nothing." *But Ben Queen* (I'd been going to say) *said it was an accident, too. The boat had a leak in it.* But of course there's no way I could know that unless he'd told me.

It was in my mind to say it would make a good hideout, and I sat up and dropped my hands. The cat's cradle went limp. I was thinking again about who'd been in Brokedown House. It was the Girl or Ben Queen and I couldn't see him shining a light in my face, since he knew me. But she might have wanted something from me, or maybe she wanted to scare me away.

I stood up. "I didn't know it was so late. I've got to get back to the hotel and wait tables. I really, really enjoyed talking to you, Miss Landis."

She rose too and walked with me to the door. "So did I, Emma. I wish you'd come again."

I think she meant it, too. "Well, I'll tell my brother that the orphans would like to see the show." Will would kill me.

"And some piano playing, too," she said.

I nodded. Mill would kill me.

"Both," she said.

"Both."

They'd both kill me.

Tracking poachers
24

At seven-thirty the next morning I was in the big kitchen heating up sausage patties and pouring buckwheat pancake batter on the griddle. I had punched it down and let it rise again. (Most people don't know this about buckwheat: to get that wonderful sour taste, first you've got to use real buckwheat flour, and second, the batter has to rise, like bread dough.)

Walter wasn't in yet, so there was nothing to do but eat, which was fine with me. Mostly when I eat, I eat, preferring not to talk so I can enjoy the food without distraction. I'm not sure why the sour taste of real buckwheat cakes appeals to people who know their pancakes; maybe it's that the syrup supplies a little pool of sweetness for the sour taste to rest in.

As I ate my highly spiced sausage patty, I thought about my new freedom. Freedom can make a person lightheaded. But freedom brings a lot of anxiety with it, for to spend my time doing whatever I wanted made me feel responsible for myself. If I frittered my time away I would have only myself to blame. I reminded myself I didn't have *complete* freedom, for there was always Miss Bertha three times a day to attend to, so I could still blame her if things went wrong, which was a relief.

Still, in a way it was good having guests in the place, for without any, there'd be just me and Aurora Paradise, who I don't think would be handy at getting rid of an intruder. Will and Mill are just as useless, as they wouldn't know there ever was an intruder unless he went up to the Big Garage to audition.

Walter isn't live-in help. He lives in a big un-Walterish house, a big blue-and-white-painted Victorian with a wraparound porch and a lot of gingerbread detail around the roof over the porch. It looks as costly as any of the important houses in Spirit Lake, and I wonder if Walter is secretly wealthy. I like the idea of Walter having suitcases full of money. I like thinking he isn't beholden to the Hotel Paradise for his living (though I can't understand why anyone would work here if he weren't).

Halfway through my pancake stack (which was pretty high), my thoughts turned to White's Bridge. I wondered if Mr. Butternut knew Dwayne. Dwayne was around there a lot, but as he was poaching, he wouldn't be dropping in on people to pass the time. He must live somewhere near there, though. The Sheriff would know, as I suppose Dwayne might have had one or two encounters with the law. How could I ask the Sheriff, though, without him suspecting anything?

I tried to make short work of Miss Bertha and Mrs. Fulbright's breakfast, but I didn't get very far at it, with Miss Bertha complaining about that rude man who waited on them the night before, and why was it my mother was taking off for exotic places when she had guests to feed, and how could I cook her eggs the way she liked them if I couldn't do anything else right?

I stood my ground and tried not to yawn (the buckwheat cakes having made me drowsy) as every so often Mrs. Fulbright put in, "Now, Bertha," making me wonder again how Mrs. Fulbright had stood it all of these summers they'd been coming here. I put their breakfasts together—boiled eggs and toast and sausage (which Miss Bertha had said she'd never eat again, after the sausage had nearly poisoned her) and the thanks I got was that Miss Bertha poked the egg all over her plate, saying it was tough.

Well, I took it for as long as I could, and finally told them Walter would be bringing more coffee, as I would be late for Bible class if I didn't leave right then. Even though Miss Bertha is a church person (for all the good it does her), she still managed to slow down my leaving by complaining about the camp meeting grounds over across the highway and its members, "a bunch of heathen dimwits."

I went back to the kitchen and asked Walter to please take more coffee in and pay no attention to her, and Walter just said, "the old fool," and picked up the coffee pot.

Delbert drove me into La Porte, thinking he was funny saying things like, "You oughta have your own cab, number of times you go back and forth." Ha ha ha ha. I answered, "I'd put Axel out of business." Ha ha ha ha. I asked to be dropped off at St. Michael's Catholic Church.

Although I seem to do a lot of it, I really do hate to lie when it comes to religious matters. I don't think this is because I'm so respectful of religion; it's more that offending God makes me nervous. Also, Father Freeman might be around. He's another adult I really like, though I keep forgetting about him since I'm not Catholic or a churchgoer. I wondered if my mother could be blamed for being lax in my religious training.

What I intended to do was just sit in a pew for a minute and apologize for not coming here right away after Bunny didn't tell the Sheriff about our trip to the Silver Pear, which was a miracle if there ever was one. I also apologized for giving Bible class as an excuse to get away from Miss Bertha. I could have stopped on a street corner and delivered up this apology, of course, but there is a lot more to look at here in the church. The stained-glass windows are beautiful.

Finished with apologizing, I exercised my face muscles by pulling my mouth back and trying to move things around in a kind of circle. I had heard a woman guest at the hotel telling another one that your face will fall if you don't exercise the muscles. Think of women singers, she said—Lena Horne, for example. You won't catch her face falling, not with all the singing she does.

Since my eyes were tight shut, I didn't see Father Freeman standing there until he said hello. Then I jumped and said hello to him. I hoped he hadn't seen me exercising. He was smiling and leaning on the

143

pew in front of me. Father Freeman always gives the impression of having all the time in the world, which makes him very relaxing to be around.

"Mind if I sit down a minute?"

I told him of course not, and he sat down in front of me, twisting around to face me, his chin on his fist, the way I do in the Pink Elephant when I feel too tired to hold my head up on its own.

"How's your mother, Emma? I wish I saw her more."

"Fine." Then, surprising myself, I said, "My mother and Mrs. Davidow and Jane have all gone to Florida." I said this in a rush, as if I were admitting to something awful, maybe the kind of thing people admit to in confession. It was almost as if I were ashamed I hadn't been invited.

Father Freeman looked at me and (as he always does) thought for a few moments before he said anything. I like that; it makes me feel I've said something deep, something deserving of thought. Finally, he said, "You know, it's my experience vacations never turn out to be as good as you expect. It's really thinking about the places you want to go, reading about them, imagining them that's the great thing. You don't actually have to go. Really, you could be better off *not* going."

To this I listened openmouthed. He seemed to have read my mind. He seemed to have been looking over my shoulder, down there in the Pink Elephant. "No kidding? Do you believe that?"

"Absolutely. At least, that's how I am."

I thanked him sincerely and left, feeling lighter than I had when I got there.

When I walked into the Rainbow Café, Shirl was perched on her cash-register stool, smoking. Through a puff of smoke she leveled a look at me that said she couldn't place me but hardly cared. I said hello to her, and she nodded, uncertainty shading off into suspicion. Then Charlene called to her for a couple of Danish and Shirl slipped from her stool to reach into the pastry case and slide two apple Danish onto a plate. I offered to carry the plate to Charlene to save Shirl from exertion and she was glad not to have to walk the six steps to take it herself.

There was never much talk in the Rainbow on mornings except for ordering breakfast, and even that was very subdued. Throat clearing, cigarette smoking, and checking themselves in the long mirror to see what bad humor looked like took the place of wisecracking and giving Charlene a pat on the behind. Everyone seemed sore at morning for

144

making them go through it all over again. As the day wore on, the customers would loosen up and by lunch be downright jolly, kidding around and telling bad jokes. It was kind of like the progress Mrs. Davidow made through her martini pitcher.

Maud, though, was always the same; she didn't have a morning person who differed from her afternoon one. You could always depend on Maud. Right now she was taking orders in the rear booths while Charlene worked the counter.

The Sheriff would have been in probably by seven A.M. What I was hoping was that he'd come back, and I'd no sooner thought it than he walked in the door. More than anyone else I know, the Sheriff walks with authority written all over him. He placed his visored cap on the pole between the booths, sat down, and asked how I was.

I felt something beneath the innocent question and decided to jump right in. "Did you find her? That poor girl who was lost?"

"Nope. No one's notified us."

He was obviously not worried, but I'd rather he'd move his not-worried blue eyes from mine. I had to look away. I shrugged and said, "I guess she must've been found." I crinkled up my forehead to show the difficulty I had working my way to this conclusion. But when I looked up again, the blue eyes were still with me. It probably was not wise, but the only other thing I could think of was Ben Queen. Casually, I said, "I guess you don't know any more about the man you think shot that woman? The one out near White's Bridge?" I added, as if there were so many shot women around he might have trouble identifying this one.

"Ben Queen."

"You know, maybe it's better just imagining you caught him than to actually do it." I realized as soon as I'd said it that vacations and catching killers didn't exactly go by the same rules of imagination.

"Whatever that's supposed to mean."

He just went on looking at me and I sighed and buried myself in the menu, which I never did because it never changed. Once I flicked a look his way to find the blue eyes hadn't faltered. I felt like a snowman melting under a hard blue sky. I suddenly realized I might work on his sympathy. "Guess what? My mother and Mrs. Davidow and Ree-Jane have all gone to Florida. I bet it's really nice there." I looked really sad. He would have to sympathize.

"They left you and Will behind?"

145

I slowly nodded and wished I had an onion. I batted my eyelashes as if I was holding back a current of tears. Funny, but this was different from the way I'd felt giving this news to Father Freeman.

The Sheriff still looked at me as he took out a cigarette (this being the smoking booth), lit it, and clicked his lighter closed. He inhaled, then exhaled, as if he weren't at all pressed for time. "I can understand why you'd stay behind."

That sounded odd. I frowned. "Why?"

"You're too busy to go to Florida."

I sat back, *thump,* as my mouth fell open. This was my *involuntary* dumb look. I thanked my lucky stars that Maud came back. She sat beside me and his blue gaze shifted to her.

"I've just been out to the Silver Pear."

"Oh? Having lunch on your expense account?" Maud said.

"No. Showing the owners some pictures." He took three snapshots from his shirt pocket, buttoned the pocket again, and set them down on the table, side by side.

Maud squinted. "How sweet. You were showing pictures of me around."

His finger tapped the second one.

Maud smiled. "Look there, that's all three of us. Did they recognize you from the picture?"

"Very funny." He turned it so I could see it. I squinted, suggesting the snapshot was so bad the people in it were scarcely recognizable.

The Sheriff said, "That's the three of us one day checking the meters."

"Interesting," said Maud, "how other people get their pictures taken at weddings, or strolling in Rome, or even just having drinks by the pool. But us? We get ours snapped by a parking meter."

I'm glad she kept talking, even though he didn't much care to hear her, for it gave me time to frown in a huge bout of failing to understand this picture. I frowned not only as if I failed to understand *this* snapshot, but as if I would never understand any snapshot ever again.

He said, "Both Gaby and Ron agreed this little girl was the one they saw the night we got called out by Asa Butternut." Pause. "How about that?" He looked at me as if he were some sculptor chipping away. His eyes chiseled my forehead into a frown. So, I guess he knew what was behind it, in there behind my forehead. But I was not going to give in just because some dumb, blurry snapshot supposedly proved things.

I said, after a lot of careful thought, "Wait a minute!" I snapped my fingers. "That was the day Mrs. Davidow and I went to the Silver Pear for lunch!"

The Sheriff leaned halfway across the table and said, "Emma, knowing your relationship with Lola, I doubt she'd be taking you to the Silver Pear."

I'd started shaking my head and kept on shaking it through this little speech. "I just happened to be with her. She had to go out to see a person who lives on the lake. Then she decided she'd give herself a treat—and me, as I happened to be with her—at the Silver Pear. That's why they saw me." I smiled, but not too widely.

"According to them, this girl was alone."

Now I sighed heavily, as if explaining something to a mongoose. "Well, they just didn't *see* Mrs. Davidow. We sat out on the porch, around the corner. They saw me because I went in to use the ladies room."

His eyes burrowed into mine. "The girl asked them for the use of the telephone."

"I didn't *say* I didn't use the *phone*. Mrs. Davidow wanted me to call my mother to tell her she'd be back a little late. By then she'd already drunk three martinis and was telling me what a pain Ree-Jane is. I could have told her that without drinking even one."

My hands were clasped on the table and the Sheriff leaned over and put his own hand around them, as if he were cuffing me. His hand was nice and warm. "Now, you listen to me, Emma Graham. You are not, I repeat *not,* to mount your own investigation here. You are *not* to go around to these places, especially the White's Bridge Road area, asking questions. This is a murder investigation and there's a killer still out there and I don't want to find you lying in a damned pool of blood—"

"*Sam!*" Maud exclaimed. "You don't have to scare her to death!"

He sat back. "Scare *her*? You're kidding."

Maybe he was being sarcastic, but it helped answer the courage question I was always putting to myself.

I had taken all of the Sheriff's remarks in, of course, and it made me feel good that he was worried about me. But it just wasn't getting me any further along and I didn't have time to waste. And now, with him being suspicious, the method I was going to use to find out about Dwayne would never work. And that left Donny. I asked the Sheriff if he was going back to the courthouse when he left here.

147

"No. I'm going out to the lake."

In La Porte, that meant Lake Noir, not Spirit Lake, where nobody goes except me. I felt suddenly very sad. "I'm sorry, but I have to leave."

"Just remember what I said, now."

"Sure." I thanked Maud and stopped on the way out for doughnuts.

"Interview a *what*?" said Donny. He looked like a squirrel when he squinted.

"A poacher."

Donny threw his arms wide as if to present this unbelievable request to everyone in the room. It wasn't very effective, as there was only Maureen Kneff, the typist, and she was cracking gum, resting her chin on her overlapped arms, which were positioned on her typewriter. Maureen's eyes were washed-out blue, the only eyes I'd seen to compete with Ree-Jane's for pure absence of thought.

I really can't stand Donny Mooma. He likes to make people think he's dangerous when all he does is hide behind the Sheriff if they run into trouble out on a call. I made sure he would not be going back to the courthouse right away, then bought three vanilla-iced doughnuts (my favorite, not Donny's), and crossed the street.

Donny was sitting with his feet up on the Sheriff's desk, looking belligerent. He thawed out a little when I handed over the doughnuts, taking one for myself first. I told him I had this school project: "I'm writing this paper on poaching. There's a lot of it going on around here, especially over around the lake. Bunny Caruso told me."

"Bunny Caruso? Your mom know you're talking to Bunny Caruso?"

I realized too late Bunny wasn't the best source to bring up. I sighed. "I'm not really talking to her. I mean we're not sitting around jawing at each other over a couple of beers."

Donny's look was clouded. "Yeah, well, you best be careful."

"Anyway, why shouldn't I talk to Bunny? She's nice."

Donny would be too embarrassed to tell me what was wrong with being around Bunny and we could go back to poaching.

"You know, places like White's Bridge, around there. There's a lot of rabbit hunting going on."

"*Poaching* ain't exactly what me and Sam would call a major event. It ain't what this office would have at the top of its list. Top pri-*or*-i-ty, if you want to know." He'd polished off one doughnut and reached into the bag for the other. "Hey, Maureen! How's about some *coffee?* You ain't too *busy?*"

Like a sleepwalker, Maureen rose from her typist's chair and swayed out of the room to wherever the coffee machine was.

Donny brushed a bit of icing from his shirt, sat back with his free hand behind his head, and started on the doughnut. He had no intention of offering them around. After munching half of it down, he said, "And what poacher would do an *interview*, God's sakes? It's against the *law,* little lady—"

(I gritted my teeth. I hated being called that.)

"—so who'd ever *admit* to it?"

"Well, of course, I wouldn't *name* the poacher. I have to respect my sources."

"*Sources?* Who d'you think you are, Suzie Whitelaw?" I got treated to that wheezy laugh of his, which if anybody else did it you'd think they were strangling to death.

"It's not my fault, is it? I'm not the . . . social science teacher." I wasn't at all sure what subject poaching would come under.

"Go to the library and bone up."

"I have. That's not going to help with poaching around *here.*" I considered for a moment. "I need a human interest part. See, the best report is to be printed in the paper. I don't mean the school paper, I mean the *real* one—the *Conservative.* So I need one poacher interview and one police interview." That should get him going.

"Oh?" The way he wrinkled up his nose pulled on his upper lip so he looked like a pig. "That right?"

I nodded. "The Sheriff says you're really good at nabbing poachers."

Donny looked astonished. "No kidding. Well."

"The Sheriff says 'If Donny can't nab 'em, they can't be nabbed.'" I pretended to be reading this out of my notebook. "I'd like to use that quote, if you don't mind."

"Nah—that's okay. But put in my last name." He shook his finger up and down toward my notebook. "And make sure it's spelt right." His doughnut now forgotten, he leaned back again with his fingers laced behind his head. He pursed his lips and blew out air. "Well, I guess it don't matter if I give you a name or two. It ain't no secret, as these've been reported anyway in the paper. One's named Billy Kneff."

149

Here he looked over his shoulder to see if Maureen was still absent. He whispered. "Maureen's cousin, but he don't mean no harm, I guess. Let's see . . ."

Patiently, I waited to be done with Billy Kneff.

"Billy lives out your way, across the tracks. We had him in three times for out-of-season deer hunting. Then there's a fella named Dwayne Hayden—"

Without moving a muscle, I came immediately to full life.

"—lives in the White's Bridge area. We—I—nabbed him, like Sam says, twice."

My pencil was poised. "Where does he live?"

Donny just flapped his arm around. "I never seen his house, but it's in that area. Not far from that fancy restaurant."

"The Silver Pear?"

"Yeah, that's it. Dwayne works over at Abel Slaw's garage. He's what you call a master mechanic. You don't really think these guys is gonna talk to *you*? Hell, girl, they'd tell Suzie Whitelaw to get lost, and she's a *real* reporter." He leaned forward suddenly. "And for God's sakes, don't go tellin' 'em where you got their names."

"I promise. Thanks."

As I turned to go, Donny was sniffing the air, like a dog sensing danger.

Master mechanic

25

I wondered how much more a "master" knew than a regular mechanic. Pondering this alternated in my mind with the Florida trip. Walter and I had calculated they'd be driving the Tamiami Trail by now. So naturally I wanted to keep my eye on the clock.

I was sitting on the bench outside Britten's store. It was the one I always sat on when conferring with the Wood boys and Mr. Root, and right now I was waiting for them to come along, for they always did about this time, after the Woods got back from La Porte and their hot roast beef and mashed potatoes lunch at the Rainbow.

Lunch in the dining room had been fairly quiet. Only once did Miss Bertha raise a rumpus and that was because I'd put a tomato slice in her grilled cheese sandwich. I told her I was just trying to make it more interesting (which I wasn't; I just wanted to see how she'd react), and she said grilled cheese wasn't supposed to be interesting.

I heard something like a shout behind me and turned. Ulub and Ubub were coming along the path that ran by Britten's. They waved and so did I. Mr. Root was limping across the highway and I could see he was hurrying, seeing me and them, and probably was afraid he'd miss something important. He waved too with his free hand. The other was carrying a brown bag which looked like one of Greg's hamburger bags.

Ubub and Mr. Root got to the bench about the same time, Ulub having gone into Britten's for soft drinks. We sat down as if we met here every day and were pretty much used to one another's complaints and comments. Mr. Root went on about the rheumatism in his knees and Ubub and I made noises of sympathy.

Ulub came across the sandy gravel with Cokes for them and a Nehi grape for me. I told him thanks and I'd pay him back. He just waved that away as he did Mr. Root's outstretched hand holding money for the soda. The Woods are really generous. They always shared, even if it was just one Hershey bar among us.

We were quiet awhile, sipping our sodas. Mr. Root examined the pickle on his hamburger and asked if anyone wanted it. No one did. Then I told them, in detail, the story of my night on White's Bridge Road, and Mr. Butternut, and Brokedown House. I must say I had them more enthralled than Will's and Mill's audiences ever were. Mr. Root even forgot to eat all of his hamburger, saying "I'll be," and "B'jeezus" every once in a while. Ulub or Ubub would echo it. They were really awed when I told them about the Sheriff coming, together with the state troopers.

Round-eyed, Ulub said, "Nay er nookin er *ou?*"

I was getting more used to Wood-speech, and figured Ulub had said, "They were lookin' for you?" I answered, "Yes. They were look-ing for me. Only they didn't *know* it. Then the Sheriff for some reason got suspicious—" (I stopped short of that "stubborn as a mule" bit) "—and he went back to the Silver Pear with a picture of him and me and Maud and, of course, the Silver Pear owner, Gaby, recognized me. I had to make up a story about being there with Lola Davidow."

Mr. Root had his railroad cap raised and was scratching his head and shaking it, sorely astonished.

"And he told me I was *not* to investigate on my own."

Well, at this, Mr. Root just looked away and made a blubbery sound with his lips, waving the Sheriff away, as if to say, "Damn fool." Ulub and Ubub watched him and they did the same thing, their blubbery lip sounds saying the same thing and somehow I was pleased that they thought I wasn't going to pay any attention to the Sheriff's order, and he could like it or lump it. I was not quite that sure of myself, and, not that the Sheriff wasn't worth paying attention to, but I was glad they thought I was doing a good job.

Finally, I got to my point. "This Dwayne Hayden works over at Slaw's Garage."

Ulub and Ubub started talking a mile a minute to each other and to us. "E fenz eye ruck!" said Ulub.

Ubub nodded quickly and said, "Eye'n oo. On ut eye'nm ill air."

Mr. Root worked this out fast, snapping his fingers. "This Dwayne's fixing their trucks—right, fellows?"

They both nodded.

"Well," I said, sliding off the bench, "I think we should go see how they're doing."

———

Abel Slaw was a wiry little man who'd had this garage since time began. Lola Davidow brought her station wagon in here and had nothing to say against Abel Slaw. This alone was a huge recommendation. Ree-Jane took her convertible in even if there was nothing wrong with it, and now I knew why.

Whether the master mechanic worked on their cars, I don't know. There were two other ordinary mechanics walking around with tools in their hands and grease and oil-spattered coveralls. One of them I think was named Rod and I never did know the other one's name, for all they called him was You-boy, as that's what his mother had called him all his life ("You-boy, come on away from that!"). They both stopped when they saw us and pulled grimy rags from their back pockets and wiped their hands. Abel Slaw came over to us, also wiping his hands on a rag, though I didn't see he was working on any cars. Maybe there's something special about wiping your hands on a rag pulled from your back pocket that sets you apart as a mechanic.

"Evenin,' Ulub, Elijah. You too, young lady."

I managed a smile.

"S'pect you're here about your ve-hic-le." He turned to look at the truck. Dwayne Hayden must have been the pair of legs under Ulub's truck; the license plate read ULB, so it was definitely Ulub's. "Hey, Dwayne," Abel called as if they were on two sides of a huge canyon. "That truck 'bout done?"

Whatever Dwayne answered was lost on the far side of the canyon. It was being underneath a truck that garbled the sound of his reply. But Abel Slaw understood it, maybe in the same way Mr. Root understood Ulub and Ubub. Master mechanics didn't have to make smart conversation. Abel said, "Not quite, but he will be mebbe in a hour? Or thereabouts."

It sounded like a question, which only made the amount of time even more vague. "Sure, we can wait, can't we?"

Abel kind of raised his eyebrows at this coming from me, but he just shrugged and said, "You want to set down, you k'n go into the office."

Mr. Root said, "Thank you kindly, but we'll just hang around."

"Folks ain't supposed t'be out here, what with all the equipment and stuff lyin' around. But suit yourself." He retreated as if at the end of a long argument.

I hadn't worked out exactly what I was going to say to Dwayne; all I knew was, I needed someone there when I went back to Brokedown House. I mean, someone with a gun.

For a while I chewed the inside of my mouth, then I walked over to the side of the car, closer to where Dwayne's head should be. I was wearing a skirt today and made sure to knife it down between my legs when I squatted, in case he looked up it.

"Hey, Dwayne," I said. "I just want to talk to you for a minute."

"Who're you?" There was more clanging underneath.

"Emma Graham."

"Don't know anyone of that particular name."

"Yes, you do. We never got properly introduced." I whispered. "I wanted to talk to you about where we were—you know—a few nights ago, and the rabbits?"

The pallet he was lying on rolled out from under the truck pretty fast. For a minute he looked at me and frowned, and then, apparently deciding there was no thrill in it, he eased himself back under the truck. Maybe he still didn't recognize me. (According to Ree-Jane, mine was the most forgettable face in the universe.)

But Dwayne's face wasn't forgettable; you'd have thought I was telling—or living in—a fairy tale the way the handsome men lined up: the Sheriff, Ben Queen, Dwayne Hayden. Any one of them could have stood in for the prince who saves the girl (me)—that is, if you go just by looks alone. I, of course, do not. I tried to get down as far as the running board to look under it and see his face. "I only wanted to ask you something."

The pallet slid out again. He just looked at me.

"Can't you at least get off that for a minute?"

I didn't think he'd pay any attention to that, but he surprised me and stood.

"I gotta look under the hood, anyway."

He said this as if he wanted to be clear he wasn't coming out just to see me. Then he pulled a cloth out of his rear pocket—confirming my impression that mechanics always have to do this—and began wiping his fingers with it.

"The way things went, I'd think you'd remember me. How many kids do you meet up with out there?"

He didn't smile; I should say he gave me the impression of someone trying not to smile.

"I was just wondering if you go around there much on a regular basis? Where I saw you night before last?" When I get nervous I sometimes stand on the sides of my feet the way little kids do. I'm embarrassed when I catch myself doing it. I stood up straight.

Still wiping his hands free of oil, he said, "Uh-huh. And just what do you want to know that for? You planning on turning me in?"

I thought of Ben Queen and felt a sudden bleakness. "I don't turn people in. Anyway—" I lowered my voice. "—I carried the rabbits, so that makes me a . . . accessory co-conspirator." I frowned. Was that the word?

"So why do you want to know?"

"I've got a really good reason." I made myself look as earnest as possible.

"Yeah. You keep saying."

I looked around at where I'd left the Woods and Mr. Root. They were all taking to Abel Slaw as if they'd been in some car graveyard for years and were just now surfacing.

Again, I lowered my voice. "I can't tell you *here;* it's too public."

"Well, better you come over to my place later on and we'll split a beer."

I frowned. "I don't drink."

Now, he stuffed the rag back in his pocket. His hands didn't look much cleaner.

"I'm surprised."

I guess he was making fun of me, but I would ignore that. "Listen: I could meet you out there at Brokedown House. But you'd have to *promise* that you'd come."

He screwed his face up in the most utter surprise I'd ever seen, except when Will was playing innocent. "Promise? You're talking like you're doin' *me* a favor."

I shook my hands in impatience. "Well, but *will* you?"

He paused for some moments, watching me and probably thinking I was crazy. A crazy kid.

"Hey, Dwayne!" Abel Slaw was calling him. "Ulub wonders will he get his truck back this year?"

That, of course, was ridiculous. Ulub wouldn't have strained himself putting that into words.

"Yeah, Abe. Won't be but another few minutes."

And he went around to look under the hood. I followed. "Will you do it? Meet me at where we were before?"

"My Lord, girl, you are crazy to go around asking strange men to meet you in some deserted place at night."

I laced and unlaced my fingers, another nervous habit. "That's just it. It's not deserted."

Tamiami Trail

26

We set the meeting for seven-thirty that evening, which would allow time for serving dinner at six. It was an annoyance to have to stop my life just to wait on Miss Bertha, but I couldn't make Walter do all the work. Also, I didn't want Miss Bertha reporting back to my mother that he was doing it.

When I got back to the hotel I checked my Florida map again with Walter looking over my shoulder as he wiped a big oblong pan. (I wondered where he found all these dirty dishes and utensils that had him washing and drying all day.)

"Where do you think they are on the Tamiami Trail?"

"Along in here, mebbe." Walter poked a finger in the middle of the red line I'd drawn.

I told Walter my vacation plans and that if he wanted, he could share them. He'd be sharing by waiting on me, but I didn't exactly put it that way. He said he always wanted to go to Florida, which I doubted, for I didn't think he was even aware of it until everyone decided to go there. Right now, I asked him to mix up some of the coconut drink and I'd be back as soon as I changed clothes.

My swimsuit was over a year old and too little by now and flouncy, with its gathered skirt, which I thought was babyish, and its bright daisy design, which I disliked also. But I wasn't about to go to the expense of buying a new swimsuit. I forced myself into the daisy design and wrapped a big towel around me, which I'd taken from a guest room. I stuck my feet in sandals, gathered up my reading matter, went down to the kitchen to pick up my drink, and made my way to the Pink Elephant.

I imagined the Tamiami Trail. It was straight and white and lined with royal palms stretching away into the blue distance. We were too far inland to catch sight of the ocean yet, but I still thought I could make out the sigh of the waves coming from the invisible sea, as well as the rustle of the palm fronds. Cooling breezes holding the smell of the sea washed through the open car windows and stirred up little eddies of sand by the road. The day was as soft as a feather bed; it was a day you could lie down in and be comforted.

The car sped along, passing shacks and stores that didn't come clear in my mind until we passed a petting zoo and Ree-Jane chimed in that we weren't going to stop, thinking I wanted to. I didn't because the animals I glimpsed looked awfully sad. I had enough sadness going on without adding more to it. We went through a little town that I didn't want to bother with. On the other side, though, was a coconut grove and a stand where a girl was opening coconuts and carving up pieces from the shell. She also had a big pitcher of the coconut drink sitting in ice. I said we should stop, and we did stop. (This was clearly one of the benefits Father Freeman was talking about.)

Ree-Jane howled with impatience and my mother told her to shut up, a thing she would never do if left to her own devices. But these were now my devices. We got out and all had a glass of the coconut drink. (I picked mine up from the picnic table before me.) I told them all it was excellent. Mrs. Davidow said a little rum would liven it up and we all laughed, except for Ree-Jane, of course, who was in a mood. The coconut milk was really good. We piled back into the station wagon and Mrs. Davidow said we should look out for a place to eat lunch.

I thought it was really too bad that the graceful palm tree landscape had to be broken up here and there by clapboard buildings selling souvenirs, surfboards, and conch sandwiches. Boys in shorts and sneakers were milling about in front of one, and Ree-Jane, of course, wanted to stop there, and got into a real snit when her mother said No, she had no intention of eating a conch sandwich.

A little farther along, I spied a hamburger place. It was impossible to miss, for a giant hamburger atop iron legs stood outside like a water tower. There was something about this hamburger that awoke in me a rush of nostalgia, but I couldn't grasp for what. And I think it was the bun instead of the hamburger itself that did this. It was silky smooth, a light brown running into copper at the edges. Where had I eaten such a hamburger? How was it I could still taste it in my mind?

But Ree-Jane didn't want to stop at a "kids' place" and her mother was on the lookout for somewhere that served cocktails, so I was outvoted, even though my mother would have been willing to have hamburgers. It was not really a tie, though, as my mother's agreeing with me was pretty weak.

Not too much farther along we passed—well, nearly passed—a place called Trader Bob's. The sign outlined in neon sported a martini glass, also in neon and winking on and off. Lola Davidow slammed her foot on the brake so hard it nearly sent me through the front window. It was a little way off the Tamiami Trail, and we drove up a rutted road to its fake island-cottage front.

Inside, it was dark, dark even after my eyes adjusted from the brightness outside. The shadowy interior made it hard to report on what I saw, except for Mrs. Davidow's drink when it arrived. It looked stronger even than one of Aurora Paradise's Cold Comforts. It seemed to sit in rainbow layers of liquor and was as tall as her forearm. My mother had something with a splash of rum in it and Ree-Jane hautily asked for a wine spritzer. I had a Trader Bob's Special, which left out the alcohol but put in everything else. All the drinks were decorated with tiny paper umbrellas in turquoise and pink.

The six-piece band started in playing.

(Here, I left my chair and put "Tangerine" on Ree-Jane's phonograph.)

The band in Trader Bob's didn't have a female singer and I offered my services. They were delighted when I sang:

Tan-ger-eeen,
She is all they claim,
With her eyes of night and lips as bright as flaaaame . . .
Taaaan-ger-eeen . . .

I was up now singing and swaying to the music, a little in the way of a palm tree, I hoped. The customers (who I couldn't see clearly and it was just as well) applauded many times. They didn't want me to sit down but I explained we were driving the Tamiami Trail and couldn't stay. I returned to the table where Ree-Jane was laughing in that dark and soundless way of hers that was more like charades than an actual laugh. My mother told me I was good, and Mrs. Davidow ordered another drink and shrimp salad.

There was a knock at the door of the Pink Elephant and I called, "Come in!"

Walter entered carrying a plate of grass I had told him to cut and set it on the table. "Here's your seagrass salad, ma'am." I thanked him, and he left. I did not eat it, of course.

My mother and Ree-Jane were now arguing about which one would drive as we more or less had to support Lola Davidow out to the car and slide her in the passanger seat while she sang "Tangerine" at the top of her lungs. My mother won, naturally. She might have entrusted a plate of fried chicken to Ree-Jane, but she wasn't about to entrust our lives to her.

So eastward we drove on the Tamiami Trail into a deep coral sky, the sun going down behind us, darkening into a grainy blue dusk with the black silhouettes of the royal palms vanishing into the distance. It was just like the picture I had tacked up on the wall of the Pink Elephant. It was just like it, down to the faintest bluish-pink line of the horizon.

It was a relief to know that some things are real, that some things don't lie.

My real life

27

My real life is what I thought about, standing at the stove watching Miss Bertha's dinner heat up.

My mother had cooked a lot of food (having no faith in Mrs. Eikleburger) and put it in the freezer, clearly marked. She had left oven temperatures and cooking times for me, too. Tonight it was to be meat loaf with mushroom gravy. I had told her Miss Bertha's favorite, or one of them, was meat loaf, which it wasn't. Mrs. Fulbright liked it a lot. As for the mushroom gravy, Miss Bertha really hated it because she was sure all mushrooms were dangerous and called them toadstools. She was certain she'd get a poisonous one, which she probably would if I knew where they were. Since she wouldn't eat the mushroom gravy, I cut her square of meat loaf open, scooped out some, and stuffed the sauteed mushrooms inside. I sealed it back up. You really couldn't tell.

Now I stood before the stove, watching the peas warming in one pot and the mashed potatoes in the other, thinking about my real life. Was it now, waiting for the food to heat up? It made me uncomfortable to think my real life was watching over Miss Bertha's dinner.

I walked over to the tin-lined counter at the end of the draining board, where Walter was washing dishes, and set down some dirty utensils and the frying pan in which I'd resauteed the mushrooms. I asked, "Walter, do you ever wonder what your real life is?"

"Uh-uh." He shook his head.

He could be so annoying. "Well, wonder *now*. Wonder what your real life is."

"Okay." He went around and around a glass platter with a dishrag.

There was this exasperating silence. I didn't know whether he was wondering or not. Probably not. I was scraping bits of blackened onion grit from the frying pan, waiting.

"Well?"

"I guess it's washin' this here dish."

Deesh, he said. Walter was *so* practical about life.

"Not just your *life*. Your *real* life. What you're *meant* to do."

He was silent for a moment, then he said, "Washin' these here pots and pans, looks like. Looks like the same thing to me."

I heard Miss Bertha's cane smarting the wood floor of the dining room and picked up their basket of rolls from the serving counter. I took them in with the water pitcher.

As she looped her cane around a third chair at the table, Miss Bertha complained again that the "two of them" had no business going off both at the same time, and what was for dinner?

Meat loaf with mushroom gravy.

There came a sound of satisfaction from Mrs. Fulbright and a big grunt from Miss Bertha. She complained that my mother wasn't there to cook her something else, and wasn't that part-time German cook here?

No, not tonight.

I let Walter dish up the food, as he really enjoyed doing that and was very neat about it. After taking in their plates, the steam rising from the potatoes, I went back to the kitchen and waited.

There came a yell and a chair overturning and I started for the back door, asking Walter to go see what was wrong.

Then I ran across the grass to the other back door and up the stairs to my room.

As I changed my skirt for my jeans, I wondered again what my real life was. Or what it should be. I stared in the mirror, pressing my fingers into my cheeks, and watched as the skin whitened and the color returned when I took my fingers away. Then I pressed my finger tips against my forehead. I was seeing how solid I was. I felt ghostly, as if the inside of me had been scooped out and replaced with nothing, not even mushrooms

———

I was told to keep Aurora happy and that meant Cold Comforts. And that meant getting another bottle of Southern Comfort out of the storage room. I knew Mrs. Davidow kept the key way back in a cubbyhole in the rolltop desk in the back office (which would have been the first place I'd look if I'd been a thief). After I knuckled it out, I stuck my head into the dumbwaiter opening in the wall beside the desk to listen to what might be going on. Aurora could make more noise for her single self than any human being I have ever encountered. It often sounded like she had a party going on.

I went up to the third floor and got the bottle, stopping among the clothes and blankets to admire some of Ree-Jane's clothes. I always had a secret hankering after one of her evening dresses (she had several): it was the one my mother had made for her for her Sweet Sixteen party. It was white tulle and chiffon, the skirt spangled all over with sequins, very small ones that seemed to show not themselves but their reflected light. It was white and silver. I took the dress down and put it over my arm and carried it, along with the Southern Comfort, to the kitchen.

After I poured the Southern Comfort and brandy, I mixed in the usual ingredients of fruit juice, some gin, and my secret ingredient, which changed every time I made it. I took the glass back to the office and called up the dumbwaiter shaft: "Aurora Paradise, I'm sending up your Cold Comfort!"

Then came a scuffling and a creaking and her voice bellowing down the shaft: "'Bout time you did!" She gave two knocks with her cane, the all-clear signal, though why it wouldn't be clear was more than I could say. I set the glass—which reminded me of Lola's drink at Trader Bob's—in the box and pulled on the cord. Up it went.

"You got it?" I called, half of me in the shaft, looking up at semi-darkness. She yelled back that she had. "I'll have Walter bring up your dinner." Silence. I guess now that she had her Cold Comfort she saw no need to put herself out by answering. "I have to go out," I called up.

Then I heard her whine: "Go out? You? Wherever would you have to go to? It's evening."

"I do have a life of my own."

"No, you don't."

That really irritated me. But the irritation only masked something else. A cold center gathered inside me. I was afraid she might be right.

Brokedown House, revisited

28

The Woods and Mr. Root were already at Britten's when I got there a half hour later. They were gathered by the truck, talking at a great rate as if they'd just discovered a common language in a country of foreigners. Maybe they had.

As it was Ulub's truck, he drove and I insisted Ubub sit in front as he was the brother and they could talk (which would save me from trying to talk to them). Mr. Root and I argued briefly over the jump seat; he said his rheumatism was really acting up, and I had nothing to go up against that, so I sat on a blanket on the floor.

"Dwayne must not have gotten around to fixing this truck," I said, after we'd driven through La Porte and were bumping down the highway. My voice was as bumpy as the ride. Then I was sorry I'd commented, as both Ulub and Ubub went into the details of the repairs, none of which I understood, and Mr. Root was chawing at tobacco and seemed miles away. I never realized before how much Ulub and Ubub talked to each other. Their speech kind of fitted in with the choppy ride.

"Turn off!" I said. Nobody was paying attention.

Ulub swung the truck right to the narrower road, and soon I saw the Silver Pear, its big silver sign turning everything in its surroundings an eerie, ashy shade, flashing in and out among the trees like a knife that might at any moment bury itself in the ground, and I wondered if it would draw forth silver blood.

I was hanging over the front seat giving directions that the pond was just over the bridge. The bridge rumbled beneath us as if every plank was loose. It was just the truck, though. We braked to a stop beside Mirror Pond and got out and stood looking at the muddy, weed-choked pond.

"Ain't much of a pond," said Mr. Root. After delivering a stream of tobacco off to one side, he wiped his mouth with the back of his hand and added, "Ain't much of a place."

"I never said it was." I was secretly offended but didn't want to show it. "It doesn't have to be fascinating to have somebody killed near it."

Mr. Root warmed his hands beneath his armpits and didn't comment.

"Ar eh aunt'd owz?" Ubub said.

I scratched my elbow, frowning. It was "Where" something.

Scarcely hesitating, Mr. Root repeated, "'Where's the house?' That it, Bub?"

"Aun'd, aun'd!"

I frowned. "Awning?"

"You sayin' 'haunted,' ain't ya?"

Ubub nodded enthusiastically and it kind of irritated me that Mr. Root could always figure it out. But then I reminded myself I'd never have gotten this far without his ability to do that. "It's not exactly haunted, Ubub."

"Uhn abow neh ite?" This was Ulub this time. It was hard to tell between them, although Mr. Root thought Ulub spoke more clearly.

"'Tonight'?"

"That ain't it," Mr. Root said again, with more authority than I liked. "He's askin' about the light. You know, you told us some sissy showed a flashlight right in your face."

"Oh, but that was no ghost, Ulub."

I stood looking down White's Bridge Road, looking for something familiar, but there was nothing familiar. With all that had happened that night, with all of the people and commotion, I expected things to be burned into my eyes—the mossy tree, the spot in the road where I'd dropped the rabbits, the oil drum, the bed of black nasturtiums, the ruts the police cars had angled into the dirt—why, this place had been *crowded.* Tonight it was empty, as if all the life had been sucked out of it.

Mr. Root must have seen me as being uncertain and said, "Maybe we ought to stop and get this Butternut feller to show us—"

"No!" I said. "He was the one reported me missing, don't you remember? Anyway, Mr. Butternut would only spend all the time talking. Come on, it's just right down here." I'd say I led the way except there wasn't more than one way to lead.

As dusk seemed about to cave into dark, the road and the things along it grew more familiar, as if they would only make themselves known at night, like the stars, one or two of which were showing faintly, near the vague moon. "Some of those stars are a billion—a lot more than a billion—miles away. It would take us thirty years to get to them. Shooting stars are bits and pieces of broken-up planets." We had stopped while I delivered this information and now we picked up walking (Ulub and Ubub still with their eyes clamped on the sky). Then I told them there were many more universes than just ours, and planets that had more than one moon going around them. "Every planet has moons. Some a few, some many." I thought a bit. "That's where that expression 'many moons' comes from, from planetary language." This was most of what I knew of star lore, and some of what I didn't.

Mr. Root stopped. "Now, that ain't so. 'Many moons'—that's some old Indian sayin'."

"I *know* it's Indian; it's what the Indians said about moons."

We walked on.

"Hey!"

We all turned.

"Wait up, now!"

I groaned. It was Mr. Butternut. If he was the spirit of the place, I might as well go home.

Hobbling up to us, he didn't look in too good shape. "Mr. Butternut!" I tried to make it sound like there was no more pleasant a surprise for me than seeing him.

After I'd introduced him around, he started in asking questions. "Where you been? I had to call the *po*-lice on you."

I looked really concerned, though puzzled. "Why's that? Did something happen?"

"Well, a'*course*, girl! You was missing! You sayin' you don't recall?" He took out his tobacco and bit off a plug. Remembering his manners, he offered it around. The Woods shook their heads, but Mr. Root accepted, having run out of his own.

These few seconds gave me time to think, all the while keeping the puzzled expression on my face, which was still there when I answered: "Missing? I was never missing or lost."

Mr. Butternut heaved a sigh: "Girl, we was both down there—" He pointed with his cane down the road. "—near to Brokedown House and you went on that path to it and just disappeared."

I sighed myself, meaning to register as much impatience as he had. "Well, of course I know *that*. I dropped my flashlight and couldn't find my way, so I wound up back on this road and just walked back to the Silver Pear. I never saw you so I figured you'd gone on home to bed." I smiled more at myself than anyone else for it was really a plausible story. Was my life becoming a pack of lies?

He looked at me in a squinty way and chewed. Mr. Root looked at me squinty-eyed too, as if he knew Mr. Butternut better than he did me. I guess they'd forged a tobacco bond between them. Ulub and Ubub weren't paying much attention but were looking up at the darker sky and the handfuls of stars now scattered there, probably thinking of the long trip to get to them.

"And I went and called the *po*-lice. I thought that *Deg*-un fellow—"

"It's not '*Deg*-un,' it's 'De-*geen*.'"

"I thought he was goin' to throw a fit."

My eyes widened, really interested, now. "Why? What'd he say?"

"Well, it ain't so much what he *said* as the way he *looked*. I was tryin' to describe you and I couldn't recall too much how you looked. I did tell him you was real headstrong. Then *he* described you. Light-haired, blue-green eyes, freckles across your nose, and real pretty." Mr. Butternut frowned, looking at me as if testing that description.

My mouth fell open. *Pretty. Real* pretty! It was worth a trip to

White's Bridge Road to hear that. It was worth a trip to a brokedown planet to hear that. I tucked this away in my mind to look at later. And it made me feel kindly toward Mr. Butternut. I apologized for causing him so much trouble and he said never mind, only he hoped I let it be known to that Sheriff I was okay.

I said I would, and now we were all looking up at a black sky where the stars were a drift of white that made me think of that tulle dress of Ree-Jane's that hung now over a chair in the Pink Elephant. But it was all so far away it was hard to say which was drifting, the stars or us.

"Ah i'ky 'ay," Ubub said.

Mr. Root gave him a pretend punch on the shoulder. "Milky Way; you got it, Bub."

And in the next moment I knew what was meant by night falling. For it did. I think it's the sort of dark that waits in all our closets, mine being a wardrobe that I hardly ever had to look in any more to see if anything's there.

We got to the overgrown path that led to the house and Mr. Root stopped us with a fierce whisper: "Lookie there!"

A dim light moved through the trees. It was probably a flashlight or maybe a lantern and reminded me of those lanterns Ulub said the Devereau sisters carried as they made their way through the woods beyond their house. We were all quiet, even me, and watching in a wondering kind of way. I said, "Maybe it's Dwayne."

"Dwayne?" said Mr. Root. "What the hell's—pardon my French— Dwayne doing here?"

"Let's go see." I pointed to the path. "You can be first if you want."

"Me?" Mr. Root clapped his hands to his chest. "It's *your* ex-pe-di-tion."

"I don't want always to be hogging first place." I turned to Ulub and Ubub. "You can lead the way." I smiled brightly.

But Mr. Butternut stuck his cane in the ground. "Don't you do it, Bub. Nor you neither," he said to Ulub.

Now, I was getting really irritated with Mr. Root and Mr. Butternut. Mr. Butternut, of course, didn't want to go anywhere; he just wanted to link up with us so he could talk.

"Oh, for heaven's sake," I said, and in what I thought was a high-born, queenly manner, lifted my chin and walked the path to the cottage. I thought surely they'd be following on my heels, but when I looked back, the four of them just stood there as if struck in stone.

I gestured for them to follow and finally they did, single file, coming up the path. I said, "What we should do is, each one of you should take up different positions around the house in case whoever was here comes back."

Mr. Butternut didn't like that, but the other three were perfectly agreeable. Mr. Root asked if I was really going in the house.

I wasn't. "Yes," I said. "In a minute. Right now I'm going around back."

Which I did, and found Dwayne. *"Dwayne!"* I tried to breathe the name, but in this silence I might just as well have yelled.

He turned, looked first one way then the other, then at the rhododendron bush I was peeking over. "Oh, Christ a'mighty! You near scared me to death."

I couldn't make out whether he was glad to see me or wished he never had. "Shush!" I said, coming around the bush. "Keep your voice down. Listen: was that you?"

"Was that me what?" He was lighting a cigarette, hands cupped around a match. It had a good effect on his face, the light and the shadow.

"We saw a light, a flashlight, probably, over there—" I pointed off to the stand of maples.

"Who's 'we'?"

"Me and and Mr. Root and so forth."

"Brought your goons this time, did you? So what'd you want with me?"

I didn't answer. Instead, I asked, "Was that your *flashlight* we saw?" There was a big square one sitting on the ground beside his sack. "Is that rabbits?" Tentatively I touched the sack with my toe. "I didn't hear any gun go off."

He didn't comment. I supposed he didn't want to bother. I sat down on a nearby stump, regardless of the others who were waiting at their appointed places. Dwayne had opened the bag. There was only one rabbit.

"Defenseless little creature," I said.

"More'n I can say for you."

I was impatient. "Well, did you? See it?"

"You mean that light? Well, we're not the only poachers here. Ever think of that? Easiest answer is the right one, usually."

No, it isn't, I thought. Still, I felt deflated, thinking in this case he might be right. But that still didn't explain whoever had been in the house. I said so.

"Why not? I've been inside that place and maybe I'd've shined a light in your face too, stop you jabberin'."

Here he did just that, and I threw up my arm to shade my eyes. "Stop that! This isn't funny."

But the light had also hit something else, judging by Dwayne's reaction. "What the hell?"

The others had appeared out of the bushes and come around the house, and even though I knew they were around, it seemed creepy even to me, as if the familiar could change in the seconds it took to shine a light in your face.

"Looks like I should've brought a keg," said Dwayne, smiling a little. " 'lo, fellas."

"Dwayne," said Mr. Root, nodding. The Woods both said hello, too.

"Now, I just got this feelin," Dwayne said to me, "that whatever spook you're after, he or she ain't about to come out to greet a group of six."

He was really annoying me. "Who said 'spook'? It's not a ghost or the Headless Horseman. It's not Creepy Hollow."

"*Sleepy* Hollow, you mean. Ichabod Crane."

I ignored this. "It's a *person. Somebody* shone that light in my face." Suddenly, I was near to tears, tired of not being understood.

They were silent and almost respectful, even Dwayne, who I bet was always just one step away from a joke. They looked almost ashamed. Which suited me fine. "You're supposed to be surrounding the house in case someone comes. They'll have to pass near enough that one of us sees who it is. And everyone's talking too loud—"

"And too much," said Dwayne, going back to his other self.

"So split up and surround the house. Dwayne can stay here."

Dwayne wasn't about to move, anyway. He was flicking his flashlight on and off at the ground.

"Du-*wayne,*" I said, the way Vera liked to say, "*Emmm*-a," as if no one could be slower on the uptake than me. "This isn't a *game.*"

"It ain't nothin, far as I can see, but okay, let's do it so I can get back to killing rabbits. What about yourself? What are you going to be doing while we're surrounding?"

Astounding myself, I said, "I'm going to be inside—" I looked over my shoulder at the cottage. "—looking around."

As far as I was concerned, now was the time to argue with me. But no one did. I wasn't going in that house again, alone. Of course, I wasn't going to admit this, so what could I say? After some thought, I said, "Well, I like that. Here's five grown men who'd let a little kid just walk right into danger!" I shook and shook my head in disbelief and only stopped shaking it (my legs were rubbery and hardly good for walking with) when Dwayne heaved a great sigh.

"Come on then," he said, looking around at the others. "You fellas are safer outside with whatever than inside with you-know-who."

I told the others as they went to take up places not to make so much noise and watch where they walked. To be truthful, I was probably making more noise than any of them. Yet it was odd how the silence out here could be shattered so easily by a twig's snap or dead leaves crisping underfoot, or the creak of a high-up branch moving in the slight wind. Each sound was distinct and seemed carved out of the night, like those profiles carved in ivory, raised against a dark setting. It was the way I think I'd feel if I'd never heard these sounds before. Was it like the world waking up and hearing itself for the first time?

"Well, come on," said Dwayne, as I was bending down to tie my shoelace, which I did so he could get in front of me.

"You don't have your gun," I said, following at what looked to be a safe distance.

"What the Sam Hill you think we're gonna run into?"

"I don't know. Snakes, maybe?"

He picked up the gun and looked at me, shaking his head. "Snakes. So I just load up my gun and draw a bead on old man milk snake and blast him to kingdom come?" He started walking again, ahead of me. "Girl, that is not how you kill a snake. You wouldn't last five minutes out in the real world."

I *have* lasted, I wanted to say. But I settled for sticking my tongue out at his back.

The back door was off its top hinge and listing to one side. "Doesn't look like this door's been used for a long time." He tried to open it, but it was warped shut.

"There's a side door," I said, pointing. "Go on," I said, urging him in. He just gave me a look, shook his head, and went in through the door. I had not meant, of course, I would go in right away. Rounding the corner I bumped into Mr. Butternut, standing stock still on the path. "You're supposed to be off there," I motioned to an off-there place, "hiding."

"I done. I hid by that old mulberry bush and didn't see nor hear a thing."

I was so exasperated. It was as if "hiding" was an activity you did in a predetermined time period, like school lunch hour. "So go back."

"Aw right, aw right. Don't be so damn tetchy." Grumbling, he went off.

I could see the spread of Dwayne's light through the side window. Since I was supposed to be inside too, I had the strange feeling I was watching myself. I walked through the door that Dwayne had left open. Inside it was black as sin and I tried to blink up shapes. It was the front room where I'd been before when that light turned on my face.

"Dwayne!" Forget about quiet. I yelled it.

"Yeah?" He yelled back.

Then I heard a tapping on the glass pane behind me, whirled around, and felt my heart fall into my shoes at the sight of a face.

It was only Ulub, but Ulub's face isn't the best-looking even at high noon in the Rainbow Café. With that lantern of his below it making pits of his eyes, well, it's not the best thing to see when you're already scared. I was surprised the window opened, but it did. Was this evidence the house was occupied?

"Ulub! You scared me nearly to death!"

"Ah een nun ah nun owin —"

"Uh-huh. Okay," I said, not understanding a word except "I." He trotted off. I wanted only to be where the gun was and hurried into the next room.

Dwayne was standing by a chiffonier, inspecting an old tin box on its high top. This room was a bedroom, and it was hard to tell whether someone was using it or not, for the disarray could be new or could be old. I'm sure the Sheriff could have told in ten seconds by observing dents in the cushions, dust on the bedside table, the warmth of the sheets. But these told me nothing. The daybed was roughly covered by a patchwork quilt. I felt to see if the bedclothes were warm, but of course they were neither warm nor cold. In one corner of the room was a chair with stuffed animals and dolls on it. I went over and looked at them: two bisque dolls that appeared to be very old, their dresses stiffened and yellow; a rag doll with one button eye missing; another doll with a pretty white dress. I thought it was peculiar they wouldn't have been removed in the course of moving. I picked up the rag doll with one eye missing. Was it a child's room?

Probably not. The room reminded me, when I looked around again, of the one up on the fourth floor, the one kitty-cornered to Aurora's room. In that room, my mother stored her own things. But it was not nearly so neat as Mrs. Davidow's storage room. My mother's jewelry and clothes lay here and there, as if she'd recently been either examining them or wearing them. There were scarves and shoes about, again as if my mother had just thrown them off. The guests' kids sometimes snuck up there, and if Aurora didn't kill them first, they crept into this room and played with all the stuff. It was never locked. It upset me, this careless disregard for family treasures and mementos. For if that's not worth standing watch over, then what is?

Dwayne held up a ring, a deep blue stone, oval and set among tiny diamonds. Or at least the bits looked like diamonds; they were probably rhinestones. "There's jewelry in here, there's even money. Other stuff too: pictures and letters."

The tin box was a more elaborate version of my Whitman's candy box. It reminded me of other things too: the box that Mrs. Louderback sorted through to get her tarot cards, and the cigar box in the back office where Lola Davidow kept small things like erasers and lipsticks. I wondered if everyone had such a box at least once in her lifetime.

"Some of it's old, some looks new."

For evidence of this he showed me an old photograph, speckled brown with age, of a young man. He recalled to me someone I thought I knew, but who? "Let me see. Hold your lantern up." He did and in the dark room it cast a sickly, bleached light across the contents of the box. There were all sorts of things: a twenty-dollar bill, coins, costume jewelry. Besides the blue stone, there was an amethyst ring surrounded by seed pearls. There were letters and cards, a valentine, its lacy doily stiff with age.

"Maybe they're love letters," I said, excited and breathless.

"Could be." Dwayne picked one up and held it close to the light. "'Darlin', I slaughtered a hog this morning . . .'" He shook his head. "I hope no lady ever writes me that."

"It does not say that! You're making it all up." I yanked the page from his hand and read: "'Wonderful to see you; I can scarcely wait until the summer.' See? He's writing how much he misses her."

Dwayne grunted. "How'd you know it's a he?"

As he turned away to put the tin box back atop the chiffonier, I made a face at him by pulling back the corners of my mouth. Making faces was something I'd pretty much given up as I got older, but he deserved it, being such a smart aleck.

"While you're getting all teary over that mail," he said, "whoever's living here might come back. And I don't want to be here when she does."

"How do you know it's a she?" I asked, smartly.

In answer, Dwayne held out a bottle he'd picked up from a cluttered piecrust table and held it out to me.

I sniffed it. It was a pleasant, green scent, the scent of grass and new leaves. "That could've been here from long ago."

"It's a half-full bottle. It would have dried up by now. The top's not even on tight."

"Should we take it for fingerprints?"

He gave me a lopsided look. "Whose fingerprints? Mine or yours? Anybody else's, what the hell would they match 'em up with? Unless whoever it is has a record."

That made me think again of Ben Queen.

I heard a haunting cooing sound like the hoot of an owl. I took a few steps toward the other room, as it seemed to come from that direction, but then just stood where I was. I was overcome with such a feeling of oppression that I hadn't the heart to move farther. A memory came back to me of ice and snow and a sloping bank somewhere, and me going down it on my sled, whooping. Then the landscape broadened and, except it was winter, it looked just like the view across the tracks from the railroad station in Cold Flat Junction that had left me feeling empty like this—a far horizon studded with trees that looked like a solid line of navy blue, and the blue trees became that white line of trees, snow-shrouded, branches packed with snow so that they made, like the dark blue trees of Cold Flat Junction, a solid line. And above both landscapes, that sky hung, grayish-white, blank, and heavy as slate.

How had I got to that slope with my sled? No one else was about and no trail led to or away from it—no tracks, no footprints. I seemed

175

to be whooping with joy in this memory, but I knew I wasn't happy. The truth was, I didn't feel anything. I think I must have been like the indifferent landscape. I fit right in.

"Emma."

Dwayne's voice jarred me out of my thoughts. I was still holding the doll with the buttonless eye.

"You're standing there like you're hypnotized or something."

"I was thinking."

"God help us all."

Then he picked up his gun, which had been leaning against the chiffonier. Suddenly, as he did this, the hairs on the back of my neck felt electric, and tiny currents of alarm traveled over them to my insides. "What's wrong?"

"Hear that noise?"

"You mean that owl sound?" Had it only just sounded? Did all of that landscape happen in my mind in only a second or two?

"Ain't no owl."

"What then?"

He was already walking out, taking the rifle and the light with him. Only the candle kept me from a plunge into darkness. Then came a light outside in the window. Ulub's and Mr. Root's faces showed on the other side.

"'Ru ne'r, 'ru ne'r!" Ulub said, when I went to the window. He was motioning wildly to the woods on one side of the house. I left through the side door to see what the trouble was.

Mr. Root and Mr. Butternut had come around from the rear of the house. "'Hell's he saying?" Mr. Butternut frowned at Ulub.

Mr. Root said, "You just mind your own talk." Then to Ulub, he directed, "Now, Bub, say that again."

"'Ru ne'r. A ent 'ru ne'r." But poor Ulub sounded like all the starch had gone out of him, just trying to get this across.

Mr. Root said, "You're saying 'They went through there'?"

Ulub nodded, starchy again and pointing off to that part of the woods.

"More'n one person, Ulub?" asked Dwayne.

Ulub shook his head. "O'ney un. U ub en af er um."

"Only one," said Mr. Root. "You're sayin Ubub took off after them?"

Ulub nodded again.

There was that beaten path through the trees which came out on White's Bridge Road, the path we had taken when the police were outside Mr. Butternut's. So my story to Mr. Butternut before as to how I had missed him was perfectly plausible. It's nice to have a lie confirmed.

"Never mind," I said. "You were really brave to run after him in the first place. You don't even have a gun or any weapon at all." I hoped Dwayne would not take this personally—that I thought he should have gone after this person himself.

He didn't. He probably was not even paying attention to what I said. He was squinting off into the dark as if taking the night's measure. His jaw was quietly working; he was chewing gum and concentrating.

Mr. Butternut decided to build on my compliment to Ulub, saying, "That's absolutely right—what'd you say your name was?"

"'On-no."

"Alonzo," said Mr. Root. "Nickname's 'Ulub.'"

Dwayne said, "I'm having a look." Off he went, on the narrow path into the trees, and I felt something like what I'd felt when Ben Queen walked away from Crystal Spring. We all stood around silently, waiting for him to come back. I think we were all really tired. Yet, it was pleasant in its way, this waiting sleepily among friends.

But Dwayne came back in a couple of minutes with nothing to report, "Except I picked this off the ground."

He held out a small tube. Atop it was the little painted head of Niece Rhoda. I caught my breath. "Mr. Ree," I said. "Where'd you find it?"

"On the path." He hitched his thumb back over his shoulder. "Who's Mr. Ree?"

"A detective. It's a game." I was rapt. It was a game and someone was playing it with me.

My Florida vacation II

29

If anyone ever needed a vacation it was me.

The next morning, I was checking into the Rony Plaza, wishing I'd brought more than one suitcase, as there were plenty of bellhops.

I gave my name to the desk clerk, informing him I was one of a party of four, and gave their names, too: Davidow and Graham. He asked where they were, and I was vague. "Held up," "Around," "They'll be here."

I was annoyed with myself for not having planned where they'd be, but last night I was too tired, and this morning I'd had to deal with Miss Bertha, who was trying to make an egg sandwich with her soft-boiled egg. She threw her toast on the floor after she'd got the egg all over everything. I told her for an egg sandwich she needed a fried egg, and I would fry her one. I helped Mrs. Fulbright clean the front of Miss Bertha's gray silk dress and then went out to the kitchen.

As he dried a roasting pan, Walter watched the egg fry. I stood with the spatula, waiting to turn it over. "That there egg's tough as shoe leather, it looks like." Walter smiled as he said this.

"After it fries on the other side, we can take it to the roof and use it for a shingle."

Walter laughed his gasping, braying laugh.

I did not wait around to see Miss Bertha's reaction to her shingle sandwich but instead whipped up to my room and got my bathing suit on again.

Down in the Pink Elephant, the first thing I did was turn on the fan aimed at my palm tree, and once I got the crepe paper fronds fluttering in the wind, I sat down and (as I said) walked into the Rony Plaza.

It really made me gasp, the lobby, as it was even more opulent than I had imagined. The ceiling was domed and inlaid with bits of gold and lapis lazuli and other semiprecious stones and looked something like the ceiling of St. Michael's in La Porte. I didn't want to linger on the ceiling as I didn't want to add any kind of religious stamp to the lobby. Between the high windows on either side of the long, long lobby were frescoes of flowers and fruit, sand and sea. Potted palms sat everywhere. Their fronds made lacy patterns on the faces of some of the guests who sat around on champagne- and cocoa-colored leather sofas and chairs, sipping vodka martinis or pastel-colored drinks from fluted glasses. I noticed (for Lola Davidow's sake) that the martini glasses were as big as skating rinks.

The desk person handed over my key to the bellhop—or he might have been the bell captain, as he was rather snooty—and inquired again about "the others." Oh, they'll be along, they'll be along, I said breezily, deciding as it was my vacation I didn't see why I should take up mental space figuring out what they were doing. (Though I would, of course, reserve plenty of space for Ree-Jane later on, as she nearly drowned, got bitten by a coral snake, or drank too many of those pastel-colored drinks and got arrested for being drunk and disorderly.)

Yes, my mother and Mrs. Davidow might remain vague presences at the Rony Plaza, wispy figures swirling here and there, but Ree-Jane would be rock solid in every detail of her soon-to-be-exposed modeless-ness. Ree-Jane was in for it.

But right now I was more interested in my room, and its balcony, and the filmy white curtains billowing in the open casement window, and the sea air coming through, and the wonderful view of the wrinkled sea. I stood on the balcony astonished by a blue that I had never seen before except in stained-glass windows. It was a blue that farther out turned to amethyst and purple. Royal palms lined the beach for what must have been a mile, for I could not, even leaning over the balcony balustrade, come to the end of them. They had no end, at least not in my Miami Beach.

I came in from the balcony. While I was unpacking my suitcase, I noticed a square envelope leaning against the mirror of the bureau. It was addressed in an elegant hand to me: *Miss Emma Graham.* I slipped the card from the envelope. There was to be a private dance, by invitation only, in the ballroom the next evening. How wonderful! I turned and regarded the closet with a sigh of relief. I was so glad I'd brought my white tulle dress with the sequins. From somewhere in the distance, the sounds of "Tangerine" came floating toward me—(Here, I jumped up and put the record on and poured my bucket of sand across the floor.)—and I practiced my dance steps, sliding across my room's champagne-colored carpet until it was time to change and go to the beach. I collected my suntan lotion, my big towel, and a copy of *Vogue.* I was wearing my wraparound sunglasses. Downstairs, I sailed out the door (a bellhop behind me, lugging my beach chair) onto the hot, white, Florida sand.

At this point my mind was too tired to actually go swimming, but I gave myself a kind of preview—like the "coming attractions" before the feature movie—hitting the high spots I'd see later, like when Ree-Jane goes in swimming (in her old black bathing suit), and the people on the beach see a big fin cutting through the water. I think it's called a "dorsal fin"; anyway, it's the one in movies you always see knifing the water and aimed right at you or, in this case, at Ree-Jane. But it was time to stop for the day. Ree-Jane's fate could be decided later. I planned also on giving my mother many new colorful dresses. Lola Davidow would wear nothing but brown.

Rainbow

30

I told Walter I had to go into town and would he please give Miss Bertha and Mrs. Fulbright and Aurora their Welsh rarebit for lunch. He said he sure would, and asked me how my vacation was going. I said I was going to a dance tomorrow evening and he said that was nice, and would I like him to wait tables at that hotel in Miami Beach? Or did they have enough help? Walter could really fall right into things.

Forgetting I was still in my bathing suit, I called Axel's Taxis and ordered up a cab. His dispatcher said Axel was right there. Then she must have turned around, for her voice got farther away. "Ain't doing nothing, are ya, Axel?" There was laughter. He'd be to the hotel right away.

I rushed up to get into my jeans and T-shirt.

When Delbert showed up, I told him to drive me to the Rainbow. I sat in the back and chewed my thumbnail, wondering how I could talk to the Sheriff without actually talking to him. My life was too complicated, and I was glad in between times I could rest up in Miami Beach.

––––––

The Rainbow was full as usual during lunchtime. Maud was in the act of setting their hot roast beef sandwiches before Ulub and Ubub. But I was surprised to see Mr. Root, who generally took his meals up at Greg's, which was across the highway from Britten's. The Woods must have brought him to the Rainbow; I was pleased to see his social life was expanding. Mr. Root was having a hot roast beef sandwich, too, and calling Maud "young lady," which made Maud smile.

They all said hello to me with real enthusiasm. Others at the counter also greeted me—Dodge Haines and Mayor Sims and Dr. Baum. It was nice to have all of these people happy to see me around.

Maud motioned me to the back booth as she filled a Coke glass. I sat down and she came along with my Coke and her cup of coffee. "Sam says your mother and Lola Davidow went off to Florida." She took out her cigarettes.

"And Ree-Jane, don't forget her." I told her they'd all gone to Miami and Will and I were supposed to take care of things at the hotel. I blushed; I felt oddly ashamed, but did not know why. Did I feel it was a judgment on me, having to stay behind? Did I feel I wasn't worthy of this trip?

"Well, that's—too bad that you couldn't go."

But her look was angry, and her clipped tone suggested she'd been going to say something else entirely.

Maud lived in a little cottage on Lake Noir. I thought she must know the White's Bridge area. "You wouldn't happen to know Dwayne Hayden?" I asked her. "The master mechanic?"

"Sounds like a magic act to me."

"He lives out your way is all."

She frowned in concentration. "The name sounds kind of familiar. Where's he mechanic at?"

"Slaw's Garage."

"Ah! Yes. I think he worked on my car once."

"But you don't have a car."

"Once I did. It was really old, but he did get it going for me. Told me it needed a new—something—and I couldn't afford it, so ever since it's been sitting at my house up on blocks. I kind of miss the poor thing."

Maud could even sympathize with inanimate things. She was really sensitive. But we were off the subject. "He lives somewhere near White's Bridge."

"Dwayne does? I didn't know that."

"No reason you should." I thought for a moment. "Mrs. Davidow and I stopped and ate at the Silver Pear once. It's really fancy, I mean the way they decorate their dishes, especially desserts."

"That's for sure. Decoration is most of the dinner. Leaves me hungry. Your mom's a better cook."

I didn't respond to that because I could see us getting off the subject again. "Well, while Mrs. Davidow was talking to some friends out on the porch there, I kind of wandered on across the bridge to have a look at Mirror Pond."

"You did?"

"I recall there was this old man there, and I wonder if it's the one the Sheriff was talking about. Anyway, he said he'd lived in this same house all his life, and his parents before him. His name's—" I pretended to be searching my memory.

"Butternut."

The Sheriff was standing right there. I hadn't heard him come up to the booth. Nor had we seen him approach because we were both sitting facing the wall and he'd come up behind us. "Asa Butternut. He's the one who called in about that lost girl," the Sheriff said, still wearing his black sunglasses, so I couldn't read meaning in his eyes.

"Oh, *yes*," I said. "I forgot he was the one."

"But you didn't know him when I asked before. You'd never heard of him."

He removed his sunglasses and the blue of his eyes scorched me like the hot sands of Miami Beach. "So what about this Butternut?"

"Nobody but him, he says, lives along White's Bridge Road anymore, at least not up at his end. But of course it goes for miles, I think all the way to Spirit Lake. So he was telling me all about his family and how long they'd lived there, and of course we started in talking about the murder. This Mr. Butternut doesn't have a lot to do with his time, I guess, and so the murder was all he talked about. He talked to the police he said, but he didn't know anything much; I mean he'd never seen this Fern Queen before in his life."

The Sheriff only looked at me. I bet this was his way of dealing with suspects. You just look at them glassily and it makes them so nervous they finally give up information they want to keep. I wondered if his dark glasses were some protection for him. It was hard to think of the Sheriff needing any, but maybe we all did. I went on:

"Mr. Butternut told me about this house you were talking about: Brokedown House, I think. And he wondered if maybe someone might be—" Here a dilemma presented itself: I wanted the Sheriff's help, but if the person who might be using Brokedown House was Ben Queen, I sure didn't want to go leading the law to the door.

The Sheriff leaned toward me and broke the silence. "Someone might be what?"

I shrugged. "Using it, maybe?"

"Butternut didn't mention that to me. And that's where he took me. That's where he'd last seen this girl he called us about."

I should have known we'd get around to that again.

He said, "I doubt she was ever lost, not really."

"Brokedown House," I said, ignoring the lost girl. "Did it look to you like somebody might be living there?"

"We weren't looking for that. What makes you think somebody is?"

"*I'm* not saying it. Mr. Butternut was saying it." I certainly couldn't tell the Sheriff about someone shining a light in my face. But if Ben Queen were hiding out anywhere around here, I'd think he'd use the Devereau house, where I'd seen him. He might have gone to Louise Landis's. Her house was about the most private I'd ever seen. She'd have to be a pretty good actress, though, not to give anything away when I was there.

It was Maud who said, looking at the Sheriff, "Maybe you should take a ride over there, Sam. Maybe *we* should. Then you could drop me off at my house."

He looked at me. "You know, you ought to get together with this lost girl—if she ever gets herself found. You're two of a kind."

Lazy days at the Rony Plaza
31

Two *of a kind.* Those words stayed with me. The Sheriff was kidding, but still it set me to wondering. I thought again about that day in Cold Flat Junction when I'd looked across the railroad tracks at the bench where I'd been sitting and thought I could make out myself on the bench, or maybe a ghost of myself. Could we have ghosts of ourselves before we're even dead? And if we can, are those ghosts like the ghosts of others who are dead? Not that I believe in ghosts; I was only wondering.

Fingerprints, footprints; the scent of perfume left behind; or charred paper, ashes of letters burned in a fireplace; a light moving in an empty house. Could the ghosts of us leave behind, like suspects in a crime, evidence we'd been there? Evidence for someone extremely smart in the ways of ghosts and suspects to decipher and track us down? Like the Sheriff or Father Freeman.

This would be a good question to ask Father Freeman, whose ability to see ghosts and spirits is a lot better than mine, his mind having been brought up, you could say, in the ways of the invisible.

All of this was making me hungry as I lounged in the Pink Elephant, so I ate the chicken-breast sandwich the beach waiter (Walter) had brought me as I studied the pop-up book of palm trees while I sunned myself on the Rony Plaza's beach that afternoon. I had found this book in the children's section of the Abigail Butte County Library. I was amazed to learn there were over four hundred varieties of palms. Comparing the pop-ups with my tree (its fronds moving gently in the sea wind), I decided mine might be more of a coconut than a royal palm, but if it was, it should have coconuts under the fronds and it didn't. So I decided I'd been right in the first place.

The book also had a pop-up of a hotel surrounded by palms but the hotel didn't resemble the Rony Plaza, for it didn't have the same kind of entrance and looked like it was farther back from the beach. I compared it with the big picture on my wall. Still, I thought the pop-ups were quite clever, even though they weren't realistic, and that children would probably like the book.

I watched the sun go down behind the Rony Plaza. It was after eight o'clock and all the sun and swimming and sea air had made me sleepy. I was glad the dance was tomorrow night as I honestly don't know how I'd have stayed awake for it tonight.

As I waited for Walter to get down here with my cocoa, I could hear Ree-Jane throwing a tantrum because she hadn't been invited to the dance by the hotel management. I did not know why (not yet, anyway). I thought about the dance minus Ree-Jane. Although anything minus Ree-Jane made me happy, in this case I wanted her to attend. I know that seems very generous of me, but it is not. If she doesn't go, I won't have the pleasure of dressing her in mud brown or watching her do numerous foolish things that will certainly not add to her popularity. I was too tired tonight to discover what she'd do, but it wouldn't be pretty, I was sure. So I saw myself leaving the beach where the floodlights had just come on and going to locate the manager—who had silver hair—and saying to him, "Look, it's the hotel's dance and all, but would you mind inviting the others in my party to it? I kind of hate to be the only one." The manager said he understood "ab-

solutely," and the other members of my party would be welcome, although they couldn't "stay after midnight." I found that a peculiar rule
and asked why. All he said was that only a very select group could stay
beyond midnight. He did not tell me why.

At least my mother would get a new dress out of it. Lola would, of
course, have to wear one of her old ones.

Scent of grass

32

As the next day wore on, I grew more and more excited, waiting for evening. Maud had called me to find out if I could drive with Sam and her out to White's Bridge Road, as she had suggested the day before. I was really astonished that the Sheriff would do this; on the other hand, as Maud had said, what did he have to lose? It was the crime scene, after all, and he'd found out precious little about who shot Fern Queen (which is what Maud had said to him, and which I didn't think was the most diplomatic way of getting him to agree to what she wanted).

Anyway, we were to meet up at the Rainbow that evening at seven o'clock. That was when Maud finished her stint. The Sheriff never seemed to finish his. He could be up until all hours on police business, as he had been when Mr. Butternut called in about the lost girl.

That brought me skidding to a stop in the dining room as I was going to Miss Bertha's table to put out the butter. If Mr. Butternut showed up when we were there—and didn't he always?—he'd certainly say something to the Sheriff about me being the girl he'd walked to Brokedown House with, the one who'd "disappeared." I pondered: could the Sheriff have guessed it was me? His description of the girl it might have been fit me, except for the "stubborn" part.

I found a rock-hard butter patty in the bottom of the bowl of ice and plopped that on Miss Bertha's bread-and-butter plate. Then I searched the butter on top until I found the softest one and dropped that on Mrs. Fulbright's.

I had made arrangements with Walter to serve them their dinner that evening and he said he thought he could manage. There was something put-upon in his reply and I figured he was just imitating my mother, who was always pressed for time but who also just "managed" whatever it was she was called upon to do. I said to Walter I was sure he could, as he had been smart enough to make my chicken sandwich out of white meat. Sometimes it's best to butter people up; in some instances I've never known the truth to help.

Maud and the Sheriff were standing on the sidewalk outside the Rainbow Café as the taxi rounded the corner. She was wearing her old brown coat, flared in a feminine fashion and buttoned at the neck with one big tiger-eye button. The Sheriff had one stem of his dark glasses hooked in his shirt pocket and I hoped that meant his mind was off duty. Not off duty in the sense he wouldn't be as smart as usual, just that he wouldn't be as suspicious as usual.

I caught this glimpse of Maud and the Sheriff through the window as Delbert slowed the taxi down and before they knew it was me. It jarred me, the way they were turned slightly to each other and how deeply involved they were in their talk. Even if the talk was just their usual banter, and though they stood in the wide, bright main street, the meeting still looked secret.

As I said, it jarred me. I hardly ever saw the Sheriff's wife; in fact, I had almost forgotten she existed until I saw her a little while ago in the Rainbow, buying pastry. He had been there too, coming in for his regular cup of coffee, and when I remembered that now, I thought it strange. For their meeting had looked accidental, like acquaintances who hadn't seen each other for some time. Florence was dark and stormy looking, her face shut down as a house would be in a storm, windows closed, doors bolted. But Maud's face was as clear and placid as lake water, so open you could have slipped right in.

We all piled into the police car, Maud remarking it was the first time she'd ever got a ride in one, and the Sheriff responding by saying it wasn't a taxi, after all, and me responding to his response that not even Axel's was a "taxi" as I never saw anybody in it.

"Fern Queen was in it," said the Sheriff.

Yes, and that made Axel's movements all the more mysterious. I reflected on this as the countryside flew by, as the same cows near the same fence looked at us curiously. It was rare being with people who didn't have to talk all the time to feel comfortable with one another. For there were stretches of silence as we drove the highway to the lake. It was rare and I liked being part of that rarity.

I saw the sign of the Silver Pear right after we turned off the highway and felt I'd spent a large part of my life by now at White's Bridge. Inside of another five minutes we had crossed the bridge and were bumping along past Mirror Pond.

There was no sign of Mr. Butternut. The windows of his house were daubs of gold in the dusk. He liked having the lights on. This road had grown so familiar to me that I felt more than just a visitor; it was as if I'd been away and now was on the road home. No, not home exactly, but I think it's how *much* you feel when you're in a place that puts your personal stamp on it. Why Brokedown House should make me feel this, I honestly don't know.

The front door was stiffer than I remembered and I wanted to creep back when the Sheriff pushed at it. I said we could use the side door and he asked me how often I'd been here; I seemed to know it pretty well. As we three filed in, I saw how unlived-in and run-down it looked, with its possessions strewn about. The light coming through the fly-specked windows now was ashy and gave the walls and floorboard a gloomy look.

The small fireplace mantle had pulled out from the wall. It was some sort of marble, but after years of its bathing in fire and smoke, I couldn't tell whether the veins in the marble were green or black.

"It's cold," said Maud, drawing her coat closer about her. "It's the kind of cold a furnace wouldn't warm up."

I nodded. "I know just what you mean."

"It's the kind of cold you hear about that's on the sills of doors you walk through."

"The cold ghosts make."

"Oh, for God's sake," said the Sheriff, sighing. He was running a finger across the spines of a row of books. There were built-in bookshelves on both sides of the fireplace. Looking at one of the dusty books, he said, "The cold's different because the place hasn't seeped up any human warmth for a long time; the warmth has leaked out."

"Oh, sure," said Maud, disbelievingly.

"It has," he said. "Probably there isn't any heating except for space heaters. It used to be a nice summer cottage."

On the way here, the Sheriff had told us he had the county clerk look up the deeding of the property. The earliest information she had found showed the house had belonged to a Marshall Thring, had passed on to his heirs, then gone through the hands of several owners— Reckard, Bosun, Wheat—bought and sold, sold and bought, the last people being named Calhoun. I was familiar with none of these names, except for Calhoun, which is the name Mr. Butternut had said. The other names were useless to me in the solving of this mystery, would be soon forgotten. I think I wished the house itself had been plunged in mystery, that the Sheriff, for all of his searching through titles and deeds and documents, had found nothing, and that the owners were nowhere. Or that it had never changed hands after the original owner, a tall, black bearded man named Crow, who, it was reported, had murdered his wife and put a curse on the house . . . well, something like that.

The furniture was wicker, similar to our own green wicker on the front porch but here a dirty white. The cushions were covered in cretonne, my mother's favorite material. The rose and lilac pattern was faded now, and dusty.

There were three bedrooms, one of them the one Dwayne and I had investigated, still with a trace of that green scent in the air from the half-full bottle of cologne. I only noticed it probably because I knew about it. The scent was very faint.

The Sheriff was looking over the letters on the bureau and had picked up one of them when he looked around and asked, "You wearing perfume, Maud?"

"Me? No, I hardly ever do. I forget to put it on." She was sitting on a footstool, looking at the stuffed animals and dolls. She was holding one, studying it.

I picked up the bottle of toilet water from the dressing table and waved it under his nose. "This?"

He sniffed. He nodded. "Yeah, that's it." He took the bottle from me, held it out to the quickly fading light of the window.

I said, "It hasn't been sitting around long. At least not all these years. It would have evaporated."

"You want to join the force? I could use a crime scene expert."

I had, as they say, the grace to blush. I wasn't about to tell him the idea had come from somebody else. So I just shrugged, as if such crime-scene-expert powers of mine were for me an everyday occurrence. If I kept up the way I had been lately, maybe they soon would be.

The room was dimly lit, as if only a vapor of light hung in the air and, like the trace of that grassy scent, evaporated as the minutes passed. Outside the light grew dimmer. Maud said, looking at the window, "I hope we have a flashlight. All I've got is this little penlight thing." She was searching in her canvas shopping bag.

He pulled a flashlight from the inside pocket of his jacket and held it up wordlessly. He appeared to be as interested as Dwayne had been in the collection of stuff on top of the bureau. He was looking at the ring with the dark blue stone set among tiny diamonds. "Lapis lazuli."

"What?" Maud turned from the doll collection.

"This ring. It's beautiful. Semiprecious, not valuable, still . . ."

I said, "Are those diamonds around it?" I could hardly see the ring from across the room, but he didn't seem to notice.

"I doubt it. Pretty, but not diamonds." He picked up one of the letters.

Do men with guns all go woozy over a few pieces of jewelry and somebody else's old love letters? If they were love letters. I never got the chance to read them, which was very annoying; I was the one, after all, who'd started investigating this place. "Do you think you should be reading other people's mail?"

He had rested a forearm on the bureau and angled his flashlight down on the paper. "In the line of duty," he said, without taking his eyes from the page. It might even be the same letter that had fascinated Dwayne.

"Well? What's it say?"

"Here—" He held it out. "You want to read it?"

"No. I don't read other people's mail." If I could ever get my hands on the hotel mail before Ree-Jane got it, that would change.

"Someone's very unhappy about leaving. I don't know if it's the leaver or the left." He had resumed his reading posture.

In spite of the cold, the growing dark, and my irritation that the Sheriff, and maybe Maud, too, were getting so much enjoyment out of this visit when I was gaining next to nothing, despite this, a warmth stole over me, stealthily, as if fearing rejection by my stiffer, glassy-eyed self. I did not know what the reason for this was.

Maybe there was a similar feeling when I was around Dwayne and the Woods and Mr. Root. The thing is, I did not have to bow and scrape to these people. Not that I'm much of a bower-and-scraper any-way, but I know I'm expected to be for Mrs. Davidow, Ree-Jane, the hotel guests, and people in La Porte like Helene Baum and the mayor. I could divide up everyone into the people who expect me to bow and scrape and the ones who don't. Most adults don't realize my feelings are just as important to me as theirs are to them. So maybe it's not so much not being taken to Florida, it's that no one wanted to listen to my feelings about not being taken—

The dance! The dance! It was to be tonight. But it didn't start until ten P.M. It couldn't have been more than eight, so I had plenty of time.

"What dance?" asked Maud.

I had said it aloud. That was so embarrassing. "What? Nothing, nothing. I was only thinking."

She just looked at me a moment longer and smiled.

Now, that's another thing about people who aren't like Maud, the ones you have to bow and scrape to. They don't really want to know how you're feeling, they want to know you're feeling the way they think you should be feeling. That's what they want to know.

I got annoyed with myself. Here the Sheriff is investigating—well, he's reading, so I guess it's investigating—and Maud is helping, in her way, and all I'm doing is going on to myself about myself. Can't I think of other people sometimes? But that question doesn't sound like me. What sounds more like me is wishing Shirl would slip on one of her banana cream pie banana peels and land on her butt right in front of everybody in the Rainbow. My wish list is long and murderous and I can only square that with my better self (I guess I have one) by saying, "They deserve it."

Maud was holding the doll on her lap when I saw her glance stray over my shoulder and heard her draw in a sharp breath. "*Sam!*" He turned to her; her finger pointed at the window. "There was a man out there, looking in."

Dwayne. I bet it was. Was he that stupid to be out there poaching with the Sheriff's car, clearly marked POLICE sitting right on the road? I positioned myself at Maud's side (for my sake, not hers).

The Sheriff went to the window and raised it. Now came sounds of a loud thrashing, like an elephant hurtling through the bushes. The Sheriff picked up his flashlight, slid his gun from its holster, and went into the front room. We followed close behind.

As he opened the front door, he said, "Stay here."

Sure. With only Maud's penlight between us? It was dark out. We waited until he was out the door and had rounded the side of the house before we followed him.

His arm was crooked, gun pointing at the sky. In the other hand he held the flashlight, fanning out light over the shrubbery, which was dark and dense. The rhododendron and mountain laurel were big enough to conceal a person; the dew-wet grass was tall enough in spots to wet my shins.

Behind him, Maud whispered, "It's probably just raccoons."

Or rabbits, I didn't add.

"Making that much noise? I don't think so. . . . Here comes—"

The dark shape coming through the weeds and bushes lightened steadily in the path of the Sheriff's flashlight and showed up as Dwayne. It didn't surprise me, of course, and I hadn't been scared, really. And Dwayne didn't seem in the least bit abashed at being caught red-handed. Well, he hadn't been *caught,* exactly, as there were no rabbits in evidence. Still, there was his rifle, which didn't look especially innocent.

"Sheriff," Dwayne said and nodded.

"Dwayne Hayden? What're you doing out here, Dwayne?" The Sheriff reholstered his gun and, strangely, I felt a rush of sadness. I was beginning to think that nothing in the world could make a person feel safer—not a parent's arms, not a million dollars, not a lifetime supply of ham pinwheels—than a man with a gun, cocked, ready to fire. Maybe I was entering my violent years.

"Nothin', really. Just walkin'," said Dwayne.

"You usually take that Winchester on your walks?"

"This?" As if he'd forgotten he had it. "Yeah, matter of fact, I do. Never can tell who you might meet up with."

"What was all that noise we heard? Maud here—"

"Maud." Dwayne dipped his head slightly in a greeting.

"Dwayne." She smiled. Dwayne had a way of making you smile even when he wasn't.

"—saw a face at the window," the Sheriff ended.

"T'wasn't me. Someone's around though, I know that. That's what the noise was, to answer your question." He turned and looked back through the undergrowth. "I was coming along from just through there—there's a sort of path through the brush that goes along more or less parallel to the road—and someone slipped past me. I don't mean on the same path; I was a little deeper in."

The Sheriff said, "Come on." They went back the way Dwayne had come, disappearing into the trees and thicket. I didn't like it, the way the woods could just swallow you up, the way the woods around Spirit Lake had swallowed up Ben Queen that night. It was black and thick with undergrowth. I heard them talking and wondered what they had found, but not enough to go into those bushes. Maud was holding my hand and I could tell she was not budging either. Their voices got farther away. Then there was silence. I looked at Maud, alarmed. She was straining to hear, too. Why was I so afraid now, when I hadn't been as much as ten minutes ago?

They came back. The Sheriff was asking Dwayne, "Did you get any sort of look at him?"

"Not really. And I wouldn't say it was a 'him,' neither. I think it was a woman. Woman or girl."

The Girl. I hope not. I hope she left this place. But she didn't strike me as a person who thought much about her own safety. Or anyone's safety, for that matter. There are some people who have a purpose, one purpose and only one, and disregard anything that's outside of that purpose. I think hers was getting rid of Fern Queen.

There was a silence as Dwayne lit a cigarette, then, remembering his manners, I guess, offered them around, including to me. At times, I thought everything was pretty much of a joke to Dwayne, probably including being arrested for poaching.

The Sheriff asked Maud, "Could it have been female, that face you saw?"

Maud seemed to be trying to bring the sight back to mind. "I don't think so, I don't . . . This face was so *heavy*, so . . . Russian."

Well, we all frowned at that. The Sheriff opened his mouth, then closed it, shaking his head. "'Russian.' So you're saying it was a man?"

After more frowning, she said, "Look, I wouldn't want to die in a ditch on it, but, yes, I think it was a man's face."

He flicked his flashlight on and off, on and off, then said, as he started walking, "I want to have a look at that window. It was this one, right?" He pointed toward the side of the house around the corner.

"That's right," said Maud. We all followed him.

The Sheriff handed Dwyane his flashlight and knelt down, looking at the ground beneath the window. He told Dwayne to shine the light on the ground as he held his hand above the faint impression of a footprint. He rose. "I'll have Donny come tomorrow morning and go over this ground."

Oh, hell! I thought. Donny. If there's anyone I didn't want messing around in my mystery, it was Donny Mooma.

"You should've brought your murder bag," said Maud. She asked Dwayne for a cigarette.

The Sheriff stared at her. So did we. "My what?"

"Your murder bag. They all use them at Scotland Yard." She thanked Dwayne for the light and blew out a stream of smoke.

The Sheriff reclaimed his flashlight. "Now, just how do you know that?"

"Books, of course. Many books."

We had started walking now toward the car, Dwayne too. It was wonderful the way he just sort of fell in with whatever the crowd was doing.

"You like William Faulkner?" asked Dwayne, who was playing his own flashlight across the ground.

"Faulkner?" Maud seemed surprised. "Well, I tried reading him, but he's awful hard."

I walked with them, not wanting to be left out of the literary discussion.

"Some are," Dwayne said. "I agree. *Sound and the Fury,* that's hell on wheels, ain't it? But *Light in August,* that's not too tough. You should try that next time."

As if Maud were always picking up and tossing away one Billy Faulkner after another.

The Sheriff offered to give Dwayne a lift home, since he was dropping Maud off.

That meant I'd have him all to myself on the trip back to town. For that I'd read *The Sound and the Fury, Light in August,* and anything else Billy Faulkner ever wrote, hell on wheels or not.

End of the pier
33

Maud's house was really nice; it looked just like where Maud would live. It was a cottage, small and unfussy, and it backed onto Lake Noir, which was huge, black, and gleaming with the moon's reflection. Some time ago I'd heard this name was not the lake's real name, that some show-offy summer people had renamed it "Noir," and that hardly anyone could pronounce it right ("hardly anyone" being the uneducated people who lived here full time). Most people called it "Nor." Ree-Jane, naturally, went to great pains to give the word its French pronunciation. Mrs. Davidow tried to and sometimes did and sometimes didn't. My mother pronounced it correctly, as she felt it was a mark of "good breeding" to do so. I called it "Black Lake" because this really irritated Ree-Jane.

In the car, Dwayne had said that he'd get out at Maud's and walk from there, that the walk wasn't very far. Probably, he didn't want the Sheriff to see all the dead rabbits. But when we got to Maud's place, we all got out; that is, the Sheriff got out when the other two did, and when I saw that, of course I got out too. This surprised me, as we were to go back to La Porte after dropping them off.

Maud started down the sloping lawn and called back that we should all go down to the pier and that she'd bring us out something to drink. Apparently, we were really going to make a night of it. Being included in this made me feel very adult.

The Sheriff was the only one of us who had actually been out on the pier, though I remembered seeing it from a distance when driving to the lake with Mrs. Davidow. From what Dwayne said about the pier and the view, I could tell he'd never been here before. Maud went inside and we followed the Sheriff. I heard him mumble something about the "damned pier." He seemed not to be in a very good mood.

I thought the pier was wonderful. It was a little rickety, smelled of damp cedar or pine (I do not really know my woods), and stretched out into the lake. Most docks are kind of stubby, but this one sort of meandered out for forty or fifty feet. At the end of it, there was the rocking chair, table, and floor lamp.

"It's like an outdoor living room," I said.

"One of these days that damned lamp's going right over," said the Sheriff.

"Great for reading," said Dwayne, looking seriously as if he wished he'd brought Billy Faulkner along.

Maud came out with a tray rattling with beer bottles and glasses. For me I knew there'd be a Coke, which there was. Maud set the tray on the little table and handed the beer around.

The Sheriff said, "You got a half dozen extension cords running up to that house and some day you're going to set the place on fire if you don't electrocute yourself first."

By the way he shook his head and the look on Maud's face, I knew they must have had this argument more than once. Out on the lake, a speedboat carved the water and the moon's reflection folded and stretched and folded again.

Dwayne was sitting on the end of the pier with his legs dangling. I sat down beside him, and we both gulped from our bottles at the same time. Maud sat in her chair and switched on the lamp, most likely to annoy the Sheriff, more than from a need for light, as the moon was casting plenty of that, its surface so hard and white-bright it looked like a stage moon. The Sheriff stood behind Maud's chair, still looking in a bad mood, especially when Dwayne spoke to her.

"I wouldn't mind coming out here to sit and read." He twisted around to see her. "What kind of stuff do you read, Maud?"

She sounded pleased as punch to talk about her chair and lamp and reading with someone who approved and with the Sheriff listening. "I like poetry."

"You're ahead of me there," said Dwayne.

It occurred to me that Dwayne's manner of speaking—I mean his words and phrases—was sometimes as good as my own. I mean, Dwayne sounded like a hayseed a lot of the time, such as in Abel Slaw's garage, with his "don'ts" and "ain'ts," but around Maud he sounded well educated. I wondered if he was. William Faulkner sounded like the sort of writer that most people around here wouldn't touch with a ten-foot pole. Maud thought it was hard reading, and she was certainly intelligent.

"Well, I guess I better be getting back," said the Sheriff, drinking off the last of his bottled beer. "Emma?"

I didn't want to leave yet, for I was enjoying sitting here on the end of the pier, swinging my legs over the edge and with that marble platter of a moon shining down. But I got up, sighing, and we said our goodnights. The Sheriff offered again to drive Dwayne to his place and again Dwayne declined.

199

The Sheriff was quiet driving, and I had an idea he was wondering about Dwayne Hayden and Maud. I looked over at him while I pretended to be really fascinated by the police radio, putting my ear close to it, which allowed me to look at his face. I thought I saw something I hadn't seen before in it, but wasn't sure what it was. It looked like sorrow.

I sat back, trying to think of some way to bring up Maud without it seeming I was bringing up Maud. I asked, "When's Maud's son coming home from school?" Maud had a son who was four years older than me, but who I didn't see much because he was away at school. He always seems to be away, which is too bad because he's really good-looking. I recalled the times I'd seen him in the Rainbow. His name is Chad. He looks just like Maud, except, I don't know—"brighter" maybe. As if he were carrying a high-wattage light around inside him. At the same time, he isn't one of those people in constant high spirits who are always smiling and backslapping, like Dodge Haines, whom I can't stand.

"He lives part-time with his dad. It's his dad that pays for the fancy school. Then he and his wife take Chad on fancy vacations, too. I think right now he's in the Seychelles. Some exclusive trip."

It was exclusive all right. I'd never even heard of it. "What's the Seychelles?"

"Islands off—Madagascar? I think that's what she said."

"That's nearly all the way on the other side of the globe! It sounds like his dad just wants to keep him as far away as he can. That's really mean." As if to ward off such meanness, I turned to the window and crossed my arms across my chest. It really did make me mad.

The Sheriff was quiet. But I could sense he thought it was mean, too.

"And all Maud's got is her job at the Rainbow." I considered this unfair distribution of wealth. It was a little like me and Vera and the tips from guests. Vera saw she got most of it. "She can't afford exclusive vacations."

"Well, she lives on the lake. He can always swim and go boating and so forth. I mean, he *could* refuse."

I couldn't *believe* the Sheriff said that; he was usually so smart about people. "Refuse? Re*fuse* to go to the Seychelles? Refuse an exclusive *trip*? They wouldn't even take me along to *Florida*. Do you think *I'd* refuse a trip to the Seychelles?"

The Sheriff coughed and cleared his throat. "Well, I don't know, Emma. You never even heard about them till a minute ago."

"You know what I *mean*. You'd have to be nuts to think somebody our age—" I was glad to link myself with Maud's son that way. "—would turn down some fancy trip because we thought our mother wanted us to stay home with her. How nice do you think we *are*?" I don't think I put that right.

"Not very, I guess."

I punched his arm, lightly. "Anyway, it's different if you *live* in a vacation spot; you can't hardly think of it as a real vacation. Look at the Hotel Paradise. Do you imagine Aurora Paradise stands out on that stupid balcony on the fourth floor thinking what a wonderful vacation she's having in this great summer resort?"

"Aurora better not stand out on that balcony period unless she wants the fire marshal shutting down the hotel."

Really irritated with him, I slid down in the seat and shut my eyes. "That's so ridiculous. That's such an exaggeration." I was amazed to see out the side window the Dreamland Motel and sat up. "We're in *La Porte.*"

"Yep. I missed the Seychelles turnoff again."

Again I punched him and he laughed, really laughed, as if he'd forgotten all about Maud.

Good.

The Sheriff dropped me off, pulling right up under the porte cochere, saying goodnight and he'd see me tomorrow. He waited until I was inside the screen door and had turned and waved.

Waiting like that was the polite thing to do, I had learned from a series of lectures delivered by Ree-Jane on boys' manners: "Anyone boorish enough not to make sure you're inside the house should not be gone out with again," she'd said.

"You must know a lot of boorish, then."

"You mean *boors,* for God's sakes!"

"You're the one goes out with them, not me."

"What are you saying?"

"Just you haven't gone out with them again. I've never seen them around."

"You're *so* stupid."

I smiled. I always like it when she can't come up with anything better than *You're so stupid.*

As the Sheriff circled in front of the entrance, he tapped the horn, saying good-bye, and I watched the car down the long driveway to the highway. And then it hit me, as if the taps were on my heart: I'd wasted it. I'd wasted the time we'd been in the car together. There I had been, alone with the Sheriff, and could have talked about anything on earth that I wanted to and got his opinions and his advice. I could have talked about how awful waiting on tables was, and how I felt like the runt of the litter around Mrs. Davidow; I could have gone on about the stars, or love, or the Tamiami Trail. I could have told him about being left all alone, and not been invited to go to Florida—

The dance! I'd gone and forgotten it again! Mad as burnt cinders, I stomped up the stairs, making as much noise as I could, hoping to wake up Miss Bertha and Aurora. That was really dumb, as Miss

Bertha was deaf as a doorpost and Aurora was probably drunk, and I'd just manage to bother nice old Mrs. Fulbright. (Nothing would bother Will and Mill except the Big Garage in flames.)

But all was quiet as I took off my jeans and shrugged into my nightshirt. Then I plopped down on the bed, pushing aside the teddy bear that sat against the cushions. I thought some more, and was annoyed some more, about having wasted all that time in the car arguing with the Sheriff, and play-punching him, after all the incredible things that had happened at Brokedown House. I had just frittered the time away, when I could have discussed anything.

Yet, I also realized you can never talk to anyone about anything you want to. You can only talk more to certain people (like the Sheriff, or Maud, or Father Freeman) than you can to others (like you-know-who). No, talks-about-anything are the talks you carry on with yourself; that's the only person you feel absolutely free to say whatever you want to.

I lay with my hands beneath my head and thought about the Rony Plaza. I found out the dance had been postponed: it was to be tomorrow night. I found another envelope emblazoned with the hotel crest, leaning against the mirror. The manager (who'd written it in a flowing script) apologized for this postponement, and assured me that one of the "hotel personnel" would make certain I got to my room safely afterward. *The Rony Plaza is well-known for its exquisite manners.*

I'm sure it is, I said to the bear, who I had picked up to see about its stuffing. He was a really old bear. He seemed not to have lost any more stuffing, so I held him against my chest and thought about the events of the night. I wondered if Dwayne was telling the truth about somebody running by him. There was absolutely no reason he wouldn't have; why wouldn't he be truthful? It was just that I knew the truth was hard to come by (especially if you were face-to-face with the Sheriff), but I decided, no, of course it was the truth.

I yawned and could barely keep my eyes open to think. I put the bear back against its pillow. I had stopped playing with him some time ago, but I kept him around, just as I kept a photo album to remind myself of what I used to look like and what I used to do.

Bartending
34

Miss Bertha threw her buttered toast on the floor at breakfast the next morning, much to Mrs. Fulbright's "mortification." Mrs. Fulbright had lived in the days when young ladies grew "deeply mortified" instead of just getting embarrassed. I think "mortify" is a nice word and does seem to suggest an embarrassment of the soul instead of the face (in other words, blushing), as if the mortified person has a lot more at stake. I did not pick up the toast.

Aurora usually didn't eat breakfast, but as I wanted more information from her, I decided she wouldn't say no to one of the "brunch" drinks listed in Mrs. Davidow's drink encyclopedia. The brunch drinks all had names meant to suggest flowers and summery flowery smells, like "Mimosa," and used a lot of champagne, all this to make you think you weren't really drinking at this early hour, at the same time knowing that champagne is just as good as anything else to get drunk on if you drink enough of it.

I knew I would need some fruit juice and knew we had orange and apple, but I had to look at the liquor supply before deciding. I made my way through the dining room, ignoring Miss Bertha's shouts for raspberry jam. I was making for the back office, where Lola Davidow kept her select bottles, the ones she liked to keep by her side in case of an earthquake. When she goes on a trip anyplace, she locks these bottles up in the black safe; I know the combination because she was out on the porch one evening and didn't want to get up herself and told me the combination. I made a note of it for future use.

Besides the Smirnoff and the Gordon's gin, there were bottles of Myers's Jamaican rum and Dewar's Scotch. I took these two out, figuring they'd be a nice change from vodka and gin. I closed the safe and marched back through the dining room with the rum and Scotch, again ignoring the howl Miss Bertha set up when she saw a slave walking by. As I slapped through the swinging door to the kitchen she was saying something about telling my mother on me. If Miss Bertha only knew how little my mother depended on her word to mete out punishments.

Orange juice and rum were probably good together, but then what wouldn't be if it was tossed in with Scotch and a thimble of brandy? I had out the orange and apple juice and was trying to think up a name. "Jamaica Juice" might do. I studied the bottle of scotch. I had it! "Appledew"! Now that sounded like a beautiful morning-after drink! I jumped up and down a couple of times, cheering myself on for originality. Walter (back in the dishwashing shadows) called over to ask if I was on my vacation up here. I called back Not yet, but I would be after I took this Dewar's and apple juice up to Aurora.

"Appledew," I said to her, as she was turning it this way and that, inspecting it as if it were a precious gem. "It's a morning drink, a brunch drink."

She *hmpf*'d and said, "You know and I know only reason people eat brunch is so's they can vacuum up the Bloody Marys."

I found it interesting that she was beginning to think of me as the hotel bartender who'd heard it all. I watched her sipping and tasting, sipping and tasting. That was just for show, to let me know she wasn't a guzzler.

"Pretty good, pretty good. What'd you say its name is?"

"Appledew. It's mainly Dewar's Scotch and apple juice. Then

there's the secret ingredient, too." Aurora loved secret ingredients. I stood as always with the small tin tray under my arm. She never asked me to sit down. She was playing solitaire and cheating as she always did. A queen of clubs sat atop a king of spades. It just exasperated me, but I told myself not to say anything. I think I got drawn in because her reasons for cheating were so ridiculous.

"You can't put black on black." I couldn't help myself.

"You can if it's the queen of spades."

"That's the queen of clubs you've got there."

"I meant the queen of clubs."

"It's no fun if you cheat."

"It ain't no fun if you *don't*."

"You admit it! You admit you're cheating!"

"I never did; I never said I was having fun."

I gritted my teeth. This could go on for hours if I let it. "Okay, never mind the cards. I have a question."

"And I have an empty *glass*."

When had she drunk it all? But I was sly. "Well, I'm not making you any more Appledew until you answer my question."

She, of course, was slyer. "Well, I ain't answering your question till you bring me another Appledew. How you like them apples, Missy?"

She thought that was *so* funny. Slapping her leg, she laughed and laughed, but it wasn't real laughter. It was put on for me. "Okay, I'll go ask Walter. He knows as much about Spirit Lake as you do."

"That man? He don't know—"

"Walter's lived here all his life."

"So've you and you don't know squat." Leaning forward in her rocking chair, she slid a ten of diamonds on a jack of hearts and looked up at me from under her stubs of gray eyelashes.

But I was sticking to my guns. I turned on my heel and marched out.

"Just you come back here, Miss! Ain't you got no manners? You don't walk away from your elders unless you're excused."

My back to her, I stuck my tongue out at the stair railing. I didn't want to push my luck; anyway, sticking your tongue out is something little kids do when they can't think of a good comeback, like Ree-Jane saying *You're so stupid!* I never wanted to get that desperate. Then I put on my blank expression, which is similar to but not exactly like my dumb look and turned back into the room.

"Oh, all right, all right, ask your question. One question." She held up a bony forefinger.

"Do you know a house over near White's Bridge called Broke-down House?" One question, she'd said, so I hurried on "... *and* whoever lived there? And the house might not have been called Broke-down years ago, as it probably wasn't broke down until—"

"Oh, stop runnin' at the mouth! Yes, I know that place. Long as I can think back that's what people called it. They was Calhouns lived there."

Calhoun. That was one of the names the Sheriff had listed.

"Last ones were Ethelbert Calhoun and his family. Had five or six kids. Kids is hard on a place as I am sure Jen Graham knows." She made shooing gestures with her fingers. "Get goin'. I'm parched."

"Well, but did this Calhoun family have—"

"*One* question, Miss Smartypants. I already answered two. You cheated and stuck an extra question onto the first one, don't think I didn't notice."

"Oh, all right." My tone was a bit too pouty for my tastes, and I turned and left and made my noisy way down the three flights of steps, running down them as I wanted to get back with the Appledew as fast as I could to hear more about Brokedown House.

Out in the kitchen where Walter was still polishing up the same serving platter, it looked like, I carelessly tossed rum and apple juice into the glass (not terribly concerned about proportions, not with all of my bartending experience) and thought about the Calhouns as I poured in the Dewar's. Calhoun: another name I'd never even known forty-eight hours ago, which now would attach itself to all of the other names, a cat's cradle of names that loosened or tightened depending how you pulled. Why is it, when you've got a mystery to solve, instead of getting answers along the way, you get still more questions? But maybe that's the way mystery goes—something like a painting, where the artist fills in more and more brush strokes, details, but the filling in makes the painting wider and wider.

I poured in orange juice, some more Dewar's, added a couple of maraschino cherries, and was off again up to the fourth floor.

———

"Ah!" said Aurora, whether to the Appledew or slapping a red king on a red ace, I don't know. She took the drink in her mittened hand.

"So, go on," I said.

"With what? This is better'n the last one. Did you add anything different?"

Only a quart more scotch, I didn't say. "Go on about the Calhouns."

"What about them?"

I squeezed my eyes shut, as if the effort would keep me from bonging her over the head with my tray. My sigh could have blown her off her balcony. "I thought you might just remember something useful about the Calhouns."

"No'm, I cannot think of a useful thing." She slurped her drink.

I would have to plod. "First off, did you know them?"

"Knew him, knew Ethelbert Calhoun, the daddy. He used to work around here doing odd jobs and such. Bert had a crush on me."

I nearly dropped my tray, I was so astonished. "The Calhouns were connected with the Hotel *Paradise*?"

"He was, so was his oldest girl, Rebecca. She waited tables sometimes. Brought her little sister with her to baby-sit."

I shook my head, so stunned by this bit of news I could hardly get off another question. "Well . . . *when*? When was all this?"

Aurora was busy poking her straw at the melting ice cubs. "Oh, forty, fifty years ago." She glanced up from her glass with that cunning look. "When I was just a girl."

Forty years ago, Aurora would have been middle-aged. But I thought it wise to let that go.

"My, yes. That was back in the days when every man from miles around was after me." She sat back and looked up at the ceiling, its plaster swimming with fine cracks. "Let me tell you the story of my youth."

Oh, no, I thought. We'd never get back to the Calhouns now. When Aurora got on herself, it meant we'd be here till the cows came home. Besides which, you couldn't tell what was truth and what was lies. But I would have to humor her if I ever wanted to find out more about Ethelbert Calhoun and his family.

She pointed behind her with her stick, too lazy to actually turn and look. "See that steamer trunk there? Got all them labels on it? I been everywhere, Miss Priss, and I mean *everywhere.*"

The old trunk, with its drawers open and spilling out silk scarves and underclothes and its small hangers holding beautiful, elaborately decorated gowns, looked to me as if it were on display, a stage setting. I groaned inwardly to think I might have to travel with Aurora to Rome and Hong Kong and India before I could get back to Broke-down House.

"It was in Sydney, Australia, when we all went to the opera house . . ." Again, she motioned behind her. "Go over to that old Victrola and put a record on. Put on the one on the top. That's Maria Callas, who invited us to supper after the performance."

Still carrying my tray, I went to the phonograph by the window and set the tray on the floor so I could wipe dust from the record with my arm. There were arias, it said, from different operas. I dropped it on the turntable.

"We traveled to the outback of Australia, then after Australia . . ."

I was prepared to be bored, not only by Aurora, but by opera. Instead, I was transfixed. As the music and Maria's voice swelled, I looked at the ceiling as if this heavenly sound were leaking through the honeycomb of cracks up there. Aurora talked and I listened. Every few seconds, Aurora's voice lapped over Maria's.

". . . Copenhagen's just full of prostitutes."

But her voice only registered for a moment, then it was gone. I dropped my head and closed my eyes, the better to hear Maria, and wondered why everything in the universe didn't sound like this record, I mean, if there was a God.

". . . then skinny-dipped in Lake Como."

Aurora cackled so hard she choked.

My thoughts seemed to turn liquid: the White's Bridge Road running into Maud's house and the end of the pier where Dwayne and I sat; light coming from the lamp moving across the Sheriff's face; the empty fields on the way back melting into the Tamiami Trail. It was all as if it was endless, seamless, with no starts and stops, no beginning and no end.

Something pointy dug at my shoulder. I lurched to find Aurora waving her stick in the air. "Ain't you payin' attention, Miss? That record's done. Put on . . . hmm . . . Patience and Prudence." Her drink finished, she licked the straw and smacked her lips.

Wearily, I got to my feet. I might have been as old as Aurora at that moment, what with the weight I felt on my back. I took Maria off the turntable, then looked through the dusty stack for the Patience and Prudence song. When I found it, I wiped it and put it on.

At the opening bars, Aurora said, "Good! We can have a sing-along!" She pounded the floor with her stick and started in:

> *I knoooow that you hoo hoo-hoo-hoooo*
> *Have fow-ow-ow-ow-ound*
> *Someone new-hoo-hoo-hoo-hoo,*
> *But to-*night *you be-*loong *to meeee.*

I just shook my head. I ought to have been more careful with that second drink. At this point I knew the Calhouns would have to wait; it was no good trying to get anything out of Aurora now. So I turned on my heel and left, saying good-bye, good-bye to her and Patience and Prudence.

> *I knooow with the daw-aw-aw-aw-awn*
> *That you-hoo-hoo-hoo-hoo*
> *Will be gah-ah-ah-ah-one*
> *But to-night—*

It followed me down the stairs.

> *—you* be loong *to meeee.*

Deaf

35

Walter had one of the kitchen aprons on and was stirring a pot. I apologized for being late and he said, as always, "Oh, that's all right," in his lumbering, uncomplicated voice. He said he was stirring cheese sauce for the "rabbit" (the Welsh rarebit, but I didn't correct him) and he could wait on Miss Bertha if I wanted, but I was feeling guilty for asking him to do so many things.

He stirred slowly; he did everything slowly. I stood next to him, watching. "We had this yesterday, didn't we?"

"Yeah. She don't like it, neither."

I watched the spoon smoothing out the sauce. "Leave some lumps in, she hates lumps."

He laughed his wheezy laugh.

It wasn't too bad at all being here without the usual kitchen drama supplied by my mother and Vera and Mrs. Davidow, who liked to sit on the edge of the white-enamel middle table where I did salads. No, it was kind of relaxing and left a lot of time and space to think in. (Also, it was nice being able to tell someone else what to do.)

I thought of what Aurora had told me. I was sure there was more. "Walter, do you know any Calhouns."

"Prob'ly. Which ones? There's Calhouns all over."

"This one's an Ethelbert and he lived on White's Bridge Road."

"Ethelbert," said Walter, in his thinking voice.

"See, he once worked here. Before your time, of course. Forty years ago. You'd only have been a baby then. He's dead, I imagine, but some of his kids might still be around. The Calhouns is what Aurora told me; she says the daughter Rebecca waited tables here."

Walter frowned thoughtfully and tapped the wooden spoon slowly on the pot to dislodge the oatmeal.

"Rebecca. There's a Becky Calhoun I think married a Spiker."

I was excited. "Where do they live?"

Walter paused for a long thought. Then he said, "I think Cold Flat Junction. There's lots of Spikers around, too. I think she married Bewley Spiker. I ain't sure, now," he said, warning me not to put my complete faith in what he said and then be disappointed.

Cold Flat Junction! This was Fate.

I figured if Rebecca waited tables here, she must have been at least seventeen or eighteen (although the management here never seemed much bothered by child labor). That would make her in her midfifties now.

There was noise coming from the dining room, though how two old ladies could make so much I couldn't imagine. One old lady, I mean. I wasn't going to fool around with her this lunchtime. I had things to do. Walter put the bacon he'd fried onto a paper towel to absorb the grease, before putting it atop the toast and cheese sauce. (I was going to tell my mother how Walter had a real eye for detail.)

"You can dish up, Walter." He loved to do this.

"What about the old fool? You just know she's gonna want an omelette or somethin'."

"She'll want anything we're not serving."

Walter tittered and got the warm plates from the shelf above the stove.

I heard laughter and talk choked with it coming from outside the

211

kitchen screen door. "That's Will and Mill," I said, surprised. I wasn't used to seeing them in the kitchen during the day.

It was laughter that could scarcely contain itself, doubled-up laughter. But the laughter ended the minute they walked through the door, as if God had cut through it with a cleaver. They were always like that; it astonished me how Will and Mill wanted everything they did to be a secret, and thus did not want to be caught out doing anything, including laughing.

"What's so funny?" I asked.

"Huh?" said Will. " 'Lo, Walter."

"Hey, Will."

Then I said to Mill, "You both were laughing fit to kill."

Mill adjusted the glasses perched on his blade-thin nose as if that would tell him who this person was who was speaking to him. "Laughing?"

Walter had spooned cheese sauce over the toast tringles, which he then decorated with the bacon strips. I picked up my tray and headed for the dining room. When I reached the swing door, I got an idea and turned. "Will, come and do your hearing-aid thing so I can get out of the dining room quick."

Will looked at me and said, "I'm too tired."

"No, you're *not*. I'll do something for you later." It was dangerous making an open-ended bargain like this with him, but I didn't have time to think up anything better.

"Okay. Come on," he said to Mill.

Wreathed in smiles, Will said *good afternoon good afternoon* to the two old ladies. Miss Bertha started in complaining when I put the rarebit in front of her.

"Where's the menu? We had this yesterday."

Will worked his mouth as if he were talking to her but no sound came out.

Miss Bertha tapped at her hearing aid and said, "What's wrong? I can't hear."

Will kept working his mouth, saying something to Mill, who worked his mouth back. They carried on a silent conversation for a few seconds.

Now, I really think this routine amused Mrs. Fulbright no end, but she did nothing except cut up her toast.

"Serena!" cried Miss Bertha. "What's wrong with this fool thing?"

Mrs. Fulbright just smiled and went for the pepper.

"Say that again!" she demanded of Will.

Will mouthed silent syllables.

Miss Bertha took the hearing aid out and shook it, even hit it several times on the edge of the table. "Damned contraption!"

Will smilingly took it from her, looked as if he were messing with it, then handed it back. She screwed it into her ear. Will spoke to her in his normal voice, "It's okay now." Mill echoed this sentiment.

Then we scattered.

Diner life

36

There are times I think all mysteries begin and end in Cold Flat Junction. Spirit Lake itself might seem the more mysterious, what with the Devereau house there and Mary-Evelyn drowning there, and Ulub's story of the lights in the woods. Or White's Bridge Road where the murder occcurred. Yes, you might think either of these places held the greater mystery.

But whenever I get off the train at Cold Flat Junction, and it pulls away, and I'm left looking across the tracks at that empty land that seems to go on forever, Cold Flat Junction seems to me the real mystery. My gaze is stopped only by that dark line of trees on the horizon, the only thing that keeps my eye from falling off the face of the earth. I don't know what word to use to describe it—"unreal," or "unearthly," maybe—but that doesn't say it, for if ever a place were "earthly," it's here. It's raw land, forgotten land, land you wouldn't give a second thought to, so why do I? Even the milky sky, colored the gray-tinged white of an opal, seems to suffer under a blight of indifference. So I sat on the platform bench and looked over there, and even grew weary with looking.

I sat there for some minutes, then walked the worn path from the station to the Windy Run Diner.

They were all there today, again, either sitting at the counter on the same stools, or in the same booth. I had the eerie impression of stopped time, the diner frozen in time and its customers turned to ice sculptures. The only person missing was the wife of the man who occupied the booth. He seemed pleased by her absence. I took my same stool at the counter, the end that butted against the wall.

Don Joe and Evren both nodded to me at the same time and the heavyset woman in dark glasses smiled at me and smoked her cigarette. They actually seemed glad to see me, but I didn't put that down to my likeability. I just figured there was so little happening in Cold Flat Junction that any news was good news.

Louise Snell said, "Well, hello, darlin', nice to see you again."

It wasn't really a question, but I said, "I'm on my vacation." This was partly true, for I really was on vacation, except it wasn't here; it was in Florida. But hadn't I told them I was from La Porte? So why would I be vacationing around here unless I was insane?

Billy was the first to comment on this: "Vacation? Thought you said you was from La Porte." He acted like he'd told a good joke, for he laughed and slapped Don Joe beside him.

"What happened is, our car broke down again over in Spirit Lake so we took it over to Slaw's Garage. It's been there now for nearly four days. We've been staying at the Hotel Paradise, which is really nice, so things could be worse."

They were all listening intently, Louise Snell going so far as to get out her cigarettes and light one up as she leaned back against the cupboard that held shelves of pie wedges. (I was planning on having the banana cream.) Maybe I liked the Windy Run because I was paid such close attention to.

"And Mr. Slaw," I went on, "employs a master mechanic, so I guess he'll spot the problem."

The heavyset woman in the dark glasses beside Billy said, "Better than Toots's trying." Everyone laughed.

Toots was the owner of the Cold Flat Junction filling station and garage where the car was supposed to have been fixed the first time I was in the Windy Run Diner. I was almost beginning to believe there was such a car, it having caused such trouble.

The woman said, "Well, Toots could sure use a mechanic like that, so maybe you could go by and drop off this mechanic's phone number." Everyone laughed.

Billy was irritated because someone else was leading things and asked, "If your folks is over in La Porte, what you doin' here? Not that we ain't glad to see you, now."

"My ma wants me to look up an old friend of hers, name of Rebecca—?" I squinched my face as if trying to recall the last name, then pulled a scrap of paper from my pocket and pretended to read it. "Rebecca Calhoun, at least that's what her name was when Ma went to school with her. She lives on—" I consulted the paper again. "—Sweetmeadow Road." I knew there was no such road. There was a Lonemeadow and a Sweet-something, but I could get them arguing over which road it was and where the Calhoun house was.

And of course they did; they fought over the right to set me straight. Billy, Don Joe, the lady in the dark glasses, and even Louise Snell said all at once: "Sweet*meadow*?"

Billy took over. "Ain't no such a road, little lady. Now, there's *Lone*meadow, and there's Sweet*water,* so your ma must of just mixed 'em up."

"Oh," I said, in my disappointed tone.

"Ab-so-tive-ly," said Billy, as if I weren't believing him.

Don Joe and Evren nodded in agreement.

Don Joe said, "This Rebecca person, she'd be living on one or the other?"

While they were all deep in this problem I requested of Louise Snell a piece of the banana cream pie.

"Sure, hon." As she pulled a wedge from the shelf, she said to the diner at large, "Well, for the Lord's sake, help her out, whoever knows where this Rebecca Calhoun lives."

They all seemed to be putting on their thinking caps, consulting one another in whispers, when a voice said, "Red Coon Rock." It was the small man in the booth. "That's where." He held his white coffee mug with his thumb on the rim. His other hand held a cigarette and he was flicking ash from it with his little finger.

Billy turned on his stool. "Now how'n H you know that, Mervin? There's no Calhouns round here. Calhouns, they live over in the La Porte area. I never heard tell of one in Cold Flat."

Mervin answered, "Her name ain't Calhoun no more, that's why. She was a Calhoun, only she married a Spiker, Bewley Spiker that was, only he's dead now."

That all of this useful information came from someone in a booth seemed to aggravate the counter-sitters.

Mervin went on: "Then Rebecca, she passed away, too."

My heart sank. I couldn't believe that my fresh lead had dead-ended.

"It's only Imogene lives there now. That's Rebecca's sister."

Sister! I was too excited by this news to stay quiet. "Which sister's that, Mr. Mervin?" I had no idea what his last name was.

Their heads all swiveled to look at me. They were not used to me taking part in the discussion, even if I was the whole reason for it.

"Rebecca's sister?" Mervin scraped the heel of his hand across his whiskers. I could hear the rasping noise even halfway across the room. "Well, I don't rightly think she had more than one. This Imogene, she'd be younger than Rebecca by a good ten, fifteen years."

Imogene must be the little sister Aurora mentioned, the one Rebecca took with her all the time when she had to work; she'd have been ten or eleven when she went to the Devereau house, almost the same age as Mary-Evelyn.

Louise Snell said, "But you was looking for Rebecca, right?"

I tried to look disappointed, and in a way I was, thinking of how Rebecca was waitress at the Hotel Paradise and I'd've really liked to hear her talk about it. "My ma will be disappointed as she was such a good friend." I looked down at the plate my pie had rested on and mashed my fork against the crumbs. When had I eaten it? "But Imogene, maybe she'd be worth talking to, for she might remember my ma. Where does she live?"

"Red Coon Rock over past Flyback Holler," Mervin said. "Where Jude Stemple lives."

Don Joe said, "Why, you was asking about Jude, too. Did you find him?"

"I did, yes."

"Huh," said Don Joe. "'Fore that, it was somebody else."

"The Tidewaters," said Louise Snell.

217

"No, ma'am. I never did find the Tidewaters."

"And there was somebody else you was lookin for—"

I broke in before he could remember about Louise Landis. "See, my ma's very best friend, besides Rebecca, used to live in these parts."

"She did? What's her name?" asked Louise Snell.

It took me only a couple of seconds to say, "Henrietta Simple. Her maiden name, of course." Where that name came from I have no idea. Names just pop into my mind. Maybe because I spend so much time making things up, my mind is really greased. Well, I could see them putting on their thinking caps all up and down the counter, for here was a name to contend with, one they could try to lay claim to.

Billy shook his head. "Ain't no Simples in Cold Flat Junction. You ever hear of a Simple?" he asked the others.

And it was kind of like one of those relay races where you hand off a stick to a team member. Even Mervin got it before handing it back to me.

"I never *said* the Simples lived in Cold Flat Junction. I said *Ma* used to live in these parts."

They had no choice but to accept there were Simples somewhere, or had been, that were outside their kin. They looked pretty defeated over this name they weren't familiar with, so I thought I should do some explaining. A cool breeze blew through the diner's louvered blinds, and I sat thinking for a moment.

"The Simples, you wouldn't know of them because they lived and maybe still do on a farm. It's really huge. They were what you'd call—or at least my ma says so—recluses. Hardly ever left the farm except for George—Henrietta's father—and he'd go into town once a week for supplies. They allowed only a few people to come to their house who they had business dealings with. My ma for years went to the Simple farm for eggs. That's how she got to be friends with Henrietta and how she found out her little brother—Miller was his name—was touched."

Well, their eyes really opened at that, and a couple more cigarettes got lit. They had perked up a lot listening to the story of the Simples. For if they didn't know the Simples, at least the Simples might be discredited and so not worth knowing.

"Touched how?" asked Evren, who sat beside Don Joe and never said much.

"Miller got kicked by a mule when he was hardly more than an infant and it did something to his brain."

"Like what?" Evren asked, and I wondered if he could be touched himself and was eager to know someone else in that condition.

"Well, he could turn really bad—violent, you know—and attack a person. He did my moth—, my ma one time. He just picked up a chair and went after her like a lion tamer. George saw and saved her. You can see how they'd be recluses. They couldn't afford to have Miller in an institution, so they kept him, like I said, at home. But they had to be really careful about visitors."

I saw all of this in my mind's eye—Miller charging my mother, Henrietta yelling, George hurrying to the rescue. The farm came clearer and clearer, the vast acres, the chickens scratching in the dust, my mother getting a basket of eggs. I blinked and looked around and for a moment wondered where I was. It was like when I come out of the Orion, wondering what world I had entered. But in a flash the diner came back and I was on firm ground. Or at least as firm as ground could be in Cold Flat Junction.

"So, you see, Imogene Calhoun might know what happened to Henrietta Simple. You said she lives at Red Coon Rock? And that's past Flyback Hollow?" I figured even if any of them ran into Imogene Calhoun and mentioned the story of the Simples, and Imogene said she'd never heard of such a family, it wouldn't matter as the whole story was so complicated they'd think they remembered it wrong or Imogene was touched too.

"It ain't far past, though," put in Mervin. "Not more'n three, four blocks."

Billy was mad at having his directions questioned. "For God's sakes, Mervin, ain't no blocks out there. You just have to measure off a length of road. I'd say a quarter mile if I'm any judge."

I asked, and was sorry I did, "What's her house look like?"

"White, with a big porch around it," said Don Joe.

Billy sighed. "It ain't white; it's this beige color."

"It's blue," said Mervin. "Spiker painted it this sky-blue."

Mervin, I thought, could really talk when his wife wasn't around. He must have lived for these occasions. "We all agreed it was the dumbest color to paint a house."

Billy swiveled around on his stool. "That ain't the Calhoun house, for the Lord's sakes! That's Wanda Leroy's. And it ain't anywhere near Red Coon Rock."

The woman in the dark glasses shoved her mug toward Louise Snell and Louise went to get the coffee pot.

Don Joe said, "It's olive green's what it is, that sour-green color." When Billy went to contradict him, Don Joe held his hand out. "I guess I oughta know, Billy, all the deliveries I made to that place."

I wondered what he delivered, though I didn't really want to know, for that would take Don Joe outside his diner life and onto that great flat uninhabited land across the railroad tracks. He could wander there forever. It was strange I should think this, when I was making it all up anyway. Or making up a lot out of whole cloth (as my mother said), spreading a little truth a long way.

"Hey, sugar."

I felt Louise Snell's hand on my arm and I shook myself.

"You all right? You had your eyes closed."

"I was just wandering in my mind."

Mervin was giving directions. "All you do's go up past the school-house and then left on Dubois and that there'll take you past Flyback Holler and then it's an easy scoot—" Here he scraped one hand off the other to mean scooting "—to Red Coon Rock."

I thanked them and took my check to the cash register by the door. The pimply-faced boy cashier who'd been there when I first came to the diner hadn't been there the last several times. I wondered if he got fired. Louise Snell came to take my money and give me change.

"Hey, girl," said Don Joe. "If you been in La Porte and Spirit Lake a while, maybe you heard some about Fern Queen getting herself shot. We don't get the news here; all we get's that *Conservative* every week."

Evren gave a tittery little laugh that shook his narrow shoulders. "'Don't get the news here'; that's funny, Don Joe. Nothin ever happens here. There ain't no news."

I wondered at this strange notion of Cold Flat Junction and just looked at Evren. Then I answered Don Joe. "Sheriff's still looking; I guess they don't make anything public until they're pretty sure of what's going on."

"Well, if that DeGheyn fella's still thinkin' it's Ben Queen, he's not ever goin' to get nowhere."

I would have asked why he was so sure of this, but I knew it wouldn't tell me more than I already knew.

Louise Snell wished me good luck.

Good luck. It was as if I was setting off on a trip that might be harder to make than Mervin allowed it was. This didn't bother me one whit; I figured if I could get all the way to the Rony Plaza, I could surely find my way to Red Coon Rock.

As the diner's screen door banged shut behind me and I had to shade my eyes against the glare of the sun in that white sky without mercy, I wished I had a diner life to anchor me to something, a place like rock in a riverbed where water just flowed around you but never moved you, a place where they didn't get the news.

Lemonade

37

By this time I was so familiar with Cold Flat Junction I was tempted to stop off and see people. Off Schoolhouse Road was the house where they kept hens and where Mrs. Davidow came to get eggs (a lot different from the Simples's farm). I passed the Queen house on Dubois Road. I followed it to its end, to the whitewashed rock with "Flyback Hollow" written in large white letters. I would have liked to talk to Louise Landis again, but decided I had too much to do.

Past Flyback Hollow the road narrowed and what showed signs of having been a hard-surfaced road had pretty much gone back to its old rutted-earth self. A distance ahead, I made out a girl who appeared to be sitting at a table, which struck me as no-end peculiar; when I got closer I saw it was a lemonade stand. A sign taped to the rim of a card table said "Lemonade 10¢." On this lonely road, business couldn't be all that good.

"Hello," I said.

"Hello."

At first I thought she was the Pick Up sticks champion, as her wide-eyed and sorrowful look was like that girl's. Maybe it was just the Cold Flat Junction look.

I had plenty of money, most of which I was going to pay whoever might be a source of information, and it looked like it would be Imogene Calhoun. That still left enough for a stop at the Windy Run Diner and for lemonade. "I'll have two cups," I said, taking twenty cents from my change purse. It wasn't lemonade, either; it was Kool-Aid and I asked about this: why had she put lemonade on her sign?

"Because it's a lemonade *stand*." She crossed her arms over her chest and scratched her elbows, which I sometimes do myself, so I guess we had something in common, except she was more stubborn than I was. I drank my Kool-Aid, a yellow color but tasting nothing like lemons. It was warm, too, but I didn't complain; I thought it kind of brave of her to set up here where she had so little chance of success. I pondered this. Or was it just dumb?

As she filled my paper cup again, I asked, "Do you get much business on this road?" She shook her head in a defeated way. "You might do better if you moved your stand back there," I pointed toward the way I'd come, "at an intersection." That was a stupid way of putting it; did Cold Flat Junction have intersections? "You could get the traffic from Flyback Hollow and the Dubois Road, too."

She nodded. "My ma doesn't like me to go all the way down there."

"Oh." I squinted skyward. Was that a reason?

I thought, if she lived here she must know the Calhoun house. "I'm looking for Imogene Calhoun's place. Do you know it?"

She pointed up the road. "It's that next house."

I made out a dark green roof, poking above the trees. The houses here, what few there were, were hard to see because of the densely leafed trees. Here and Flyback Hollow seemed to have got all of the trees in the region. I set down my half-drunk cup—I hated Kool-Aid—thanked her, and started walking again.

It was not very far. The house was set into the wood around it as if it had grown there like another tree. It was part fake brick and part real wood and the whole was painted a seasick green, as tan as it was green, and it just sort of melted into its surroundings, which I actually found rather nice.

The lady who came to the door looked a little like the lemonade girl, only older, and with the Cold Flat Junction look, unhappy and unsurprised, worn, like the long print skirt and brown sweater she was wearing. Her hair and her eyes were coffee-colored, and she was holding a can of Schlitz and a cigarette.

"Miss Calhoun? Are you Imogene Calhoun?"

She nodded behind the screen door. "You want something?"

I couldn't tell if her tone was belligerent or just bored. "My name's Emma Graham, and I live in Spirit Lake? I'm writing this history paper? It's what my teacher calls a 'project?' He wants us to *delve* (a word I really liked) into something around these parts—you know, where we live—and to write it up. I understand you once lived around White's Bridge and your sister—"

"My sister is deceased."

"Yes, ma'am. I heard she was." I dredged up what the Sheriff always said in these sad circumstances. "I'm sorry for your loss."

"Chrissakes, she's been dead nearly ten years. Come on, you best come on in."

The screen door slapped shut behind me. The living room was dark, not simply because it got only slanted light, but because everything in it was dark—walls, woodwork, furniture. She sank back into her slipcovered rocking chair and told me to sit down in one of the armchairs. The upholstery was a burnt biscuit color and kind of scratchy. Dust shimmered up from it, caught in a slant of light when I sat down.

I went on, opening my purse and taking out a five-dollar bill. "Also, our teacher told us if we interviewed anyone we should pay them for their time. So I'll be glad to pay five dollars an hour, or of course for less than an hour." I put the bill on the coffee table.

That surprised her. "Well." She smiled and the smile made her look younger than fifty, for she'd have to be in her fifties. Maybe it was the way she was dressed in that flowered skirt and sneakers, or maybe it was her long hair. I didn't know. I would have mistaken her for thirty if I passed her on the street. "It's sure okay with me, but what I could talk about for an hour that you'd want to hear beats me."

"Did your sister wait tables at the Hotel Paradise sometimes?"

"Yeah. Becky worked there part-time for two or three summers. She used to take me with her places she went to work so I wouldn't have to stay home by myself. And partly because I could do some work too and help her out." She pushed her light brown hair back off her forehead. "Lord, but that must've been forty, forty-five years ago." She sipped her beer in quite a ladylike fashion, considering she was drinking it out of a can. She tapped ash from her cigarette into a tin ashtray she kept on her lap.

I thought back too and wished I had a rocking chair to do it in, for with her leg pulled up and the foot resting on the cushion, and the smoke clouding the air around her, Imogene seemed honestly to be back there with Rebecca. I myself settled into the dark, rough armchair and listened to her talk in her dreamy way about the kitchen and the help and my mother, who she called "Miss Jen." I reminded myself that these were pre–Ree-Jane days, pre–Lola Davidow days and my scattered thoughts flew to those days I hadn't lived as if the past were a magnet.

"There were those trees up behind the kitchen, near that big garage, where I'd sneak off with the dishwasher's kid and smoke cigarettes behind one of those trees."

She went on about the hotel, the people who worked there, and the guests she sometimes ran across when she was making up their beds. Yes, she was definitely worth the five dollars I was paying. The atmosphere seemed so heavy with memories, my eyelids drooped. She might have been talking about me and Paul, our dishwasher's son, who I could get to steal brownies from where they were cooling on the pastry table, and to bring them up to the woods where we ate them, and Paul got blamed.

It was getting so I was living not only my regular life, but other little lives. It was almost as if I were everywhere. I wondered if I was going crazy to the point where I would be like Miss Ruth Porte, making candlelight suppers for myself, or being a kleptomaniac like Miss Isabel Barnett.

"... Devereau house."

My heavy eyelids snapped up. She was talking about the Devereaus and I hadn't been listening!

"They were awful hard to work for. That Isabel should have been in the slave trade."

"Wasn't that the house where—" No, I was being too direct. You have to sneak up on what you want to know; you have to peek through

225

windows at the facts so they won't run off and hide. You cannot go smashing through doors.

"My mother says some sisters lived there. Maiden ladies, she calls them."

"I guess you heard about what happened?" said Imogene.

"What?"

"That little girl that drowned? She was their niece, I think."

I squinted up my eyes as if memory were refusing to budge. "Drowned . . . yes, I guess somebody said . . . But go on." I tried not to sound overeager.

Imogene lit another cigarette from the butt of the old one and threw the butt into the empty grate. The way the sun stole through the venetian blind and lay in stripes across her face lent her a shadowy prettiness. "It was early one morning, I think. Those sisters called the police and said this little girl Mary was missing—" She stopped to take a swig of beer. "Now, this is what Rebecca told me as best I can recall. They found the little girl in the lake, that one over near the Hotel Paradise?"

I nodded and tried to be careful about believing everything I was told, for a lot of what I heard was secondhand, and the person doing the telling had heard it from somebody else. Either that, or the teller couldn't really know because they hadn't been there. Jude Stemple was certainly an example of this when he said, *Fern never had no kids.* Fern could have and he not know, which is what I was sure was the truth of it.

So far, of course, Imogene was right; the things she was saying had been part of the newspaper report.

"She was supposed to have taken out a rowboat in the night and then couldn't get back; the boat was old and leaky. Does that make any sense? Why didn't those police look into it more? One thing that clinched it for sure in my mind was—"

I knew what it meant to be on the edge of your chair. "What?"

She stopped talking, as if she were holding on to a surprise, a gift she opened layer by layer—ribbon, paper, box, tissue. She stopped and started picking at the red polish on her fingernail. It was dark red and chipped.

"What?"

She blinked. "Oh . . . sorry. I guess I just got—you know—carried back there to the Devereau house and those sisters." Deeply, she frowned. "Those *sisters.* I keep thinking of three sisters, but wasn't it four?"

She was asking not me—even though she looked at me—but the air around me, as if knowledge hovered in the room like light, like air, hovered but couldn't settle.

"Rose Devereau was the fourth sister, and nothing like those other three. She married Ben Queen from here in Cold Flat, but I won't go into all that. Rose was younger than the other three by a good fifteen, twenty years. She was real pretty, real alive. Those three, though, always seemed to me more dead than alive. There was no prettiness there." Again she stopped to drink and smoke. "There was this kitten that was so scrawny it wasn't much bigger than a pencil. Rebecca said there was always a water dish but no food."

This actually scared me. I knew about the starving kitten, for Ulub had told us, but I never heard its fate. I never wanted to.

"It was the little girl's—Mary's. They wouldn't allow her to feed it. It would've died, of course, but what Becky did was, she put the kitten under her coat and took it home with her and fed it for the week, then brought it back just so the sisters would see it and know that she hadn't stole it. Then she'd take it away again. She brought in a little box of cat food for it, but she was afraid to leave it with Mary; it just seemed too dangerous, for what if the sisters found it?"

"It was like prison. She was in prison."

Imogene laughed, but it wasn't a carefree laugh. "That's for sure. They didn't like me coming there, either. But if they wanted Becky, they had to take me in the bargain."

I was so relieved about the kitten. "Your sister Rebecca must have been a really nice person."

"Yes, she really was. This little girl Mary, she was so pale. It's funny, I can't call back her face, the features of it, I mean, but I do recall the paleness of her." Imogene frowned. "Why did they hate Mary so much? It was as if she'd been visited upon them as a punishment."

Then Imogene stopped talking and just smoked and drank. I wondered if she'd forgotten I was there, even. But I didn't want to say anything for fear of interrupting her chain of thought.

"She had these beautiful dresses, like party dresses. It's what she always wore—a dress. Never shorts or jeans like me. What we used to do was stay in her room and play with the stuff in her toy chest."

I thought about the Mr. Ree game and how Mary-Evelyn had cut faces from snapshots and pasted them over some of the character cards that stood for the people in the game: Mrs. White, Niece Rhoda,

Colonel Mustard. I knew I'd have to go back to the Devereau house and look at things in the light of what I knew now. Yet, what did I know?

"You said there was something that clinched it for Rebecca. Clinched what?"

"How she died. That it wasn't an accident. What accident could befall a child in that way? Police called it a 'suspicious death.' No damn kidding. Why in God's name would that child take out a boat at night, anyway?"

These had been my questions, the ones I'd made a list of after I read the forty-year-old report on the death in the *Conservative* offices a while back. How I wished Imogene's sister, Rebecca, was still alive! For she had got her information direct. Of course, Imogene had too, but being only ten years old, her memory of all of this would be colored by her older sister's comments.

Imogene went on: "No shoes. Now, that always got me. Or it did Becky. How was that child supposed to walk through that thick wood without shoes? And no coat, don't forget. Here it was October and the child had no coat."

"Then you think—maybe her shoes were never on? Like, maybe they carried her?"

Imogene took a sip of beer. "Maybe she was already dead, that's what I think."

My heart really leaped into my throat. This had never occurred to me. I thought of what Ulub had seen at a distance: those lights, either flashlights or lanterns, moving through the woods, a kind of silent procession. How could Mary-Evelyn not have cried, or yelled, putting up some kind of resistance with no shoes and no coat on? She was already dead—that would explain it.

Imogene was talking about the kitten again. "He was almost white but with a faint blue or gray tinge to him. Poor thing didn't even have a name. Mary-Evelyn really loved him. She told me she'd gone down at night sometimes and stolen bits of food and that's what kept it alive. But the sisters caught her at it and put a padlock on the refrigerator. And of course they punished her."

"How?"

"They had her pick up leaves. This was October, remember."

"What?" My mind, used to Mary-Evelyn's mistreatment, still could not take this in.

"From the yard. It was in October, so they kept falling. The leaves, I mean. One by one, she was to pick them up and put them in this potato sack. And when it got full she was to dump it and start again."

Here Imogene turned her head to look out the window, as if maybe she could see it out there beyond the side of the house. And I did too. Mary-Evelyn, in one of her party dresses, stooping to pick up a leaf and put it in the potato sack.

There wasn't a sound, both of us gazing out the window. By now I had moved without even knowing it and was standing by Imogene's chair, my hand on its arm, as if I could draw comfort from it.

In my mind I saw Mary-Evelyn look up at me and even though I knew it was my own imagining, I could feel her telling me or us that we had to find out what happened, get to the bottom of it, that though I might have figured out Fern Queen's death, that it might have avenged some part of Mary-Evelyn's awful life and death, it still wasn't enough. And that if I didn't do this, she couldn't be released from her terrible punishment and would be picking up leaves throughout eternity. It was like one of the fairy tales I read years ago when I was little, how in a lot of them the princess was under a spell, and the prince had to figure out what had happened before the princess could be released. So it was like Mary-Evelyn was under a spell. Or I was.

"What was Mary-Evelyn like?"

"Like I said. Quiet."

"What was she like when she wasn't quiet?"

"Oh . . . she was real sweet."

That pained me. It made thinking about her that much harder.

The clock chimed. It was four-fifteen. More than an hour had passed. I realized that Imogene was an ally, and I had the perfect reason for coming back: my history project. I also realized I owed Imogene another five dollars and took it out of my change purse.

"Honey, you don't have to give me any more money. I liked talking. It brought back a lot of things about me and Becky."

I put the bill on the chair arm. "Just say it's for feeding the kitten."

I walked back down the road. There was a terrible feeling in me, a heaviness. I felt I was dragging myself along, that my feet didn't want to move, but since they didn't have any better idea where to go, they had no choice.

The lemonade stand was where I'd suggested the girl move it to, where this road met Dubois Road, but she was gone. I guess she meant to return, for the Kool-Aid pitcher was there. It was a different color, orange instead of yellow, and I saw where she'd crossed out "Lemonade" and written in "Orangeade," which sounded like my sort of truthfulness. Anyway, that might mean she'd been doing some business. I poured a little into one of the plastic cups and put down ten cents. It might encourage her to see business was going on even while she was away. I used to do things like selling lemonade myself, when I was young, only mine was real lemonade which my mother helped me make. It tasted as fresh as if it had dripped from a lemon tree.

Flyback Hollow was off to my right and for a minute I stood by the stand and thought about Louise Landis. She knew everyone in Cold Flat Junction. She certainly knew Rose Devereau and Fern Queen. I couldn't think of a good enough reason for stopping in to see her. I guess I had made up so much of my life that it didn't occur to me to tell the truth. Even if anyone wanted to hear it.

I poured the Kool-Aid out and stood there with my paper cup, afraid I was emptying out like the cup. Looking around me I had this vision of Cold Flat Junction that I never could have explained: there did not seem to be anything in it. It was like the card table and the pitcher and the missing girl; like the lone girl in the school playground and her Pick Up sticks; the lone boy there on a different day with a basketball he wasn't playing with; like the empty train platform where I had first seen the Girl.

I knew what was both restful and fearful about Cold Flat Junction: it had all stopped. As in those old *Twilight Zone* episodes, where the street was always empty, leaves and blown paper being the only movement, and what people you finally met seemed made out of clay and in a different time and space. But such words as I could use were husks, empty of true meaning. I could put no words to it. You had to find words for it to get a handle on it. I didn't even know what "it" was.

I walked Dubois Road, passing the Queens's big house, wondering. Not that I expected to find Ben Queen sitting in the front parlor. It would be the last place he'd choose to hide out.

I heard the whistle of the 4:32 as I was walking down Windy Run Road and I broke into a run. It was moving right past me as I ran the open stretch, the beaten path there, between the diner and the station.

I saw it stop up there and knew I'd never make it, so I slowed down as I came to the steps leading up to the platform.

I was down at the far end of the platform when I saw someone boarding. With one foot on the top step and one on the bottom, she turned, and, only for a moment, looked at me. If I had run fast, I might have made it. The engineer might even have waited, seeing a poor kid running for all she was worth (one of the few advantages of being a kid), only I couldn't. I was frozen in place.

It was the Girl.

I sat in the silent landscape, thinking about her, wondering what her business was in Cold Flat Junction. This was where I'd first seen her, on this railroad platform, nearly a month ago.

I think she's Ben Queen's granddaughter. Ben's and Rose's. Anyone who saw her and knew Rose would think so, for Rose was who she looked like: she could have been Rose when Rose had been about the age to run off with Ben Queen. The trouble was, no one else I knew had seen her. But I admit I hadn't been very forthcoming in any description of her. She looked nothing like her mother, Fern—at least nothing I could tell from the pictures of Fern in the paper. I bet Jude Stemple would see it, for he had been really taken with Rose Queen, had described her pale hair and her skin and eyes so vividly I could almost see her. Jude Stemple would have known he was wrong about Fern being childless.

I sat on the platform, on the brown-varnished bench, waiting for the six o'clock train, hardly thawed from my state of frozen stupification. I was that close to finding out who she was for sure. Only a few yards of station platform between us. That close.

I was almost certain the Girl had shot Fern Queen. And one of the reasons was that I knew Ben Queen *hadn't* shot Fern that night when he'd dropped the gun on the sofa in the old Devereau house.

But if he had a gun—? I imagined someone arguing.

It wasn't his gun (I answered in my mind). *He dropped that gun like it was a snake could have bit him.*

A girl shooting her own mother? This was Lola Davidow's voice, and no wonder she might have cause for concern.

It's no less likely—the Sheriff said, who knew the score—*than a man shooting his own daughter.*

No, no, no, no, just about anybody would say, for it was, I agree, a fearful thing to have happen.

Hell! Donny was saying from his seat behind the Sheriff's desk. *Sam's right. It was him shot Fern. How in hell you know it wasn't his gun? Man walks in, drops a gun on a chair, you say it wasn't his. That don't make no sense at all!*

Maybe.

I sat there and looked across the tracks at that empty, blistered land that drew me. Why would a place so barren and exposed pull at me this way? Dry earth the color of sand, sunbleached saw grass, some scattered rocks. And far off, that line of dark trees like a distant horizon. Not a single building, not a soul.

Yet, for some reason, it gave me a sense of ease, made me less tired. Indeed, looking at it, I realized how tired I was and how much things weighed on me. It was as if over there was the place where you could stop worrying things to death, where you could finally stop caring about Ree-Jane's taunts, where you could set down the tray of dishes, where you could stop the lies and the connivery, where you could finally own up. Where you could drop the gun on the chair.

Solitary blue

38

The train ride was only fifteen minutes long, three minutes shorter because I was getting off in La Porte instead of Spirit Lake. I was going to call on Dr. McComb.

I spent the short train ride wondering about the Girl and why she was traveling between Cold Flat Junction and Spirit Lake. Maybe I'd have been better off figuring out what reason I was going to give Dr. McComb for visiting him. The last time I used the excuse that I wanted to ask him if there were any White Lace butterflies around this area, for I thought I might have seen one.

Butterflies were a speciality of Dr. McComb's. We had spent some time out behind his house in grass up to my chin swishing nets around. At Spirit Lake, I had certainly seen a white butterfly, and it might have been a White Lace, but it looked so peaceful, swaying on a stalk of

Queen Anne's lace, that I couldn't net it and stick it in the box I had taken for that purpose. I couldn't stand the idea of carrying it to its death.

I stepped down from the train, loving that little yellow metal stool and the way the conductor placed his hand beneath my elbow. I walked up and down the platform, looked in the station waiting room. There was no sign of her; I guess I didn't really think there would be.

One of Axel's taxis was standing by the station, its motor running as if it were a getaway car. Delbert was driving, as usual. I wondered how Axel had ever started his taxi business with only the one ghost cab he himself drove. I walked over and asked Delbert if he was waiting for someone and he said, no, just sometimes he parked here in case anyone getting off might need a cab.

"I do," I said, and got in. I told him I wanted to go to Dr. Mc-Comb's house.

"Dr. McComb, Dr. McComb. Now whereabouts does he live?"

"You're supposed to know where people live. You drive a taxi." I sighed. "You go to Red Bird Road and along it until you come to Valley Road. You go along that and his house is at the end."

"Hokey-dokey," said Delbert, and turned the car toward the street.

I settled down in back, biting the bit of calloused skin near my thumbnail. I did this sometimes when I was thinking hard. I pictured the butterfly I had seen, clinging to the Queen Anne's lace, when I had looked across the lake and seen the Girl. She and the butterfly seemed to occupy the same space.

Full of itself, the First National Bank rolled by. Banks always strike me as so self-important. Then we were coming up on the corner where the Abigail Butte County Library sat, and as it came into view, I yelled to Delbert to stop.

Delbert acted like he was having a heart attack, and I only hoped he'd get the car to the curb before it happened.

"I need to go in for just a minute," I said, poking my head through his window. "Wait for me."

Delbert said, "It'll cost you waiting time."

"That's okay." I darted across the road wondering how he figured "waiting time." I skipped up the wheelchair ramp. I knew I was too old to skip, but I wanted to see if I still remembered how. I went into the library.

The butterfly books were on the "Nature" shelves, but I had found Dr. McComb's book before in with "Local Authors and Authoresses." These books were gathered on a table prominently stationed near the oval information desk. There were any number of local authors; I'd read scraps from different books when I was on my butterfly search two weeks ago. I thought none of these authors could write except for Dr. McComb (whose writing name was L. W. McComb). His descriptions of the various butterflies he'd seen and studied were, I thought, poetic.

Since I already had nine books out that were overdue, I didn't want to try and check this book out because I didn't want Miss Babbit looking up my record. I would just copy a page or two of Dr. McComb's illustrations and comments. I carried the book to the copier, which children weren't supposed to use without supervision. It was more or less hidden at the end of the stacks. I put the page face down and dropped in my money.

From the tiny bit I'd read just standing there, I knew I would like to check the book out, for it was very pleasant—dreamy, almost, as several of his passages mentioned he had to stay still so long he sometimes fell asleep. I thought it very brave of him to admit to this weakness in his scientific procedure. I then stuck the book back with the local authors and hurried out and back to the car.

"That's going to be extra," said Delbert, starting up the engine.

"I know. You already told me."

"Well. Just so's you know."

I gritted my teeth and made some kind of throat noise.

"You say something?"

"No."

"Cause Axel, he says waiting takes time up just as good as driving does, so we got to charge for it."

He was looking worriedly at me in the rearview mirror. I could see the mirror over the top of my copied page, which I raised to blot out his eyes. Delbert would go on and on about the "waiting" charge for days if a person encouraged him. I held the page so he couldn't see my eyes and read Dr. McComb's account of a blue butterfly that was really beautiful. Here, he'd climbed to the crest of a hill called "Hatter's Hill," a place I didn't know about. Dr. McComb had gone there purely to try and see this blue butterfly. On this page, he described the scene before him:

I wondered to whom this land belonged, for it looked un-
farmed, untenanted. I gazed out over the fields which seemed
as nothing, as endless. And I sat for over twenty minutes,
nearly dropping off (a bad habit of mine, as I've said) when my
peripheral vision caught a movement near the base of a yew.
Carefully I turned my head downward and there in a patch of
some weedy nectar plant swayed what appeared to be the
Reakirt's Blue, very rare in these Northern parts. Of unprecedented hue, it was no shade of blue that I had ever seen before.
Perhaps I was partial to this butterfly, also called a Solitary
Blue, because it tends to be a loner.

"Here's Valley Road!"

Delbert's voice snapped me back to my surroundings, only mine—
the trailer home with its pink flamingos on the left, the falling-down
barn on the right—were far less seeable than the words on the page. A
blue "of unprecedented hue," no blue I had ever seen, and I guess never
would unless I saw his butterfly.

"Well, go *on*. Didn't I say it was at the *end*?"

Delbert sighed, the world on his shoulders. "Yeah, I guess."

Finally he stopped where the road ended, outside of the square
stone house. This time I told Delbert not to wait, as I knew I'd be gone
long enough for him to have a conniption fit over the "waiting time"
charge. As it was, he only charged me another fifty cents for waiting
outside of the library.

I hoped Dr. McComb's housekeeper or sister or whoever she was
would not answer the door, as she had made me feel really uncomfortable the last time. But the door was open and I just went in and called
Dr. McComb's name into the silence. The room looked just the same,
and why shouldn't it? I'd been gone from it for only a few days, not
ten years. Yet, life had lately taken on a ten-years-gone tinge. Lately,
my sense of time was stretching out to accommodate all of the trips,
talks, plans, ideas that I'd had going—not to mention that I was still in
Florida, which about doubled everything.

The silence was nice, though, broken only by a grandfather clock
ticking away. It was a place where I didn't feel crowded the way I did
in other places, as if there were room here to think, to lay things out in
your mind and take your own good time examining each one. But I
didn't stop; I went through to the kitchen where another clock ticked

quietly. I looked under a napkin covering a plate of what I hoped were brownies like the ones we had eaten before but were sugar cookies, which would do in a pinch. I did not take one. And something was in the oven, for the air was heavily scented with something sweet, a cake or brownies. I did not open the oven door.

I went out the kitchen door into the rear garden, though it could hardly be called a garden now, for it was overgrown with weeds, ivy, and bramble. Weeds stretched back to woodland. There was blue grass and buffalo grass; black-eyed Susans and Queen Anne's lace; butterfly bushes and the ones he called his "nectar" plants. I knew this because he'd told me, not because I recognized them.

Looking down the narrow worn path, I couldn't tell if what I saw bobbing above the dogbane and milkweed was a head of white hair or a cloud of tiny white butterflies he called Dainty Sulphurs. I followed the path as an arm came up ahead of me with a net and *whissshed* through the air. I took care on this overgrown path, as I wasn't quite sure just what sorts of things were living near it, unseeable, hiding. I knew there were snakes and hoped they weren't copperheads or rattlers.

"Dr. McComb!"

He turned, searching the air. It was hard, in this undergrowth, to see someone. "Who's there? Who is it?"

"Me, Emma Graham." In another few yards of bramble and brush, I made my way to him. "Hi!" I said, and waved. When I got up to him, I apologized. "I hope I didn't scare off any Little Wood Sapphires."

"You didn't. And it's 'satyrs,' not 'sapphires.'"

I did not linger over my mistake. I thought I had been doing well to remember Little-Wood-Anything. "Are you busy?" Now, there was an ultradumb question. "I just wanted to talk to you about your book." That would surely be the favorite topic of all the authors (and authoresses).

He grunted and said, "Oh, that." Then his eagle eye lit on a butterfly that swayed atop a stalk of milkweed. In the pale sunlight splashing across the dogbane and butterfly bush, this green butterfly shone as brightly as one of the neon letters in the EAT sign of Arturo's, the diner along the highway. Dr. McComb watched its wings closing, opening, closing.

I whispered, "Aren't you going to net it?"

He brought his finger to his lips and said, "Sssssh."

237

How much time passed as we watched the green butterfly, I don't know. I know I was getting pretty bored. I didn't want Dr. McComb to think I wasn't sincere about my butterfly hobby; it's just that you can't stand around gazing at them unless butterflies are the end-all and be-all of your existence.

Yet, I think they might have been the be-all of Dr. McComb's, even though you'd think medicine would be, as that had been his life's work. While he still watched, not a muscle flickering into movement, I took out my copied page and read again his description. A lot of it really had nothing to do with the blue butterfly except in an indirect way.

Then I had one of those lightbulb ideas go off in my mind—the kind you see in cartoons, bulbs above heads—that the book wasn't really about butterflies; that is, butterflies might not have been its purpose, but rather, its purpose had been to say things about life. This was such a new idea that I didn't know what to do about it, so I filed it away in my mind until I had some time on my hands (which I never seemed to have these days).

Patiently I waited, wishing the butterfly would take off or that Dr. McComb would lose interest. Neither seemed to be about to happen. And I thought again about his description of the Solitary Blue butterfly, about how he'd said he waited for over an hour to see it, and wondered if there wasn't a lesson to be learned in that. Not that I wanted a lesson. What I wanted was to know if that baking smell coming from the oven was brownies.

A drowning

39

At last the butterfly grew tired of being looked at (which seemed to be its chief occupation) and flew off. I reminded Dr. McComb that there was something in the oven that might burn up. We wended our weary way back to the house.

Overseeing the pan he took out of the oven—brownies!—I asked him what kind of butterfly it was. A Dogface, he said. I objected to that name for something so pretty. Then he told me a lot more about it than I needed to know, as he shook powdered sugar over the pan of brownies. I said my mother does that with cakes, only she places a doily on top and then the powdered sugar makes a perfect design. I went on in some detail about my mother's cakes, which was probably more than he needed to know, so I guess we were even.

But Dr. McComb didn't seem to mind at all, probably from a lifetime of listening to patients go on about their ills. (Imagine having Aurora Paradise as a patient!) He said my mother was the best cook he'd ever come across and was I one, too?

The question kind of staggered me because it was, after all, a reasonable question. Yet I can't remember ever having asked it of myself, maybe because of the hint in it of death. I don't think I really believe that my mother will die and I will then have to carry on. Me taking my mother's place in the kitchen is the most harebrained notion I can imagine.

"I can't cook worth a lick," I said, I suppose to lay that notion to rest. I sat chin in hands watching the brownie pan while Dr. McComb went about the coffee. "I'm pretty good at bartending, though," I added.

"Are you now? I like martinis, myself. Vodka."

"That's Mrs. Davidow's favorite drink. But martinis are easy; they don't take any imagination." I watched him cut the brownies into squares.

"Martinis aren't supposed to. They're supposed to make you drunk."

The brownies were now on the Blue Willow plate. I looked them over. "Well, you can get drunk with imagination as well as without it, can't you? I'm talking about drinks that take two or three kinds of liquor. Among other things, of course. They're my inventions. Cold Comfort's one of them. That's made with Southern Comfort."

We both took the two largest brownies. He said, "That sounds imaginative all right. What else goes in it?"

"I'm sorry. The recipe's a secret." The recipe changed every time I made one, which was why it was a secret.

"Maybe you can make one for me sometime."

"I'd be pleased."

I drew from my pocket the page I had copied from his book, unfolded it, and slid it across the table.

"That looks familiar." He seemed pleased.

"I got it from the library. I didn't want to check the book out because other readers wouldn't see it then. There was only the one copy."

He sat down and studied it, nodding. "I remember this day well."

"Where's Hatter's Hill?"

"Mile or two the other side of Hebrides."

Hebrides was the nearest big town. I loved it, for it had department stores and bookstores and candy shops. Stores that we didn't have in La Porte. I liked to do my Christmas shopping there.

"I liked what you wrote there."

He smiled. "Well, thank you."

"You said you looked out over fields that seemed endless and 'bereft of adornment.' That's very pretty. There's a piece of land I look at sometimes and I get that same feeling. Only I can't explain the feeling."

"Where's that?"

"Cold Flat Junction."

"I haven't been over there in a long while. It always struck me as deserted. A strange place. A sad place."

Sad wasn't really the right word, but I didn't want to waste time thinking up the right word, as I wanted to get around to Mary-Evelyn's death. The coffee tasted surprisingly good with the brownie. Dr. Mc-Comb is the only person who has ever offered me coffee. "It must take a lot of patience to watch butterflies."

"Does. It takes a lot of patience to watch anything. I mean really see it." He had polished off one brownie and was now studying the plate for another. "Most people aren't really very observant." He took the brownie I had my eye on. I guess we were both ultraobservant.

"But if you're a doctor, you really have to be. I mean, you've got to be able to tell things—oh, like about death. What people die from. Don't you always have to fill out those certificates?"

"Death certificates? Yes. Not any more, though." He sighed. I couldn't tell from the sigh whether he did or didn't miss writing out death certificates.

"It's probably not easy, a lot of the time. I mean some deaths can look like they're caused by more than one thing."

"True."

I smiled. What I liked about Dr. McComb (and the Sheriff, and Maud) was that he didn't tell me I was being morbid, or I should be out playing ball. And he didn't look fearful. I've noticed how easily adults become fearful when children say something they don't expect.

I went on: "Like, you can't tell that somebody's died of a particular poison unless you go looking for that particular poison."

"You been reading up, I'd say." He poured us some more coffee. "I'm glad I made the brownies and not you." He laughed.

Eating my second brownie, I said, "Oh, it's just interesting. Espe-

241

cially about poisons." I was getting good at this. "I guess arsenic is the most common to murder someone, right?"

He munched and frowned. "I can't say with any certainty. I haven't come upon such cases. I've come on *accidental* poisonings, of course. But poison in that case is pretty obvious. Kids getting into things, stuff like that. Or sedatives, taking too many, which of course might not be accidental at all."

I brought up shootings.

"You've been hanging around Sam DeGheyn too much. What about them?"

"Didn't you ever have someone get shot you had to pronounce dead?"

"Yeah, sure. Hunting season's full of 'em."

"But that's accidental. I mean deliberate."

He shook his head. I thought it was safe now to bring up drowning, drowning as just one way of dying among others. "How about drowning? Can you always tell that?"

"You mean tell if someone did or didn't? Oh, sure. Your lungs fill up with water, you drown. No way I'd mistake that."

I paused, frowning, as if thinking hard. "Remember Mary-Evelyn Devereau?"

"How could I forget? How could anyone forget that poor little girl?"

I stopped eating. That expression, *tears sprung to my eyes,* actually described it. It was the surprise at finding Mary-Evelyn's death was important to somebody else, and after all this time.

Dr. McComb pushed the Blue Willow plate toward me and then took out one of his cigars.

"I know she drowned—"

He sighed. "Indeed she did. No two ways about that."

"But can you be sure—" I should have led up to this question more, but I was getting impatient. "—where she drowned?"

Dr. McComb stopped in the act of lighting his cigar. "What? She drowned in Spirit Lake." He looked at me for quite a time. "You getting at something?"

I shrugged. "Oh, I was just thinking. Here's an example: what if I shoved Jane Davidow's head (it hadn't taken long to scare up an example) down in a bucket of water until she drowned. Then I dragged her dead body (I can't deny I was enjoying this) to Spirit Lake or Lake

242

Noir and dumped her in. How would you know she didn't drown there?"

"How? Well, it'd look pretty damned suspicious for one thing." He dragged in on his cigar, hollowing out his cheeks.

"Why? What if everyone knew she wasn't a good swimmer?" Which she wasn't. "Okay, so it looks suspicious, say. What would you do?"

"Analyze the water. See if it was lake water. See if it was *that* lake water." He rolled his cigar around in pouty lips and gazed at me. "What you're talking about is the Devereau girl, isn't it? You're saying maybe that girl didn't drown in Spirit Lake, but elsewhere."

There wasn't much use beating around the bush, I guessed. "I'm saying—" I chomped my brownie "—they killed her."

Dr. McComb finished lighting his cigar as he stared at me. He seemed unable to say a word. He did not make fun of me or try to dismiss the idea. I knew he wouldn't.

"You thought it was strange too, you said so."

He nodded.

I went on: "Of course, they could still have done it in the lake, only probably on the other side, the side their house was on, for it would have been nearly impossible to take her through the woods and get her into a boat without her yelling or crying. If she was alive, I mean. Ulub would've heard her if she'd yelled. You know he was there because he came with Ubub to tell you." Carefully, I cut the last brownie on the plate in half. I took one half and pushed the plate across to him. But he didn't seem to notice. He sucked in on his cigar. I ate my brownie, trying not to swing my legs under the table the way I did when I was little. He was looking around the kitchen as if it weren't his and he couldn't make out whose it was. Then he studied the ash end of his cigar as if he wasn't sure whose that was either. I suppose because I wasn't used to being taken so seriously, or giving any adult something worth thinking about, I was surprised by his silence. I wanted to ask him if he felt guilty about Mary-Evelyn, but I didn't. It wasn't my place to.

By now what was left of my coffee was cold, but I drank it just the same, not wanting him to think I didn't appreciate his trouble.

He said then, "I should have done something."

He knew. That was probably why I'd told him. I knew he knew. "I should have done something," he said again.

I was quick to disagree. "The *police* should have done something. It was their job, not yours."

He blew out a thread of smoke. "It's the job of anybody who thinks there's a wrong been done to try and right it, I'd say. It being your job makes it only one more reason." He said, "I remember that sheriff. He wasn't like Sam DeGheyn."

Who was? I wanted to say.

"He was just a toady, spent most of his time at the pool hall or licking the mayor's boots. He wasn't about to mount an investigation."

"Wasn't he even suspicious?"

Dr. McComb shrugged. "Beats me. He didn't let on if he was." He held his cigar over an ashtray and flicked the long ash from it. "No one I knew of knew the Devereau sisters very well. They were considered very odd. They left Spirit Lake right after. I heard later one of them died, don't know which one. But I guess they're all dead by now." He frowned. "Maybe not. At least one of 'em was probably my age, and I'm still alive. Seventy-six, I am." He sighed.

Seventy-six. But of course Aurora Paradise was a lot older still, and it'd be some years before he caught up to her. Somehow, as he sat back, he looked older, his eyes now not bright as they had been out there chasing butterflies. He asked, and it seemed more of himself than of me: "Why would three grown women do such violence to a little girl?"

I looked up from the Blue Willow plate. And the word locked in my brain as if it were a puzzle piece that I'd been looking at sidewise out and upside down and every which way but the right one. But now it locked in perfectly.

"Revenge."

A word, a space to fill a lack.

Waiting time

40

"Again?" Delbert whined when I told him I wanted to stop at the library. "There's waiting time—"

"I *know*."

He pulled out, saying, "It's your money."

"Well, then, stop acting like it's yours."

I watched the same scenes go by in reverse outside the window on the other side of the cab. The trailer, the plastic flamingos—

Flamingos! I pounded my head with the heels of my hands, picturing them out there in the center of Hialeah racetrack, where I hadn't gone as I'd planned this afternoon. I sat back, sighing. I'd just get Walter to call the bookie.

Inside the library I said hello to Miss Babbit and made my way to the history shelves. I looked for Greek history. I cannot say why I was going about solving the mystery this way, when what I should be doing was gathering evidence. But what evidence was there to gather in Mary-Evelyn's story?

Yet, I knew it wasn't only Mary-Evelyn's story; it was also Rose Devereau's and Fern Queen's; it was Ben Queen's and Lou Landis's; it was Rebecca and Imogene Calhoun's story. It was also mine.

I dragged book after book off the history shelf, but I couldn't find Do-X-machine. One reason was because I couldn't spell it. I couldn't look it up for that reason. I really hated asking Miss Babbit because you should be able to do your own research and also (mostly) because I was embarrassed to.

I leaned back against the stacks. Mill had said it was a Greek idea and I thought: if Will and Mill are using it in a play, then maybe I should look under Greek plays. I went to the drama shelves, where I found an anthology of Greek plays and ran my finger down the index under "D." I couldn't find it, again, because I couldn't spell it, so I went back to the top and started looking much more slowly.

Here it was, or must be: *deux ex machina.* Wow. Seeing it that way, it looked even more important. Mill certainly hadn't pronounced it right, though he did know what it was. Here it was explained as "God-from-a-machine" and Mill was right about this character (God) coming down in some contraption to set things right. But it didn't tell you how to pronounce it. I guess the book figured if you were smart enough to know what it was, you must know how to say it. I took the book to Miss Babbit.

She adjusted her glasses and smiled down at the page. Miss Babbit always seems in a lovely temper, never harsh or saying things to make you feel dumb. "I *believe* you pronounce it 'day-*uus ex* mack-*in-ah.*'"

My eyebrows slid upward in wonder. Wow, I thought again. I tried it out: "Dayus-ex-MACKinah."

"That's right. Only the first word is more of a 'day-u.' Think of two syllables."

"'Day-you.'"

"That's about right. It's very difficult, I know."

She only said that so I wouldn't feel dumb. I smiled. "Thank you, Miss Babbit." I knew I had to get back to the taxi or Delbert might just take it upon himself to leave. "Now, would you happen to have a picture of Hialeah racetrack?"

———

All the while we drove through town, past Miller's and the Prime Cut and Souder's Drugs, up Second Street and past the Rainbow Café, I watched out for the Girl. She could have gone on to Spirit Lake as easily as alighting in La Porte, or she could still be traveling to some stop up the line, some stop she knew but I didn't.

I could have danced all night
41

Walter told me when I came in the kitchen that he didn't call my bookie because I never told him how much or what horse. I said that was okay, and I might have time to go to Hialeah tomorrow and place my own bets. He then said that Miss Bertha was mad as hops she never got her dinner at the usual time. "They was settin' down in there," he nodded toward the dining room, "and I just went in and told 'em you got called away on an emergency."

I tied on my apron. I hadn't bothered changing my clothes as it was nearly seven-thirty.

As I filled a water pitcher, Walter said, "I set the rolls to warm and put them butter patties on the bread plates."

The rolls were in a basket on the ledge above the stove. My mother never served cold bread. I thanked Walter and asked him if he'd take

Aurora Paradise her dinner. I'd make her a drink, but if I started fooling around with her I'd never be done. He said sure he would.

"I don't want to be late again for the dance," I said, and pushed the swing door through to the dining room where Miss Bertha waited like a big gray spider.

———

Ree-Jane came to the dance (as my guest), wearing a mustard-colored long dress with puffed sleeves and a sweetheart neckline. The style was more that of a ten-year-old, which it was, as it had been my first long dress. If I do say so myself, I had looked pretty cute. Ree-Jane didn't.

My mother wore a black linen dress with a string of (real) pearls. This plain but perfectly cut dress shot from shoulder to floor and looked grand. She looked free and unburdened for once.

Lola Davidow wore a dark brown satin two-piece dress, the top straining across her bosom and the bottom straining across her stomach.

I, of course, wore my white tulle with the sequins and the moment we all stepped through the door, I was asked to dance by the son of the Rony Plaza's owner. My mother twirled off with the owner himself. I asked the son (whose first name I hadn't caught, but what do names matter at times like these?) to dance me by Mrs. Davidow and Ree-Jane so I could wave to them, which he did and I did. Ree-Jane was as red as fire from falling asleep in the sun (again) and her face was peeling. The mustard color against her hair and skin made her look like a big hot dog. Mrs. Davidow stood at the rim of the dance floor pursing her mouth in and out like a fish, wanting either a dance or a drink.

The ballroom was immense. The twenty-foot ceilings had vaulted marble arches. The chandeliers turned the sequins of my dress into tiny stars and I looked like the Milky Way. The orchestra sat on a platform at one end of the room, all of them dressed in black pants and flamingo-pink jackets. In the very center of the ballroom was a circular pool planted with royal palms and poincianas. In this pool flamingos waded up and down and around, more graceful than anyone on the dance floor (except for me and the son).

The band was playing "Poinciana" as Ree-Jane, who had finally been asked to dance by a short bald man, stumbled by. Her partner was not more than five feet five or six. Ree-Jane sported a phony smile on her empty face as she looked over his head, pretending she enjoyed all this. He stepped on her foot. She gritted her teeth as the son and I floated on by. I called out, asking her if she was having a good time.

Lola was. By now she'd had three or four martinis, and she'd found herself a drinking buddy. They were doing some dance that wasn't a jitterbug but also wasn't anything else, that involved dancing in place and shoving the index fingers of each hand up and down and up and down. They were both laughing. That was fine with me.

On several occasions, new dancing partners had cut in on us, and each new partner twirled me away. The son looked disappointed when this happened, but we always got back together again.

The bandleader brought a fast number to a close and then announced a special treat for the dancers. They were now to hear a rendition of "Tangerine" sung by Miss Emma Graham.

Imagine! It seemed my fame had spread all the way from Trader Bob's to South Florida!

Breathless, I moved up to the stage, passing Ree-Jane and the bald man. You could tell she was just beside herself, seeing me get all of this attention.

At this point I got out of my beach chair and put the needle on the record and swayed to the music.

And down in the Pink Elephant, while my royal palm fluttered in the breeze stirred up by the fan, and the waves lapped the beach of the Rony Plaza, and the flamingos bunched among the poincianas, I belted out—

> *Taaaan-ger-ene,*
> *She is all they claim,*
> *With her eyes of night,*
> *And lips as bright as flame;*

> *Taaaan-ger-ene,*
> (Here I was joined by three backup singers.)
> *Da du de da*
> *When she dances by*
> [I trucked along the stage]
> *Do do de do do*
> *Senoritas stare and caballeros siiiiiigh!*

And I've seeeen—
  (Boo be boo be boo)
Toasts to Tangerine
Raised in every port across the Ar-gen-teeeeen—

Here all of the dancers raised their champagne and martini glasses in a toast. I was a tremendous success.

And the night, as they say, was still young.

Psssst! from overhead

42

The next morning I lay in bed an extra few minutes casting my mind back to Brokedown House, to Maud and the Sheriff and me in that fusty old bedroom, and something I was trying to remember. I saw the room, Maud, the Sheriff reading, the ring he'd held out. My mind's eye roved that room, but I couldn't discover what I needed to remember.

I got out of bed and padded down the hall to the bathroom. The stairs to the fourth floor are near the bathroom and I could hear Aurora banging around up there and talking to herself. I sat down on the toilet with my head in my hands, still seeing us in Brokedown House. I tossed cold water on my face and swiped my toothbrush across my teeth a few times. I studied my face in the mirror for signs of dis . . . another "dis" word, dis, dis, *dissipation!* I left the bathroom.

"Pssst! Psssst!"

I looked up. Aurora was hanging over the fourth-floor bannister. I honestly couldn't remember ever seeing her out of her chair before.

"*Pssssst!*"

"Why are you going 'pssssst'? There's no one else around."

"Don't you get fresh with me, Miss! I want an Appledew."

"But it's hardly more than seven A.M.!"

She responded to that by saying—fluting, more—"I have something you'd like to see."

I hadn't noticed she was holding a book, or journal, until she patted it and looked really smug.

I'd been standing at the bottom of this last flight of stairs up, and as I started up them, she yanked the book back. "Oh, no you don't! You don't get to see it till I get my Appledew!"

Stopping on the third step, I said, "What is it? You can at least tell me that." More than likely, what she had was of no interest to me. But then I thought, no, if she tried tricking me with it, then I'd never know whether to believe her; I'd always think she was tricking me and wouldn't fall for it.

"It's a picture album." She patted it again.

Now, photographs have a lot of promise in them as far as information goes. I said, "I've got to serve Miss Bertha and Mrs. Fulbright their breakfast before I can make any drinks."

"You mean that Bertha is still coming here? Crazy as a bedbug, that old lady. Okay, then bring it after, but don't make me wait too long. These pictures might just waltz away if you don't come back soon."

And here, Aurora began to waltz around, reminding me of the dance last night. Maybe I should have invited her.

———

Miss Bertha wanted pecan waffles with orange syrup and I said I was sorry (which I was, but not for her sake), we didn't have any, that we did have grits and hot biscuits (one of Mrs. Fulbright's favorites), and eggs, of course. "Any way you want them," I generously added, knowing how she'd get them.

After much grumbling and tomfoolery and moving things around on the table—her silver, the water pitcher, the vase of wildflowers—and stabbing her butter patty with her butter knife, she said, "I'll have eggs over easy, since you can't boil an egg. Mind you get the grease off."

I put my pencil behind my ear and minded I wouldn't and returned to the kitchen.

Walter was standing at the stove stirring the grits in the top of a double boiler. That's what my mother always used to keep things hot. The biscuits were in the oven heating up. He was wearing one of my mother's aprons. He turned to me and said, "What's the old fool want?"

I laughed because he sounded just like my mother and almost looked like her too, as he stood with arms splayed and hands resting on the long counter.

"Eggs over easy, no grits. Can you do it without breaking the yokes?"

"Sure can, I watched Miss Jen do it."

"Well, don't. At least break one."

"Got it," he said, just as my mother would have.

"I've got to make Aurora Paradise an Appledew."

"Ain't no more apple juice, but there's pineapple. You could make a pineapple dew." Walter broke two eggs into a small bowl. They both ran. Calmly, he picked up another egg and broke that and the yoke stayed whole. He heated up the frying pan.

I considered a Pineappledew, leaning on the counter as Walter had done and as my mother did. It was her thinking position. Vera would march in and rattle off four totally different orders and my mother would stand arms akimbo, her head bowed a little, eyes shut, nodding. When Vera was finally done, she'd say, "Got it."

A feeling wrenched me, almost as if someone had literally grabbed me around my waist. It was a terrible feeling, no doubt caused by her absence, that there would come a time when my mother would not stand so, arms splayed and eyes tight shut. Vera would come no more to bark out her food orders nor would Mrs. Davidow come to sit on the center table, to smoke a cigarette and gossip. It was the same feeling that had washed over me in the upstairs storeroom where cobwebs floated in the thin light that slanted through the grimy windows, the same feeling as I had got when I remembered the Waitresses. In this lingering absence, it was as if something knocked loose within me to roll across a green baize table, like the one in the poolroom next to the *Conservative* offices—to roll away and out of control. I could not find words for it, or maybe I did not want to find words for it, for they might give it a shape (as William Faulkner says) and I did not want to see the shape. Then I wondered if not wanting to see it was just my cowardly way. I hung my head and wondered if anything could set all of this to rights.

"Is this broke enough?"

Walter's voice snatched me back from this hard place and I'd half forgotten what we were doing. I looked at Miss Bertha's fried eggs. "Yes." One yolk had spread flat and hard and the white was tough and stringy. Just the egg my mother would never have allowed into the dining room, not if they tortured her for a spy.

"Sorry," I said to Miss Bertha, when I'd set the breakfasts before them. "We used the last egg on that." But somehow I didn't feel as gleeful as I usually did nor think the joke as jokey.

An album

43

Whatever had knocked loose from me had rolled out of sight by the time I'd finished making a Bombay Breakfast for Aurora. What inspired this new drink was the bottle of gin in the back office safe called Bombay. The finished drink, I thought, surpassed the Appledew. Besides the rum, the Jack Daniel's, and the Curaçao (which I discovered had an orange flavor), I put in orange juice, pineapple juice, and half a mashed banana, which I whisked together with one of the broken eggs Walter had saved. (This also felt thrifty.) The whole thing struck me as a very healthful drink. The egg especially gave it an honorary breakfast standing.

"This ain't an Appledew," said Aurora Paradise, complaining right off.

Still, she looked at the tall glass with an air of expectation. For had

I ever let her down? I had also found among Mrs. Davidow's souvenir swizzle sticks one with a camel sitting atop it. It made, I thought, a nice Bombay-ish touch.

She sipped and smacked her lips. "This is a *good* drink, Missy." She took another, longer swallow and said it again.

"I'm glad you like it, but don't expect it every morning. It takes a lot of trouble."

She flicked her fingers at me. Today her crocheted mittens were pale olive green with tiny darker green leaves done in satin. I wondered if she had made all of these mittens herself. I couldn't imagine her having the patience. "Oh, you're just so all-fired lazy."

"No, I'm not. Listen: I can't be making you drinks every time you get a mind for one, remember. Mrs. Davidow will be back soon and I can't be getting stuff out of her safe all the time."

"Well, I'll give you some money and you can go to the liquor store."

I rolled my eyes at this crazy suggestion. "I'm *twelve*, remember?"

"Then send that man."

"Look, we had a bargain you'd show me that photo album, there." It sat on the side table at her elbow.

She slid a glance that way, then gave me a sly look. "How about doing the pea trick first?"

"No! It's not even a trick because you hide the walnut shells right from the start."

She sighed. "Oh, all right, if you're going to be contrary." She set aside the drink and picked up the album. It was covered in an olive-green silk the color of her mittens. It was water stained and a little threadbare. She turned a few pages quickly as if she knew exactly which one she wanted, and said, "There!" Her finger tapped one of the snapshots.

A young pale-haired woman sat on the top rung of a wooden fence; the dark-haired young man leaned against it. They were both smiling happily.

I gasped. They were Rose Devereau and Ben Queen.

"Couldn't've been more'n twenty when that was took."

Questions tumbled in my mind. I picked one. "Where are they?"

"Spirit Lake, looks like."

"There's no sign of the lake."

Aurora looked again. "Could be Paradise Valley or Cold Flat Junction." She shrugged. "Could be anywhere, I guess."

257

Most places seemed to be so hard to pin down they did seem "any-where." It was important to anchor the two to a particular place. While I was studying the snapshot for clues, she whipped the album out of my hands.

"That ain't all!" Now she flipped to another page and turned the album so I could see it. Here was another couple, and this snapshot was older than the one of Rose and Ben. They were posing, she awk-wardly, he easily, as if used to the camera's attention. He was dressed in a dark blazer and light trousers and was very good-looking. She was wearing an embroidered white dress. His smile was brilliant. He was the young man in the old photograph Dwayne had shown me.

"That there is Isabel Devereau."

I couldn't help it; I snatched the album from her. Isabel Devereau! Younger than in the snapshot my mother had of the sisters, and almost pretty—at least, not as grim. Her expression was softer. "Who's *he*?"

"Jamie Makepiece is what I believe his name is. I *thought* she had a beau. That's him right there. I remembered when I found this album. I thought it was lost and I found it over there where Jen Graham keeps her stuff. *Someone* had removed it from amongst my possessions."

"Well, don't look at me." She sounded so self-righteous, but I didn't want to get her off on another subject.

"When I saw this picture, it all came back. Isabel Devereau and Jamie Makepiece. Why, that was fifty years ago. When I myself was eighteen—" She slid me a glance to see if I bought this point, which I didn't, but again I didn't want to argue.

"There was talk of marrying. But then they didn't. He was from New York and you can see by how he dresses he's a city boy. A sharpie and a ladies' man. This was taken," here she tapped the snapshot again, "when he come to visit one summer, visited some relation in Spirit Lake, I don't know who. "Actu'ly—" She primped her hair with her bony, mittened hand. "—he was sweet on me, I could tell."

I kept from pointing out that Jamie was a good twenty years younger than she was, like Ben Queen (who, she'd said, also had a crush on her).

"But that ain't the reason he left before any marrying could take place. No sirree!"

I waited. She was silent. "Well, why did he?" I shifted my small tray from under one arm to the other. I must admit I was on pins and needles for I was sure there was more to come. But her thin mouth had swung shut like a letter box. I should have known.

She snatched up her empty glass and moved it back and forth. "I'll just have another Bombay Brunch before I continue my story."

"'Breakfast,'" I corrected her. "It's too early even for brunch. How could you drink another when it's hardly nine A.M."

"I'll push myself." She raised the glass.

This was *so* maddening. I went through some pretantrum motions of whining and stomping my foot, knowing it would do no good but not being able to help myself. It might be surprising to hear that when I was little I had a leaning toward temper tantrums, though not any more of course. It got to be all I wanted to do was throw my physical self around, even while knowing this wouldn't get the outcome I desired. But here I was so irritated the tale of Jamie and Isabel was being interrupted I could hardly keep myself from doing something physical. My feet seemed to have a mind of their own, like Frankenstein feet. They stomped several times. Aurora just sat with her album clamped to her chest, her lips sealed.

"Oh, all right!" I grabbed the glass and left with my tray and stomped downstairs until I was out of earshot. Then I ran.

Walter had gone up to Britten's store, so I was alone in the kitchen watching the liquor, a banana, and a fresh egg I'd broken sweep around in the blender. I decided to pour in everything and let the blender whirl it all together.

Jamie Makepiece. Another character added to the story, an even older story; another player to add to the Mr. Ree game. Jamie Makepiece and Isabel Devereau. It was hard imagining one of the Devereau sisters having a romance, especially with a good-looking New York society ladies' man. If Aurora remembered all of this right. Back then she would have been in her thirties, I figured, and fifty years ago— why, Rose Devereau would have been only ten years old. Younger than I was now. And the same went for Ben Queen. And my mother would have been just a girl. It was so hard to imagine these people as children. It was hard to imagine one of the dour Devereau sisters in a party dress, to tell the truth.

I was pouring the frothy drink into Aurora's glass and nearly dropped the pitcher. I saw the awkward Isabel in her white dress, embroidered with dark little flowers whose color didn't show in the picture but which I'd bet several years' worth of tips was blue.

The same material as Mary-Evelyn's dress, the same blue silk flowers, only a different design. I remember how Miss Flagler, who owns the gift shop, had talked about one of the Devereau sisters as being an accomplished seamstress, and how a Devereau dress was to be coveted then much more than anything Heather Gay Struther could come up with now. Miss Flagler had said whenever she saw Mary-Evelyn, the child was beautifully dressed. And I'd seen those dresses, for they were still hanging in the closet of Mary-Evelyn's room. Still in mint condition forty years later. I had tried them on, so I knew.

Floating in the thick water growth of lily pads and grass, Mary-Evelyn had been wearing her white ruffled dress, made from the same material Isabel Devereau must have kept for ten years. But it was not this which had caught my attention—the two dresses made of like material. No, what kept me standing and staring out of the window by the icebox was what I'd been trying to remember when I woke up. It was the doll Maud had been holding in that bedroom of the house on White's Bridge Road, dressed in white organdy with little blue flowers sewn onto it. What was that doll doing in Brokedown House?

The picture, the photograph. Was *that* where I'd seen Jamie Makepiece?

It was in a kind of stupor that I walked the Bombay Breakfast up to the fourth floor. I think I might have walked it all the way to Bombay and hardly noticed. It kept going through my mind: the doll, the photograph—what were they doing in the Calhoun house? For I have no doubt the doll was Mary-Evelyn's. Miss Flyte hadn't said the Devereau sister made doll clothes to sell. And the Calhouns were a whole different society from the Devereaus. They wouldn't have mingled. It appalled me to think I would have to go back even further in time and consider things done then, fifty years ago, but I recollected the story of Agamemnon and his family and realized fifty years of revenge was just an eye blink for the Greeks.

"You in a coma?"

I had got to Aurora's room and handed her the drink (at least I guess I had, since she was drinking it) and must not have been wearing my usual know-it-all expression. I wondered how much the album had shaken loose in her memory. If nothing else, there was still more of the

Jamie Makepiece story. "You agreed to tell me why Jamie left," I said testily, to let her know I was out of my coma.

Slowly she sipped her drink, then set it aside and made a few small movements, such as resting her hands in her lap, as if gathering herself together. She looked pleased to death with herself, as she usually does when she has information I want. "There was talk."

"About Jamie and Isabel?"

"About Jamie and *Iris*." She delivered up this name with a little hiss as if the name were dangerous.

Wide-eyed, I jumped back. "*Iris?* But you said Isabel before. Isabel was Jamie's girl."

She nodded. "Um-hmm."

It was almost as bad sometimes as talking to Ree-Jane, the way she held on to information I wanted, but was quick to give me information I didn't want, like what was on my X-rays, if I'd had any taken. "Are you saying he was *both* of theirs?"

"That was the talk, that Iris got him away from Isabel. Now, I can't say if he broke off with Isabel and picked up with Iris, or if he started seeing Iris on the sly behind Isabel's back. But then he left real quick, that's what was said. Talk was, all the girls were after him. Well, as you can see, he's right handsome. I didn't have time for him; I had other fish to fry."

"How long was he here?"

"All that summer, if memory serves."

Memory wasn't serving very well if she couldn't recall this when I first asked about the Devereaus several weeks ago.

"That was one fine summer, indeed. We went swimming almost daily in Lake Noir—" (Surprisingly, she was one of the few people around who could say it right.) "—and had weenie roasts nearly every night beside the lake. That water was cold as ice and clear as glass. And we'd take boats out on Spirit Lake, too. At night when the moon was up, we'd just drift and drift around."

It sounded more like some movie about high school kids than something that really happened. Why would she be attending weenie roasts at her age? That was the trouble with her stories; you never knew what part to believe in. But something told me it was true about Isabel, Iris, and Jamie Makepiece.

"Then Elizabeth stepped in; Elizabeth took over like always."

This detail surprised me. "What did she do?"

"Why, she sent him packing's what I heard. Elizabeth was pretty much boss, being the oldest. I guess he went back to New York and his New York ways. Elizabeth sent Iris off to relatives. That was her punishment. I can believe it." Here she slewed a look around at me as a relative, then picked up her drink and sipped it.

I stood looking at her intently, as if my look were a kind of hypodermic syringe that could siphon more of the Iris and Jamie story out of her. Imagine Iris going back finally to the Devereau house and that grim fate.

"Did anyone ever see him again?" I was getting concerned for Jamie for some reason. Isabel, of course, would blame Iris and hardly attach any blame at all to Jamie, as she would want to think it was her, Isabel, he truly loved and had just slipped for a moment. At least that's the way I'd do it if it were me.

Aurora held up a mittened hand, palm out, as if to push my questions back. "That is all I recall."

I was frowning in simple frustration at not getting more details. "Why didn't you tell me this when I first asked about the Devereaus."

Complacent, she was shuffling her tattered deck of cards. "When you get old you start remembering things that happened long, long ago."

"You're hardly three weeks older than you were when I asked."

She didn't reply, just started laying out the cards. I couldn't stop here forever hoping for more of the story, and I had no desire to watch her cheat at solitaire, so I left.

My mind ran down names of people who were old enough to have been here and heard this "talk." There weren't many. Miss Flyte and Miss Flagler, in their sixties and seventies, respectively, would have been young, back then. Miss Flagler owns a gift shop in La Porte, and Miss Flyte has a candle store next to it. The two of them would sometimes invite me to their morning coffee breaks. It was more often cocoa for me and coffee for them. I knew Miss Flagler recalled something of the Devereau sisters, certainly of the one who was the seamstress, for she gave me a description of an ice-green organdy and silk dress sewn by one. So she seemed to remember that time pretty clearly.

Miss Flyte, though, was the one with the greater imagination, so even if she'd only been in her teens, things might have impressed her more. I'm only twelve, and things impress me, though I tend to be more literal and go by evidence more (somewhat in the way of the Sheriff). Miss Flyte (for instance) could probably take a trip on the Tamiami Trail and to the Rony Plaza without even having to tape up pictures or make a palm tree, or bring in a fan or play records on a phonograph. Her imagination is such that she doesn't need props.

What other seventy- to ninety-year-olds did I know? There was Dr. McComb, of course, but he would have mentioned it if he knew about Isabel and Iris and Jamie. It would have been a bit of a scandal, I would guess. There were probably dozens of people still around who might have heard about Jamie, but they were probably all in Weeks's Nursing Home. No, I could think of no one more likely than Miss Flagler, so I called Axel's Taxis to come and pick me up just before ten.

———

The Oak Tree Gift Shoppe is the next shop up from the Candlewick, separated by a narrow alley. Inside, it appears not to have changed in a hundred years, though I know Miss Flagler changes her window display every week. I studied it now. That thing that makes it look always the same is that what Miss Flagler puts in looks like what she takes away. The little silver fox that sat beside the porcelain bowl looks like the silver pig she had moved somewhere else. The blue-flowered bowl sat in the same place as had a pink-scrolled china bowl; a gold bracelet had taken the place of last week's silver; amethyst earrings had replaced emerald; a single strand of pearls replaced a double. I loved to look in this window because I found it restful. No, a better word is "comfortable." It was the comfort of seeing small changes occurring within a background that never does, that was dependably always the same. This was the opposite feeling to what I'd felt yesterday, leaning on the kitchen counter—the feeling that enormous changes would come. I placed my palms and my forehead on the gift shop window, willing the fox to come back if the pig left, the amethyst to replace the emerald earrings—anything like that except to find the window barren, swept clean.

I saw Miss Flagler coming through the curtained alcove behind the counter and I suspected it was time for her to change the OPEN clock-sign to the one that said BACK IN. She always moves the hands to show "15 minutes," which was never enough time, for her tea and coffee breaks always took a half an hour to forty-five minutes. But she explained that she did not want to discourage trade, and any customer happening along would go off and do something else for an hour or so, and then return.

She was surprised to see me at the window and gave a little wave, which I returned. She opened the door and told me that Miss Flyte was in the kitchen and invited me to join them. She turned the clock hands to "Back in 15 minutes."

Miss Flagler is tall and thin and Miss Flyte is short and thin, but aside from that, age seems to have made them sisters. I've noticed this age thing the few times I've been to Weeks's Nursing Home to deliver cakes and pies my mother donates. The old people all look strangely alike, as if age is another country, a country of relations, and anyone not a relative (such as me) stands out like a sore thumb.

Both Miss Flagler and Miss Flyte have gray hair, worn similarly in a bun, and filmy blue eyes, like one of those rainy-day skies where the blue is glazed over. They dress differently, though. Miss Flyte likes wool sweaters and skirts and Miss Flagler always wears gray dresses and cashmere cardigans. (Her dress indicates family money, or money from another source than her gift shop, whose profits wouldn't run, probably, to silk and cashmere.)

Hello, hello, hello, I said, the third hello being directed to Albertine, Miss Flagler's queenly white cat, who also joins us during coffee breaks. Albertine likes to sit on a painted shelf right above my chair, sometimes lightly chewing at the crown of my hair. Miss Flagler busied herself at the big cast iron stove, having offered me, as she always does, a choice of tea or cocoa. (Dr. McComb is the only one who has me down as a coffee drinker.) I chose cocoa, as always. Miss Flyte must have started the percolator, for it was perking away.

"Emma," said Miss Flagler, "has something to ask us. Some business."

It seemed to please both of them that I was there on business and not simply in my cocoa-drinking capacity. Even Albertine sat alert instead of lying down on the shelf.

"Really?" said Miss Flyte, with enthusiasm. She made it sound like my "business" was important (which shows how uneventful life can be around here, aside from the ongoing recent mystery). She laced her fingers on the table as Miss Flagler set down her coffee. The cocoa had been made earlier and had only to heat. My cup was served with two marshmallows and I was glad Mr. Butternut wasn't here to compete for them. I quickly stirred the cocoa to keep a skin from forming.

We three settled now, I began: "It's those Devereau sisters. You remember, we were talking about the Devereaus. They were Elizabeth, Isabel, and Iris—"

"Iris!" said Miss Flagler. "That was her name; Iris was the one who sewed so wonderfully. Do you remember her?" Miss Flagler had turned to Miss Flyte.

Miss Flyte pursed her lips. "Vaguely. I'd have to think." Her brow furrowed.

"Iris Devereau made me a dress. I believe I told you that?" said Miss Flagler.

I nodded. "You said it was ice-green silk or organdy. It was a garden party and Mary-Evelyn Devereau was there, handing sandwiches around."

"Indeed, she was. Such a solemn child. But such pretty clothes. Her Aunt Iris must have sewn them too. Iris was quite famous for her dresses. Everyone wanted a Devereau dress. She wouldn't sew for just anyone, either. I remember Helene Baum—well, she wasn't Baum back then, of course; she was Helene Smith—anyway, Helene, who was only a teenager then, nearly had a fit when Iris Devereau wouldn't make her a gown to wear to some dance. I myself felt quite flattered that she made one for me."

"What was she like except being a great dressmaker?"

Miss Flyte said, "What I remember is I thought it just a shame she lived with the other two. Elizabeth and—?"

"Isabel," I said.

"Yes. Well, Iris was the youngest and pretty, while the others were plain—grim, really—and I imagined they resented Iris. All three of them living together like that, and with that little niece to take care of, I'll bet they were rife with resentment."

It was strange to me that again Rose had been left out. "Four of them."

The two looked at me, quizzically, at first. Then Miss Flyte said, "You mean Rose? Yes, that's right. But Rose was a Souder, only a half sister, and she looked so different. She was blond and quite beautiful. You recall her, Eustacia?"

This was Miss Flagler's first name. I thought it suited her.

"Now, didn't she run off and get married?"

Neither recalled this so I told them.

"Queen?" said Miss Flagler. "But that's the name of the woman who was shot over near White's Bridge, isn't it?"

I didn't want to get off on that as it would keep us sitting here all day. "Yes. But I was wondering about Iris. Going back, going back ten years before, do either of you recollect a man from New York City. His name was Jamie Makepiece. He might have been engaged to one of them." I didn't want to put memories in their mouths.

"You know, I always wondered why those girls never married," said Miss Flagler. "I mean none of them. Especially Iris. But now you mention this Makepiece fellow . . . Yes, I do recollect something. There was a row—now, where was this? I honestly think it was at the Hotel Paradise. Yes, it was. Fifty years ago, how it does take me back."

Her voice was sad now, whether at what was there fifty years ago, or what isn't here now, I don't know.

"Your own mother was just a child, back then. It's hard to believe, isn't it?"

Miss Flyte said, "Jamie Makepiece. At the time, I could only have been, oh, thirteen. But I remember him. He cut an elegant figure, let me tell you, and I think all us girls were a little silly about him, flighty. Tipsy." She smiled. "Even me, young as I was."

In my mind's eye I pictured that old photograph on the wall in the Devereaus' parlor. It was hard to imagine those women in their high-necked dresses and pulled-back hair and serious, reproachful faces as ever having been flighty or tipsy. Except, that is, for the fourth one, Rose.

Miss Flagler had stopped, back there fifty years ago. I wanted her to go on. "What about this row you overheard. Was he—Jamie—fighting with someone?"

She had started to raise her coffee cup, and, perhaps realizing it was cold, put it down again. "Yes, with one of the Devereau women."

"Did you hear them?" My cocoa almost forgotten (I was letting the marshmallows melt), I scrunched forward on my chair.

"Well . . . no . . . I honestly can't remember. My goodness, I'm amazed at any of this coming back after fifty years."

"My great-aunt Aurora Paradise says that as you get older you remember more from the far past." I hastened to add, "Of course she's a lot older than you."

"Elizabeth." Miss Flagler's look was vacant, as if her mind were seeing, not her eyes.

We both looked at her. "Elizabeth?" I said.

"It was she, the one who was arguing with Jamie Makepiece."

I waited, but it seemed her mind wasn't going to turn up any more of this scene. I thought for a moment. "What happened to them? To the Devereaus?"

Miss Flyte answered: "They just left, didn't they, Eustacia?"

Miss Flagler nodded. "After the drowning death of poor Mary-Evelyn, yes." She added, "No, but wait: one of them died, remember? I think Iris. Yes, it was the youngest one. I recall that because people commented that it was a pity it should be the youngest. The most talented. Mind you, the other two weren't all that much older—five or ten years, perhaps. They just acted so old, so set in their ways. As I said—grim. Even Iris soured, later in her life, like milk gone off." Miss Flyte picked up the snapshot and gazed at it. "Can you imagine the life that poor child would have led in that house? With those dour old maids?"

Miss Flagler poured more coffee, which had been sitting forgotten on the table between them. "I suppose people say the same of us."

Miss Flyte laughed. "Not 'dour,' not 'grim,' I hope."

"Nobody ever says anything about you that's not complimentary," I said. It was true, except for Lola Davidow, who got mad because the McIntyre wedding party wanted Miss Flyte to light the reception for them. I said, "The Devereaus left nearly everything behind. They even left Mary-Evelyn's dresses."

"How do you know that, Emma?"

"I've been there."

"Really? It's sad to think, but perhaps they wanted no reminders with them."

I was suddenly overtaken by a surge of loneliness. There were pictures in the house of the three sisters and even of the black sheep, Rose. But none of Mary-Evelyn. This hadn't occurred to me before. All we had to remind us of her was this snapshot under the porte cochere, this and memory. And the sisters even wanted to wipe out memory.

267

Light in August
44

My life had become crowded with people I hardly knew existed a month ago; I counted them up and it came to twenty-one new people. This was even leaving out Rose, since my list had to be people I had actually talked to. For that reason, too, it left out the Girl, even though she might have been the most important of all.

Twenty-one new people! It was staggering, since these are not people I met and only said hello and good-bye to; these are people I am *involved* with, such as Dwayne and Louise Landis and the folks in the Windy Run Diner. Yes, I was staggered by this. The next time Ree-Jane makes a comment about my lack of social life, I will tell her this.

After I left the Oak Tree Gift Shoppe, I decided I needed to think for a little before I talked to Dwayne later on, so I walked down to Second Street to McCrory's, which was usually a relaxing place to be, es-

pecially the makeup counter. I liked to look at the lipsticks and powder and eyeliners, deciding what I'd wear if I wore makeup. Ree-Jane
said that makeup wouldn't do you any good if you didn't have the
bones to begin with.

None of this was getting me closer to how I would convince
Dwayne to go to Brokedown House again, so I left. But then I got
some notion of what I might do and hurried to the Abigail Butte
County Library, a couple of blocks up Second Street.

Inside the library (where I should have gone in the first place), I
headed for the literature shelves, where I started looking for William
Faulkner. I was amazed to find he wrote so many books. Where did he
ever find the time? For one thing, he didn't have to wait tables. I had
decided I would take down just one instead of piling a bunch of his
books on my library table and thus confuse myself. Also, it was working its way around to noon and I had to get back to the hotel. It was irritating to have to get back and serve lunch to Miss Bertha, but I
couldn't keep putting this off on Walter. After lunch I would go to
Slaw's Garage.

I ran my finger along the spines of Willam Faulkner's books, reading the titles. *As I Lay Dying* (no thanks, unless it's being told by Ree-
Jane); *Python,* which I didn't know what it was; *The Sound and the
Fury,* which I read the opening paragraph of and put back; *Sanctuary,*
a title I really liked, for it sounded peaceful. I leafed through it and
found one of the characters was named Flem Snopes and put it back,
too. *Light in August.* This title I thought was the prettiest, and wasn't
that the book Dwayne carried around? I took this book to my favorite
reading table, which sat by a sunny window. I liked the way the sunshine made a latticework of light coming through the little square
panes. It must be fate, for here I was, reading *Light in August.*

On the very first page, the woman named Lena is remembering
when she was *twelve years old.* I could scarcely believe it. Talk about
fate! Here's a double dose of it! She thinks about her mother and father, who died when she was my age. William Faulkner described her
house and rooms lit by a "bugswirled kerosene lamp."

Bugswirled. What a wonderful word. I looked up and I could see
above me the thick whiteness of our porch light and small moths cir-
cling and fluttering around it as if its whiteness were some sort of moth
landing, like a landing on the moon. I read on. "Stumppocked." Here
was another wonderful word. Since he was describing where the trees

had been cut, I suppose it means stumps that look diseased. Then there's "hookwormridden." I did not want to linger too long over Lena's condition. I guessed she must be going to have a baby. I suppose all writers get around to sex sooner or later, only Faulkner got around to it on page two.

It was noon and I had to get back. Holding the book, I went up to Miss Babbit where she was working behind the checkout desk and asked if I could please have a sheet of paper and borrow a pen or pencil. Of course, she said, and reached to a shelf and brought up the paper and handed me a pen. She noticed the book I was carrying. My, my, she said, Mr. Faulkner. Faulkner-country is not an easy place to be, she said. Neither is Graham-country, I said, surprising myself with this comeback.

I thanked her and went back to my desk, where I started going through my book, just looking anywhere, quickly running my eye down a page here, a page there, stopping if I found something and copied it down. After I'd taken down three different things, I went back to "hookwormridden" and wrote that down too. Then my eye fell on the paragraph that followed:

> There was a track and a station, and once a day a mixed train
> fled shrieking through it.

This was Emma-country. Wow!

270

In Slaw's Garage, the mechanics were all wiping their hands on oily rags, so I guess they must have seen someone coming.

They weren't very impressed seeing the someone was me. Especially Dwayne, who made a huge production out of getting down on the flat board and sliding under a gray car. I said hi to Abel Slaw and the rest and walked over to the gray car. "Dwayne?"

"Yeah?" His voice sounded miles away. There was a lot of metal clanging on metal, the sounds of being busy.

"Come on out from there, will you?" I sat down on the running board of an old Ford pickup that looked like Ubub's but wasn't, for the license plate didn't read UBB. You-boy was whistling, searching under the hood of an ancient convertible up front.

"Why? I got work to do."

"I can see that. Come on out anyway. It's important."

"You think everything you want's important."

"That's kind of dumb, Dwayne. Everybody does."

He didn't answer. I pulled out the sheet of paper with my three quotes to see which one best fit the situation. None of them really did, but I decided on:

> There were words that never even stood for anything, were not even us, while all the time what was us was going on and going on without even missing the lack of words.

I knew Dwayne favored words. So did I.

As he shot out from under the car, I quickly folded the paper and shoved it in my pocket. I wanted him to think I knew it, and had recited, not read, it. I sat with my chin on my updrawn knees and tried to look heartfelt.

"What'd you just say?" Prone on the board, he bent his head back as if he thought maybe Billy Faulkner were under the car with him.

I wasn't at all sure what I'd said. "You heard."

Dwayne got up off the wood flat as if he were rising from Lake Noir, buoyant. The oily rag came out and he stood wiping his hands.

"Don't you recognize it?"

He grunted, but he was near to smiling. His eyes already were. "Recognize the writing. I have not memorized everything Billy Faulkner wrote."

"I thought you'd like that, as it's about words. You remember what you said about words being 'a shape to fill a lack.'"

"So do you know what all that means? What you just said?"

I couldn't even remember what I'd read, much less what it might mean. "No, but it sounds good. It's from *Light in August*."

Dwayne stopped wiping his hands and shoved the rag in his back pocket. It hung limply over the edge and was a dull rose color.

"I decided I really like him. Billy Faulkner, I mean. William." I hadn't yet read enough to be on a nickname basis with him.

"He'd be pleased."

"When do you get off work?"

"'Round seven this evening. I still got a truck to do. Why?"

"We need to go to Brokedown House."

"'We' do, do 'we'? And why's that?"

271

"I need to go in that room again to see some things. You're going home anyway. White's Bridge is hardly any detour at all."

"So where's all your buddies? Night before last, it looked like a Fraternal Order of the Owls meeting."

"There's too many of them. They get in the way."

"What about your good friend Butternut?"

I sighed. "Du-*wayne*. You know Mr. Butternut wouldn't have any idea what to do in an emergency."

"And just what emergency might announce itself?"

"I don't know. But you do recall the police came that time."

"From what I gather, a missing girl was that particular emergency."

I ignored that.

"What's in this house that's so all-fired important?"

Abel Slaw shouted from the door of his tiny office, "Dwayne, you better come on and finish up Teets's truck. I promised he could pick it up before we close."

I said, "So I'll come back at seven, okay?"

"Emma!" called Abel Slaw. "Now you shouldn't be hanging 'round the cars."

Dwayne said, "Okay, come ahead."

I answered Abel Slaw: "I'm leaving, Mr. Slaw."

"Yeah, well, it ain't I don't want you around, but it's dangerous out there where all the machinery and stuff is."

Some idea of danger he had.

Miss Bertha found another reason to complain, with having to come into dinner at six instead of her preferred time of six-thirty. It was as if she had a schedule of events on her social calendar that would be completely thrown out of kilter by this earlier time. She demanded to know why as she and Mrs. Fulbright sat down at their table.

Pouring the water, I knew if I said it was because I had certain plans for the evening, she would do everything in her power to make me at least a half hour late, so that I would gain nothing from the change. I had to make it worth her while. When I'd set their menus before them, I told her that our candy supplier (for the display case at the desk) had called up and said they just got in the York peppermint patties—which was Miss Bertha's favorite—that we'd been out of for so long and that he'd be there till seven this evening if I wanted to pick them up. It was a special trip I'd have to make but seeing how much she liked them I would make the effort.

I love going to the candy wholesaler when Mrs. Davidow goes to pick up boxes of Hershey bars, Butterfingers, Snickers, Mounds, and Three Musketeers, my favorite. It's because the bar is in three sections of chocolate, vanilla, and strawberry. Candy boxes, each containing one or two dozen bars, are stacked in the warehouse ten feet high, row after row. I often wonder how they sold all of that candy. To Miller's and the five-and-dime and the drug stores, I guessed—all around.

When I'd told her this, she didn't know how to respond. She was on what is called the "horns of a dilemma" (a state I myself am often faced with), as she wouldn't want me to miss delivery of her York peppermint patties, but then she'd have to go along with this time change. The York patties won out, for she told me to get their first course (fruit cup) and be quick about it.

I smiled and told her "Coming up!" and made for the kitchen. Miss Bertha would not be happy when she saw the display case tomorrow, but I'd worry about that tomorrow. As Scarlett O'Hara liked to say, tomorrow is another day.

Master mechanic II

45

It really bothers me sometimes, this life of lies, but more times it doesn't. I thought this while bumping along in Dwayne's pickup. It was noisier than either Ubub's or Ulub's trucks. It sounded like every little pipe and wire was getting jostled loose.

"How come with you being a master mechanic your own truck's falling apart?"

He shifted gears and they ground as if they were hammering into the highway. "Don't have time."

"I don't want to be rude, Dwayne, but it's not a very good advertisement for a master mechanic to have a car like this." We had passed what city limits there were and were rumbling along the highway.

"Yeah, well, of course, I don't often get the extreme pleasure of a customer driving around with me listening."

What childish sarcasm. "What is a master mechanic, anyway?" I looked out my window and thought those were the exact same cows standing and looking at us over the rail fence. I wondered what they thought. I wondered *if* they thought. For a moment I shut my eyes and put myself in cow-mode, me behind the fence looking as the truck passed. But nothing came to mind and Dwayne was talking.

"It means I'm good."

"Well, You-boy is *good*. I guess so is Abel Slaw." When he didn't bother answering, I said, "I bet you could easily do something to a car so it couldn't run." Naturally I was thinking of you-know-whose. Then I realized the Dewey's Do-Nuts hut wasn't far off. I said, "Suppose we were being chased and we all stopped for doughnuts. I'll bet you could just nip out to the chaser's car and put it out of commission." I could see the blue neon Dewey's sign ahead. "Couldn't you?"

At the doughnut hut, he pulled his truck over. "I always stop here. Got nothing to do with you dropping big hints."

We piled out and piled into Dewey's Do-Nuts. I was starved. I had sacrificed my own dinner for this.

On our way again—I had insisted on paying for the doughnuts and coffee and was glad he didn't make some remark about me drinking coffee—I ate my vanilla-iced doughnut and decided Dwayne was mysterious. I didn't actually know anything much about him, I mean about his life so far. He didn't talk about himself, which was awfully unusual in a person. I inspected my powdered-sugar doughnut; I've always loved powdered sugar from watching my mother make designs with it on cakes. I like to watch the powdered sugar drift down from the sieve like sweet snow.

We were just a short distance from the turnoff. I wondered if Dwayne was running from the law and that was the reason for his secrecy. But he hadn't been at all bothered when he'd met up with the Sheriff that night.

We turned off and I saw the Silver Pear sign casting its moonish glow on the branches, turning them pale and unearthly looking. The restaurant's parking lot was crowded as usual.

Dwayne said, "You can buy me dinner there some night by way of repaying this favor."

"Oh, sure. Listen, maybe you shouldn't park by the pond."

"Why's that?"

We were trundling over White's Bridge now. "Because Mr. Butternut will see the truck and come to Brokedown House and we'd never get anything done."

"Just what are we trying to get done?"

"It's a long story." Mirror Pond came up ahead and Dwayne stopped and braked in the same spot as the first night. So much for my advice.

"I like long stories. Come on." He opened his door and I opened mine and both of us climbed down.

He went around to the back of the truck and pulled out his shotgun. It looked absolutely lethal. Well, it was, wasn't it? Just ask a rabbit. He broke it over his arm and jerked his head at me in a "come on" gesture. We crossed the road and went up a small embankment. We were taking the way through the woods instead of the road.

It was dusk, the same part of the day as when I'd been here before. Dwayne was carrying his square flashlight with the handle and switched it on. I love the woods but not if I'm walking through them. With Dwayne there I felt considerably more comfortable, even more than with the Woods and Mr. Root. Every scraped rock, every snapped twig, brittle leaf, wind rustle sent a chill down my spine. It was dark activity of such a level I really thought God ought to be notified. (When I said to Father Freeman I didn't hold with the belief that God knows everything, he said back, Maybe that's just wishful thinking.)

There was this beaten path that we kept to. I wondered how a path had ever gotten trampled out here, with so few people in the place, and no one living in the houses farther along than Mr. Butternut's.

"How come you brought your gun, Dwayne? I mean, you're not going rabbit hunting, are you?" Frankly, I wished he'd say yes, he was, for I didn't like to think he'd want to carry it for protection.

"Always do, going in here."

I didn't care for the sound of that, so I kept quiet. Matted leaves, rotted and wet, squished unpleasantly beneath my feet. Narrow ribbons of water ran down the bark of an oak we passed as if the trees were raining after the sky had stopped. Every so often a shower of drops lighted on my head. Dwayne played his flashlight on either side of the path.

"What are you doing?"

"Just lookin' to see."

"See what?"

"You might recall I saw someone the other night."

I certainly did recall it. I edged closer to him. The path was really too narrow for two people walking abreast, but I wasn't going to hang around behind him. "You're not the only person that comes out here hunting, I guess. Maybe it was another poacher you saw. Or heard."

"This ain't hunting season, as you were quick to remind me. No, it wasn't another poacher."

I heard running water. We must have been near a stream. I asked him.

"That's the creek, one that runs under White's Bridge. It runs into the lake. So if you ever get lost, just follow this creek, you'll get out okay."

Lost? I had no intention of getting lost.

He left the path and I was right beside him. In another forty or fifty feet we'd come on the creek. Dwayne looked up at the sky. "Full dark in another fifteen minutes." He leaned his gun against a tree and set his flashlight on a stump.

"Stumppocked, this place is," I said.

"Where'd you hear that word?"

"Light in August."

"You're one for details, aren't you?"

Beneath the tree was a wide flat stone, its surface as fine as pewter. He fingered a cigarette from the pack in his shirt pocket. He sat down on the slab of rock and motioned for me to sit, too. "I always stop here, take a cigarette break, and think."

I sat down. The rock was worn perfectly smooth and was big enough to hold us both.

"Cigarette?" He reached into his pocket.

I just gave him a look, ha ha ha.

"You gave it up? Wish I could. Here." He held out his hand.

It was a piece of candy, a Caramellow, that I love just as much as Miss Bertha does her York peppermint patties. Caramellows are hard to find. I felt less anxious when I bit down into its softness. "Thank you."

"You're welcome. Now, what the devil is it inside that house you want to see?"

"You know that letter that you read and the picture of the man?"

"I remember the letter. Yeah, so?"

"It's just possible it was written by the man in the photo. *Just possible.*" I made it sound as if I didn't want Dwayne to build his hopes up.

He frowned and sucked in on his cigarette. "So what you're saying is you think you know him."

"Know who he is. *Maybe.*" It amazed me that Dwayne didn't ask the next question: who? He must have figured he wouldn't know him anyway, so why ask the name? He was leaning forward, one arm across his knees, chin in the other hand. I kind of copied how he sat, my legs drawn up, my skirt pulled down over my knees. It occurred to me if anyone (my mother, for instance) knew I was out here in the woods with a strange man, she'd be totally horrified. (But what would she do about it?) I could hardly be afraid of Dwayne since I was the one who talked him into coming. Maybe if his mother knew he was out here with me, she'd be horrified too. I felt I should say something else. "It's just a hunch." But it was more than that.

"Most things are."

I had no idea what he meant. Dwayne said strange things a lot of the time that seemed unrelated to what was happening. I would like to talk to him sometime when we hadn't so much to do.

"You finished your smoke break?"

"Yep. You finished your marshmallow break?"

"*Cara*-mallow."

He smiled and crushed his cigarette on the stone, then brushed the bits away.

I couldn't say if the wood was darker than before since whatever light had filtered through the trees had stopped before it hit the ground. Upward it was dark. Except for the squelch of our feet, sounds were blanketed so that the *too-whit* of a barn owl or the scraping of branches or the snap of a twig seemed awfully insubstantial in all of this creaking darkness. He was still checking the undergrowth beside the path.

"How much farther?" I whispered for no reason. I had hold of the hem of Dwayne's bulky wool shirt. When he stopped and knelt down, I did too. He pulled something from a thick bush of mountain laurel, dwarfed I guessed from a lack of light. It was a piece of cloth I saw when he shone the light on it. In this light it was hard to tell the color, though I could see it was dark—dark red or blue, or a kind of plum color. The material was heavy, probably wool. It had been torn off by the small sharp branches; threads had unraveled from one end.

"So what do you think, looking at that?"

I felt complimented that he was asking my opinion—seriously, too, for his expression bore no sign of the usual Dwayne-mockery.

"It's from clothes," I said, "somebody's shirt or dress, maybe."

"Uh-huh. Last month, last year, when?"

I frowned. "When was it caught here, you mean?" He nodded. "Can you tell?"

"Sure, whether it's old or recent. Look at the tear. The threads haven't stiffened up with cold or anything. You can tell that even without a magnifying glass."

"So it's just been torn recently?"

"Recent as a couple of nights ago, maybe."

I handed the bit of cloth back. "Dwayne, that's really jumping to conclusions."

"Sometimes conclusions can't be got at any other way."

It was then I realized that Dwayne was taking this whole thing seriously, that he wasn't seeing it as just some crazy twelve-year-old's notion. He pushed the cloth into his shirt pocket and we walked on, me clutching his shirt again. It wasn't long before I could make out the roots of the big oak, where I'd hidden that first visit, just coming into the edge of the flashlight's light. It seemed months ago, years even.

"You've got to be realistic, Dwayne." This coming from *me*? "It probably doesn't mean a thing."

"Sound and fury is all. That's what Billy Faulkner said about life. Or what Shakespeare said; I believe those were his words, originally."

I was having enough trouble with Faulkner. I didn't want Shakespeare adding to it.

Dwayne stopped and stopped me, too. He put on a listening face, the two of us standing a few feet from the rear door. He shone the flashlight carefully, seeming to walk the light from right to left and back again. Nothing moved, nothing sounded. I wished for some sign of life, even a rabbit scurrying (though I guessed what its fate might be). Both the screen door and the back door protested when Dwayne creaked them open and we went in.

What I noticed first was the scent of grass, the toilet water that first Dwayne and then the Sheriff had opened. This faint scent had escaped the bottle and stayed.

"Dwayne, you smell that?"

He nodded. "Probably from the other night."

I stopped as he had and listened.

"There's no one," he said.

"How do you *know*?"

"Used to be a cat burglar. Come on."

I looked at his back, openmouthed. He was kidding. Wasn't he?

There were two bedrooms we had not paid any attention to before. Dwayne swung the light across the bed, dresser, and bureau. The surfaces were empty of what small items they might have held before:

jewelry, brush, comb, mirror, stuffed animals, a doll. There were no bedclothes except for a blanket folded at the bottom of the bed. The second bedroom was much the same, except here there were curtains at the window and a closet on the side of the dresser. I stayed in the doorway while Dwayne went to the closet and opened it.

Anxiously, I asked. "Are there clothes and stuff in there?"

He shook his head. "Nothin' except a couple worn-out suitcases." He pulled them out; they were cheap plastic or the cardboard that suitcases used to be made of a hundred years ago.

"Come on," I said, "into the other room."

Still looking at the cases, one of which he'd opened—it was empty—he grunted and rose up.

The third bedroom was as we'd left it. The bottle of grass-scented toilet water stood in the same spot, tightly stoppered. The dolls and animals sat back in the same corner. While Dwayne lighted the two thick candles, I headed for the doll Maud had been holding. It was true: the doll was dressed in the white organdy, a little yellowed and stiffened by time, that had made both Iris's and Mary-Evelyn's dresses. The tiny, faded, blue satin flowers were the same ornaments as on the dress that had been Mary-Evelyn's shroud. The fact of this doll was dizzying. I turned away from the night beyond the window full of woe, woeful. I was making way for the blue devils, misery's misery. It was never going to go away. It was the return of the feeling I'd had in the kitchen the day before, and again tonight. I felt the end of something.

"This is it, here." Dwayne was holding the letter he'd read to me, the same letter the Sheriff had read. "You want to read it?"

I shook my head. "You read it."

He read:

> "My dear, I have faith that we will be together again and soon. It has become too much for me and, I'm sure, too much for you. It's better I leave for a little while until this fury quiets down. I suppose a century ago, my faithlessness would have been shouted in all the newspapers!"

"It's signed, 'Your, J.'"

He handed it to me, that and the photograph. "Now here's a guy more interested in saving his own skin than being true to her."

I studied the man in the photograph. There were differences between this picture and the snapshot Aurora had shown me—the color of his hair and the shape of his eyes. The snapshot had been taken in bright sunlight, the hair lighter, the eyes squinting against the sun. In Aurora's picture, he had a hand raised, covering his eyes. But I still was sure that this was Jamie Makepiece, this was he. I think I had found out more than I expected, more even than I wanted to know.

My dear I Have faith that we will be together again and soon.

I didn't make the mistake Dwayne did, only because the "I" meant something to me.

"Dwayne, it's not 'I have faith.' The 'H' is a capital. He's saying to her, 'Have faith.' See?" I handed it back.

Dwayne looked at the script, frowning. "Who's 'I'"?

"Iris or Isabel, and I'd say Iris because I don't think he felt that way about Isabel."

"Who the hell are Iris and Isabel?"

"They were sisters. They were both in love with the same man, him." I held out the picture.

He took it and sat down in the rose slipcovered rocker. His gun was leaning against the side of the chest of drawers. "Which one did he take to?"

"Both."

"Well, hell, there's trouble right there comin' down the road."

"First he was engaged to Isabel, then Iris came along."

He smiled a little. "That sounds romantic: the real thing came along. There's a song goes like that. So he broke off with Isabel and got engaged to Iris."

This butting in annoyed me. "Dwayne, will you let me tell it? This is *my* story." With that momentary irritation I was once again overcome with that feeling of woe. The woe, the sorrow I know was part of the fear. What was coming to an end was my story.

"Sounds like something out of Faulkner." He fingered another cigarette from his pack.

I thought about *Light in August*. "Maybe it does, except they hadn't got in this Lena's, you know, condition."

"What?"

I shrugged. "Her 'condition.'"

"Oh, you mean she was fixing to have a baby. Sometimes I think every woman Faulkner writes about is in that condition." He struck a match, inhaled. "How do you know?"

I frowned. "Huh?"

"How do you know they weren't—or one of them wasn't—in that 'condition'? This Jamie would have to be a hell of a fella if they both were." Dwayne got up. "I'm going out to have a look-see round the house." He picked up the rifle. "I'll be right outside, don't worry."

He left. I followed, all the time thinking.

Was that what it was? Was it only a story?

For what did I really have—as the Sheriff would say—as evidence that they had killed Mary-Evelyn? She drowned in strange circumstances. Things were left unexplained, such as the party dress and her not wearing shoes. But all of Mary-Evelyn's dresses were beautiful; any one of them could have been a dress for a party. As for the shoes, she could simply have removed them because it seemed the natural thing to do if she was going out on the lake in a boat.

It all might be just as Elizabeth Devereau had told the police: they didn't realize until late that Mary-Evelyn wasn't in her bed and had then gone looking for her. It could have happened that way. And did they actually hate her so much? Could Ulub and Imogene have misunderstood what they saw?

And then there was Rose. As beautiful as people say she was, there must've been more than one man to make Ben Queen jealous. But that didn't make any sense if Ben Queen was innocent of her murder. And he was; I was sure of that. It was Fern who had the motive. In this light it made sense: Rose was going to send Fern off to an institution and Fern got in a rage and stabbed her. Over and over, if the accounts were true. Stabbed her the way someone worked up into a crazy frenzy might have done. It made horrible sense. I would have to go back and talk to Louise Landis, who struck me as the person with the most sense in Cold Flat Junction. Only it was tiring, making up reasons for talking to people. Oh, of course I *could* tell the truth about what I was doing. But imagine how they'd react: *Hello, I'm inquiring into a forty-year-old murder of a little girl. And two other murders besides.* Yes, I can just imagine the folks in the Windy Run Diner hearing that.

About Fern's murder. I asked myself if she couldn't just've been going to the Silver Pear; she was all dressed up. Maybe going to the restaurant to meet someone. But there was nothing to show that; the Sheriff had asked everyone in the area around White's Bridge (not that there were many to ask) and no one had seen her. So what made another kind of awful sense was that she was going to meet her daughter and wanted to look her best. After twenty years, her daughter might not have been too impressed. I mean, if Fern just left her child somewhere twenty or so years ago. If she just abandoned her, left her in an orphanage, or worse. I didn't want to think too much about worse. Of course, there were a lot of orphans around and they didn't end up killing their natural parent, if they could even find the parent. There were a lot of blind places in this theory, but all I know is Ben Queen didn't do it, and if he didn't who did? No, it all made awful sense if I was watching a Greek tragedy.

As for the beginning of this, as for Mary-Evelyn Devereau's death: there *was* this doll, this letter, this photograph—and all in a house where there was no reason for them to be. Unless Mary-Evelyn had given Imogene the doll. I didn't think so, but I could always go back and ask Imogene. That still didn't account for the photograph of Jamie Makepiece, or the letter.

What were they doing in Brokedown House?

Dwayne came back. "Ain't nothing around I could see. You find anything else? You're good at finding things, that's for sure."

"No."

"It's about time I took you home."

"Oh." I was surprised at myself that it hadn't occurred to me Dwayne would have to do this. "You don't have to, Dwayne. I can just get a taxi to come to the Silver Pear."

He shook his head. "I'll take you. I figure you been at large enough in the world for one night."

"I'm going to take these things." I picked up the doll, the letter, the picture. "I'm taking these to the Sheriff. It's evidence."

Dwayne considered this as he folded a stick of Doublemint in his mouth and offered a stick to me. "It's some interesting story you cooked up, that's sure."

I felt complimented until I reminded myself I only just told it; I didn't "cook it up." But it *is* my story. I looked at the letter again. "I guess *you* wouldn't do that, I mean save your own skin instead of being true to a girl?"

"I should hope not. 'Course, it'd depend pretty much on the girl, wouldn't it?"

"Now, that doesn't make any sense, Dwayne." He could be so irritating. "If you were *already* involved with this girl."

He picked up his gun. "Boy, you sure are a stickler. Sometimes you're worse than Billy Faulkner, I'd say."

I took that as a compliment, though I didn't know what he was getting at.

———

I didn't mind the walk through the woods going back as much, but then I guess you wouldn't mind having danger behind you instead of before you. On the ride back I said, "What if it was true?"

"What if what was?"

"About Jamie and Iris having a baby."

"You thinking of that little girl that drowned being theirs?"

I nodded. "Maybe."

"For one thing, it'd be one of the most awful things I ever heard of outside of Faulkner."

"I wonder if his stories were true."

"Depends what's meant by 'truth' I guess."

Irritated again, I slid down in my seat. Why did adults have to make so much of a simple question. "You know what I mean. Whether it actually happened to *Lena.*"

He thought this over, then said, "Do you read much?"

"Well, of *course.* I'm reading *Light in August,* aren't I?" Actually, I wasn't, not after those first ten or a dozen pages.

"Haven't you come across characters in books so real they just wander off the page and around town, so to speak?"

I had saved my stick of gum and now unwrapped it. I had to admit Lena seemed to have stepped off the page and onto that dusty country road she meandered along, not unlike the road to Spirit Lake. I could walk along with her, hoping she didn't have that baby then and there with only me around. "Yes. I guess," I answered Dwayne. I thought of what Father Freeman told me about trips in the mind being better, maybe, than trips actually taken. They must have been talking about the same thing. I didn't know whether I believed it, though.

I looked at the doll and imagined Mary-Evelyn holding it while she stared out of her window at the rain-pocked lake and the boat dock on the other shore and imagined escaping. I wondered if Maud, sitting out there on the end of the pier, watching the boats and the water, imagined escaping, too.

I could ask Maud. Mary-Evelyn, I couldn't.

Out of the clouds

46

It did not help my state of mind much to find a note pushed under my door from Will and Mill telling me to come to the Big Garage right after breakfast the next morning. They were like that—or at least Will was—issuing orders when one of their productions was in process ("in rehearsal," Will liked to say). Despite the annoyance of being ordered around and maybe delaying my trip into town, I had to admit I was curious to know what they'd been doing in the garage.

Did they know this note read like a blackmail demand? Like, COME TO BIG GARAGE WITH $10,000 IN SMALL BILLS OR YOU WILL NEVER SEE REE-JANE AGAIN.

Oh, if only it *had* said that! To think I wouldn't have to hand over the ten thousand *and* get what I've always wanted! So I might as well do it, and quick, so I could take my evidence—photo, letter, doll—in to the Sheriff. Not that I expected him to actually do anything; I just wanted some clear thinking brought to bear. I wanted to know if someone agreed with me or thought I was plain crazy.

Walter was at the stove "aproned up" (as he liked to say) when I walked into the kitchen yawning at seven-thirty. He was frying himself eggs and offered to drop one or two in the pan for me.

"But I guess you'll want them buckwheat cakes."

I frowned. "It can't be buckwheat cakes, Walter, as it's too early in the year. You can't get the flour till the fall."

"Don't ask me; someone must've, for there she sets." He pointed his spatula at one of my mother's mixing bowls. It was covered with a damp cloth, which meant the flour was rising, or had already.

I removed the tea towel, and I'd say my eyes lit up, but it was really my stomach that did.

"Miss Jen showed me what to do before she left. It's easy." Walter transferred his eggs to a plate, scooped three pieces of Wonder Bread from the wrapper, and sat down at the serving counter to butter his bread. "I greased up that skillet for you. It's heatin'." He hooked a thumb over his shoulder. The cast-iron pancake skillet sat atop two burners, it was so big.

I looked at the risen dough as if it were Christ himself (and quickly told myself not to make that comparison when Father Freeman was around). When I try to draw up a list of my favorite foods, it never runs up and down, but kind of travels across the page:

Buckwheat cakes Ham pinwheels and cheese sauce Angel Pie
Chocolate Feather Cake

and so on.

Miss Bertha and Mrs. Fulbright completely forgotten (I heard the cane doggedly *tap tap tapping* across the dining room floor), I shook droplets of water on the skillet and watched them dance as if they were happy about the buckwheat cakes too; I then dropped a large dollop of batter in the center and watched it slowly spread. Even in that movement there was something delicious. In a moment the outer edges crisped and shrank and tiny bubbles erupted on the surface of the batter. I waited while more bubbles appeared, until the surface was coated with them before I turned the cake over. The cooked side had that fine-line crazing that you get only on buckwheat cakes, a honey-brown crackle that always reminds me of pottery glaze.

As I slid this cake onto a plate, Walter said, "I warmed up the maple syrup."

The little pan sat on the ledge above the stove, staying warm. I thanked Walter and poured syrup in thin ribbons across the cake. It was real maple syrup, caught in a bucket tied to a tree (or however they caught it), just as this was real buckwheat. Whenever I took my first taste of a buckwheat cake—that incredible mix of sour-sweet—I could almost hear them in the Tabernacle way over across the highway shouting "Hallelujah!" I could also understand why Mrs. Davidow had to have her pitcher of martinis every evening. There are certain things that make you crave more of what you've just had, as if your taste buds suddenly woke up and said, "Gimme!"

By this time, Miss Bertha's non-Hallelujah shouts were coming from the dining room, but I went right on eating. Nothing could get between me and a buckwheat cake.

Walter got up from his stool, said "I'll take the old fool her orange juice," and went on in the dining room with the juice pitcher and two small glasses.

––––––––

Even though I had been told to appear at the Big Garage, I still had to wait through three knockings until the door opened its usual two or three inches, enough for Will's eye to appear at the crack.

"It's me," I said.

"What?" Will's tone was, as usual, suspicious.

"What do you mean, 'what'? *You're* the one who ordered me to come here." This was really irritating. "You wrote that note."

He still hesitated before closing the door enough to remove the chain, then opened it so that I could pass through. I still thought the space he allowed was very stingy. Who in heaven's name were they afraid would see what they were doing?

The Big Garage was like a huge cave with artificial lighting. They loved to fool around with lighting and they had managed to get their hands on some lights from the playhouse on Lake Noir. It was some dumb summer theater with a lot of bad acting. They covered the lights with different colors of crepe paper, today's being blue and green. The effect was eerie and it almost made some of the rafters look like stalactites. At one end of this huge cave was a stage, part of it hidden by several tarpaulins, tented across it. A piano sat near the stage. Mill came out from the tarpaulin tent, hauling a thick rope behind him. I couldn't tell what it was, or what for, which wasn't unusual. He uncoiled it as he walked.

"What's under there?" I asked.

"You don't have to know," said Will. "All you have to do is rehearse your part."

It was my turn to be suspicious. "What part?"

"You know what part. We've already discussed it."

I started to reply when a high voice came from somewhere around the rafters: "Hi, missus!" It was Paul's voice. (Paul called all females "missus," from my mother on down, except for his own mother.)

Paul seemed to be straddling the rafters twenty feet above us. It was hard to see exactly what he was doing, but what difference did that make since I couldn't imagine him up there in the first place. "What's Paul doing up there?"

"He's going to work the clouds."

"The *what?* For God's sakes, are you crazy? He could fall and break his neck! Look how high up that is!"

Will—who had never had any particular interest in Paul's welfare—just shrugged. "We tied him."

"You *tied* him up there?"

"Well, we had to. Otherwise he'd fall off, probably."

Why bother objecting? I shaded my eyes with my hand—as if that would do any good. I could see the pale skin of Paul's legs, the legs swinging away as if he were on a hobby horse. But the rest of him was bathed in this weird green light and his towhead disappeared into the dark shadows. I could also see a few white objects. These, I guessed, must be the "clouds." For a moment, Paul looked like pictures I remembered from an old book about ships. He was the sailor up in the crow's nest. "Clouds," I said. "Clouds."

Mill sniggered and ran down the few steps from the stage and plopped down at the piano. He thumped off a bunch of chords that sounded like an accompaniment through the gates of Hell, which I guessed was appropriate.

Will said, "What he does is, he lets out the string the clouds are attached to so they move along, down in front of you, so when you appear it's just like you came out of the clouds. Pretty neat."

It was not a question. Will was not asking me to attest to the "neatness" of this harebrained idea. If Will said it was neat, it was neat. Then, as my eyes got a little more used to the dark green-blueness of this cave, I repeated, "When I appear? When I appear *where?*"

"See up there? Near Paul?"

I made out a swing—an old-fashioned board-notched-in-rope swing, the sort you see tied to a high tree branch. It was dangling near Paul, up where he was. "So what's that?" As if I had to ask.

"It's the 'machine,' you know, the one God comes down in. Or Zeus, or whoever."

Mill had stopped playing his death march and come over to stand beside us. He said, "The *deus ex machina.*"

Of course he pronounced it wrong—"Do-X-machine"—as we all had been doing. "You mean 'DAY-*us ex* MACK-*in-ah.*'" I must admit I simpered a little when they both looked at me, and repeated the phrase in the labored way one must do with fools and babies. "DAY-us *ex MACK-in-ah.*"

They were both chewing gum, Will slowly, Mill, fast, and they stopped. "Nah," said Will.

I continued laboriously, "Well, go look it up in a Greek dictionary." I did wonder why the proper pronunciation of this seemed to be more important to me than what the *deus* did. "If you think I'm getting on that swing, you're crazy."

"You're going back on our bargain?" said Will. "You swore you'd play a role in this production and we took Jane's car and drove you to White's Bridge. You *promised.* You gave your *word.*"

Will liked to make it sound as if a person's entire value in life was honor, was his word, when actually a person's value was measured in how useful the person was to Will. If Will ever made a promise (which I can't remember if he ever did), he would break it as fast as my mother breaks eggs if it served his purpose.

"I said I'd play a role; I didn't say I'd be willing to go up there in a swing." I looked rafter-ward.

"Hi, missus!" Paul called down again.

"Okay, okay, we'll show you how safe it is. "Let the swing down, Mill."

At that, Mill whistled himself off to some sort of pulley he'd rigged up out of rope, rope cranked around what might have been an old car wheel, and in a minute the swing descended. With a disconcerting tilt and knock when it hit the stage.

"See how simple it is?"

"Sure, without me in it."

"Christ!" said Will, walking over to where Mill and the swing were. I could hear them talking about all of this in low voices. Will got on the swing, then. Mill started cranking away and Will and the swing swayed upward. He shouted to me, "I can't believe you're such a coward."

This insult was, of course, to appeal to my vanity. It didn't. "Well, now you can!"

I could have just turned around and left, but that would be a bad idea because I never knew when I would need their help, and if I didn't do what I promised, they'd never do anything for me again.

Will must have been telling Paul to start moving the clouds around, for as the swing descended, so did two of the clouds. For the clouds it was a much jerkier descent than the swing. The swing didn't look all that dangerous, I told myself. But the idea that Paul—probably the most homicidal person I had ever come in contact with and one who'd grow up to be a serial killer if it was possible to serial-kill people by accident—was up there (tied on or not) manipulating the clouds or anything else having to do with my descent really made me nervous.

The swing tilted when it hit the stage and Will got out. "You see! Would I do it if it wasn't safe?"

"You'd do anything. Both of you are like mad scientists. Paul's one of your experiments."

A huge, dramatic sigh from Will, as he turned, hands on hips and paced back and forth shaking his head. He has always been *so* dramatic.

"I'll go up halfway to see how it feels," I said.

"Good, good!" said Will. "She's going up!" he called over to Mill.

"Good!" said Mill. They were always echoing each other.

Gingerly, I sat myself on the swing, then told Mill to pull it up just clear of the stage, which he did. I bounced on it to see how sturdy, how firmly the plank fit into the rope that curved around it, and decided it was pretty good. Anyway, I guess if the plank fell off I could still cling to the ropes. "Okay," I said. "Slow!" The swing started its ascent and I reminded him to stop in the middle to see how I felt. So he cranked and cranked and didn't stop in the middle (why did I think my orders carried any weight?) although I yelled and yelled, Stop! No one paid any attention. I finally got all the way up to Paul and the clouds, which I think he was trying to slice the top off with a razor. Oh, that was wonderful! Paul was up here with a *razor.*

"I want to go back down. Back down! Right now!"

"Okay, okay!" called Will. "Paul, start lowering the clouds!"

"Hello, missus!" he yelled, as if I were still thirty feet down.

I looked to see if the rope was tight enough around his chest to keep him from leaning any closer to me. "Paul! Don't you *dare* do that!" He was whittling at the rafter with the razor, or maybe it was a pocket knife; it was too green-dim up here to tell. Between his legs sat a brown grocery bag.

"What's he doing?" yelled Will.

"Only cutting up the clouds with his razor !" I was happy to shout back.

Mill yelled at Paul. "Any of those clouds damaged you won't leave here alive, Paul!"

Paul stopped and he laughed.

"I'm lowering the swing, Paul. Understand? *Understand?*"

I heard paper rustle. It must have been the grocery bag. Then as I slowly descended I felt something light falling on my head. I shook myself. Then it was falling all around me, falling thicker. I saw a flurry, what going through a cloud might actually look like.

Flour. I looked back up at Paul just as he was dumping it and got a blast in my face. I was fuming, I was furious. I yelled down, "Damn it! You didn't say anything about flour."

"Yes, I did," Will yelled back. "We had to experiment to see if it added anything, what with the clouds, too."

"Experiment with yourselves!" I said this as the swing dumped me on the stage.

"I don't want to get flour all over me. Boy, do you look funny."

"What's this stupid production *about* that you need to go to these lengths?" I wiped some of the flour from my face. The top of me was pretty much covered in it.

Ordinarily, they wouldn't have answered this question, but perhaps because they'd made a guinea pig of me, they felt they owed me something.

291

Will said, "It a Greek story. It's about Medea. She got jealous of Jason and killed their kids to get back at him. That's just like the Greeks," he added, with a sniff.

"Well, if she murdered them, what's the purpose of the Do-X—I mean *deus ex machina*?"

"We'll think of something."

Now I was really beside myself. "Think of something? You're just going to tack it on at the end? It's because you like it, that's all, even though it serves no purpose. I just went through all of that for no reason *at all.*"

Mill pushed his glasses up his nose with a fingertip. "The Greeks always had a Do-X-machine."

(I noticed he made no attempt whatsoever to pronounce it correctly.)

"It wouldn't be a true Greek tragedy without one. What we really wanted to do was that story about Agamemnon's father and one of his enemies' fathers. See, Agamemnon's father did something, I forget what, so of course the friend's father had to exact revenge. He killed his kids and served them up in a pie."

Will said, "That's a great story. The Greeks were always killing off their kids right and left."

Mill said, "And other family members. They were a really bloodthirsty bunch."

They both sounded as if this was the best news they'd ever heard. I shook my head in disbelief. "So who's playing Medea?"

"June."

My mouth dropped open. "June *Sikes*? You know we're neither of us to have anything to do with her! She's worse than Toya Tidewater."

"No one will recognize her, not in the weird clothes and all that makeup. And the long hair. June's pretty good, actually, the way she handles a knife."

Mill said, "She slits their throats. The kids', I mean."

Will chewed his gum faster, as if the thought excited him. "We've got a lot of fake blood. A lot."

"Who plays the children? How many are there?"

"Two. Paul plays one. But we've got to train him to stay still. We kicked his butt several times."

"Who else?"

They both looked at me and slowly chewed their gum.

My eyes widened and I stepped back. "Oh, no you don't. If you think I'm going to appear on stage with June holding a knife and Paul with a razor—*forget it!*"

As if I'd said nothing at all, Will said, "We got to double up some roles, actors have to be in more than one part. I'm playing Jason and also a Greek messenger."

"Well, you can play the other kid, too." I turned and stomped out. It's hard to look indignant when you're covered with flour.

———

"You musta been up in the Big Garage," said Walter as I fumed into the kitchen.

"How'd you know *that*? Is that towel clean?" I pointed to one in a pile Walter kept near the dishwasher.

"Uh-huh. I know because they ax'd me to do it, come down in that swing thing."

I glared. So I wasn't even the first choice. I rubbed the flour from my face.

Walter went on: "They got Paul up there tied to the roof some way. I ain't seen him for nearly three days and his ma come lookin' for him, but I never said nothin' about where he was."

"You think he's been tied up for *three days*?"

Walter picked a big serving platter from the rinse rack and began drying. "They might of let him down nights. I seen a cot back in a corner I expect they got for Paul to sleep on. Maybe they lock him in."

I shook my head. "They wouldn't do that. Not, mind you, because they're so nice. It's because they'd be afraid to have him around their scenery. He'd ransack the place. You know Paul. He's like Wile E. Coyote only without the brains."

Walter placed the platter with the other dry dishes and said maybe I was right. I asked if I'd got all the flour off and Walter said yes, and I went to call a taxi.

Deputy Dawg
47

With the evidence on the seat beside me in a gym bag, I leaned back and closed my eyes and hoped Delbert wouldn't talk all the way into town.

"You fixin' to see Sam?"

I had told him to drop me at the courthouse. "Yes."

"I think maybe he ain't there."

I didn't comment.

"Thing is, he got his hands tied with all that's been happening. That murder you know."

I clinched my eyes shut. "I know. Well, if he's not there, I'll wait."

" 'Course he might just've stepped across to the Rainbow, him and Donny. Donny loves Shirl's doughnuts."

I sat silently, willing him to shut up.

"On the other hand, Donny'd more'n likely know where Sam's at."

Sliding down in my seat, I plugged my ears with my fingers. I wondered if there was ever a cab driver in any Greek tragic play. Probably not, but there must have been an equivalent. If it were China, it might have been a rickshaw operator. I could hear Delbert even over my stopped-up ears.

"There's the Teets's place, so we're almost there." He nodded toward a big yellow house behind us now. What was he saying all this for, talking as if I were a stranger to La Porte? Finally, finally, he pulled up in front of our grand white courthouse and I gave him the fare, hauled myself out of the cab, and fled. He was still talking.

Donny sat at the Sheriff's desk, leaning back in the creaking, leather-cushioned swivel chair. He always did this when the Sheriff wasn't around, as if he, Donny, were the law in La Porte. "Sam ain't here, he's out at Lake Noir. He pronounced it 'Nor,' as did most people. Having myself learned *deus ex machina,* I could certainly "N'wah."

"I'll wait."

"For God's sakes, girl, he could be out there for hours."

"Then I'll wait for hours." It was now a point of pride that I not move from this chair. I knew it would be really hard not to go across to the Rainbow for some chili. It was way after lunchtime and I didn't know how long I could hold out. I had never been tested in this way, what with my mother's cooking always available. That made me wonder if they had started back from Florida. Which day was it? I hoped I could get to the Pink Elephant in time to say good-bye to my dancing partner and the staff of the Rony Plaza. These thoughts held me for a while—dreaming on palm trees—and I didn't bother commenting when Donny said "Suit yourself."

He didn't want me waiting because he didn't want me to know how little there was for him to do. For a while he stayed in the swivel chair, opening and closing drawers with a yank and a shove, as if whatever he was looking for better give itself up. Then he got up and swaggered around, his thumbs hooked into his Sam Brown belt, one close to his holster to impress on me how dangerous he could be. This all went on for a good ten minutes.

It's best, I've found, to remain silent with someone you can't stand so that they just fizzle out or give up. But it's so hard to follow my own advice. "Don't you have anything to do?" I just couldn't resist it.

At that he swung around from where he'd been messing with Maureen's In and Out boxes. "I got puh-*lenty* I ought to be doing but Sam wants somebody here, in the office, case he needs backup." He adjusted the holster looped over his belt, adjusted his gun, adjusted his height. He managed to stretch himself an inch taller by leaning over slightly backwards.

"Backup for what? Has he gone after the killer?"

Donny paused. "Could be." He narrowed his eyes in a threatening manner, or at least what he thought was such a manner.

"No, it couldn't. He doesn't know who killed her. Fern Queen," I added, as if he might have forgotten.

His eyes got even more squinty looking. "And just how do you know *that?*"

"I know."

Donny half sat his butt on the Sheriff's desk and fake-laughed. "You know somethin', Emma, you always have been too big for your britches. Think you know everything. Hell, you're but twelve years old, chrissakes."

Maybe I'd tell the Sheriff Donny worked the Devil and Jesus Christ into the same sentence that he said to a twelve-year-old. I stuck my tongue in my cheek.

"You don't know *nothin'*!" he said.

It all sounded so much like Ree-Jane, just the kind of thing she'd say. How pathetic that an officer of the law couldn't come up with better put-downs. "Well, I know more than you do."

Now he was up and stalking about, as if that would give his reply more weight. Only, he couldn't think of anything to say. He sat down again and pushed a few of the items on the desk around and started talking about their search for Ben Queen.

"We catch him and put him away, you got a dead man walking." Donny looked at me, looked pleased with himself that he'd come up with something that might scare me.

I made my face expressionless and didn't comment.

"You know what that means, I guess. Dead man walking?"

I could tell he was irritated I didn't ask.

"Means when a killer's going to his execution," he said. "When he's walking that last mile, so to speak. Guards call out 'Dead man walking!' Yep, that's what's comin' down the pike for ol' Ben Queen!" He smiled, showing a bottom row of crooked teeth.

He had sensed something—I guess the word is "intuited" something—of the way I felt about Ben Queen. It was then I realized that Donny was like Ree-Jane in this respect: he had a way of ferreting out the beliefs that kept a person going—like Ree-Jane knew I did not want to know the report in the newspaper about the death of Fern Queen, and so proceeded to read it to me. It was this uncanny grasp of what was important to me that had her figuring out ways to get at me; it had nothing to do with being clever. No, it was like they'd both received the same blessing from Hell.

Had this been Ree-Jane talking, I would have thought up rejoinders that would really get her goat. But Donny wasn't worth the thinking up. Donny was not a constant thorn in my side; he was by way of being an occasional mosquito bite. Still, he got to me. It was important not to let it show in my face or voice, but I felt I had at least to stick up for Ben Queen. "How do you know he did it?"

Donny had risen again to go to Maureen's desk for nothing in particular and now he swaggered back to the Sheriff's swivel chair and re-sat himself, fake-laughing as he did this. "How do I *know?* Plain as the nose on your face. Right after he gets free of prison, another family member gets murdered, which is exactly what got him twenty years in jail. That time it was the wife he murdered. Now, don't that strike you as just too much of a coincidence?"

"No. It's a coincidence, but not too much of one. You think maybe it's just a habit Ben Queen got into—killing off family?"

This irritated Donny no end. "What're you talkin' about? You don't know one damn thing about it."

"Sure I do." I still kept my face and voice expressionless. Your expression and your voice, those are the dead giveaways to a person who's trying to undermine you. I'd had lots of practice at this sort of thing; I pretty much had to know it to survive.

Well, Donny just didn't know how to handle my being so cocksure. He stared at me, then he pointed his finger at me. "I can't hardly wait to tell Sam he's been barking up the wrong tree."

"What tree's that?"

Donny snatched up this question, which betrayed my ignorance, finding in it an opportunity for sarcasm: "With you and him being such friends and all? You don't know what Sam thinks about all this?"

Again, it was the brand of sarcasm Ree-Jane stooped to. Then it suddenly struck me—it was the strangest sensation—that Donny was jealous of my friendship with the Sheriff. So I said that: "You're jealous."

Well, at that he looked like he'd turned to wax (his natural coloring, only not usually hardened into immobility). He couldn't think of a response weighted enough to do justice to what I'd said. Finally, after a few moments of pursed-mouthed movements, he blurted out, "Of you? I'm jealous of *you*?"

He made sounds, blubbered his lips, shook his head. Finally, he came up with, "Okay, you just take care of things here while I go across the street and get me a cup of coffee and a doughnut. Anyone stumbles in here bleeding or shot, you just take care of him. If the mayor calls about the budget, you can fill him in, too." Donny grabbed up his black-visored cap and snapped it on his head.

"Sure," I said. "If the Sheriff comes back I'll just tell him you left me in charge while you went for coffee."

For a flicker of time he looked frightened, his water-colored irises freezing up, congealing. But all he did was give me a flip of the hand, as if he were done with answering fools. He walked out.

I moved over to one of the windows that looked out on the street and across to the Rainbow Café and watched. Donny was in the middle of the street stopping the one approaching car. He just thrust his arm out, palm flat against space, as if he were a comic-strip hero like Superman. He strutted on. There was only this single car, and he couldn't even wait for it to go by. Why did the Sheriff keep him on? Maybe because no one wanted the job of "deputy." Was he good at anything? Paperwork? Organizing?

I turned and looked across the room at the banks of file cabinets. Did Donny realize he'd left me alone with all of their reports?

The drawers were arranged first according to the violation; second, alphabetically. There were a lot of drawers, the cabinets stacked with a row on the bottom and one on top. Two of the bottom drawers, the ones at the end, were devoted to old cases. They went decades back, back to the 1920s. These files were pretty scruffy and stuffed in without much care taken and little arrangement. On the tabs were written what I guessed was the key word in each case, or the key name. I went through them quickly. Towards the back was a file marked "Devereau." I yanked it out.

I was not prepared for the pictures; it hadn't occurred to me there would be any, but of course it was logical that there would be. Two of Mary-Evelyn's face, two of her face and torso, one of her whole water-logged body.

And then I realized that I had never seen her except in the snapshot taken of the sisters in the shadowy vicinity of the porte cochere. I had made her up in my mind, building on what I could see of her in the snapshot. In some ways I had caught her, in other ways, missed her completely. But then the girl in these pictures was dead.

I took the doll out of my gym bag, smoothed its dress and held it next to the picture that showed Mary-Evelyn's dress most clearly. Though the wetness of it had turned it dark in places, there was no mistaking the clothes were the same. The same dark little handsewn flowers marched down the front.

Statements made by the Devereau sisters: that's what I wanted to read. Elizabeth, the oldest, told the sheriff (a man named Win Whittle, back then): "We dined at the usual time—seven—after which Mary-Evelyn went to her room and, we supposed, to bed."

I frowned over the 'we supposed.' Was Mary-Evelyn allowed to drift around like a little pile of leaves, with no one knowing what she did or where she blew? And besides, how could she have gone to bed so early? For they couldn't have spent more than a half hour or forty-five minutes eating dinner. (With me, ten minutes would do it.)

I set aside Elizabeth's statement temporarily and went to Isabel's. Her statement matched Elizabeth's, and added a little more. Neither did she know how Mary-Evelyn had slipped out at some point in the night. "After dinner, Elizabeth played the piano and I sang; we often do this in the evening. Iris was in her room, sewing. We have no idea why the child walked to the other side of the lake and took out that rowboat. Why on earth would she do that? She never liked to swim or have much to do with water sports. But she did, and that was that," Isabel's statement read. "Iris woke us sometime much later, around midnight, I think. She told us Mary-Evelyn wasn't in her bed."

I turned to Iris's statement: "I sleep poorly. That night I was up late sewing. I'm a dressmaker. I found I needed some material that I'd shown to Mary-Evelyn for a new dress I was making her, and remembered I'd left it with her. So I went across to her room."

If she went "across" that meant the room exactly opposite was Iris's. I remembered the rooms, how the second floor was laid out.

"That's when I discovered she was gone," Iris continued. "Her

299

bedspread wasn't turned down and her pajamas were under her pillow. She was gone."

Elizabeth: "We dressed and we went looking for her. We searched the grounds around the house and when we didn't find her, we searched the woods. It was a black night and we had only hurricane lamps and a flashlight."

Isabel: "When we went up to bed, about nine it was, Mary-Evelyn was in her room, lying on the bed, reading. The door was open; we always insisted she keep the door open."

(Imagine. *Imagine.* Never to have any privacy, always to have to be public. That might have killed her if the water hadn't. It certainly would kill me.)

What I wondered was, if Mary-Evelyn's room was across the hall from Iris's and both doors were open, then how could Mary-Evelyn have sneaked out without being seen? I remembered the room that was Iris's; I closed my eyes and pictured the furniture. Besides a bed and dresser, hadn't there been an easy chair near the door of the room? And a sewing machine? I had concentrated on Mary-Evelyn's room and hadn't paid much attention to the other bedrooms, other than to just give them a quick look. The easy chair, I thought, could be seen through the open door, which must mean Iris would be able to look into Mary-Evelyn's room. I would have to go back there and look. For if this were true, there is no way Iris would have failed to see Mary-Evelyn leaving her room.

I was disgusted with this Sheriff Whittle. You could only believe the sisters' accounts if it was too much trouble *not* to believe them. The Sheriff—my Sheriff, that is—would have punched the living daylights out of the Devereau sisters' statements. Their story made me wonder, too, why they hadn't gone to more trouble over the details of Mary-Evelyn leaving the house. And why hadn't they questioned Mary-Evelyn's getting in that boat, if she was afraid of water? After all, she wouldn't be around to contradict them. She wouldn't be around for anything anymore.

The answer, I guess, is that they didn't think their version of events would be questioned, no matter how fickle it sounded, and they were right. They were right. It all made me feel like crying.

I looked at the photographs again, wishing I could see Mary-Evelyn's eyes, the eyes that were lost in shadow on the snapshot. But the eyes were closed. Her face was kind of heart-shaped, a valentine face. She had freckles across the bridge of her nose, not going wild over her whole face, as if even the freckling had been kept within strict boundaries. I rolled up the photograph and walked over to Maureen's desk to get a rubber band to hold it. It fit into my gym bag easily. That I shouldn't be stealing police documents was perfectly clear to me and perfectly meaningless. I stopped short of taking the entire file, settling for using the copy-maker in the room. I copied the sisters' statements and also the doctor's report, Dr. McComb's. There wasn't anything in it that would throw light on the case; he had already told me pretty much what was in his report. But I thought I would show it to him and see if it jogged something loose in his memory. I stared at the copier as it *whicked* away. It was very slow. When I had all of the sheets I wanted, I put the originals back into the folder and the folder back into the file cabinet, where it had been before.

Where was Donny? I'd had the file open for forty-five minutes or so. Not that I wanted to see him; I wondered if the Sheriff knew he left the office for long periods of time. Or that he left the office in the hands of someone who might want to go over police reports.

I sat down again to wait for the Sheriff. The office was strange with no one in it. Hanging on the opposite wall were framed pictures of the police forces in neighboring towns. These consisted of two policeman in Hebrides, eight in Cloverly (where the Davidows went for their clothes). The pictures must have been turn-of-the-century, for the unsmiling men were dressed in heavy, old-fashioned uniforms and several of them had handlebar moustaches. (This was a fad I was very glad had gone out of fashion.) The Sam Brown belts across the dark, heavy material seemed wider than the ones today.

In the room were four desks, the fourth minus anyone to sit at it. I guessed this desk was for the extra deputy that the Sheriff hadn't acquired because the mayor wouldn't allocate the money.

My head felt leaden. I must have dozed off. Was it dusk already? The light at the window had turned as gray as granite, and seemed heavy, too. Then I must have slept a second time, but surely not for more than a minute. What dragged me awake was the advancing voices. What time was it? I looked wildly around. Was it dinnertime?

301

Inadmissible evidence

48

The door to the office opened and the Sheriff walked in, followed by Donny, who was in the middle of bragging about how he'd "cuffed" the Snavely boys that morning.

"Emma?" The Sheriff was taken aback. It was hard to take him by surprise, but my being there certainly did.

"You still here, for God's sake?" Donny said. A look from the Sheriff cut him short. "She's been here all afternoon. I told her you were over White's Bridge way."

"I was just waiting. There's something important I need to talk to you about," I said, holding up my gym bag.

The Sheriff turned on Donny. "You left her *alone*? Now, listen up, Donny: you don't leave this office when somebody's in it, and for God's sake, you don't leave *Emma* alone in it."

I considered. There were two ways of taking what the Sheriff just said: one way was that he was concerned for my safety. I might be here alone when there was a jail break (the jail being on the opposite side of the building) and the escaping prisoners would find me here and hold me hostage. The other way of taking the Sheriff's order was that he didn't trust me around the filing cabinets. I guess I'd have to go for the second interpretation, since he was right.

He had by now removed his cap and uniform jacket and had sat down. He motioned me over to the chair beside his desk. "Must be *really* important if you waited all this time."

I looked over to see what Donny was doing. He was at his own much smaller desk and was pretending to be busy pulling out drawers and taking files out. What he was really doing was listening. I shifted around so my back was to him and whispered to the Sheriff, "In here—" I unzipped my gym bag. "—is evidence." I pulled out the letter, the photo, the doll.

Frowning, the Sheriff picked up each in turn. "I've seen these things before, haven't I? In that old Calhoun cottage?"

"Brokedown House," I said, nodding.

Donny just couldn't resist getting in on things. "You talking about that old falling-down place near Butternut's?" Now he was out of his chair, moving toward the Sheriff. "Ain't nobody lived there for years, not since old man Calhoun moved out. You recall him, Sam—"

"Donny. You were supposed to check out that fracas at the Red Barn. And that complaint from Asa Ledbetter about someone messing with his stock. Have you done it?"

"Well, I was just about to when—"

The Sheriff tossed him the keys to the cruiser. "Good. So do it."

"It's almost six—"

"We don't keep regular hours, Donny. You want a nine-to-five, get a job at the Second National."

It was so much a point for my side, I didn't even bother gloating.

"I'll say one thing," said Donny. "She tells you anything that trans-pired here before I left, you better take it with a grain of salt, hear?"

How stupid of him. He'd just let the Sheriff know, just with that comment, that something had "trans-pired" which would put Donny in a bad light.

"See you later, Donny."

Donny, unhappy, left.

"Okay. Now what were you doing in that Calhoun house? You aren't going over there alone?"

"No, of *course* not. I was with—Mr. Butternut." Something kept me from saying Dwayne Hayden.

"Same thing. What about these things?"

"The doll is wearing a dress like Mary-Evelyn Devereau's the night she drowned. I mean—what's that word the police and papers use when they can't come right out and accuse someone?"

"'Allegedly'?"

"That's right. Allegedly drowned."

The Sheriff looked surprised. "You're saying she didn't?"

"I'm saying she didn't." I weighted the words.

"A doctor has to sign a death certificate," said the Sheriff, "and drowning is pretty easy to identify. Especially when you take the body out of a lake."

I wasn't in the mood for his smile (for once). "It shows she drowned, but not where."

Puzzled, he said, "You're saying she drowned somewhere *else*?" He leaned forward, as if getting closer to me might explain me.

"If somebody held your head under water, it could look like you drowned, couldn't it?"

Leaning back in his swivel chair, he nodded, but his eyes widened.

"When they put her in that boat she was already dead."

Never had I seen the Sheriff appear so astonished. His chair crashed forward. "*What?* You think the Devereau women killed that little girl?"

Since I had just said it, I sat there.

"*Why?* Why would they do such a thing?"

I shrugged. "I don't know, yet. I know they hated her, is all. I know from what Ulub said. He used to do odd jobs for them." From his expression, I could tell the Sheriff might be just as suspicious of Ulub's brainpower as most other people around here. "Ulub said he was looking through a window one night when he'd been raking leaves and saw Mary-Evelyn playing the piano and crying. The sisters were eating dinner. She wasn't allowed to eat dinner with them that night. She was being punished. If nothing else, I think playing the piano is a funny way to punish somebody, don't you?" But I could tell the Sheriff wasn't putting much stock in what Ulub might say, and that made me angry. But I tried not to let it show. I tried not to get emotional, since emotions weren't convincing. "You probably don't think you can believe what Ulub and Ubub say; but I know them better than you. They're perfectly sensible and sane. Then there's Imogene Calhoun."

The Sheriff sat back. I must be switching topics too fast for him. He said, "You mean the ones who lived in that cottage?"

I nodded. "Imogene lives in Cold Flat Junction. When she was ten or eleven, she'd go with her sister Rebecca to the Devereau house. She told me how they mistreated Mary-Evelyn. Things like they wouldn't let her feed her kitten. And other things."

Instead of being shocked, he pondered. "But if this Imogene was only a little girl then, could she have misunderstood—?"

I shot out of my chair. "You don't know anything about all of this and you're already arguing *against* it! Why? It's not as if you'd given Mary-Evelyn Devereau any thought because you haven't. I pointed at the filing cabinets. "There's old cases in there. I'll bet, I'll *bet* one of them's Mary-Evelyn's. You don't have any *history*. For you, they were just born yesterday. They came and went in an eye blink. But you're wrong. *They'll be around forever.* You're wrong about Ben Queen, too. He never killed his daughter Fern."

As if he'd only been waiting for this topic to arise, the Sheriff said, "What do you know about Ben Queen? What haven't you told me?"

I was still standing. "You haven't heard a thing I've said. All you want to know is stuff that you think will be more evidence for what *you* believe. As for *my* evidence, I'm taking it with me." I picked up what I'd brought and shoved it back in my gym bag and walked to the door. But before leaving, I said, "You're wrong about Ben Queen; you're wrong about him killing Rose. And you're dead wrong about him murdering Fern Queen. I know who killed her." I yanked the door open.

The Sheriff had risen when I left his desk. "Who did, then?"

I turned. "Her daughter." I added, "If you ever read a Greek play, you'd understand. Good-bye."

Hell-bent

49

Her daughter.

Saying it out loud made me shiver in the icy light that looked more moon than sun. But who else could she be but Fern's daughter? The Girl looked exactly like Rose Devereau, to go by Jude Stemple's description of Rose. Fern, the mother, was a plain woman, and this was a case of what I guess is called beauty skipping a generation. It had skipped out on Fern altogether.

And Ben Queen was protecting the Girl, just as he'd protected Fern and kept her from the jail sentence he then had to serve. I remembered what he'd said when I told him that night I'd seen this Girl:

> "Maybe this girl you saw, or thought you saw, maybe she was just a figment of your imagination."

He was pretending not to believe the Girl was his own grand-daughter; I was pretending to believe he was right, when both of us knew who she was or, at least, *that* she was. He knew either that she'd shot Fern Queen or that she could be blamed for it. But *why* the Girl had shot Fern—it must've been revenge for being abandoned.

I thought all of this as I was making for the Rainbow Café, for I wanted to talk to a sympathetic person. My anger at the Sheriff had not lessened one whit, but what added to it, or was maybe a feeling riding sidesaddle with it, was the misery at being let down. He had *really* let me down. Ben Queen had made me feel just the opposite when he'd said, *If it goes too hard on you, turn me in.*

The Sheriff, I thought, as I walked through the door of the Rainbow, had done just that—had ratted on me, had told the enemy where I was, had broken faith, had let me down. Had turned me in.

I sat down in the back booth. In a couple of minutes, Maud came back carrying a cherry Coke to where I sat with my head in my hands. She sat down and placed her cigarettes on the table, as usual. When I said nothing but a mumble she tapped the pack and slid out a cigarette, lit it, and gave me time.

When the squall of tears started I dug the heels of my palms into my eyes to stop their flow, but of course, I couldn't. Tears have a life of their own and pay no attention to whether you want them or not, or whether they'd embarrass you or not.

Maud went off; when she came back, she set something before me. I looked through my fingers to see if it was a bowl of chili, but it was only a glass of water, so I dug my hands into my eyes again. Finally, I raised my head and shook and shook it and the tears weren't so much falling as flying off my face.

Maud handed me a handkerchief that looked so fresh and new I didn't want to dirty it, though I did dab at my eyes with it; for nose-blowing I yanked a paper napkin from the stainless-steel holder on the table.

She put an arm around my shoulders and said—as if it would be a real comfort to me—"Sam just walked in."

What? I looked up to see him nodding to friends along the counter as he passed it. Then I grabbed up the glass of undrunk water and tossed half of it on my eyes, and, no longer caring about the new hand-kerchief, I wiped it all over my face. I yanked out a menu and was studying it hard when the Sheriff came up to the booth and said hello.

I did not return this greeting, as I had to begin not speaking to him sometime and it might as well be now. I read the menu.

He sat down opposite me. "Emma," was all he said and he said it very nicely.

With my eyes still on the menu and aware that my T-shirt was sopping wet, and also aware that it was nearly six-thirty and Miss Bertha might be banging her cane on the dining room floor at any minute, I said, "I believe I'll have a bowl of chili."

"Sure," said Maud, who got up before I could stop her. The chili hadn't been a good idea, as it would mean I'd be left alone with the Sheriff. I looked up at the slow-circling ceiling fan.

"I'm sorry, Emma, sorry I hurt your feelings."

My *feelings*? I just sat looking at him, mouth agape. He thought all that I had said was nothing at all; his concern was not for what I'd told him, but only for my feelings about what I'd told him. He didn't care about what I knew (for he probably didn't think I knew anything), but for what I felt. Unused to having my feelings considered, I suppose I should have been grateful. Only I wasn't.

"It's not my *feelings*," I finally said. "My *feelings* were only because you didn't even take in what I was telling you." I pulled my gym bag up from the seat beside me and set it on the table. "You didn't give a thought to this."

"Look, Emma—"

I heard him dismissing it all over again.

"Look: this half-a-century-old Devereau business that for some reason you're hell-bent on solving surely can't have anything to do with the murder of Fern Queen."

It was just too much. "How do you *know* that? You haven't talked to people like I have."

"This is important, Emma. This isn't a game. Where did you see Ben Queen?"

I just stared. He was doing exactly the same thing again. On top of that, he was accusing me of thinking it was all a game. A *game!* If Ben Queen had been the shadow on the wall behind him, I wouldn't have pointed it out.

Maud returned with my chili. "Good Lord but you two look grim. What's going on?"

I would not be so babyish as to "tell" on the Sheriff. I was not even going to produce the doll, which Maud had held and would remember, for what good would it do unless I produced one of the police photos to show her it was the same dress? Even then, what conclusions would she draw from it, knowing as little as she did about the Devereaus and Mary-Evelyn. No, it was my story and I was stuck with it. "Is it six-thirty yet?" I asked.

"Not quite. Have you got dinner guests?"

"Yes. I'm sorry, but I won't have time to eat the chili."

"Don't worry about it. You go on. What's in the gym bag?"

I didn't answer; I looked at the Sheriff.

He said, "This child is hell-bent on getting into big trouble. You might even call it obstruction of justice."

I slid across the seat of the booth, hauling my bag with me. "Obstruction of something, maybe, but not justice."

I was enormously pleased that this was my exit line. My head up, I walked out of the Rainbow, haughty and hell-bent.

She's Medea

50

I apologized to Walter, who was set to take in Miss Bertha's V8 cocktail (into which I usually shook a few drops of Tabasco sauce because I liked the way her mouth pursed up when it hit). Tonight was meat loaf again, and I couldn't think of anything I could do to Miss Bertha's portion. I had overworked my mind today and I guess it balked. Standing at the serving counter, looking at the harmless meat loaf and pan of gravy, I asked Walter could he come up with anything?

He was silent, thinking. Most people have no patience with Walter but I do, as I think he makes a good accomplice. Also, he can share the blame, or even take the whole of it. He never rats on a person.

"Well," he finally said, "there's them mushrooms still. You could put them in that gravy. Miss Bertha hates mushrooms."

"Except I used the mushrooms once, don't you remember?"

"How about I make her an omelette and you use some of that Spanish sauce (tomato sauce with diced up vegetables) and cut up one of them hot peppers—" Walter had left his dishwashing station to root in the refrigerator. He drew out a small can. "These is hot as blazes. I know because Will tricked Paul into eating one. Paul run around like a house on fire."

"Paul does that anyway. Walter, that's a great idea. I'll just dice one up if you make the omelette. I'll take in their V8 juice and tell her."

Walter reached in for the eggs and I went to the dining room, set down the juice, and said to Miss Bertha that as tonight was meat loaf and she didn't like it, we were making her an omelette. Mrs. Fulbright heartily approved of this idea when Miss Bertha didn't do anything but go "umpf." Mrs. Fulbright, of course, preferred the meat loaf; it was a favorite of hers.

"I want a *Spanish* omelette," said Miss Bertha.

Oh, how wonderful! I told her absolutely, she'd get a Spanish omelette.

Returning to the kitchen, I told Walter. He gave his choking kind of laugh and drew his spatula carefully through the eggs, just as my mother does. As the omelette cooked, I chopped up a hot pepper and tossed it in the sauce Walter had heated. Then I fixed Mrs. Fulbright's plate, tossing a plump morsel of parsley on the meat loaf. Walter whisked the omelette onto a plate. I poured the doctored Spanish sauce over it.

"You make a beautiful omelette, Walter," I said.

"I watched Miss Jen do it enough times I got it memorized. You ought to tell Miss Bertha not to drink any water to try and cool things down as that only makes it worse. I read that somewheres."

So dinner went off without a hitch. I mean, from Walter's and my point of view. Miss Bertha nearly fell out of her chair when she got her first taste of that jazzed up sauce and I enjoyed patting her back (or her hump, I guess) and saying I had no *idea* Spaniards liked things so hot. She was shouting she was on fire. I shoved her water glass closer to her.

There was nothing else I could do, so I let Mrs. Fulbright handle things. She was waving her lacy handkerchief uselessly in front of Miss Bertha's mouth when I returned to the kitchen.

Because I was upset with the Sheriff, I didn't have much of an appetite and ate only one helping of everything, except of course the Spanish sauce. Dessert was Peach Blossom Pie, one of my mother's cloudlike confections the color of the sun coming up over the Rony Plaza's stretch of beach, just that first flush of rosy-gold fast disappearing. Tiny bits of peach and pecans were scattered through the meringue crust.

Walter, who'd been standing with an ear against the dining-room swinging door, now joined me at the kitchen table for the pie. "*Um-umm!*" he said, taking a bite of the pie.

"Unbelievable," I said, taking one too.

———

There was another note under my door:

Rehearsal after dinner

Not *again!* I groaned. Why did I need a rehearsal, anyway? I didn't have words to say. All I was supposed to do after I got down to the stage was get off the swing and bop Medea with my silver wand. This sounded a lot more like Cinderella's fairy godmother than a *deus ex machina*. I told Will. He replied that they were taking certain "liberties" with the original. I could imagine. I didn't bother asking him if they'd even read it.

I had agreed I'd play a role. In return for them driving me to White's Bridge, I had to do this. Considering how much I'd learned as a result of that first visit, I guess getting flour thrown on me wasn't too much to ask. I tied a scarf around my head and pulled it forward a bit over my eyes to keep as much off me as possible.

Tonight in the cave of the Big Garage, instead of blue and green lights slicing the darkness there were pink and gold cones passing back and forth across the garage, something like pictures you see of Hollywood premieres. There had to be someone making them move. "Who's up there?"

"Chuck."

Chuck was a boy maybe a year older than me and really dumb. He was good at following directions and that made him useful to Will and Mill, more useful than he ever was to his family. Will and Mill loved nothing more than giving directions.

"Hi, missus," yelled Paul.

Will called up to Chuck: "Try the blue and green . . . let's put them all on just to see." He turned to me. "Go up there and stand." He gestured toward the stage.

"Why?"

"Do you have to question everything?"

"Yes, if it comes from you. And where's Medea? If this is a rehearsal, why isn't she here?"

"She's coming. Go *on*." He gave me a little shove.

I clambered up to the stage and turned and saw watery reaches of pink and gold, blue and turquoise, their paths crossing and in combination creating even more color. It was probably very pretty from out there, but with these colors crossing and recrossing my face, I felt a little seasick. Will called up to douse the blue and green for a while. I wondered what I looked like in this eerie light.

June Sikes was, I guess, what you'd call hard-pretty, the kind of prettiness you'd find in a woman whose past was a little too full. She wore so much makeup it was difficult to tell just how much was her and how much was added color. She had walked in a moment ago and was stopped now by Will's side.

"Where's my costume?"

Changing her clothes (Marge Byrd once told me) was pretty much all June Sikes was good at.

Will had gone off and was back now with June's "costume." This Medea-gown looked familiar to me, though I couldn't for the life of me think where I'd seen it. It was really pretty—a flow of dark blue tulle shot through with silver and a satin top.

Then, suddenly, I recognized it. It had belonged to one of the Waitresses and had been, when they'd worked here, my favorite article of clothing. They must have left it in a storage room over the kitchen, and I couldn't understand why I'd never seen it. June Sikes wearing it! I wanted to fall on her and rip her eyes out, even though it hadn't been her choice.

That the Waitresses had years ago left this gown behind and I hadn't seen it, hadn't known it was there in that storage room where I go far more often than Will and Mill—that this dance dress should hang now on the back of June Sikes—was too much after all of the disappointments of the day. *No!* June was *not* going to wear this particular memory! But I would have to pretend this wasn't important to me. I thought for a moment and frowned at Will and said, "Medea wouldn't wear that."

Will, who was not as sure of things as he appeared to be, asked, "Why?"

"It's too dark. The Greeks almost always wore *white.* You ought to know that if you're putting on a Greek *play.*" My mind was outracing my words. I tried to be casual. "I know just the thing. Give me that dark dress and I'll go get it." I held out my arm.

"No," said Will. "Get it first."

How stupid! "Okay." I walked out of the Big Garage and ran all the way to the Pink Elephant, pulled Ree-Jane's white gown off the hanger, and ran back to the Big Garage. I slowed down for the last little way, not wanting to appear hurried.

Will looked at the white dress and shrugged. "It's okay with me. But where'd you get it?"

"Nowhere in particular," I answered, as I exchanged the white dress for the midnight blue one.

June went off to a dark corner and changed clothes. She came back. Ree-Jane's white gown was too long for her and too tight across the top, making her look mummified. But I guess she was so pleased to have a fancy dress to wear on stage she didn't much care. "Where's a mirror? Have I got this on right?"

I assured her she did. There wasn't a mirror.

She went traipsing around holding the skirt bunched so she wouldn't trip. I did not make the point that she couldn't do this the night of the performance because she might insist on having the blue dress back again. I decided to take the blue dress out of harm's way and rushed back to the Pink Elephant, where I put it on the hanger and the hanger on a hook in the wall. I stood back and looked at it. Once, they had dressed me up in it and danced me around the room. The Waitresses. They flashed in and out of memory like sunlight striking the turquoise ocean along the shore of the Rony Plaza, for what I recall mostly about them is their color: their bright clothes, their glossy red and blond and dark hair. I closed my eyes.

Once I had asked my mother whether they were good waitresses. "Oh, they were all good waitresses, I expect, but silly girls."

Silly girls. I do remember they were always laughing. They put on records and danced me around. My mother didn't know how much time I spent with them, since she would have stopped it. She did not care for our befriending the "help."

If my days now are mostly black and white, the days of the Waitresses were technicolor. For before they left, everything, I sense, was different: my father was still alive, my mother did not have to work so hard, the Davidows were unknown. Imagine! Imagine a time without Ree-Jane. It was almost impossible to, for Ree-Jane is one of those people you must have around to test yourself on. I sometimes wonder: without her, would I have been up to a challenge?

June was up onstage, and Will was calling for Paul to come down and to be careful doing it. I could see him up there maneuvering from rafter to swing, the rope around his middle in case he fell. Thank goodness for that. I think his foot slipped once on the rafter. But he managed to get into the swing, and Mill told him to untie the rope so the swing could be lowered onto the stage.

Will said, "You go stand beside June."

"Hi, missus," Paul said to June. She didn't answer.

I asked, "What's he going to do?"

"Nothing. It's not a speaking part."

"Well, what's he going to be, then?"

"He's one of Medea's kids."

I looked around. "Where are the others? Because I'm not going—"

Will crinkled up his forehead in exasperation. "Oh, relax, will you? Since you were so testy about playing one of them, we rewrote. In our rewrite, the other kids are dead, she's already bumped them off. Paul's the only kid we can make do what we want." Will's head was bent over his "script," chewing gum.

Mill was at the piano, standing before it, barking orders. "Okay, Medea, sing after me: 'I'm Med-e-a—' Go on."

June, still holding up the white tulle, sang:

"I'm Med-eee-ah."

This, I thought, was crazy; it was crazy even for Will and Mill. "What *is* this?"

"Be quiet," said Will.

Now Mill was pointing at Paul. "Now, after June sings that line, you're supposed to echo it—"

"'Echo it? I'm sure that's crystal clear to Paul. Echo—"

"Oh, be quiet," said Will.

Mill went on: "Echo it and sing, 'Sheee's Med-e-ah.'" Mill brought his arm down, slicing up air and saying, "GO!"

"Hi, missus," said Paul. He had the tune down right; it was just the words.

"No!"

Mill rarely yelled; he left that up to Will. "You're supposed to sing, dammit! Mill sang, " 'She's Med-e-ah.' Will, go up and take care of him. We'll be here all night."

Will marched up onstage and got behind Paul and placed both hands on Paul's shoulders. He shook him. "Sing it right."

Mill came down on the piano again, and sang, "She's Med-e-ah."

Paul nearly turned his head upside down to gather in Will's face and got himself a good shaking. Then he sang—shouted, rather—"Sheee's Mud-a-uh."

Will shook him. "Med, Med, not Mud."

Paul sang it again, correctly this time.

Mill ordered, "Okay, now from the top—first June, next Paul. Paul you just have to sing what June sings."

You'd think he had the Gospel choir up there.

Mill played the chords and pointed. June sang (with feeling) "I-I-I'm Medea."

Paul sang (as my brother's thumbs dug into his shoulders) "Sheeee's Mah-de-a."

"Great!" Mill yelled. "Terrific!" Mill was a much more positive person than Will. Mill believed in getting people to do things by encouraging them. Will believed in hitting them. He left Paul to his singing and returned to stand beside me.

"Now!" Mill brought his hands down on the piano again. "Here's the second line: "Mama mia!"

June sang, "Mama mee-ah."

Paul sang, "She's Medea."

Mill ordered him to stop. "No, no, Paul. You sing 'Mama mia' for the second line."

I gaped. "That's crazy! That's Italian!"

Will was tapping his foot in time to what music there was and didn't answer.

I grabbed Will by the arm. "You can't have Greeks singing that. 'Mama mia'—that's an Italian saying!"

Will chewed his gum and thought. "It's . . . international."

Mill was still playing and baton-ing the air like a symphony conductor and the two were still singing. Then I said to Will, "If you think God is going to come down in any machine to save *this* mess, forget it!" I turned and marched toward the door.

Will called after me, "God works in mysterious ways!"

"Not this mysterious!" I slammed the door behind me.

Golden girl
51

Back in the Pink Elephant, I took everything out of my gym bag and lined it all up. From my Whitman's candy box I took the Niece Rhoda tube Dwayne had found, and the snapshot of the sisters and Mary-Evelyn. I balanced the photo of Jamie Makepiece against one of the fat bottles that served as a candleholder, the hardened wax dripping down its side. My hands crossed on the table, my chin lowered to them, I ran my eyes over this little collection. I got down to eye level with Jamie Makepiece. Where was he now? He'd be in his seventies if he was still alive. How I'd love to talk to him! Not just for the things he could tell me about Iris and Isabel, but because he inhabited a period of time from which I was excluded.

I read again the statements of the Devereau sisters to see if there were any other clues. I looked at the photo of Mary-Evelyn, her closed eyes, her water-scattered hair, water-darkened. Darkened. I frowned. What had Imogene said about Mary-Evelyn? *I thought she was so lucky, having that pale hair and the bluest eyes, and having all those dresses.* Pale hair. Only Rose had that kind of hair. The other Devereau sisters had dark hair. I thought of the photograph hanging on the wall in the parlor. The three sisters grouped around light-haired Rose when she was only a child. Their hair was almost black.

Sitting back, I tried to recall something Dwayne had said when we were talking about Lena from *Light in August* and her "condition." Dwayne had joked about nearly every woman in Faulkner being in some kind of "condition." I looked at the photo of Jamie again, saw how handsome he was, saw his golden hair. And I thought of Lena, walking along that dusty road in Tennessee, hoping to find the baby's father.

I looked up and stared at what was in my head. Mary-Evelyn couldn't have been Rose's child because Rose was only a child herself back then. But she could have been Iris's. Iris's and this golden-haired Jamie Makepiece's child. It made sense of all the attention Iris had lavished on Mary-Evelyn's clothes, since she wouldn't dare lavish it on the girl herself, even if she'd wanted to, not living as she did with Isabel and Elizabeth watching.

Mary-Evelyn was their scapegoat. That was why they hated her, especially Isabel. Imagine every day having to be reminded you'd been thrown over for your own sister. Worse, that Iris's and Jamie's child made sure she'd never forget.

That was why they wanted her dead, at least why Isabel did.

I picked up Jamie's letter and read it over again.

> *My dear I Have faith that we will be together again and soon. It has become too much for me and, I'm sure, too much for you. It's better for me to leave for a little while until this fury quiets down. I suppose a century ago, my faithlessness would have been shouted in all the newspapers!*
>
> *Your, J.*

Did he ever know about Mary-Evelyn? I doubted it. But what happened to him?

He had not come back.

319

I lay in bed that night, weary with thinking, and still thought. Where was Ben Queen? He was around; I felt it. If the Girl was still here—and I'd seen her boarding the train just two days ago—if she was still here, so would he be. Ben Queen was not the sort to leave on account of trouble. He was not a Jamie Makepiece. Ben Queen would never desert a person.

I think he really did believe that what happened to Mary-Evelyn was an accident. He believed it because Rose believed it. Even though she had lived in that house for years, still Rose believed it was an accident because she couldn't bear not to. You do that sometimes; you slam the door on the truth because you don't want it inside overturning tables and knocking photos off shelves.

That's what I felt the Sheriff was doing—shutting out the truth. He was seeing my gym bag as nothing more than a bag of tricks. Or maybe he was angry with me because he thought I knew something and had refused to tell him what it was. That was true. I had let him down. Maybe our way of seeing this was that we'd let each other down.

I suddenly felt very old and reached over for the teddy bear that was always on the bed. I had to check to see if the stuffing was still in place.

We remember it well

52

"Well, my goodness," said Louise Snell as I took my place at the counter in the Windy Run Diner, "a person'd think you moved to Cold Flat Junction, hon. You want the roast beef sandwich? It's real good today."

"It's always good. Yes." I had become a regular; I had my own stool and my own story. Maybe I'd tell them another chapter about my mother's friend Henrietta Simple and the Simple family, if I could recall what I'd told them before.

Billy asked if I had found "that Calhoun gal," and I told him I had and thanked them for such good directions.

Don Joe gave me a wide smile that showed a lot of broken and nicotine-stained teeth. "So who you lookin' to find this time? Seems to me you spend half your life lookin' for people."

Everybody laughed. I smiled back displaying my own perfect, white teeth. "Seems like it. Well, today I'm not looking for anybody." Saying that, I almost felt I was here under false pretenses.

"What's goin' on over in La Porte about Fern Queen? They any nearer to finding who done it?" asked Mervin from his booth bench. He was here without his wife again; I'm sure he was happy about that.

I had been trying to think of a way to bring this up, so I was grateful Mervin had done it. "I don't think so, at least I haven't heard. But I do know the Sheriff's looking for Ben Queen. That's who he thinks is guilty."

"With Fern being his own child?" said Louise Snell, indignant. She had given the cook my order and was waiting for it, leaning up against the Plexiglas pie shelves. "Your sheriff mustn't have kids of his own to think a man could shoot his own child."

"The Greeks did it all the time," I informed them. "Killing off kinfolk (a word I loved)—kids, mothers, dads, all sorts. It was like a way of life with them. Didn't think a thing of it." The little window barrier shot up and the roast beef sandwich appeared. Louise set it before me and I got my nose right into the steam coming off the mashed potatoes. I wished my mother would make it, but it was a dish she thought "common."

"Greeks? You sayin' like that fellow outside La Porte has that restaurant—?"

"It's Arturo-something," said Don Joe.

"Yeah. That Arturo fella."

"He's Italian," I said, eating instead of thinking.

Don Joe, wanting to broadcast his superior knowledge said, "Hell, yes, Billy. He's one of them I-ties. Arturo ain't no Greek name."

Billy was irked. "He sure *looks* Greek."

Why did I have to open my big mouth? We were getting miles away from Ben Queen.

"Looks?" said Don Joe. "How come?"

"That real dark hair and what's called 'swarthy' skin. And his eyes looks like black olives. Yessir, Greek to the core, far as looks go. Just because his name's Italian-sounding don't mean he is."

It was like being back in the Big Garage.

"Well, why in hell would he have an I-tie name if he wasn't an I-tie?"

I stepped in. "I think you're both right. He's half Greek and half

Italian. His mother was Greek. I think his middle name is something that ends in -opolis. You know, like so many Greek names. 'Acropolis,' that's Greek. And so on." I shoveled a forkful of mashed potatoes in my mouth, feeling quite proud of my mastery of nationalities.

"Well," said Billy.

"Well," said Don Joe.

Frankly, I think they were both glad I'd put an end to that discussion. Now, I would have to work the talk around to Ben Queen again, so I picked up where I'd left off. "All I meant when I brought up the Greeks was pointing out that their plays often have characters killing off their kinfolk." (I managed to work that in again.) "Kinfolk (again) being children sometimes."

"That's horrible, hon. Why, you ought not to be seeing things like that! Where's it at? They got this summer theater in La Porte, I know."

When she looked away, I rolled my eyes. Then I said, "No, they don't put on the Greek tragedies at the summer theater." Maybe I should invite them all over to the Big Garage. "All I'm saying is it's perfectly possible for a mom or a dad to kill their own child. I'm not saying Ben Queen did it, though." I decided to ask a jackpot question. "Were any of you here then?"

You'd think this was a perfectly simple question, but they had to argue about whether they were or not. It was Mervin who said, "I can tell you everybody who *was* here acted like they'd been hit by a truck. Yessir."

Don Joe agreed and tried to get in on the telling of it, but Mervin just ran right over his words. "First person they thought of—the sheriff's people, I mean—was the husband, Ben, for as we know, it's most often the husband or wife." Here Mervin got out of his booth and came to the counter to sit beside Billy on the stool that was usually occupied by the woman in dark glasses. Billy didn't like this one whit, Mervin moving to the counter. He went on: "When Ben Queen come in, there wasn't a spot of blood on him. Yet the crime scene was covered in it; there was like a lake of blood and it was ev'erwhere. So that told me right there it could not of been him."

Just to argue, probably, Billy said, "So? He coulda just changed his clothes. Mind you, I ain't saying Ben done it, for I definitely *don't* believe he did."

Mervin said, "How's he goin' to change his clothes without the Queens seein' him? He'd have to come in from the barn and get past

Sheba and his brother George. That's when Ben and Rose was livin' with them that time. When their house was bein' built."

Louise Snell interrupted. "That's all beside the point. The point is Ben Queen never would've harmed Rose. Never."

Evren said, "Except they was fighting, him and Rose. There was this big row they had the night before."

Billy flapped his hand at Evren. "Be quiet, Evren. You wasn't even here, so you don't know."

"I'm only goin' by what Toots said, over to the Esso, that's all. Toots was here, wasn't he?"

"Where was Ben Queen when Rose was killed?' I asked, feeling something significant was being left out. They all looked at me as if this question had never come up.

Mervin, now back in his booth, answered me. "Hebrides. That's where he was at."

"But then somebody in Hebrides must've seen him."

Billy held up his cup for a refill. He said, "Nobody come forth to say."

I frowned. If the Sheriff waited for somebody to "come forth" he'd never be arresting anyone. "But didn't the police investigate?"

Mervin was up and over to the counter again, this time on the empty stool nearest me. "That's just the thing," he said to me. "That's what's so damned fishy. There was hardly any questions asked, and after they took in Ben Queen, then there was none. So as you see there was precious little 'investigatin' ' going on." He slapped the Formica countertop.

Louise was pouring refills and said, "That's because Ben never put up any resistance. He hardly even said a word, according to Boyd Spiker."

Don Joe said, "Oh, hell, Boyd Spiker's an injit."

What I was thinking now was that I should have paid more attention to the details of the police investigation of Rose's murder. I knew Ben Queen didn't do it and so did people like Louise Snell, but the law didn't. "Who's Boyd Spiker?"

Mervin answered, "He's a trooper. Troopers got there first. When Ben come back, they took him in. First thing."

"But if he was *gone* from Cold Flat Junction, then how could he have killed her?"

"That was my point," said Louise.

"Cops just figured Ben was fixin' to alibi hisself," said Don Joe.

For me, this was just like Aurora and her find-the-pea so-called trick. She just told you you were wrong no matter what walnut shell you chose. She wouldn't lift the shells, either. That's what all of this sounded like. The *obvious* conclusion for the police to draw was Ben Queen *didn't* do it. One, he was in Hebrides, two, his truck was being worked on, so how did he get back? And, three, he adored his wife. It was crazy, and I said so.

"I'm with you, hon," said Louise, giving me a fresh Coke.

I asked, "Didn't the Sheriff from La Porte investigate?"

"Not really. Come around, asked a few questions. But like I said, Ben never put up any fight."

Louise asked, "Who'd have the gumption after finding the wife you dearly loved had been knifed to death?"

That wasn't exactly logical, but it was a point. "Did he confess?"

"'Cording to Boyd, he just said, "Let's get it over with," said Billy.

Mervin was still determined to get his first point in. "Witnesses said him and Rose'd been fightin' somethin' awful."

"What were they fighting about?" I asked.

"Their girl, Fern. You know, the one that was killed out your way. They went round and round about her, Rose and Ben did. She wasn't playin' with a full deck—" Here Billy made circles near his ear.

Louise was annoyed. "No need to make fun, Billy; the woman was just retarded, and you shouldn't be speaking ill of the dead, anyhow."

"Anyway, they fought a lot about Fern. Rose wanted to ship her off to an institution but Ben didn't. That girl was a handful."

Louise wiped the counter, absently. "It was a real shame. They'd only the one child and she turned out that way. Didn't seem to get nothing from Rose and Ben, certainly not looks."

Don Joe said, "I think you had a crush on him."

"Oh, don't be ridiculous. I wasn't more'n eight or nine years old then."

"Still, every woman around was sweet on Ben."

"Like every man was sweet on Rose," said Billy, tapping ash from his cigarette with his little finger.

Billy must have been older than he looked, for he said this as if he remembered. Remembered it well.

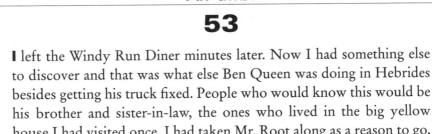

An alibi

53

I left the Windy Run Diner minutes later. Now I had something else to discover and that was what else Ben Queen was doing in Hebrides besides getting his truck fixed. People who would know this would be his brother and sister-in-law, the ones who lived in the big yellow house I had visited once. I had taken Mr. Root along as a reason to go, for Bathsheba Queen had once been his "girl," he said.

Today I stood outside their house trying to make up what I would give as the reason this time for visiting. My mind was as blank and smooth as an eggshell. It was still blank five minutes later when George Queen, Ben's older brother, came out on the porch with a newspaper, meaning, I guessed, to sit and read. I thought about the newspaper.

"Hello, Mr. Queen!" I called, as if I had just then been passing by.

I didn't want him to find me skulking outside his house. I waved as he got up from his chair and kind of squinted down the path between fence and steps. "It's just me, Mr. Queen, Emma Graham. I guess you don't remember me." I'd found that the elderly don't like it if you suggest their memories are slipping, so that comment might get him up and going. Mr. Queen came right down the path and unhooked the garden gate.

"I sure do remember you. Come on up to the porch. I bet Sheba will rustle up some lemonade and cookies. You just sit yourself down and I'll be back in a flash."

I hoped Sheba would produce store-bought cookies, as her own were so bad. I settled into an old wooden rocking chair and waited for him to come back. I saw he was reading the Cloverly paper, which was a daily. Our own *Conservative* was a weekly, out every Thursday. I don't know how much was in it now about the White's Bridge murder, but I didn't need to read the paper to find out, as I knew more than the paper did. I looked through the first two pages of his paper but saw nothing about the murder or about Ben Queen. I folded the paper back carefully and returned it to the seat of his chair.

Mr. Queen came out then with a pitcher of lemonade on a little tray with three glasses, which meant his wife would be joining us. "Sheba'll be out in a minute. She's taking the cookies out of the oven." I winced as he drew over a round table and set the tray down. "Nothing like fresh-baked cookies, I'm sure you'll agree."

Depends who baked them, I didn't say. "I surely do, Mr. Queen."

He poured out lemonade and handed me a glass and sat down with his own.

"This is really good," I said, which it was. Then for some reason I remembered the girl with the Kool-Aid stand. It was only two streets up and over from here. I pictured her there with a drink nobody much wanted and with nobody much passing her way. I wished she had some of this lemonade to sell. I looked at the paper and asked, in an offhand way, if there was anything in it of interest.

"Not much. I was looking for mention of Fern—you know. The city paper thinks it's old news."

Cloverly hardly rated as a "city." I said, "I'm really sorry about her, Mr. Queen. And I'm sorry about your brother, too."

Just then Sheba Queen came out carrying a plate of the same kind of cookies she'd served before. "Well, hello, Em'ly. How are you? How's your mother? You came just at the right time. Here I was baking cookies and only us to eat 'em.'"

"Thank you, ma'am." "Ma'am" was a word I was never to use, as my mother considered it common; so in her honor I corrected myself. "Thank you, Mrs. Queen." I took a cookie, the smallest I could find, wondering why Sheba Queen seemed so much more friendly than the last time. But I guess people can have on-Em'ly-days and off-Em'ly-days. I wondered where I could slip the cookie.

Sheba Queen sat down in the third rocker and munched her own cookie. I bit into mine and gave her a big smile back.

"We were talkin' about there not being any news." George fluttered the paper a little.

Sheba put on her *hrr-umph* look as she resettled her shoulders. "Police ain't done a lick. That sheriff of yours is just dragging his feet."

"I think he's really trying, Mrs. Queen." Even though the Sheriff and I were on the outs, I would still defend him. I made a note to tell him what we said here to show how objective I could be.

"Well . . . maybe," said George Queen. "Depends how hard he's looking for anybody *besides* Ben."

That was a good point. I would add this to my defending him. "Yes, sir. I know what you mean." I did, too. I could have kissed him for bringing Ben up, but settled on another bite of the cookie to express my gratitude. There was a silence into which I dropped Rose's name.

Sheba stiffened, for she had always disliked Rose Devereau; I had learned that plain enough from my visit here with Mr. Root.

George just shook his head in a woebegone way. "That poor poor girl. Ben never did that, and I'll say it with my dying breath."

"'Course he never did it." Sheba looked away, out over the garden.

I took the opportunity to break my cookie into little pieces as I pursued my point. "I was overhearing some people talk about it in the Windy Run Diner—"

Sheba had to butt in and comment about the customers there. "That Billy and Mervin and Don Joe. All's they do is sit around and talk silliness."

I winced. "Anyway, they were saying your Ben went to Hebrides that day."

"He was in Hebrides, that's right," said George. "He always went on Thursdays."

I waited. *To do what?* I silently urged. I was afraid to get too technical on them, as that might make them wonder about my reasons for coming. "They said in the diner he had to go to get his truck fixed." George set down his lemonade glass as I dropped some cookie bits between the slats of the chair.

"Not exactly. His truck got something wrong with it while he was there in Hebrides. So he took it into the shop."

I frowned. "But if he was in Hebrides, how could he have been in Cold Flat Junction and killed Rose?"

"They said at the trial there was time after he picked up the truck to get to the house here and after he killed Rose to go back to Hebrides. They claimed Ben had used the truck as an alibi, but the alibi didn't work, as it turned out. Those police doctors can figure times pretty good. Anyway, they didn't have to do much figuring out because Sheba saw Rose go out to the barn to feed the chickens and after an hour or more when she never came back, I went looking for her." As if the vision were rising up before him, he closed his eyes against it. "Blood everywhere. Awful." He dropped his head. "Poor Ben. What they say in ninety percent of the cases where a man or wife is murdered, it's the spouse that's guilty. That's what started 'em in thinking about Ben."

I could understand how it might have *started* them, but not how they could have *ended* with thinking it was Ben Queen. The Sheriff once told me that when you've got a homicide staring you in the face, you begin by going for the most obvious explanation, for nearly all homicides can be explained that way. You don't do what mystery writers do: you don't hit on the *least* obvious, or one that's so all-fired complicated only a damned fool would try it. So here we were: the police hit on what struck me as the least obvious explanation. Ben was in Hebrides, but others were here. So why not Sheba Queen, who was known to have taken a powerful dislike to Rose? Why not Fern Queen, who was in a rage over being sent to an institution and who was kind of crazy anyway? As far as I was concerned, Fern was the obvious choice. She had a motive; Ben didn't.

I guessed in the end you couldn't blame the investigation if Ben Queen never denied he'd done it. But you'd have thought his own lawyer could have worked out that he was protecting someone. Then, again, maybe the lawyer did figure it out, only Ben Queen told him to keep his mouth shut. There's only one kind of person you'd do that for and that's someone you feel responsible for. It leaves out, of course, how good Ben Queen's judgment was to let a homicidal killer run around free.

But I just couldn't tackle the matter of Ben Queen's judgment right now. Right now I wanted to know what he'd done in Hebrides. "You said your brother always went into Hebrides on Thursdays. Was it some kind of regular thing he had to do?"

George said, "Well, he always picked up the feed Thursdays. Always went to Smitty's outside town."

"Did he get it that day? I mean with the truck acting up, did he have time?"

George frowned, concentrating. "Yeah, I think he did."

Sheba had to butt in again with her thoughts. "That day, that day will live in infamy."

She could live in infamy with it as far as I was concerned. Why hadn't they done something? If they'd believed their brother Ben's innocence so much, why hadn't they questioned the times? Maybe it was from hanging out with the Sheriff so much and listening to him talk about past investigations that made me suspicious of conclusions. *You've got to be sure you have every scrap of available evidence before you can draw your conclusion.* (I wish he'd reminded himself of this in *my* case.)

I asked, "How long after it happened did he come back?"

"Couple hours, I guess. Of course, police said he came back *before*. You recall, Sheba?"

"Three o'clock. I remember because I noted the time that sheriff came."

"So she was killed like around noon?"

"Well, police put it at between eleven and three. But of course we knew closer than that. I saw her at noon when she went to the barn. George here went out to the barn around one-thirty."

George nodded. "That was the time all right. I never saw such a scene in my life. It was terrible, terrible. I tried to keep you from goin' out there, Sheba, but you would insist."

"Well," was all Sheba said as she rocked more intensely.

"He got the truck fixed okay, though?"

"Yeah. Carl's one of the best mechanics around."

Carl. "My mother's in need of a good mechanic. I guess he's not there any more. It's been so long."

"Sure is. Carl's had that Sinclair station for fifty years and his dad before that. But you got Slaw's over in Spirit Lake. That Wayne . . . what's his name?"

"Dwayne Hayden?"

"That's the one. Nobody's better'n him. Not in Hebrides, Cloverly, or any place in a hundred miles."

"I'll sure tell my mother about him. We're looking for a good feed store, too. We've got a mess of chickens out back." We did have four, actually.

"What you been feedin' 'em?"

"Ah, corn. And stuff. See, I don't actually do it myself."

Sheba said, "Well, you should. It's good for youngsters to get a start on finding out what the real world's like."

They thought this was the real world?

Solace

54

I stood on Louise Landis's porch thinking up a reason for coming. How I wished I'd chosen the history project I had told Imogene about. But couldn't the project have started after my first visit to Louise Landis? No. I had to stick with what I had.

"Hello, Miss Landis," I said, when she opened the door.

She seemed really pleased I'd come. "Emma! Come in, come in."

"Thank you. I just wanted to tell you about the entertainment for the orphans' lunch." I said this as I followed her through the cool, dark hall and into the living room. It was exactly the same as it had been when I'd left, down to the last detail, which included the length of orange yarn I'd been using to make a cat's cradle. Did I suppose she'd move all the furniture around and hang wallpaper after I left? (This question was asked by my sarcastic self.) No, of course not (my more patient self answered). Perhaps it was more that everything seemed to have stopped and had just started in ticking now, like the mantel clock.

I sank into the deep armchair and considered curling up and going to sleep, it was so comfortable. Instead, I said, "My brother Will and his friend Brownmiller—he's a real musician—would be happy to entertain the orphans." Was I crazy? Why hadn't I asked them yet? But wait! There was another way to approach this. "Now, what they said was they weren't sure if they could come to the lunch, but they thought you could all come to their production. As their guests, of course. (They never charged anybody anyway unless it was someone they didn't like.) They put one on every year in summer."

"How nice of them to suggest it. What day is the performance?"

"The day's not quite certain, but it'll be in the next couple of weeks. Usually they do two or three performances. I have a part in it; I'm to be the *deus ex machina*."

She looked truly surprised. No wonder. How many people had ever heard of a *deus ex machina*, much less could pronounce it? "How ambitious of them! Is it Sophocles? Euripides? Is it *Oedipus*?"

I'd forgotten to find out who wrote it, though I imagine what Will and Mill were putting on didn't have a lot of the original in it. "*Medea*. I mean it's *about* Medea."

"A Greek tragedy. My word, but your brother and his friend must be very well read."

I could have argued that, based on the comic books and magazines under his bed. "It's a lot different than most Greek plays because it's a musical. That's what Brownmiller is an expert at. He writes lyrics and is a musician. He plays just about every instrument you can imagine."

Louise Landis's expression didn't give away much of what she was thinking and I supposed that came from teaching all these years, making your expression coolly polite like that. I went on: "Brownmiller writes all the words for the songs and just borrows the music from over there at the camp meeting or from other composers." I sat forward a little to make my position clear: "I don't think you should really do that—I mean, it doesn't seem exactly right, *morally* right (how nice to toss that word in!) to have this woman that's just killed or is going to kill her kids sing, "'I'm Medea. Mama mia'." I sat back.

She coughed and said, "Why—Emma, would you like some tea?"

"Yes, thanks."

She rose rather carefully, as if trying to hold herself in check and

333

walked out, just as carefully. I hoped I hadn't upset her, though I couldn't imagine why Medea would. I got out of my chair and turned to the wall of bookcases. I didn't see *Light in August,* but there were a couple of others by William Faulkner I wasn't familiar with. I wondered if he spent his whole life writing books and how he managed to do that, what with life being as busy as it is. I looked for Greek plays she might have, but didn't see any. I would like to see a *deus ex machina* in action, instead of just hearing it described. (I certainly couldn't depend on the one in Will's play to be a good example.)

Miss Landis was back with our tea. As she poured I watched and commented on all of her books. Then we both sat down and I added three spoons of sugar to my tea. "There's a lot of killing of family members down through the years in Greek plays. They're always after revenge, it seems to me."

"Well, the Greeks were certainly caught up in the notion of retribution."

I blew on my tea (a habit my mother didn't encourage), then said, "Do you think, if you wrote a play and needed a *deus ex machina* at the end that it's a very good play? I mean, shouldn't you have to get out of the mess on your own?"

"In some circumstances, perhaps you can't."

But that was just saying it again, it seemed to me. "How come?"

"It might be like running a fever. Eventually, it either breaks or it kills you. You can't do much about it. Except to wait."

I thought about this. "But—" I tried to put words to what I was thinking. Sometimes words just walked out on you and left you stranded. I went back to the murder. "What about that murder that happened here forty years ago?"

"Rose Queen?"

I nodded. "And then somebody comes along and kills this Fern? Her daughter?"

"Yes."

"Well . . . you don't think it was him do you?"

We seemed both to know who I meant.

"No. No, I don't."

There was a silence. I tried fashioning a cat's cradle again and said, "At the diner I had lunch, and I overheard people talking about this Fern Queen's murder. The Sheriff in La Porte thinks her father did it, but he can't see any motive. Why would her father murder her?"

"He wouldn't; Ben Queen would be incapable of such a thing. As your sheriff says, there's no motive."

"He doesn't like coincidences."

Miss Landis raised an eyebrow. "'Coincidences'?"

I tried snapping the yarn taut, but I hadn't done it right. "Like Ben Queen getting out of jail just days before the murder of Fern."

She looked over my head at the wall of books behind me, so long that I turned to see what she was seeing. "Sorry. I was just thinking that it might not be a *coincidence;* at the same time it doesn't mean Ben Queen did it."

I thought about that, frowning at the orange thread as if it had some part in the matter. "Have you lived here all your life?"

"Yes, I have."

"What about your mother? And father?" I sometimes forgot fathers, as I didn't have one. I wondered if that made me, as a person, lopsided.

"This house goes back to my great-grandparents. I think he's the one who built it."

"Nobody else has lived here, then? Nobody came along to interfere, did they?"

She didn't answer for a moment, then she said, "You mean—?"

"To move in, to try and take it away."

"Oh, no. I can't imagine that happening."

"I can." I concentrated on my hands. Finding something to do with them, like the cat's cradle, helps you not look at the other person.

"Interlopers?"

That was a good word, good enough to repeat. "Interlopers." I smiled.

"You must be referring to the Davidow woman."

"You know her?"

"Yes. I've often seen her in La Porte. I go there to buy groceries and things."

"Well, I mean, more her daughter is the interloper." I pulled the cat's cradle as if both ends were Ree-Jane's arms.

"Interlopers are extremely hard to take."

Well, *that* didn't tell me anything new. I said, "But you should be able to do something about them."

"There should, you mean, be a *deus ex machina*?"

I looked over at her. She was not being sarcastic. And it suddenly came to me that a *deus ex machina* was exactly what I thought should come along. "Yes."

"But remember what you said."

I frowned. What had I said? I said so many things it hardly bore remembering.

To my blank (or perhaps surly) look, she said, "You said the playwright must not be very good if he couldn't find a way for his characters to get out of the mess on their own."

I wished I hadn't said it; now I was stuck with it. Still, it was nice to have your words remembered. "Yes, but this isn't a play."

"All the more reason to be able to depend upon yourself. And wouldn't you rather, in the long run?"

I slipped down in the chair, something I had a habit of doing if talk got around to my character. I didn't want to talk about depending on myself. For one thing, it made me lonesome. I changed the subject. "Have you read all of these books?"

"No. A lot of them, but not all."

"Do you like William Faulkner? Right now I'm reading *Light in August*." Actually, I hadn't picked it up after it came in handy for getting Dwayne to go with me to White's Bridge.

"That's wonderful. You must like words."

"'Words'?" But I right away knew what she meant. For I loved sitting in the Abigail Butte County Library with an open book, or several books, feeling they were consoling me, somehow. "I guess I do, yes."

"They're an idea of home, I think. Words are. It really is like opening a door, isn't it, to open a book. If that's not too sentimental to say. Books, words, stories are a kind of solace."

I frowned, taking it in. This was definitely a new idea, one worth coming back to, when I didn't have this mystery to solve.

Words, stories, solace.

Smitty

55

Instead of going to Spirit Lake on the 4:32 from Cold Flat Junction, I got off in La Porte. I figured Delbert would be waiting in his cab, hoping for a fare.

He was, but not for me. "You goin' to the hotel?" he asked in a hopeful tone, suggesting he didn't want to take another unscheduled trip with me.

"No." I slammed the door. "I need to go to Hebrides." It wasn't yet five o'clock and that meant businesses would still be open, as I was sure a feed store would stay open until five-thirty or six. I'd try the feed store first, and then Carl's garage, though I didn't think Carl would do much toward establishing an alibi, since the police knew about the truck being fixed.

"*Hebrides?*"

Did he have to make out that any destination outside of La Porte and Spirit Lake meant he'd have to trudge over sand dunes and mountains for a year? "You know where it is, don't you?"

He half turned in his seat to present a worried face to me, to let me know just how much he didn't want to do this. "That's like a twenty-minute, even a half-hour drive."

I sighed. "Delbert, why do you always have to argue about where your customer wants to go. This is a *taxicab*. Axel has this business to drive people where they want to go. Not where you want them to go." I fell back against the seat. "So, go."

He let out this enormous sigh, then grunted a little, then began pulling away from the depot. "Where at in Hebrides?"

"The feed store. It's called Smitty's, I think."

This was so outlandish to him, he turned to look at me and nearly got hit by Helen Baum's yellow Cadillac. I enjoyed this, for she was really mad and waving her fist at him. After we crawled out of the depot and turned left, he said. "There's a Smith's. J. L. Smith's Feed and something. Is that the one? On the outskirts?"

"I guess. I wouldn't imagine there's more than one in Hebrides."

"Yeah, I think J. L. Smith is called Smitty by people."

I wondered how much more conversation we'd have before he was confident we had the same place in mind. "How far is it from Cold Flat Junction?"

"Why?"

I raised my hands, clawlike, to the back of his head as if to rip his neck open, but simply said, "I just want to know."

"You plannin' goin' to Cold Flat Junction, too?" He sounded affrighted. "I ain't got the time for that."

"No, I don't want to go there; it's just a *question*, Delbert."

"Oh. Well, it's about the same as from here. Same distance. We're south of Hebrides and Cold Flat Junction's west."

"Like a half hour from either place?"

"Yeah. I guess."

I settled back in my seat and rode northward. If you were the police, you'd time it exactly to see if an alibi held up. There didn't seem to be all that much exactness to the investigation of the Rose Queen murder, though.

Out of my window, farmland slipped by like a length of green silk unrolling. Barns, farmhouses, fences. Horses, their tails swishing away flies, came up to a white-painted rail fence to watch. I wondered why the cab interested them. The farmhouse sat way back, maybe a half mile from the highway, on a straight-as-a-die dirt road, hemmed on both sides by more of the white rail fence. More horses grazed within its boundaries and I guessed it was a horse farm. By this time it was behind us and I could see it only in my head (where I saw most things).

I decided Henrietta Simple and her family lived on just such a farm. I wished I hadn't told the Windy Run crowd that Henrietta had a retarded brother, for I now felt he might disturb the tranquility of what I saw as a peaceful scene. But it was too late, too late to get rid of the brother unless I just killed him off. He could be up in a tree, maybe swinging from a limb, and fall into the creek below.

Then I started wondering if William Faulkner had similar problems with his characters. Once he'd created one, if he decided he didn't like him, could he just go back and erase the person altogether? Most people would say "Sure," but I wondered. It might appear that if a writer was making the person up anyway, then he should be able to go back and unmake him. Maybe it wasn't that simple; maybe it was more complicated than that. Once William Faulkner (who was an incredibly powerful writer—look at the effect he'd had on Dwayne and me: I still thought of Lena even after only a dozen or so pages)—once he made you up, you stayed made up. Yes, you stayed and stayed and if you were yanked out of the story, you'd just come back as somebody else. There must have been characters William Faulkner was sorry he invented. Take that "Flem" person. How disgusting. But I also imagine William Faulkner's disgust threshold was a lot higher than mine. The idea, though, was worth thinking about when I had more time: that a person could peel right off the page and go wandering around (causing trouble, mainly) until William Faulkner found another place for him. Even the name of the character couldn't be changed after a certain point of getting used to. Names were like barnacles and limpets, crusted to you so it would need a saw or ax or something to get the name off.

"Why you goin' to the feed store? You ain't got animals at the Hotel Paradise, last time I looked."

Delbert must have been trying to work this out all the while we'd been driving. It really annoyed me, as I'd been having a nice time until he broke in. "I just want to talk to him."

"Smith?"

"Yes."

"We're goin' all this way just to talk? Well, my goodness, girl, why not just call him up on the phone?"

"Because I want to talk in person. There's a difference."

Delbert grunted. "Beats me. Words is words far as I'm concerned."

I was sorely tempted to grab his neck and squeeze. *Words is words.* William Faulkner turned over in his grave. I could feel it.

"We're in Hebrides," Delbert called like we'd just landed on the moon.

Houses flashed by, big trees lining wide streets, and driveways, cars, bicycles, basketball hoops—all let us know Hebrides was a thriving city, which it was, about as far from Cold Flat Junction as you could get in prosperity. We waited at a traffic light that marked the town's center where my favorite store stood. This was the Emporium. I loved this store, the way the headless mannequins posed with their hip bones jutting. We turned right and were soon passing the Nickelodeon, which showed the latest movies a week before our own Orion got them (if it ever did). Across from the movie house was Barb's Beach House, although there weren't any beaches around; the nearest one might even be in Florida. Barb's was where Ree-Jane had come in her white convertible to get her bright new swimsuits. (Too bad she lost them in Miami Beach and had to wear that old brown one.) The windows of Barb's were always covered with sand and shells and whatever else caught her fancy as she dressed them. I bet she had a fake palm tree somewhere I could have borrowed.

I really liked Barb; she seemed to live in a sun-and-sand fantasy land, which was swell with me. In the window today was a huge blue and green striped beach umbrella with nothing but four feet jutting from under it, one set wearing flippers. Barb sold water-sport equipment too. Indeed, except for boats themselves, she had furnished out her shop (and her mind, I guessed) with just about everything relating to beaches and cruises.

We were now past the Hebrides town limit, going east, and Delbert was asking me if I wanted to drive back with him.

"Of course, what did you think?"

"There's a charge for waiting time, you recall."

"I know because you must have told me twenty times when you waited at the library the other day. There it is!" I pointed to our left.

Delbert turned into the big parking lot of J. L. Smith's Feed and Garden Supply.

I got out and walked to the wide open garagelike door, thinking that I should have been spending my time during the ride rehearsing what I was going to say instead of thinking about William Faulkner. What *was* I going to say? *Mr. Smith, I would like you to search your memory . . . Mr. Smith, twenty or so years ago . . . Hi! Mr. Smith. You don't remember me—I'm kin of Ben Queen . . .*

I stood stalk still in front of bags of fertilizer and pruning shears, thinking.

"Hello, little lady!"

I wanted to snub whoever'd said that. I squeezed my eyes shut to get control of myself.

"What can I do you for?"

He seemed to be all teeth. The teeth glistened white above his red apron. Oh, how I hated expressions like that old tired "do you for" phrase, supposed to be funny. But I put on my phony smile and asked him if Mr. Smith was here. (Mr. Smith, I suddenly realized, could easily be dead.)

"Which one?" he asked, and laughed as if he were just the funniest person on God's green earth (as my mother likes to say). "I'm one of 'em. Then there's Pa and Grampa. All three of us in business like beans in a row."

I stretched my mouth in a wider smile imitation. "It's not you, but it might be your dad, if he was here twenty years ago."

This really stumped him, not whether his dad had been here, but that he didn't have a set response to fit the occasion. He was worse than Delbert. "Why'd you want to see someone from back then?" He struggled with the question as if he were just learning to read.

"I just do, Buddy." That was the name stitched in blue on the bib of his red apron.

Buddy scratched his neck as if I'd just given him a rash and finally said, "Yeah. They both were. Store's been in the family for over seventy-five years. Yeah, they were both here back then. He's over there."

I got the impression that Buddy felt he came up lacking because he himself hadn't been here, and wasn't of interest even to a twelve-year-old kid. I guessed I should feel sorry for him, being this insecure, but I didn't. He was standing here wasting my time. Then he turned and walked off, and I went over to where his father was standing, passing the time with another man who looked like a farmer in his feed hat. This Mr. Smith wasn't wearing an apron (probably thinking it against his dignity to do so, which I agreed it was), but his name was stitched on the pocket of his shirt: *Smitty.* This definitely was the right person. And he was obviously old enough to have been here twenty years ago, or thirty, even.

It was kind of hard to browse in a feed store. I wandered over to the wall behind him and looked at some gardening tools. Every once in a while, Lola Davidow would don some of these "Greenthumb" gardening gloves and go down to our big garden along the gravel road that went by the Pink Elephant. It was usually after a brunch of several Bloody Marys that she did this and would bring back a cabbage or runner beans. Once she even got Ree-Jane to go with her and I tagged along just to see what would happen. What happened was Mrs. Davidow would pull up potatoes or snap off beans and hand them up to Ree-Jane, who just stood there being bored.

I don't know how long I stopped there, running over this scene in my mind, but in a while a voice said, "Hello, there."

Mr. Smith—Smitty—I liked immediately. He asked "Can I help you" in exactly the same voice he'd use talking to an adult, instead of that stilted, slow-paced, singsongy manner adults use for retarded people and children.

I said, "Yes, sir. The Queens over in Cold Flat Junction asked me to pick up about fifty pounds of fertilizer? But I'm not sure what kind, and you seem to have several kinds here? Something else they wanted, too, but I can't remember it right now." I squinted up at him as if they'd told him, too.

"Fertilizer's easy. Maybe you'll recall what the item was after we've dealt with the fertilizer."

This was a very sensible and relaxed person, I thought. I was immediately calmer. It could be nerve-racking, thinking up ways to get information.

Mr. Smith looked the fertilizer over, searching, I guessed, for a certain kind. He found it and said, "Here we are. Fifty pounds, you'd want two twenty-pound and a ten-pound bag." He started hauling the bags out to the aisle.

This was going too fast and I better think quick. "Maybe there was other stuff they usually get you might know about?"

I was trying to think of a way to introduce Ben Queen into the fertilizer pickup when he said, "Well, when George picks up he gets chicken feed, usually. Could that be what they wanted?"

I smiled widely and said, "That's it. Thank you. I guess you know the Queens pretty well."

"Oh, yes. Known Ben and George for years and years. Ben'd come in every other Thursday like clockwork. Right here's the feed. It's good quality."

Like clockwork. That's what I was interested in. "I never knew him. Of course, now he's out of jail, maybe I'll meet him. That all sounded real bad, what happened."

Smitty shook his head and his eyes looked as if a pool of sadness had gathered in them. "Ben Queen. I just could hardly believe all that business. You know, he was in here that day and not a trace of any behavior that would have said he was upset or bad tempered. He was just as usual. We caught up with each other like we always did, could've talked the afternoon away." Smitty laughed. "I'm a terrible talker. "

"That must've been the day he had to get his truck fixed?" I kind of held my breath, hoping he'd forgotten I was only twelve and what interest would I have in that day?

"I do believe that's right; he said he'd had it over to Carl's shop that morning. Something wrong with the carburetor. I guess I remember pretty good because of what happened."

He was pulling out the chicken feed and didn't notice that I was nearly doing a tap dance. *He was here, he was here, I knew he was here.*

"I was mighty puzzled when Ben confessed. You'd never have made me believe it otherwise."

That was the reason Mr. Smith hadn't said anything to the police: the so-called "confession"—which hadn't been a confession at all, but a silence. I looked at him, a very nice man, and wondered how he'd feel, finding out he could have supplied Ben Queen with an alibi.

Mr. Smith called his son over to load the fertilizer into the cab. I could take the sack of chicken feed. I figured Buddy could take Delbert's one hundred questions as well as I could, about what was being put in his cab and why. I went to the cash register and paid for all the fertilizer and feed. Mr. Smith had said he could just put it on the Queen's account, but I said, no, I'd rather pay. I told him I'd really enjoyed meeting him and he seemed pleased at that.

Delbert went on and on about the three bags of fertilizer as we drove to La Porte. His talk was more a humming in my ears as I stared out the passenger's window—I'd slid over to the other side to watch everything go by in reverse. I was so elated that what I'd believed to be true, was true, and now all that remained was to convince the Sheriff. "All"? It wouldn't be easy.

It was so strange that what Ben Queen had been doing that afternoon had been here all along in Mr. Smith's mind and no one had known. But Ben Queen knew it, knew he had an alibi and would have used it, I suspected, if he hadn't thought it would call down even greater harm on someone. So where he had been or *if* he had been anyplace other than at the house made no difference as far as he was concerned. He was determined to take the blame upon himself.

It was almost funny about Mr. Smith. Smitty, a *deus ex machina,* come out of nowhere to finally straighten things out. And he didn't even know it. I wondered, as we again passed the horse farm, if you could be God and not know it. If God didn't know he was God.

Here was a question for Father Freeman.

The fertilizer had taken all my taxi money and then some. Delbert would love that.

Cold Turkey

56

Delbert was really put out that I'd spent all my money on fertilizer. He had to wait until I ran in and took the fare from the cash box in the back office. I asked since he had to wait anyway, why couldn't he unload the fertilizer? He argued it wasn't like suitcases, that suitcases were part of a person's trip, but fertilizer wasn't. I got him to do it by saying I'd give him a big tip (which I wouldn't). Finally, he left, mumbling curses which I would report to Axel, if Axel ever got within speaking distance.

It was time for dinner. I left the fertilizer on the front porch and half walked, half ran to the kitchen, taking the short cut on the wooden walk to the kitchen's side door.

Walter, dependable as always, was just taking Salisbury steak out of the oven, a more dignified version of hamburger. There would be my mother's dark rich gravy to pour over it.

"I took 'em in their first course. Melon balls. I didn't have much to do so I made some."

In a glass dish were perfect little rounds of watermelon, honeydew, and cantaloupe. I congratulated Walter on his inventiveness.

"Miss Jen called, too. They're on their way back. Miss Jen said the sun was something fierce."

"Did you tell her it was Florida?"

Walter hawked a laugh around and shook his head.

Of course, Miss Bertha objected to her Salisbury steak, fussing her fork around her plate as if poking and prodding meat and potatoes would turn them into whatever glamour dish she had in mind.

I told her, "It's not hamburger; it's a high-quality ground beef. Ground round, I think I heard my mother say."

Mrs. Fulbright had taken a bite and proclaimed it delicious. She did this all the time, like a fond parent trying to get a baby in a high chair (a pretty good description of Miss Bertha) to mimic her actions. But Miss Bertha only demanded, as usual, something else besides "this muck" to eat.

Referring to anything my mother cooks as "muck" is the same as calling gold or silver shavings "sawdust," but my day had been so spectacularly successful (at least as far as I was concerned) that I could rise above my daily and ordinary self and offer something else. My mother had left, exclusively for me, some ham pinwheels. These are made of pastry dough spread with perfectly seasoned ground ham, and then rolled up and sliced (something like icebox cookies). After baking they are lathered with rich cheese sauce. This scrumptious dish, beloved by me, is also a favorite of Miss Bertha's, at least as much as she favors anything.

So this dinnertime I offered Miss Bertha a ham pinwheel in place of the Salisbury steak. This was such an instant success that I decided not to mix a lot of fiery English mustard into her cheese sauce as I was tempted to do. And I reminded myself to divide the cheese sauce three ways (for I was also going to let Walter have a pinwheel), which did not mean an equal three ways, for my portion would be biggest. (Now, I will say this for Aurora Paradise, and that is she eats just about everything. I mean, unless she throws it at you instead, like the chicken wing and the stuffed tomato.)

The two old ladies' meal proceeded in relative peace after Miss Bertha got her ham pinwheel. My own and Walter's dinners were also peaceful. I had the largest pinwheel, half a Salisbury steak with my mother's lucious gravy, the au gratin potatoes, and peas as green as an Irish meadow. I saw to it Walter got just the same meal, except for not as much cheese sauce.

Following dinner, I stayed in the Pink Elephant saying good-bye to all of my new friends at the Rony Plaza, who pleaded with me to come back next year, telling me I was the most entertaining guest they had ever had. The manager said he would hold "my room" and was even considering putting a bronze plaque on the door with my name. I think he would even have offered to hold a sunset.

What a day, what a day.

I wrapped the cord around the fan and lay the palm tree against the wall and scooped sand back in the bucket. Will and Mill had been agitating to get their fan back, needing it (they said) to "create a disturbance." I told them please to keep it away from me.

I hauled the fan up to the Big Garage and knocked at the door. The noise behind it quickly subsided as if someone had shot it dead. When Will finally came to the door, he refused to open it more than an inch or two, as usual.

"Here's your fan."

"Good. Leave it."

"Why not open the door and take it inside."

"Just leave it."

"This is *really* stupid. I've already *seen* what you're doing, haven't I?"

"Leave it. Good-bye."

I heard laughter. There was a girl's voice, probably June's, and Paul's crazy laugh. As I walked away, I thought it wasn't *what* the secret was but the whole nature of secretive-ism that Will and Mill loved. It didn't matter that I'd seen some of the "production." Simply leaving it behind restored the secret of it.

When I went back to the kitchen Walter told me Aurora Paradise had been hollering down the dumbwaiter when he went into the back office. "It was way past the cocktail hour is what she said and she wants her Cold Comfort."

I sighed. Then I went to the office to sort through the bottles, and found no Southern Comfort, only gin and vodka and Wild Turkey. Well, the Wild Turkey would do, so I took it and miniatures of crème de menthe and brandy. Back in the kitchen I mixed up a couple of juices and ice in the blender, then dumped in the liquor. I poured it, frothing, into a tall glass, speared some melon balls on a long swizzle stick and held it up for Walter to inspect.

"Cold Turkey," I said.

We laughed.

Ghosts

57

First thing after breakfast I got a taxi into La Porte. Because of yesterday, Delbert was in a really sour mood, which would have been fine with me if only it kept him from talking.

"Courthouse don't open till nine-fifteen; it ain't even nine yet."

"The Sheriff will be there. He goes in early."

"Maybe. But that don't mean the sheriff's *office* is open. I know for a fact Maureen ain't there yet, for I just got a call to pick her up over in Spikersville."

His bad mood was evaporating in the face of his need to disagree. I didn't comment. I refused to say anything else in our trip to the courthouse. Now I was in a sour mood, but it faded as soon as I was out of the cab.

The Sheriff was there, as I thought he would be, looking as if he hadn't shaved in a couple of days and hadn't slept in a week. I felt sorry for him.

Donny was also there. "Uh-oh," he said, "here's trouble."

Actually, that was a compliment, but he couldn't see it. I ignored him and said to the Sheriff. "Could I talk to you for a few minutes? Please?"

Donny answered: "Sam's got enough to do without you dragging in more—"

The Sheriff leveled him with a look, I was pleased to see. Then he said to me, as he unhitched his jacket from the back of his chair, "Come on."

"Where?" I picked up my folder and wondered if I was under arrest for file-drawer theft.

"Over to the Rainbow. Donny can hold down the fort." He turned at the door. "Donny, you hear *anything*, let me know."

"Well, sure, Sam," he said, as if to say, *Don't I always?*

As we walked down the steps of the courthouse, I said, "What I have to tell you is kind of private."

"The best place for telling that kind of story's in the midst of a crowd. People are so busy listening to themselves they can't be bothered with somebody else. "Of course, there's Maud—?"

He meant she might sit down with us at some point, and did that bother me? "No. Maud's okay."

We had started across the street, but had to wait for a car to pass that had just rounded the corner. The Sheriff would never hold up his hand to stop a car just so he could cross a street.

The regulars were pretty much settled at the counter, having their morning coffee. Morning coffee sometimes ran into early lunch and I wondered how people like Dodge Haines ever did any business. As we passed them, they said hi to the Sheriff, who said hi back again. Maud was taking a breakfast order from some man who was probably just passing through. She winked. And Patsy Cline was kind of presiding over all of this, as she often did, singing "I Fall to Pieces," one of my all-time favorites.

We sat down in the back booth and I lay my folder on the table. I still hadn't shown him anything in it, but that would come as I told my story. I said, now, "I'll make a bargain with you if you hear me out before you get mad, for I know you will, at least on the inside."

Smiling, he settled back in the booth. "I'll try and reign in my temper."

"Because part of this is about Ben Queen. There's evidence he never murdered his wife Rose. It's not just my imagining things."

The Sheriff started in: "That old case isn't mine and I don't see how it's important—"

I held up my hand. "The reason it's important is because you think Ben Queen killed Fern and you think that because you think he killed Rose."

"Wait a minute, that's not altogether true—"

"What's not true? Altogether?" Maud was standing there with her order book and a Coke, which she set before me.

"It's true you're looking for him. Why are you looking for him?"

Maud said, "So he can help the police with their inquiries. That's always what they say. Sam?" She sort of waved her order book back and forth. "Breakfast?"

"No, and sit down as long as you don't interrupt."

"Well! Emma?"

I didn't know if she was asking if she could, or if I wanted something. But she sat down beside the Sheriff.

"What's this proof you've got, Emma?"

"Ben Queen was somewhere else when Rose got killed."

Maud raised her eyebrows, but didn't interrupt.

"Where?" asked the Sheriff.

"He was in Hebrides. He went to Smith's Feed Store, it's out on 219 the other side of Hebrides. I was hoping you'd go and talk to Mr. Smith because he's the alibi. The old one, not his son, who's kind of dumb. If Ben Queen didn't do it, don't you think his name should be cleared? Twenty years in prison for nothing; I think he should get back his good name."

"Absolutely. But what's your part of this bargain?"

"I'll tell you what I know about Ben Queen." It struck me, though, that for a person who wasn't there that night and hadn't heard him, I didn't know much. Ben Queen hadn't out-and-out denied killing Fern. It was like the murder of Rose all over again. And he did have that gun with him. If the Sheriff had been there, he might have agreed with me.

Maud had her chin propped in both hands. She turned her head to look at the Sheriff, who was surprised.

351

"That's fair. Tell me what you know."

I shook my head. "Not until you go talk to this Mr. Smith."

"You don't trust me?"

"Of course not," said Maud. "Why would she? You haven't believed anything she's said up to now."

The Sheriff looked, I can only say, crestfallen as he studied Maud's face, as if he couldn't imagine she'd think he was untrustworthy.

The thing was, it wasn't because I didn't trust him to keep his part of the bargain, it was because I knew if I told him about Ben Queen being at the Devereau house, he'd be out of here like a shot. I couldn't have that. "That's one part of your bargain. The other is to go back and look at what happened to Mary-Evelyn Devereau. It wasn't any accident. That sheriff back then was an idiot, or plain lazy, or was cowed by the Devereaus. Even Dr. McComb thinks the whole thing was peculiar and maybe hushed up. The way she died?"

The Sheriff said, trying not to sound impatient, "I haven't got the reports on that case, so how could I—?"

I opened the folder and took out the police report.

"Where'd you get this?" The Sheriff was astonished.

"It's all in your files. I just took this stuff out."

"Did you get this out of the files?"

"Sam—"

"When Donny took one of his seven-hour coffee breaks."

"Sam—" Maud said again, her hand closing on his arm.

"I'm sorry," I said. "But you weren't paying any attention to me."

"I *wasn't?* Well, who went looking for you when you *disappeared?* Who took—"

So he *did* know the missing girl was me! Well, I hadn't time to bother about that.

"*Sam!* Stop being ridiculous!"

The Sheriff turned to look at Maud, and somehow, some way, the anger seemed to drain out of him.

"Listen," I said, trying to get my story back on course. "The way Mary-Evelyn died, why would anyone *not* think it's peculiar for a little girl to take a boat out at night. If it'd been *you,* wouldn't you have investigated?"

"Of course he would have," said Maud.

The Sheriff's face was down, but he held up both hands in a silencing gesture. "That case is forty years old, Emma."

"What difference does *that* make? They shouldn't be allowed to get away with it. Mary-Evelyn's good name is be-, be-" I couldn't think of the word.

"Besmirched," said Maud, indignantly.

"Right. They were so spiteful toward each other, those three sisters, they took it all out on Mary-Evelyn. You should go and talk to Imogene Calhoun that lives over in Cold Flat Junction, too. She actually went to that house when she was a kid, and she'll tell you. They hated each other. Isabel and Iris hated each other because of *him*." I slapped down the photo of Jamie Makepiece.

The Sheriff picked it up. "Who is this?"

"His name is Jamie Makepiece. And this letter—" I took out the letter the Sheriff had already seen. "—is a good-bye letter to Iris Devereau." The "I" could have meant Isabel, but what reason would he have to write it? He no longer cared about Isabel. I didn't go into this for it would just complicate things more. "That's reason enough for Iris and Isabel to hate each another. And for both to hate Elizabeth for breaking up the romance. And listen to *this*—Mary-Evelyn wasn't their little niece, I bet you. Mary-Evelyn was probably Iris's *daughter*. *Now* do you see why they'd hate the sight of her?"

Maud had a paper napkin scrunched in the hands she held up to her mouth. She was wide-eyed. The Sheriff's frown I can only describe as exquisite. Exquisitely wondering. Boy, I really had their attention. "Just look at her." I pushed the picture of Mary-Evelyn around so both could give it a good, hard look. I also took out my one snapshot of the Devereaus under the porte cochere. "Look at her, then him, then them. Everything about her looks is like him, especially the hair. You can't tell in the police picture because her hair's wet and looks dark. But you can certainly tell in the other picture." I tapped it with my finger.

We were all silent for a moment. Then Maud asked, "What about Brokedown House, Emma? These things were there. Where does that come into your story?" All she had heard, I could tell by her look, by her voice, had seeped into her as if, like Mary-Evelyn, she might be drowning.

I thought of that light shining in my face. "Somebody's there."

"Ben Queen," said the Sheriff, always ready to blame the man for the state of the whole world. "It's Ben Queen, isn't it? That's where you saw him."

"No!" I said. "But there's someone. You know from being there that night. Remember?"

"Dwayne Hicks said there was somebody, but—"

"You think Dwayne was making it up?" asked Maud, irritated. "You want to bend everything to fit your own theory?"

"No, Maud, I didn't say he was making it up. I'm only thinking he might have been mistaken." He drummed his fingers on the table, looking at me all the while. "Who would have a motive for killing Fern Queen? I've got to say, it doesn't sound like her father would. Unless maybe Fern killed her mother."

"Revenge?" said Maud. "That doesn't make any sense if he'd gone to prison himself to protect Fern."

"Fern must've killed her mother. That's the only thing I can see would account for it." Ben Queen wouldn't have any motive. But the Girl might, since her mother had abandoned and betrayed her. "There's a Girl—"

Maud leaned forward as if not wanting to miss a single drop of this story, and I thought, even more than the Sheriff, she was the person to tell it to.

"What girl?" asked the Sheriff.

I started to remind him about that afternoon a few weeks ago when I'd seen her through the window of Souder's Drug Store and run after her. I'd collided with the Sheriff and asked him if he'd seen her. I started to say this, but didn't. After those few words I'd uttered, it was like I got stuck. Was I afraid he'd go after her? Was I afraid she wouldn't come back if I talked about her? I studied my hands folded on the table, then my untouched Coke glass. My mind just seemed too empty of words. Words can abandon you just like people can. I had to get my mind going again. I said, "She looks like Rose Devereau. She looks *exactly* like Rose Devereau." I opened my mouth to say more, but fell silent again.

"Where?" asked the Sheriff. "Where have you seen her?"

"In Cold Flat Junction. At the railroad station. And here." But I didn't want to say where here. I had told Dr. McComb more than anybody and that was precious little, but I had told him about seeing her across Spirit Lake, in front of the Devereau house. And I saw her again, when I was in the house, outside, standing just within the rim of pines out there. I did not want to tell anybody that I believed she was getting closer. For a moment, I thought she might know about being lost, know the secret of lostness. It all sounded crazy, even to me it sounded crazy, the whole story—wild, weird, nightmarish when you heard it like this all at once. I can't say how far away my mind had traveled from the Rainbow Café, for Maud's voice pierced me like an arrow.

"You look," she said, "as if you've seen a ghost."

Dead man walking

58

Two hours was plenty of time to get to the Devereau house and tell Ben Queen, if he was there, what had happened. Warn him off, only he didn't strike me as the sort of person that needed warning off, the sort who would hightail it out of town when trouble came his way. The Sheriff's pursuit of Ben Queen would still continue, even if the reason for it had changed, even if the reason were only to ask him some questions. For there was still the murder of Fern and she was still, after all, Ben Queen's daughter.

But I had to lie down for a few minutes; I was more tired from telling my story to them than from all the running around I'd been doing. Maybe what tired me was the end of it. Or maybe what tired me was knowing the Davidows would be back soon to flatten everything. Or maybe I was just afraid my story was just a story, full of what

William Faulkner said was sound and fury. (Or at least what Dwayne said he said.)

I lay in bed, thinking all this while holding my bear who, I discovered, did have a very small hole in its stomach that could leak stuffing if I didn't pinch it closed as I was doing. I found a tiny safety pin and closed the tear with that.

To make up for being so lackadaisical, I ran down the back stairs, taking care to use the route that bypassed the dining room. Miss Bertha and Mrs. Fulbright would be heading in for their dinner, if they weren't already seated at their table.

I took the wooden walk to the kitchen and announced to Walter I had to do something really important and would he mind waiting on the two for dinner? I also told him where I was going just to be on the safe side although I wasn't sure the safe side of what.

I didn't mean to be dramatic about things; I left the drama to Will and Mill who were dramatic enough for all of us. I wanted to be more like Lena, who was the most *un*dramatic person I had ever come across (except maybe for Walter), considering everything wrong in her life, and being about to have a baby and looking for the father (and even inexperienced me could see *that* disappointment coming a mile away). Imagine walking all the way from Alabama to Mississippi, taking a whole month to do it. Imagine having that kind of faith in your feet.

My own feet were carrying me down the half mile of dirt road to Spirit Lake and another quarter mile or more to Crystal Spring. I stopped to look at the old boathouse and remember back to when my father brought us here and further back to the night of Mary-Evelyn's drowning. At Crystal Spring I stopped to get a drink of water. The tin cup was where it always was, shoved back in against the rock by me so no one could see it except the ones who knew it was there. I drank and looked off into the woods where a look didn't penetrate very far. I figured I had been through there eight times already, coming and going, so there was no reason I couldn't do it the ninth and tenth times. It was still daylight, but however light out here, the woods were closer to midnight. And it had begun to rain, not much, but enough to veil the available light.

In the woods the rain did not penetrate any more than the light. I was glad there was this rutted old road, even though it was mostly overgrown, narrowed to just the ridge of earth between tire tracks. A lot of tires and a lot of feet had trampled it down. The Devereau sisters had passed this way the night they had brought Mary-Evelyn through. Brought her, not gone looking for her. I believed that now.

My feet scuffed up cold wet leaves, making as much of a squelch as they could for comradely noise. I had picked up a sturdy stick and battered and whacked the beeches and pines as I passed, again, I guess, to make noise, as if to scare something off. I moved as fast as I could and as noisily as I could through the laurel bushes and tangled vines, through pines and heavily laden oaks that littered the ground with acorns, past ash trees whose bark was like cold gray marble, through patches of wildflowers I couldn't name, but which my mother could.

I even stopped and thought of my mother as something more than my cook, as a person making her way through the Carolinas with crazy people, almost as crazy as Aurora Paradise could ever be. I marveled that my mother had been brazen enough or had enough starch in her to put up with them for all of these years without much help from Will or me.

I tore bark from my stick as I thrashed along, getting it down to white bone. An uneven runnel of light showed above me where thin branches fretted the sky that was nearly canceled out. Then the trees opened up ahead and I was at the dark line of pines that edged this end of the wood and the Devereau yard.

I crossed it and went around to the rear, to the kitchen door. The kitchen had been used again, which made me think Ben Queen was around. In the sink were a couple of plates, a bowl, and two cups. On one plate were the remnants of egg and toast. If only Walter were here! He could tell me not only when all of these dishes had been eaten off of, but what kind of person had done the eating! The drying baked beans that had been a careless puddle? "Ain't Miss Bertha, she's too mean to leave them beans behind." Or the asparagus spear sheared cleanly in half? "Someone got a grudge on, it's Aurora Paradise, most likely." Yes, Walter could tell more from the state of uneaten food than an Irish famine. (I should tell the Sheriff to add Walter to his list of crime-scene people.)

On the stove there was a frying pan in which the eggs had been fried, a quart of milk and bread standing by it. Crumbs lay on the white enamel counter and a bread knife, such as my mother uses, with a serrated edge. My mother is horribly particular about which knives cut what. Vera once used her meat-cutting knife to slice lemons. It's the only time I recall my mother giving Vera hell (which she very often deserves, as far as I'm concerned). What I was seeing here looked like the remains of a breakfast. It must have been Ben Queen's.

I walked through the dining room without stopping as I doubted the intruder would have set himself a place. With a table setting I would probably be as good as Walter was with food when it came to figuring out what kind of person had been sitting at the table. Cutlery shoved all anyhow? Miss Bertha, for sure. Knife and fork aligned perfectly on a plate? The Poor Soul, definitely.

The living room produced in me the same mixture of gloom and nostalgia I had felt before, only now it was weightier, as if the room itself were inconsolable. I stood looking at the picture of the sisters that hung on the wall near a sideboard, the only picture there. Three of them with their dark hair worn loose or in plaits, and Rose herself, not more than a child and much younger then the Girl was now, but still with that light bright hair, incandescent if the sun hit it, otherwise shining with a cool and moonish glow. The sisters must have been in their late teens; it was hard to think of them that way, so solemn they looked, their dark hair against their black clothes.

The piano and a small table were studded with candles stuck to small plates in their own wax, as if there had been a power outage. I looked at the sofa where Ben Queen had dropped the gun like a toy. I could see him doing it, as if tossing it off himself. He seemed himself almost affrighted by coming face-to-face with a little kid, no more dangerous to him than one of Dwayne's rabbits. I could only think now he was afraid of my fear of him. I had never known an adult to react so quickly to something in a child, not even Maud or the Sheriff.

I looked through the screen door that opened out onto the porch, across the yard for any sign of either of them, the Girl or Ben Queen. The rain fell sluggishly, or that was just me seeing my own tiredness in the rain.

I climbed the stairs. I wanted particularly to see the relation between those two rooms, the one I thought to be Iris's, since there was a sewing machine, and the one I knew was Mary-Evelyn's. The doors were opposite one another, as I had thought. And there was a rocking chair in Iris's room in direct line with the door. I sat in it and looked across the hall into Mary-Evelyn's room at Mary-Evelyn's bed. Had she been lying in it, I could have seen her clearly; had she been sitting by her toy chest, I also could have seen her. There was no way she could have left without Iris seeing her. I suppose Mary-Evelyn could have said she was going downstairs to get a glass of milk or something, but that was not in any of the sisters' statements. There were other possibilities, such as her sneaking out when they were all asleep, but with the open doors upstairs and locked and bolted doors down, I doubted it. This house, after all, was geared to imprisonment.

I left the rocking chair and Iris's room and went across to Mary-Evelyn's. She might still have lived here, for the white iron bed was made up with its yellow and white chenille bedspread and her beautiful dresses hung in the mahogany wardrobe.

I really was in awe of these dresses and the fine workmanship that had gone into their making. But had they scared her into a carefulness of behavior she wouldn't have felt if she'd had my old clothes to wear? Ice-blue taffeta, pale yellow cotton with tiny pleats and satin-covered buttons, rose-colored wool, as soft as cashmere.

Then I went to the toy chest, opened it, and rummaged through puzzles, stuffed animals, cotton dolls, and a Ouija board until I found the Mr. Ree game. I removed the board and the cards and the tiny weapons and lined up the hollow tubes with their molded plastic heads, marveling at the care that had gone into the making of this game, as much care as had gone into the sewing of the dresses. I lined up the tubes: Mr. Perrin, Butler Higgins, Aunt Cora, Miss Lee. The tubes were used by the players to conceal the tiny weapons which you had to have in your possession to murder somebody. It was the best game I knew of.

Niece Rhoda, of course, was missing. Dwayne had found her on the path. It brought up the same question I asked about Mary-Evelyn's doll and Jamie's photograph: how had they got to Brokedown House? The Artist George piece had been in the alcove in the wall of Crystal Spring where the tin cup was kept. There hadn't been any message because—I thought this now, but hadn't then—it might fall into the wrong hands. All of the character cards were here, though. Mary-Evelyn had cut the faces of her aunts from some old snapshot and pasted them over the card faces. I had discovered this the first time I'd looked in the toy chest. Somehow, I found that a totally terrifying act on the part of Mary-Evelyn.

I sat absorbed, trying to make something of all this, and probably making too much, as I guess I tend to do about everything. I was not facing the door, but sitting sideways to it on the floor. I felt a kind of shadow hovering over the room and though there had been not the slightest noise, not even a disturbance of the air, I knew someone was in the hall. If I moved my head scarcely an inch outward, I would see the person. I moved nothing, not a scrap, as if my stillness might void the shape that I knew was filling the doorway. Whoever it was had been in the house all the while, and had kept quiet, which was the scariest thing of all.

In seconds my mind would collapse under a weight of fear if I didn't stave it off by just going blank. Blank. Any thought I had ran before my inner eye as if it were coming by ticker tape, from outside.

"Why are you here?"

It was a woman's voice. There was no way I could pretend I was deaf. I was shaking, I couldn't help it, but I could try and cover it up by pretending stupidity. I did turn my head then and said "Huh?"

"Get up from there."

She was tall, gaunt, and plain, as plain as the dark wool dress she was wearing. It was an ugly plum color. She was fifty years older than she was in the picture with Jamie Makepiece, but she was still unmistakably Isabel Devereau.

I had stared at the pictures of the sisters and Jamie long enough to know to a fault who was who. But her question was strange. Shouldn't it have been "Who are you?" and not "Why are you here?"

I could not hold the cards because my hands shook, but I could handle the tubes. I dropped the miniature gun and knife into the Miss Lee tube, as if I were continuing to play, and when it rattled, no one would know it was my shaking hand causing it. It wasn't until then that I saw the gun. She was holding the gun Ben Queen had dropped on the couch, loosely, as if it were an afterthought.

She appeared to look over my head and take direction from something or somebody. I resisted the urge to follow her look. The "huh" which had registered as stupidity or emptiness was frozen there, which probably made it that much more convincing. If I could keep her from doing anything for another minute I might come up with something from the mental ticker tape. One thing on it was that question, "Why are you here?" What threatened to upset me from this tightrope walk was the terrifying notion that Isabel Devereau took me for Mary-Evelyn. Here I was, the same age and size. My face wasn't Mary-Evelyn's, but I didn't think that would matter to Isabel. After all, here I was in Mary-Evelyn's room, with Mary-Evelyn's things.

She was crazy. I don't mean the Davidow craziness or even the Aurora Paradise kind. I mean *crazy* crazy. Insane. A craziness perhaps shared by a few of the old people in Weeks's Nursing Home, the ones who talked to the air and hit whatever was around to hit, even empty space. No, Lola and Aurora weren't even in the running if it was Isabel Devereau they had to beat; they weren't even close. She seemed to be listening to something. Although I knew nothing was there, still it was an effort not to turn and make sure nothing was coming up behind me. Her eyes widened and narrowed.

Then she was standing over me and reaching down to grab my arm. "Get up! We have to go." Pulling me to my feet, she shook me as if I were one of Mary-Evelyn's cotton dolls, the gun at my back.

I couldn't have put up any resistance even if I hadn't been numbed by the fear I was trying to hold at bay. It would flood in like the news of a death if I so much as opened my mind for a moment to it. My blank self was pushed and prodded down the stairs. My hand was all this time glued around the Miss Lee tube.

I mustered up some will to act as if this were just one more occasion of angry-adult-disciplining-willful-child. "What are you *doing*?" My feet clattered on the stairs. She didn't answer; I hadn't really expected her to. I wanted to hear the sound of my own voice.

The screen door was at the bottom of the stairs and on the last step I gave a terrific yank, freed my arm of her grip and rushed the door. But she was just as quick, pulling me back, and this time her iron grip was on my neck.

"Isabel!" I yelled.

Her hand fell from my neck. I hadn't the vaguest idea what to add to the shouted name. I turned and looked at her and wished I hadn't. She was standing with the gun raised.

"Go on," she said, prodding me forward.

With the gun at my back we came to the living room screen door. That I had managed to control her actions by calling out her name made me feel momentarily elated. If I had done it once, maybe I could do it again. Right now, I saw myself running. *All you need to do is break the point of contact.* No, I thought, running was instinct, and instinct was too dangerous. Anything without cold reasoning behind it was too dangerous. I realized right then that the enormous practice I'd had all these years in controlling my feelings would be to my advantage. I *had*, after all, controlled Isabel for a few seconds when I'd said her name. If I was patient, I could do it again.

But patience with a gun at your back isn't an easy thing to practice. I did what the gun wanted and it wanted me to cross the yard and enter the woods. Into the thick darkness we went. It was not the time to think of Donny Mooma and what he had said about the last mile.

For here I was, dead girl walking.

The boathouse

59

I wondered how much time had passed, for it felt like half my life. As I went by the few landmarks I knew, I thought the woods had never seemed such a friendly and familiar place, one I really would hate to leave. Something life-threatening does that I suppose, throws up a different face to things. I looked up briefly to that narrow bit of sky and saw that there was still a scrap of light and was relieved.

Out of it, we came to the spring. We had to pass the little stone alcove where the cup sat, and, without knowing why, I reached out my stubborn fist and shoved Miss Lee into it.

Why did I do this? Did I think someone would find it, like a message in a bottle, and come like a lightning bolt to knock mad Isabel down? Why had I taken the chance, when any sudden movement could have got me shot in my back? I think it was because of that fairy tale I told myself when I was little, that there are certain places that can't be got at by the wrong people. That stone alcove was a charmed place. I think that's why Artist George had ended up there. I knew it was why the tin cup was there in the first place. I had told myself back then a drink from that cup would arm me against evil. That was back when I knew what it was.

But Isabel hadn't noticed; she was too intent on getting where we were going. I was sure we were headed for the boathouse. The gun had dropped farther down my back as we walked; it was now at my waist. I imagined it as some tiny burrowing creature looking for a hiding place.

Behind me, she spoke not a word. All I could hear was her ragged breathing, as if she'd run a race. Quick, short jabs of breath. I think I knew what she intended to do, and it was certainly preferable to the gun at my back, although it carried its own hazards with it. We had come to the boathouse.

As in those old stories of pirate ships and mutinies, I was being made to "walk the plank"—the boardwalk to the boathouse. The boats, some of them, were still there, though I hadn't seen anyone ever using them. Whether the one that had carried Mary-Evelyn like some old Eskimo woman sent out to sea to die was among them. I counted four rowboats, all of them old as the hills, none of them looking like it could bear any weight, but I hoped they could, even though they were oarless. My heart hammered; my stomach fell another foot as we left the boardwalk that stretched out over Spirit Lake, which I saw now, as I had the woods, with a fresh vision. I seemed to grasp the story all at once, as if my mind closed around it as my fist had closed around the Miss Lee tube.

In my heart-hammering dread, I was surprised I could still talk, surprised I could still make out language. It wasn't talk; it was more like an echo of talk, more like a memory of it.

"She was dead before you put her in the boat, wasn't she?"

"Elizabeth drowned her first. Not I. I hate death up close."

"Why did you kill Fern Queen?" I choked this out, feeling as if a wasp were in my throat, stinging it closed.

"She murdered our Rose."

"Our Rose? *Our* Rose? You hated Rose Queen!"

Isabel smiled and her smile was dreadful, a blackened crescent, moon lava. Once she had been a handsome woman, cold but dignified.

Her mind had ravaged her face, now. "Rose was under his spell. It wasn't her fault."

I knew how much of a lie all of this was. But the Devereau sisters had managed to shore up each other's beliefs with lies. There were things she wanted to believe, most of all in Jamie's love for her.

The gun touched my chest. Her tone was actually friendly as she talked about how I was a bastard child, how they had to get rid of me, even Iris thought so. (I had nearly forgotten that to her I was Mary-Evelyn and so was a hateful thing. I was proof of Jamie's and Iris's betrayal.) Her smile was impenetrable, as if me being a bastard child was of no consequence. She said Iris blinded Jamie with her beauty and then stole him away. It was then it occurred to me that she wanted to believe in Jamie, that there are things each of us wants to believe and could believe in spite of there being no evidence for it. If this weren't so, she wouldn't be doing all of this talking; it was nervous talking, the kind that keeps things at bay. What I thought was it wouldn't be too hard to convince her of what she wanted to be convinced of.

"Jamie. What about that letter Jamie wrote you?"

She paused, uncertain. "What letter?"

By now I had read it or heard it read enough times I could almost recite it. I did, coming down hard on the "I" of "My dear I."

"Iris is who he meant."

"How do you know if it only said 'I'?"

"Because Iris told me—"

"She told you it was to her." My teeth had finally stopped chattering. I was almost beginning to believe myself. Even with that gun pointed at me, I had a taste of power, which was what people usually had over me. Now I saw why they used it. It felt good. "You believed her and you shouldn't have. He came back. He must have gone to that old Calhoun house where you've been living. Where you brought the photograph. Where you brought the doll."

"Jamie's gone. Elizabeth sent him packing. She controlled all of us, excepting Rose. Rose was the lucky one—she ran off. Even though it was with that no-account Queen fellow. Too bad he got blamed for what his awful daughter did. But I fixed her."

For that minute she'd been seeing events in her mind. Now, she was seeing me. She shifted the gun. I could not look at it any longer. The moon was caught behind cloud cover and the stars were hidden. There was usually such a bright rash of them I could hardly believe they'd retreated on me, too. I thought of a hand shutting the eyes of the dead. I felt as if we were talking underwater, where words scarcely rose to the surface. Maybe I was drowning in the wake of a boat. I could hardly keep my head above all of this imaginary water.

It's as though all these years never were. Had she said that? Or had I thought it? I felt I was getting farther and farther away, drifting away across Spirit Lake, out of reach of everyone. I felt this more strongly even than fear, fear had almost nothing to do with it. It was loneliness, pure and simple. It was the blue devils.

Yet I thought all of this while I was talking, telling things I could only guess at, but kept on talking, for that fixed her mind on that long-ago summer when for a while she had the power that happiness lent her: with Jamie she could have done anything.

"My own sister." That's what she kept saying, in a dead voice, over and over again, *My own sister.*

My mind tried to race to a way out of this, but it could only plod. Then I thought, *Wait:* she knew I—or Mary-Evelyn— was Iris's child, but she didn't know I was Jamie's, not for certain.

"I'm not his; I'm not Jamie's. Iris lied."

At this the gun dropped to her side, but she still had a quick enough hold on it that I didn't dare move. She was mad, but she wasn't addled.

"Lies."

"No. Iris was really bad. There were other men besides Jamie." Then for some reason I came upon this lucid patch in my mind that said: You're twelve years old and here you are trying to take charge of your own life and maybe death. I would sooner be sitting in the Orion with my bag of popcorn and my eyes silvered by the reflection of the silver screen, as if I were up there too in that fantasy land of men and women going mad for love or lack of it.

It made more sense than this. I should have been merely an observer of life that I couldn't possibly understand, instead of stuck down in the midst of it as an actor, a player, a participant. It wasn't fair. *Whine, whine,* my player-self said. *Nobody twisted your arm, did they?* Then my mind rushed past this lucid place and I felt its weight again, trying, trying to get myself out of here.

She had been uttering a storm of epithets, heaping abuse on Iris's head, apparently partly convinced that what I'd said was true. She raised the gun again. "Just you back up, now."

I did.

"Get down into that boat." She pointed to the one closest, bobbing slightly, though Spirit Lake seemed deathly quiet.

There were no oars and I was a poor swimmer, but any place was better than here.

A short wooden ladder that was used to get to the boats was attached to the dock on both sides. I climbed down into at least six inches of water sloshing around in the bottom; it looked pretty old, and I'm sure it was. I can't recall ever having seen anyone using this dock in the last several years. I could swim to shore from here, as it wasn't more than fifty or sixty feet. Certainly, I could, except she could get there quicker than I and I'd just be back to where I was. So I watched her undo the rope from the post it was tied to, toss it into the boat, then pick up one of the oars lying on the dock and shove the boat. I floated on quietly moving water toward the center of the lake. She stood on the dock, watching, and I had no idea, none, what she meant by all of this. What I felt was the most incredible relief I'd ever known, getting away from her. Even though there was water in the bottom of the boat, I think it had come perhaps from rain, or disturbance of the lake which had sloshed over the side. For it didn't get any deeper, and although I had nothing to scoop it up with, I could do a little with my hands, and nothing came to fill it up again. I didn't see any sign of leaks. I kept bailing water with my hands, feeling if I had to bail all the rest of the night, I'd still be lucky. Shore got farther away; I wouldn't want to have to swim from where I was now.

I was looking down and bailing when I heard a shot and beside the boat the water caved as if someone were skipping big stones. I looked toward the dock. She was firing at me. I dropped down, terrified, my face in the water. So this was what she had in mind. I put my hands over my ears, which did no good for I heard the second shot as clearly as the first. More clearly, because it was closer. The frightening thing was, she didn't even have to hit *me*. All she had to do was hit the boat and then it *would* sink. Able or not, I might have to swim toward shore, and I could imagine the shots in the water. How many bullets did that gun hold?

I was a sitting duck. I couldn't stand it, just to have thought I was safe from her, and now I find that this was what she had in mind all along. *I hate death up close.* It was Elizabeth who'd had to hold Mary-

Evelyn down. I could just picture vicious Isabel walking away from the scene, hands over her eyes.

Another shot that didn't split the water, but came with a cry. I raised my head just enough to see over the bow. What I saw astonished me more than anything else that night: Isabel fell, flailing, into the water. A figure emerged from the brush along the road and walked the boardwalk to the dock.

It was Ben Queen. Even from this distance, and in the dark, I could tell it was him. He had a certain way, a certain walk. He shouted something, but I couldn't understand it. I had come to save Ben Queen, and here he was, saving me.

I tried to use my hands as oars, but made precious little progress.

I could see her, floating there near the dock, her ugly purple dress turned black by the water. Holding one of the old white lifesavers stacked on the dock, Ben Queen jumped into the water and started toward me. He swam like a sewing needle running up a seam, scarcely parting the water, dragging the lifesaver with him. When he got close enough he shoved it to me.

He was treading water and raking his wet hair out of his face. "Glad I happened along."

"Me too."

"You can swim some?"

"Some."

"Paddle with one hand and give me the other and let's get the hell outta here."

———

When I'd spotted the police car fast arriving along the road, my main concern was not for Ben Queen's welfare, but whether I looked like a drowned rat. You'd think being held at gunpoint would overcome a person's self-consciousness and vanity, but not mine.

"Emma, long as you're all right, I think it might be best for me to vamoose."

I insisted I was all right. I thanked him and thanked him.

"I owed you, Emma. Looks like I might again." He was looking at the car a short distance down the road, its red bulb flashing, aimed here. Ben Queen picked up his shotgun and vamoosed.

The two of them were out of the car, and the Sheriff was running

369

along the boardwalk, calling out my name. I'd forgotten: Walter knew where I was and the Sheriff would have come looking for me once he got back from Hebrides.

He sounded really worried—Good! *And just wait until you hear about what you failed to save me from!* I wish the body of Isabel Devereau hadn't chosen that moment to float up and bang against the dock. I nearly screamed, but caught myself.

"Hi," I said, casually. "She's down there."

The Sheriff kept an arm around me, saying things like *My God, Jesus Christ, holy hell,* and a few other blasphemies which I might have to report to Father Freeman. Donny swaggered around with his thumbs hooked in his Sam Brown, chewing gum and generally giving the impression that he knew right away nobody was in danger. The Sheriff told him to get the hell back to the car and call in for an ambulance and the coroner. Get things going. Donny reluctantly left.

The Sheriff kept his arm around me and asked me if I was okay. I said, grandly, of course, hating that I looked soggy and caked with water and lily-pad muck. But I was flattered that he asked me about me before he asked about the body floating in the water, whom he didn't recognize.

I said, "You've got a really bad memory, considering all those pictures I showed you." But he hadn't spent as much time as I had looking at them. "Isabel Devereau," I said, shivering, while trying to look blasé and modest but only managing to look dripping wet. The Sheriff saw me shiver and immediately removed his uniform jacket and whirled it around my shoulders.

Well! I thought. This was worth getting wet for! Was it worth almost dying for?

I guess not.

Ree-Jane goes spastic
60

I was a celebrity. Glasses were being raised to me so much and so often, you'd think I was Tangcrine. There were all these reporters come from newspapers for miles around, from our nearest big city a hundred miles away, and someone even suggested the New York papers would pick it up.

I was a celebrity not just in Spirit Lake and La Porte, but in Cloverly, Hebrides, and you-name-it. My fame was spreading.

The three returned to find me rocking on the front porch, in the company of reporters from three newspapers also rocking on the front porch, and all drinking Cold Comforts and having an hilarious time interviewing me. I thought perhaps their laughter and clear enjoyment of the assignment might have been suppressed in view of the danger I had been placed in, but then I put that down to my mixing too much

Jack Daniel's and Wild Turkey in their drinks. (I had ransacked Mrs. Davidow's storeroom.)

Now: imagine Ree-Jane.

Imagine Ree-Jane getting out of the car (hideously sunburned) and walking up the front steps into this scene. For here I was at the very center of her own daydream. Her daydream become waking reality, not for her, but for me: Famous Adventurer, Famous Heroine, Famous Actress (for Hollywood must be on its way). Famous.

Famous, Famous, Famous, Famous, Famous.

Me. It was all happening to *me*, Emma Graham, not to *her*, Ree-Jane Davidow.

Even Walter was there, leaning against the porch railing, smiling to beat the band, for he had been interviewed and photographed, too. It was Walter, after all, who had sent the police car to Spirit Lake.

Walter! Walter, who was so low on the totem pole. Walter, who was mere background music. Walter had stepped out of the shadows into the story of a lifetime.

"Now, be sure you tell them, Walter," I'd said when I was whipping up the Cold Comforts for the reporters, "you be sure to tell them that *you* were the only one who knew where I was and that *you* would have come looking for me if the Sheriff hadn't turned up."

"Well, it's true, ain't it? I woulda."

Ree-Jane stayed spastic for two days. Lola, who took her fame where she found it, even if it was being lit by reflected glory (and extra martinis), had me in the back office going over the story again and again. Laughing in the wrong places, of course, but who cares? One of the funniest things was watching Lola and Ree-Jane compete for the most "print" (as the reporters called it). Elbowing Ree-Jane aside, Lola told the reporters she had always said I had more gumption than anyone and that she had raised me always to assert myself. To another reporter, with whom she was sharing martinis, she came very close to adopting me—I was as good as her daughter.

The only ones not jumping on the bandwagon were Will and Mill, who could have got a lot of free publicity for their production out of it, but who didn't seem to care. When I mentioned this, Will put his hand on my shoulder and said he wouldn't want to intrude upon my success. That was the *biggest* lie. They'd intrude all over the place if they thought it would get them something they wanted, and publicity wasn't it. But why would it be, if everything they did was a secret?

I was there when a reporter approached the two—searching them out in the Big Garage, which was nervy—and to her questions, they both said, "No comment."

No *comment!* Oh, for heaven's sake!

"But aren't you thrilled that your little sister has done this?"

Will favored her with a tilted smile. "Like a *deus ex machina,* you mean?" He even pronounced it right.

The reporter stumbled over that. "A *what?*"

Mill answered: "You really ought to bone up on your Greek tragedies."

They turned, unconcerned, and walked away. Back to Paul and the bucket of flour.

But Ree-Jane went wandering around in her new blue dress like a wilting delphinium. I knew she would make a nasty recovery, though, and she did.

She started laughing when she saw me, pointing and laughing, fit to kill as if she knew a version of my exciting story that others didn't. It was that silent fake laughter she'd got down so well.

But it didn't last long.

One morning shortly after their return, Mr. Gumbrel called me up and asked me if I'd mind coming into the *Conservative* office; I said I'd be glad to, and did not ask him what this was all about. But I had an inkling something else was about to be added to the list of Me.

Famous Reporter.

Poor Ree-Jane.

Star reporter
61

"What I'd like you to do, Emma, is write this up for me." Mr. Gumbrel held up his palm as if I'd been going to object. "Don't say it's already been written up until we're blue in the face, because it hasn't. Don't tell me that you don't have a lot more to add, and don't tell me these reporters didn't include a pile of misquotes and mistakes—*including Suzie Whitelaw!*" She was passing by his little glassed-in cubicle, and he wanted to make sure she heard this.

She did. Her face went cherry red. She'd been walking by just to find out what he had me in there for.

"Oh, yes, there were mistakes all right." I did not give as an example the city paper that had spelled Regina Jane ReeJane (as suggested by me), this spelling having been picked up and flaunted by a dozen other papers. "But I'll correct them." Except for that particular mistake, I didn't add.

"Good! Wonderful! What I have in mind is your in-depth history of this whole affair. Maybe begin with telling how you came in here over a month ago, wanting to read our report on the death of the Devereau girl. It's stuff like that, it's the details I want. And I want it spread—" His hands measured off a width of air. "—through at least three and maybe even four or five issues."

I was really excited, but kept it in check. "Yes, I can see a story like this could take a lot of print."

"You betcha! I'm going to sell more papers with this than I have in the last two years!"

"I wonder," I said suavely, "if it'll go on the wire?"

Mr. Gumbrel said undoubtedly, as he lit his cold cigar. "You know, ReeJane—"

(Would *everyone* now be calling her this? Would it turn up on her headstone? How wonderful!)

"—she'll take offense I turned her down," Mr. Gumbrel went on. "But obviously she can't write it."

"You mean—she *asked* to write this story?"

"Oh, my goodness, yes. Came in here like the Queen of the Nile, telling me she was a lot nearer the source than Suzie Whitelaw and so could do a better job." He plugged the cigar into his mouth, took it out again. "I had to remind her the one little thing she wrote a couple years ago didn't constitute 'experience.' Which is what she says she has. There's a girl could turn a silk purse right back into a sow's ear."

"Can I quote you?"

He guffawed.

———

My progress from the *Conservative* up Valley Road was marked by bursts of jumping and laughing. I guess anyone who might see me would conclude that fame had driven me mad.

No one did see me, though, for both Valley Road and Red Bird Road were so empty of houses. On Red Bird Road, the mobile home with its half-moon garden had set a plastic goose family among the zinnias and petunias. A pink flamingo had been added to this plastic family, and I had to admire the owners' attempt to draw what color out of life they could.

Dr. McComb's house seemed, as always, to be drowsing in its acres of tall grass, weeds, gladioli, and Queen Anne's lace. The lack of a front porch or a cellar gave it this submerged and sleeping look. The front door stood open, so I didn't have to knock, which might have summoned the strange, tall, voiceless woman, who I personally thought was as crazy as a loon, but then I'd been too long among stories of the Devereau sisters to have a good slant on madness.

I walked through the kitchen to see if any baking was going on. It was; from the oven wafted the smell of lemons. I went out to the back.

"Hi, Dr. McComb," I called.

His head came up and he waved, "Over here!"

I plowed through buffalo grass and strange tall winged flowers until I got to him. He was wearing his floppy broad-brimmed straw hat the color of burnt grass, which he swept off as he made me a courtly bow amid the butterfly bushes. "Brilliant! Brilliant! How'd you do it?"

"Thank you. That's what I came for—to thank you for the autopsy information you gave me."

"*Autopsy* information?" He looked swiftly around as if he had overlooked a dead body. "Did I dig someone up?"

I gave an exaggerated sigh. "You know. About drowning."

Slapping his straw hat back on his head, he said, "Emma, as I recall, all I did was *confirm* what you'd already figured out. That the child could have been drowned beforehand and someplace else." Then he put his arm around my shoulders. "This is at least a two-brownie topic. Let's go." He picked up the net and we walked back to the house.

"I didn't smell any brownies," I said. "I smelled lemon. Is it cookies?"

"Good grief! Does your investigative prowess never take a holiday? Right now what's baking is a citron pound cake. I already made the brownies, especially for your visit."

As we pushed through the weeds and Queen Anne's lace I said, "There's something else I wanted to thank you for, though."

"Um? What's that?"

"For not laughing."

Hearsayist
62

As I walked up the street to the Rainbow Café, I saw, of all people, Ree-Jane coming down the steps of the courthouse. Upon seeing me, she stopped. She did not cross the street to say anything; she merely stood there, pointing at me and laughing. Even as far away as she was, I could tell it was one of her fake, soundless laughs, but she really acted as if she would split in two with it. She had done this before, of course, but she hadn't done it coming out of the courthouse. What was going on? Who had she been talking to?

Shirl gave me a blistered look when I walked into the Rainbow (she being another one unaffected by my fame). I made my way to the back booth, slower than usual, as the counter sitters kept stopping me to comment. Mayor Sims enjoyed telling me that maybe I should be sheriff instead of Sam (ha ha ha), whereupon Ulub, sitting next to him, gave him a verbal thrashing, or as near as Ulub could get to it. We were so pleased with ourselves we nearly knocked Ubub off his stool with all of our friendly pats and punches. Patsy Cline was singing "Crazy."

Maud brought me a Coke. It was nice, always being fed by people. It almost made me want to be a wandering orphan or a matchstick girl, for then I would really have appreciated it.

I hadn't seen much of Maud in the last several days because the reporters (and the police) had kept me so busy answering questions, and because there'd been this big increase in business at the hotel. Today, I had been let off serving lunch when I'd told my mother I had really important business to attend to. Such are the benefits of being a celebrity that my mother had neither questioned the business nor why it was important.

Will certainly questioned it, since I would be missing another rehearsal. "You'll never get anywhere in the theater if you can't be serious about it."

"Why do I have to rehearse, for heaven's sake? All I *do* is come down on that swing thing."

"It's the *timing*, for fuck's sake."

I refused to lower myself to tell him he'd just said the f-word. That was really more because I wanted to say it myself and waited for him to pave the way. Yet, he said it so calmly, and without emphasis, that you'd think it was just another old word. Maybe it was.

"What timing? Mill just lowers the contraption with me on it. That's all."

Will put his hand to his head and groaned a little as if weary of dealing with amateurs.

"You producers are all alike," I said. "Temperamental, egotists, rude. Really fucking rude."

I turned away and marched off, the tart taste of the word on my tongue.

Maud said, putting down my Coke and her cigarettes, "You look as if you're holding up pretty well."

"Outside I ran into Ree-Jane."

"Everyone calls her that, now." Maud lit up a cigarette. "It's hysterical."

"That's what she was. Hysterical, I mean. She was laughing at me, pointing and laughing. It's like she knew something. And she was coming out of the courthouse."

"But she does that—I mean, you've said she laughs at you just to make you think the way you're thinking now: that she knows something, when she doesn't at all."

"Still, I'd like to see the Sheriff."

"Well, honey, your prayers are answered, for here he comes now." She looked toward the counter, where the Sheriff was stopping to talk to the Mayor.

The Sheriff broke out a smile so beaming it was like my Florida vacation all over again, but I was too suspicious of what Ree-Jane had been doing in the courthouse to appreciate it.

"Why was Ree-Jane in the courthouse? Were you talking to her?"

He frowned. "Nope. All I did was pass her outside, just a minute ago. I'd say she was talking to herself. Laughing to herself. Does she act like that often?"

I could have gone on at length about her actions, but I was focused on the most recent. "Well, if she wasn't talking to you, was she to Donny?"

"Donny knows better than to discuss police business." The Sheriff looked a little concerned, now.

Why would he think about "police business" in relation to Ree-Jane's weird behavior? I didn't like the sound of this.

Neither, apparently, did Maud. "And just what 'police business' does Donny know not to discuss, which he would discuss anyway, if it made him look at all good to discuss it?"

I leaned up against the edge of the table hard enough it dented my chest, waiting to hear him answer.

"Nothing. There's no new evidence. Nothing."

"*Evidence?* Evidence of *what?*" I demanded. "You know *everything*, more or less, and I can repeat every single word to you of what Isabel said. She admitted she shot Fern Queen. She admitted they murdered Mary-Evelyn. You said her prints are all over that gun."

It was rare for the Sheriff to look uncomfortable, but he did now. "That's right. Of course, so are Ben Queen's prints. We still haven't found him, even though—"

Wide-eyed, I literally fell back in the booth with a thud. "Ben Queen's *prints?* Why are you concerned about Ben Queen's prints?"

The Sheriff looked down, frowning, as if he'd expected to see a cup of coffee there.

Maud said, "Sam?"

379

She knew. So did I. "But it's *over*. It's solved! I *told* you—" Then it hit me square in the face and I stood up in the booth, jammed between table and seat. "You don't believe me. I told you everything. *You don't believe me!*"

"Listen, Emma—" the Sheriff began.

I said to Maud, "Let me out, please."

Immediately, she rose and I all but threw myself out of the booth.

The Sheriff looked really unhappy. "Emma. It's not that I don't believe you. It's just that in police work there's something called hearsay—"

Maud shook and shook her head. "Oh, for God's sake, Sam."

I glared at him. "You're telling *me* about police work?" I turned and walked off.

But I heard Maud say to the Sheriff something I couldn't imagine her ever saying to him. She said it calmly, without accent, the way Will had said "fuck."

"Asshole."

I had a coin out and as I passed the jukebox, now silent, I plugged it in and stabbed a button for Patsy Cline.

Let *him* fall to pieces for a change.

Ree-Jane rousted

63

I told Delbert to drop me off not at the hotel but at Slaw's Garage. Of course he wanted to know "what-all" kind of business I had at a garage, but I ignored the question. I didn't tip him either because he'd asked it. I was not in a good mood as I walked into the garage, where Dwayne was working by himself on the engine of some big old car. The hood was up and he was leaning over the engine. He didn't see me come in and I said hello.

"Well, Lord, look who's here," said Dwayne, standing up and wiping his hands on an oily rag. "That's some story, girl. I read all about it in the paper."

I hoisted myself up on a pile of new tires, as there were no chairs. I said, in an offhand manner, "Don't believe everything you read."

"Okay," he said, shoving the rag back in his pocket.

I sighed. It was just like him to say that; he irritated me to death sometimes. "I didn't *mean* that nothing was *true* in that news-paper story. A lot was. Maybe most was. Just, you know how reporters exaggerate. I mean, I wouldn't call myself 'courageous' or even 'spunky.'" Of course, I would.

"Okay, neither will I." He was leaning over the engine. He ad-justed his caged lightbulb to see into its depths.

"The *way* it happened was right. I mean, with Isabel Devereau's turning a gun on me and forcing me to walk through that dark, cold wood. It was like a death march."

"Wasn't that bad, was it?" He studied a spark plug.

"Yes. *Yes.* It was worse, if you must know. And there was *nobody* to help me."

He held the spark plug up toward the light and seemed to be regarding it as if it were a jewel. "I guessed I'd of helped, if I'd known." Then he hummed something. "You want to go rabbit hunting tonight?"

This took me completely by surprise. "With you?"

His head was lowered, half in shadow. "No, I figured maybe you could hook up with a couple foxes and the three of you go."

"Ha ha ha ha." I hated when I couldn't think of a clever response and had to resort to childish ha ha ha's. I shrugged to suggest I could take it or leave it, then quickly de-shrugged, thinking of his retort a moment ago. "Yes, I would." Besides, I wanted to talk to him about what the Sheriff had said. Even thinking about that now made me want to hit something.

"What's wrong?" He was looking at me through the triangle of light made by the raised hood of the car.

"Nothing. What time are we going?"

"I'm through here in a couple hours. I need to finish this. I can come pick you up at the hotel. In that." He nodded toward a fancy little car.

"*This?* Are you saying this's yours?"

"No. I'm saying Abel's loaning it to me because my truck's outta commission. It's Abel's."

"*This?* But it's . . . foreign, isn't it?"

"Lotus Elan. Really nice to drive."

How I pictured the reaction when he spun to a stop in this car un-der the porte cochere. I mean, of course, how Ree-Jane would react, since she's been flirting with Dwayne—or trying to—and he pays her no attention. Dwayne is handsome enough he doesn't have to be an earl to get Ree-Jane's interest.

"Okay, I'll be ready." I had been released from waiting tables that night, again, because I was famous.

As I walked lazily up the dirt path on the hotel grounds, I entertained myself with thoughts of Ree-Jane's reaction to the sight of me getting into that foreign car and purring off into the evening. This pleased me so much, I forgot for a moment the Sheriff's giving me that hearsay insult. How did I know but what he'd have me up on a murder charge? As if I'd shoved Isabel Devereau into the lake on general principle? Oh, it was all too infuriating.

When I left the leafy walk for our circular drive, I saw a smart little car that looked mildly familiar parked beneath the porte cochere, and when I neared the porch, I saw someone sitting, talking to Lola Davidow, who was rocking, drinking, and laughing—three of her favorite pastimes, at least the drinking and rocking part. The other person I was astonished to see was Louise Landis!

I stopped dead. The *orphans!* The orphans' lunch! For what day had I arranged it? Well, but I hadn't arranged it except between the two of us. I hadn't said a thing to my mother or Mrs. Davidow and here Louise Landis would be assuming they knew all about it. Thank heavens it was the cocktail hour and Lola had a pitcher of martinis close by.

Now, I figured that what Lola would think was that my mother had made the arrangements and forgotten to mention it. And if she was on her fourth martini (and by the look of the pitcher's contents she was), she wouldn't even care.

I bounded up the steps and said a bright hello to Miss Landis, who looked as happy as a lark to see me. Indeed, she did something seldom done: she hugged me. It wasn't that no one ever hugged me (Maud did a while back), but I was certainly not the most hugged person around.

"Emma!" She said, giving my shoulder an extra squeeze, "you are absolutely wonderful. You know you saved Ben Queen's reputation, to say nothing of probably saving his life!"

Now, it was just too bad that Ree-Jane chose that moment to sashay out and drop her little bomb. "Are you talking about that Queen person the police are looking for?" She arranged her pale blue dressed-up self in a green wicker chair. "But they're *still* looking for him." She gave one of her mirthless laughs.

Louise Landis asked her what she meant. It was such an innocent

383

question, I felt like socking Ree-Jane in the teeth before she said what I knew she would.

"The police need more to go on than just the story of a twelve-year-old *child.*" Ree-Jane glanced my way, laughing as if the mere idea of my story being useful was the funniest *thing.* "She might just have been imagining the whole thing. And as far as the law is concerned, what she says the Devereau woman said to her is only *hearsay.*"

The "h" word. I clenched my teeth to keep from yelling at her, but my hands made fists of themselves without any help from my brain.

Remarkably, Miss Landis's expression didn't alter one whit. She stayed slightly smiling. She was one cool customer, I was delighted to see. She said, "How do you know that?"

"You mean about the police?" Ree-Jane looked surprised, unused to having her words questioned. "Why, the deputy *sheriff* told me. Donny Mooma."

Louise Landis's smile deepened. "But that," she said, "is only hearsay, too. So I'll just go on believing Emma's the heroine of the story."

My mouth dropped open. To be hugged and made a heroine all in ten minutes' time was almost more than I could bear. To have someone stand *up* for me was a novel experience, too.

At that moment two things happened: my mother walked out on the porch and the foreign sports car crunched to a stop on the gravel under the porte cochere. My mother, surprised to see Louise Landis, gave her a friendly hello. They were glad to see each other again. And me, I was even more glad to watch Dwayne getting out of the car.

Ree-Jane twisted herself around so that her chin rested on the back of her chair in a coy sort of way, and called, "Dwayne! Hel-*lo!*" Dwayne's appearance got her over the retort from Louise Landis.

In the background, my mother was hearing all about the orphans' lunch, apparently thinking Lola Davidow and Louise Landis had just been arranging it, while Mrs. Davidow (as I thought she would) assumed my mother knew about it all along but didn't care one way or the other, having poured herself another martini.

Of course, Ree-Jane thought Dwayne had come to see her wonderful self and smiled lavishly at him as he walked up the porch steps. He nodded to her (coolly, I was happy to see), then, more energetically, put out his hand to shake my mother's, then Lola's, then Louise Landis's. I had no idea Dwayne was so very mannerly. I could see in my mother's eyes he had climbed a rung or two up the breeding ladder. Of course, it might not get him a seat in what I sometimes believed my mother fantasized was her Paris *salon* life, but he was still a cut above most of the uncouth inhabitants of Spirit Lake.

Ree-Jane was craned around, staring at the red car. "I haven't seen your *car* before, Dwayne. It's really something!"

He smiled a little. "Not mine; it's a borrower. I drive a broke-down truck."

It was then I knew Dwayne was a man who didn't need the world's favor. Most men would have let us think the fancy car was his. Not Dwayne. He didn't need to impress us, he didn't need our approval. I thought of how rare this quality was. *I* sure didn't have it; no one on this porch had it with the possible exception of Louise Landis.

Dwayne was turning down—very politely—the offer of a drink, as Ree-Jane asked him what brought him here, certain it was her baby-blue self.

He smiled at me. "To pick up Emma."

Oh, for a snapshot of Ree-Jane's open mouth! Wondering if I could stand another moment of glory, I crimped my mouth shut against shouts of glee and tried to look nonchalant.

My mother, understandably, I guess, raised an eyebrow. Mrs. Davidow would've too, except her eyebrows were engaged in looking sober. "Emma? What for? Where are you going?"

As if he were looking at cue cards written by God, Dwayne gave the perfect answer. "Scene of the Crime. Emma has to look it over again."

Ree-Jane, who wasn't getting cue cards, worked her mouth, but couldn't come up with anything, and just sat twisting a lock of her blond hair so madly I thought she'd pull it out. Goody.

Between Louise Landis and Dwayne, my day had really improved. If tomorrow I said "Dwayne Hayden came by in his red Lotus Elan to drive me to the scene of the crime," it would not be hearsay.

My mother was discussing the food Louise Landis would like for the orphans' lunch. Neither she nor Lola had figured out the source of this. Of course, Miss Landis now was pretty sure no one had sent me to Flyback Hollow to check on the details, but if she did, she wasn't talking.

So, before any of them could ask me any embarrassing questions, I said to Dwayne it was time to get going, and we got. Ree-Jane did not want to stare at the car disappearing down the drive, or me turning and waving to her, but she couldn't help herself, and I almost felt sorry for her.

But it's a long way from "almost" to "most," as long a way as from here to the Rony Plaza.

Bugswirled, stumppocked

64

"That is one helluva story, Emma."

We were sitting on the wide smooth rock on the path near White's Bridge Road where Dwayne always stopped for his cigarette break. The air was soft and cool and the moon had risen as we sat there.

I was leaning over, my chin resting on my knees, pulling up grass and weeds. It helped me think. "Well, but do you *believe* it? Because the Sheriff I don't think does." I told him about our talk in the Rainbow. "He said it was hearsay; I'm a hearsayist."

"It's probably a lot more complicated than that. You know what the law's like."

"No, I don't."

Dwayne pulled over the small insulated cooler he'd brought along. It was one of those six-pack-sized ones. "Want a beer?"

That made me *so* impatient, when here I was, telling my story. "*No.* You know you wouldn't give me one even if I did."

"Want a Coke?"

"Yes, thank you." It surprised me that Dwayne must've thought about me when I wasn't around. Although a lot of people probably would have preferred me that way.

He flipped off the caps with a bottle-opener he took from his back pocket. He handed me the Coke. "Maybe you should've heard DeGheyn out, instead of stomping off like you did."

"I did not *stomp* off!"

"Uh-huh." Dwayne tilted the bottle of Rolling Rock and drank off nearly half.

"I *didn't!*"

"Sure you did. Takes one to know one." He turned and smiled. "I'm a prime stomper."

"You? But you always act like nothing ever bothers you."

"Well, it does." Dwayne exhaled a big smoke ring and then sent smaller ones through it.

Smoke could do so many things, I thought. I watched the rings dissolve and said, "But you never answered my question. Do you believe it? You think I'm making it all up?"

"Did I say that? What the sheriff is probably thinking is the only witness to all of this is Ben Queen, and he can't be found."

"The *only* witness? What about me? That's what I mean; you think I'm making it up!"

"You're not a witness; you're the victim."

Victim. I liked the sound of that. It was so much more than being just a "witness." I leaned my head against the stumppocked stump and thought about it. "Well, how do I know but what he thinks *I* shot her?" The idea excited me, though I didn't believe a word of it. "Shot her, and then just threw the gun in the water?"

Dwayne scratched the back of his neck, thoughtfully. "Well, I wouldn't let it worry me. You'd be tried as a juvenile and probably get off with ten, fifteen years."

"Du-*waaaayne!* Stop that!"

"This Queen fella—he's probably fled the coop, what with everybody looking for him."

"No, he hasn't." I said this without thinking. "He's looking for someone, too."

"Oh, yeah? Who?"

"I think she's his granddaughter." I told him about the Girl, about the five times I'd seen her. For some reason he seemed to be the right person to tell it to.

He shook his head. "My Lord."

I was glad he was impressed. "It's like a Greek tragedy." I stashed my Coke by the stump.

"What about this girl? Anyone else know she exists at all? Anyone else seen her?" He turned to look at me in a way that could be described as "meaningful." The look was full of it, I was annoyed to see.

"Don't look at me like that. She *exists*. I *saw* her those five times."

"Oh, I'm not contradicting you saw her."

"Then what? *What?* You think she's a figment of my imagination?"

"That's what you said Ben Queen said."

"But he didn't mean it! He was only *pretending*." I was really irritated. "William Faulkner would believe it. He would. Maybe she's a shape to fill a lack."

Dwayne looked from the sky down to me. "A word? Yeah, but maybe Faulkner meant it the other way. That a word itself don't amount to a hill of beans. Like the word "love" can't take the place of the feeling. The word's a shape, a husk, an empty shell."

I was absolutely astounded he'd think such a thing. "But of course he believed in words. He was a writer, after all. How could he not?" I recalled Louise Landis talking. "Words are home."

Dwayne stopped in the act of setting his beer down to finger out another cigarette. "That's pretty deep. Where'd you hear that?"

"Oh, I just made it up," I lied.

Before he put the cigarette in his mouth, he said, "One of the deepest things I ever heard."

"Actually, I didn't. Someone else said it." Whatever provoked me to tell the truth? "That lady you met, up on the porch. Louise Landis."

"She must be interesting. She's sure good-looking for a woman that age."

Quickly, I said, "Well, she's too old for you. A lot too old."

"Yeah? Well, you're too young for me, yet here we are."

I put my chin on my knees again, for I was blushing, and he, being a poacher, could probably see straight through the dark to my insides. "Don't be stupid."

389

He was handing me a cigarette. "Hate smoking all alone."

My jaw dropped as I took it. I sat up and watched him light his and then pinch out the match. I wiggled my cigarette at him. "Well?"

"You can just pretend. You could go through a whole carton just pretending."

I think that was a compliment, but, knowing Dwayne, I thought I'd better leave well enough alone and not ask.

We were silent now, both looking up at the moon. "Hunter's moon," he said. "That's because of the brightness."

"Poacher's moon, you mean."

Dwayne laughed. "That's pretty good. It looks silvery, looks the color of a gun barrel tonight."

We were silent again. I disliked the wet taste of the tobacco in my cigarette. "I've smoked before, you know. You can't get to my age without doing it at least once."

"Oh, I can see that."

We grew silent again, and I thought about my story. Mr. Gumbrel believed it. All those reporters believed it. Even Ree-Jane believed it, for heaven's sake. So I could stop worrying about that. I went over everything that had happened, thinking about what to put in and what to leave out for my newspaper write-up. I wondered where the beginning began. Was it down in the Pink Elephant, going through my Whitman's candy box? Was it my first glimpse of Cold Flat Junction and that horizon of dark trees? Or was it even further back? Was it back before our playhouse burned down? Or when my dog got run down out on the highway? Was it back with the Waitresses?

I said, "I wish the past weren't dead and gone; I wish things weren't over."

Dwayne smiled. "The past ain't dead; it ain't even past. Billy Faulkner."

I thought for a moment, and then I smiled too. "This is *my* story, and it's not over till I say it's over. Emma Graham."

We laughed.

I watched Dwayne's real smoke and my pretend twine upward toward the gunmetal poacher's moon.